Also by Susanna Allen

SHAPESHIFTERS OF THE BEAU MONDE
A Wolf in Duke's Clothing
A Most Unusual Duke

a Duke *at the* Door

SUSANNA ALLEN

sourcebooks
casablanca

Published by Sourcebooks Casablanca, an imprint of Sourcebooks
P.O. Box 4410, Naperville, Illinois 60567-4410
(630) 961-3900
sourcebooks.com

Printed and bound in Canada.
MBP 10 9 8 7 6 5 4 3 2 1

Prologue

THE SATURDAY NIGHT PATRONS' LACKLUSTER cheers faded as Jack Bunce crept through the backstage gloom to the beast wagons. Not content to mimic Wombwell's tour of zoological curiosities, Bunce's employer aped Astley as well: Phineas Drake's Equestrian Spectacular and Exotic Traveling Menagerie wed equine arts with ferocious creatures; if you asked Bunce, the combination was less than the sum of its parts, much like the animal who was his prey this evening.

Like the rest of his ilk behind the scenes of Drake's Spectacular, he knew when a tide was about to turn. They were newly returned to London after a tour of Scotland, where they'd been welcomed with less than open arms, not to mention purses. If the box office continued its decline, Drake would be hard-pressed to keep things ticking over.

If he packed it up, went bankrupt…well, that was not Bunce's problem.

Bunce's problem was about to be solved, thanks to a keen eye and an utter lack of fear.

Animals rustled in dry straw, stirring themselves at the sound of an unexpected visitor. The beast wagons ranged in a semicircle for the punters to view in promenade before the main event, but one was off on its own, in the near dark, the better to frighten the spectators with the shadowy threat of the greatest predator of them all.

While covering for the lion keeper, Bunce had clocked a golden chain fixed around the animal's paw, and he was after having it tonight; he feared no creature, even if the one he crept up on was the king of them.

"Some king you are." He slithered along to reach the sturdy lock on the cage. "Look at this, will ya? Could keep in ten of your kind. Won't keep me out." He slipped a slender lockpick from his sleeve. "Someone as clever as me can take a bit o' gold off an old cat like you. Old, innit? That's why you're all gray, yeah."

Though the horses were Jack Bunce's main responsibility and did not require cages, he made sure to keep up skills that had served him well in previous enterprises. A fellow like him did not come of age in the worst stews of London without having a trick or two up his actual sleeve. He coaxed the padlock open, and light as a feather, with the ease born of slithering through more than one second-story window, he climbed into the beast's den.

The lion stirred, and as confident a chap as Bunce was, he hesitated. The cat's great paws ended in greater claws, blunted though they were. As the creature rolled his head to look at the intruder, Jack's skin erupted in gooseflesh. For it was as if the lion *saw* him, and that was not possible, to be seen for what he was—a man on a mission of ill intent—by a mere animal.

The creature yawned, and it was all Bunce could do not to laugh. "My apologies, Your Highness, for disturbing your slumber. You'll be on to your eternal rest, you will, if Drake doesn't shape up this show. Won't be chucking in a whole deer for your tea, no, he won't."

The great eyes blinked as though the animal understood every word the man said. "Speak English, do ya? Here's some news for you, then. You're to be sold on, and by *sold on*, that's to the abattoir, once they figure out how to feed you enough opium. Your days are numbered, old son. And you won't be needing that shiny…ah, yeah, there we are."

It had taken a sharp eye to catch what Bunce spotted, as the lion's grooming was a disgrace: the once luxurious mane was tangled and filthy; its whiteness and that of the lion's coat was the result of old-fashioned wig powder, and cleansing it between the creature's performances in the equestrian revels was not on the cards, due to the keeper's laziness and fear of the beast. *Performances* was putting a fine point on it: the lion was dragged out by its handlers acting as though they were trying to keep him in check rather than convince him to move. The sight of the beast outside of his cage was sufficiently impressive, even for the short traverse upstage; it didn't matter if he was not in the least bit threatening in practice: he was in theory, and that was enough for the watchers in the stalls.

The thief edged forward and reached for the chain that lay beneath the matted fur of the beast's ankle. A credulous observer, had there been one, might have thought the creature helpfully angled his paw in aid of the thief's light fingers. Bunce smiled and slid his smallest pick into the lock, a complicated clasp made to stand up to wear and tear. It would not stand up to him: he shimmied the pick right, left, right again, and the chain slid away.

When the porters from Bedlam arrived to fetch Jack Bunce, naked and screaming, he swore over and over that the lion had become a man.

One

ALWYN AND THE DAWN WERE OLD FRIENDS.

As a boy growing up in Anglesey, he had counted down the hours until he was free to roam; as a captive, he would wake before first light, after an uneasy sleep, to another day in the beast wagon. Since his recent liberation, his rest was continually disrupted by the desperate need to ensure he was still not trapped at Drake's, for proof that he was free.

Even after nearly a month dwelling on the grounds of Lowell Hall's park, he did not trust his instincts.

He ought to be better by now.

Alwyn sat on the doorstep, unaffected by the brisk spring air. His abode was simple and easily managed without outside interference: Alfred, Duke of Lowell, had assumed he would not want to be tended by maids or footmen, and Alwyn gave the wolf credit for his prescience. The cottage sat on the highest vantage in the park, which was very high in comparison to the low, rolling hills of Sussex; he had the lay of Lowell's land, from the River Eden to the village of Lowell Close, over the entirety of the wild park to the London Road. He was once again removed from the rest of the company, but unlike Drake's, he was free to come and go, or to prowl and lurk, as he overheard more than one denizen of the village mutter. How they would tremble if he were able to scale trees as he once could, concealed amongst the leaves, ready to attack... Although it had to be said, a sturdy branch also made for a superior napping place; it was as much in his nature to loll as it was to pounce.

When he roamed, he kept well away from the flocks and colonies and herds who sensed him, no matter the distance between them; no matter that he inhabited his manskin, he was given a wide berth once spotted. And spot him they did, for the bright yellow coat Alwyn often wore was impossible to miss.

His essential self was naturally prideful and would have resisted the eccentric picture he made, but the reasons behind it were not only down to alerting the prey to his presence. The coat was loose enough that he did not need a valet to wrestle him into it; the shirt was flowing and easily donned; and the cravat, a cursory length of fabric hung loosely around his neck. When he had raided Georgie's storerooms, he'd taken only what he could put on without assistance.

How his ragtag ensembles had irritated his sovereign. The pleasure Alwyn took in it was out of proportion but familiar all the same: one had an inexplicable desire to annoy His Highness even as one applied to him for aid. There was help that only the prince could give, the only one to whom Alwyn could go once he had fled, dressed as he was in clothes stolen from a thief. The regent showed unexpected patience, cloaked in diffidence, for Alwyn's inability to speak with fluency or abide in company; his native Welsh contrariness required he return the favor in flights of sartorial fancy sure to send the prince into the boughs.

Was that why Georgie had banished him to Sussex? His Highness had insisted it was for Alwyn's own good, but one never knew with him. How swiftly he had been dispatched after landing on the royal doorstep...

———

Alwyn skulked behind one of the yellow marble columns that lined the main corridor of Carlton House. He had been pressed into service as a witness to Arthur, Duke of Osborn, marrying the small, canny human known in the *ton* as Lady Frost, the widow of that lunatic wolf, the Marquess of Castleton; now, he wanted nothing more than to disappear into the bowels of the royal residence.

The Prince of Wales had made a dramatic exit, as was his wont, and Alwyn hoped the royal retinue would hide him even as it swept past. He had managed to get this far without drawing attention but did not fool himself in thinking his presence went undetected. As stunted as his own senses were, His Highness's were extremely acute; he held his breath and waited for Georgie and his escort to move on to the next order of business.

"Alwyn ap Lewin," a voice intoned.

Drat. It appeared he was the next order of business.

"The Wild Lion of Wales." His Highness paused, meaningful and portentous. "Descendant of the House of Aberffraw, in the line of succession from Rhodri the Great."

Yes, yes, Alwyn thought, alone in his head without a whisper from his lion. *Let us not trot out my entire lineage.*

"Walk with me." It was an order, and one Alwyn was not convinced he could fulfill. The column was for support as well as camouflage: going about on his human legs remained a challenge.

In addition, being at the beck and call of the prince made his feline nature revolt—but only in spirit, in muscle memory, for his lion had disappeared, leaving nothing behind but silence.

Disappeared, to the concern of the prince and two of his dukes.

Why Alwyn had been called upon to witness Arthur's hole-in-the-corner nuptials was beyond him. Georgie had obviously orchestrated the whole thing against the will of both participants. If Alwyn recalled correctly—and it was a miracle he could do so—Osborn's mother had been killed by hunters, and his father, diminished in his grief over the loss of his mate, had fallen in battle to a rogue Shifter. Arthur had disappeared from society, refusing to take up the mantle of duke; Alwyn wished him the best of luck in his marriage to that little cannonball—what havoc she promised to wreak. She appeared as though butter wouldn't melt in her mouth, but anyone could see the banked fire in her eyes. If he remembered Arthur correctly from their childhood days, the bear Shifter was quick to react to the smallest provocation in a melodramatic fashion. Blessed Palu only knew what Georgie held over each, to force them into an indissoluble union.

Not that he cared about their future life. He would never see them again. With any luck, his torment would end. He and his lion would be free.

The prince, as ever, stood on display, decked from head to toe in showy attire that was the height of sophistication, unlike Alwyn's own madcap apparel. He fluffed the ostentatiously lacy cravat that hung limply around his neck; the plaid waistcoat beneath it clashed quite violently with his striped knee breeches.

"Alwyn." The royal tone remained light, which never failed to lure the listener into a false sense of security. Alwyn slipped from behind one pillar to the next, which had the added concealment of a large fern. "How distraught we were when we learned what you had suffered."

Right under your nose, wasn't I?

"To be fair, we did think you had returned home to Anglesey to take your place and do your duty. There was a letter to that effect, if I remember correctly."

Fate intervened.

"To think you were lost to us and could have been so forever." The prince's voice nearly broke from an abundance of sentiment. "I can tell you the stipend gifted to your family has increased in your absence. There is much we owe you in recompense, not least the years of your captivity. For it was likely my however-many-great-grandfather who brought your ancestors to England—"

Likely? Certainly.

"—and installed them in the Tower menagerie. Although I do not believe you are quite that ancient. One does wonder that *versipelles* at the top of our hierarchy should find themselves captured so often, but you and your kind are the highest prize of hunters, human and Shifter alike. I have only to think of the decimation of your pride…" George fussed with his ceremonial sash. "You have my apologies."

George apologized to no one. Alwyn allowed himself to be flushed out.

The contrast between them had ever been there: a bear Shifter, the Prince was large, crowned with a profusion of curls, the center of attention, immaculately dressed. Alwyn was equally blessed when it came to hair, but his mane was straight and thick; he was tall but not nearly as wide. Both aspects of his person were now taken to the extreme: his locks were long and tangled and rough, nowhere near the elegant tresses he sported in his youth, and he covered his diminished frame in tatterdemalion vesture to hide his lack of flesh.

"And what form will this apology take?" Even to his own ears, his voice was barely human. "For words will not suffice."

"The words of your prince—"

"Are wordy and princely. You know my wish."

George resumed his stroll, the only indication of tension displayed by a tightly clenched fist. "It has been decided that you will be the honored guest of Their Graces of Lowell," he said. "The duchess has a deftness with those of our kind, an empathy. But Lowell is not keen to spare her in the full efforts your return to health requires."

So Alfred did not trust him with his new bride. Could Alwyn blame him?

The regent continued, voice as airy as though proposing a jaunt to the seaside, "Nevertheless, he is all that is eager to make you at home, and a suitable abode is being prepared. He is, of course, on his journey back to Sussex with his new bride, and his attention will be taken up with her." Georgie winked salaciously then sobered. "Given we do not know if your escape will result in pursuit, we have determined it safer for you to remove from London. As it is, the days of Carlton House as a royal residence are numbered." Georgie surveyed the gilded ceiling with a jaundiced eye. "We shall hide you in plain sight."

"Clever. Imagine if there were an industry based on this notion."

The royal fist tensed further. "We cannot be blamed for something we knew nothing of."

A defense against guilt, Alwyn supposed, was to become offended. This offense was doubly rich, given the royal family's history of displaying so-called exotic creatures. "I recall your mother and her lineage's penchant for zebras," Alwyn rasped. "Whatever became of the Queen's Ass? Did you both not share a birthday of sorts?"

Georgie's face flushed a deep scarlet, and Alwyn saw the threat of his Change, the claws peeking out from the tips of his fingers, a ruff of fur sprouting around his neck. The queen, Georgie's mother, had been gifted one of the striped beasts on the occasion of her wedding; it became a symbol of the displeasure the populace had for its current monarchs.

The animal was loathe to obey its handlers and often ran rampant, prone to kicking out. The gutter press dubbed it the *Queen's Ass*, and thanks to George's mercurial behavior, which was much like the zebra's, the nickname soon became his own. Caricatures of the prince and the zebra were still displayed in the windows of print shops; Drake's roustabouts had passed them around with spiteful glee. Reminding him of it was a calculated blow to George's vanity, and yet the regent was equal to it and dampened his choler.

For all his faults, and they were many, the prince's control of his bear was impeccable. The claws retracted, the fur disappeared, and his essential self was tucked away like a hand into a pocket. A pity, as a brawl would bring Alwyn to the resolution he desired. *A consummation devoutly to be wished…*

"I know what you intend." The prince's tone was as frigid as a winter's day. "I will not be goaded."

"Then I insist I be left to my own devices at Lowell Hall, as I am here." He ignored the pang of loneliness. It was what he wanted. It was for the best.

"Oh no, my dear Duke. We cannot let it be said we did not do everything that could be done to bring you back to the fullness of your health." Alwyn recognized the glint in the regent's eye; it promised a very long game indeed. "You will be taken into the care of the Honorable Miss Tabitha Barrington."

"An unmarried lady? And human, presumably?"

"She is quite unusual. As learned as a man when it comes to potions and palliatives."

Alwyn scoffed. "There is no potion or palliative in this wide world that will be of any use to me."

"So dramatic, Llewellyn." Georgie smirked. "Have you taken Osborn as a pattern card?"

"There is no pattern card for me." This was more human contact than Alwyn had had since he escaped Drake's, and it began to tell: his head swam, and he would be damned if he fainted at Georgie's feet. His body was weak and his mind exhausted; there was only one solution to his situation. "I am no better than Castleton, who ought to have been put down."

"I say you are." His Highness turned to face him; Alwyn hadn't noticed Georgie had not been looking at him full on.

"There is no reason to believe there is a way back for me."

"You were not in your right mind when you arrived on my doorstep, but arrive you did, proving you are capable of rationality and forethought." The prince looked down his nose at Alwyn. "You will repair to Lowell Hall and bow to the lady's knowledge."

And put the entirety of Lowell's pack in danger? "If in one month there is no change, you will put me down."

"I will not." The bear threatened again if the growl in Georgie's voice was any indication.

"I shall call upon Lowell to do what you will not."

"The man who rescues every runt on my island?" The regent laughed. "He would not lift a paw against you."

Alwyn snarled, but where there ought to have been a rumble that doubled his displeasure, there was nothing, nothing at all since he had Changed to his manskin. "I am no better than Hallbjorn, who challenged Arthur's father and won, leaving that sleuth scattered to the four corners of the earth. It was your father's duty to put him down, to put Castleton down, and he did not do so. Will you follow in his footsteps? Is this failure to do your duty a feature of your bloodline?"

Had he been at full strength, the *dominatum* of another Alpha would not have affected him. As he was now, he was not equal to it. The fury of his regent did not manifest in a Change but in the power of an Alpha to suppress and control another through sheer force of will. It swirled around Alwyn and caught him as though in a vise; it stole his breath, and if not for the marble column at his back, it would have driven him to his knees.

"I am not my father." Despite the force emanating from him, Georgie was as calm as a sea at rest.

"You will be informed when the cottage is prepared and the lady has arrived. Help is at hand."

Alwyn was beyond help, much less from a *lady*.

————————

Apart from an escapade requiring he once again attend an Osborn-related event, in which the prince did sort out Hallbjorn and install Arthur as the rightful Alpha, Alwyn had not wandered beyond Lowell's boundaries once settled within them.

Now, with the sun fully risen, he roamed, as was his wont.

He had been welcomed with warmth and fearlessness by the duchess. She was yet known as *Fallen Felicity* with some lingering scorn by the *ton*, no doubt envious that the only fall she took was into a title and the arms of the young (ha!) duke. Lowell was his usual lupine self, exuding power as easily as he breathed. How did Alfred prevent the lower orders from going mad with fear? Due to the strength of his *sentio*, perhaps? Lowell's heart connection with his diverse pack was strong enough that even Alwyn could sense it, though he was not woven into it. Was this the common way of things?

Having had no experience of his own *sentio*, he could not say.

Having had no experience being an Alpha at the height of his powers, he did not know.

Having lost his pride at so early an age… No, he would not dwell on it.

He was not entirely without awareness of what he should and should not have at his disposal as an Alpha. He was fully acquainted with his *dominatum,* as much good as it had done him at Drake's, which was none at all. The *vera amoris* legend was robust across all species, deeply desired and wished for…but for his kind, those who roamed, felines at the top of the hierarchy, it was the *coniunctio* he had hoped to forge before his freedom was stolen.

He had once dreamed he might be the first in generations to make that bond. An old dream he must release, for he was not fit for company.

At the start of his residency, Her Grace insisted upon his attending every meal at the Hall, then reduced it to the evening repast…then Sunday lunch only, accompanied by glowers and grumbles from the duke, who took Alwyn's unwillingness to dine with them daily as an insult to his duchess. They were lucky he managed the Sunday Meal at all; sitting at table with humans was a foggy memory. He saw to his daily fodder, foraging like a rabbit, and thanks to Blessed Palu, meat appeared on his doorstep, already prepared. There was an excess of sauce, which he blamed on Lowell's fancy French chef, but he ate it and was grateful, grateful he could eat it in peace, alone.

Alwyn paused in a familiar spot, his view through

a lattice of sycamore branches, and observed that Barrington woman—no: that Barrington Woman, styled as one of Mrs. Anchoretta Asquith's heroines. No, yet again: an antiheroine, for no wilting debutante was she, and therefore no heroine. The lady apothecary was more in the line of a duenna or chaperone, her sober garments of little note, her willowy figure nowhere near *au courant* as determined by current society, her hair a diffident blondish brown, her eyes...oh, but those eyes, dark chocolate and doe-like yet without a shred of innocence. They lit upon everything in their path with a measuring gaze, removed and considering. What would it take to inspire them to lose that detachment?

He watched as Miss Barrington moved back and forth behind the large window of the odd little outbuilding behind her cottage. She spent much of her time there, when she was not wandering the grounds, carrying her equally odd little basket thing, kneeling amongst the low-growing plants, her head tilted as though she were in conversation with them. Alwyn had eluded her as handily as if he were in accord with his essential self. She did not see him unless he allowed her to, to prove he was beyond her grasp.

The lady apothecary left her shed and set off toward the deepest part of the park, where the wolves and the stags and the boar often went to

Change. Had she no sense of self-preservation? Lowell Hall may appear beyond breaching, but he knew what the wide world was like, how quickly a situation could turn, how evil moved about disguised as innocence.

Nowhere was safe. Not even the grounds belonging to an Alpha wolf who commanded a growing pack that was likely the greatest in all these islands and the Continent.

He grumbled as he shadowed her into the heart of the park. It fell to him to keep her in sight.

Two

TABITHA ADORED THE DAWN. IT WOULD FOREVER remind her of that first day in France after she and Timothy executed their plan and made their escape. She had woken, in a run-down guesthouse in Calais, to sunlight creeping over the windowsill, luminous and sharp, so unlike the light in middle England, landlocked in their homeplace of Worcester.

In that morning light, she had determined she too would rise and be unlike the self she had been, be luminous and sharp and new.

She had slipped out of doors to be greeted by the scent of the sea and of strange French food cooking, the sound of hooves on the cobbled road, made foreign simply because it was a French horse on French stone. The flowers were not unlike the ones she'd known all her life, the architecture not entirely exotic, the people scurrying about their early morning business not all that strange to look upon… Yet it had all been unfamiliar enough to be thrilling, the very air redolent of freedom and hope.

It was not as though she and Timothy had embarked upon a conventional Grand Tour;

they were light in their pockets but rich in skill and determination, with no intention to remain idle. They had the gift of time for Timothy's broken heart to heal, and distractions aplenty as their journey unfolded. There were any number of folks, who were not of the typically educated classes, who wished to learn English; Timothy was more than happy to take them in hand. Every day, she watched him come back to himself and, even better, live without fear due to whom he wished to love. She had her apothecary knowledge and the willingness to learn more, and she had reveled in their liberation, if not the circumstances that brought them there.

That was in the past. As was her Continental adventure.

Bundled up to her ears, she set off into the morning chill. The park at Lowell Hall was a wild cataclysm of plants and trees, of paths and switchbacks, of rolling hills and verdant dales. She doubted anyone cultivated it but for the birds who dropped seeds as they traveled over the south of England; she'd hardly scratched the surface of the variety of greenery surrounding her.

As she had hardly scratched the surface of the task she faced.

Tabitha gamely trudged up an incline. How she adored life in the country. It was easier to be poor in the country, for the outdoors contained bounty for those who knew what to look for. The fresh air, the long walks, the flora—and here, of all places, a previously unknown species that defied human logic.

Oh, but being in a city…the culture, the salons, everything one could need at one's fingertips. London was not so far away after all, but where would she stay, with whom would she go about? Did the duke and duchess keep to the *ton*'s calendar? Society was not Tabitha's favorite thing—nor she, its. One as firmly on the shelf as she had no place there.

Would she make a place here? Explaining her skills to the populace of Lowell Close had been met with polite smiles and assurance she would be the first to know when her aid was required. If the strength and longevity of *versipelles* was as she suspected, her knowledge would largely be wasted. There were a few humans—no, *homo plenum*—who were spouses of Shapeshifters, so it was for them she would keep her stores fresh.

Felicity had been incredibly helpful in instructing her in *versipellian* characteristics. Tabitha's unexpected audience with the prince had alerted her to their swings of emotion, and her friend had told her it was down to their dual natures, of having to negotiate their heightened senses even in their human forms, which alerted them to things those with duller capacities could not fathom. Even the smallest of them was stronger than any human, and the eldest was older than any *homo plenus* would ever be. The Lowell Pack was woven together by the *sentio*, a heart-based connection that allowed the duke, their Alpha, to ensure their well-being. They followed the holidays of the lupine species, and some of the larger groups within the pack— the mice, the bees, the cats—held their own deities and ceremonies dear.

Verispelles could see in the dark, hear a pin drop from miles away, and were ever true to the natures of their animal selves. Creature aspects? Tabitha did not like to call them *animals*, it seemed uncouth, and *creature* even more so. For they were as civilized as any human she met, perhaps more so: to keep themselves safe, to keep their secret secure, they had to behave above reproach in every instance.

Tabitha was honored more than she could say and respected their law that forbade inquiring after an individual's species; in any case, their second nature was very obvious once one knew what to look for.

For example: no one would mistake the Duke of Llewellyn for anything but a predator and, with that head of hair, nothing but a lion.

A predator who even now tracked her as she went about her morning. The feeling of eyes upon her was tangible, an instinct that had not proven her wrong in Arcadia, the Humphries' home manor, when the prince regent set her upon this path…

———

Years of keeping her composure when faced with either her choleric father or fractious clients stood her in good stead when she was called into the presence of His Highness. Rumor had it George IV was mercurial at best, splenetic at worst; despite having provided palliatives for more than one Continental potentate, Tabitha was intimidated by an audience with her native sovereign.

Not that she would allow it to show.

A chance meeting on the way to Lowell Hall saw Tabitha joining Felicity on her journey to Arcadia, the seat of the Duke of Osborn, ahead of a ceremonial event and on the heels of a dangerous situation involving a missing child. As ever, Tabitha was happy to provide aid as best she could. Timothy continued on with their belongings; he would be happy enough to unpack for both of them, delighted at having a secure place at last, at home, in England.

Tabitha had been curious about life at the Lowell ducal seat and all who lived there. Felicity had become secretive upon her marriage, speaking in a roundabout way about the traditions and protocols found in her new home. Tabitha and Timothy had seen more than one strange thing in their travels, and a part of her was hoping for more than usually met the eye in a traditional English village.

When they arrived at Arcadia, the forecourt was as bustling as the port of Liverpool. His Highness had already arrived and was currently repairing his appearance. She and Felicity forded their way to the door through waves of footmen scurrying about on royal business; immediately upon entering, Felicity began discussing accommodation for Arcadia's newest guests with the housekeeper and was swiftly swept away behind the green baize door. Tabitha found herself alone in a room that contained a single footstool and nothing else.

Thanks to the lack of a door, a footman clearing his throat on the threshold was all that prepared her for the royal presence.

"Miss Barrington." The prince's toilette was a roaring success, his abundance of curls and luxuriant sideburns groomed to perfection; his person exuded a clean, woodsy scent. His pantaloons, embroidered with a riot of sweet cicely, would send Timothy into ecstasies. The royal coat was a sober bottle green until it caught the light and one noticed its iridescence, and his cravat a waterfall of dazzling white lace. The waistcoat alone, its field of delicate anise flowers the perfect complement to the cicely, deserved the deep curtsy she proffered.

"Your Highness." Good Lord, she was not as fit as she had been when they lived in Greece.

Beatrice, the Duchess of Osborn, cultivated a signature curtsy that brought her so close to the floor, her eyelashes nearly swept it. Tabitha did not know how her friend managed: even with all the walking and foraging she did, she was struggling to keep her balance. She hoped the prince would release her from her obeisance, or else she didn't think she could return to standing with dignity.

"Rise," he commanded.

She rose. The attending footman stood in the doorway and turned his back to the room.

His Highness scrutinized her. "The Honorable Tabitha Barrington," he intoned. "She of the single unfinished Season, nigh on, oh, what is it, twenty-five years ago?"

"Seventeen, Your Highness." That stung in a way it had not for ages. "It transpired that my father had need of me."

"I confused the length of time ago with your length of time away."

"That would be but ten years, Your Highness." Was he goading her? "I am thirty-five years of age, and we departed for France in 1807." They had, through sheer luck, managed to avoid the worst of the Napoleonic conflict, having made their way through Spain well ahead of the armies.

"And now you are returned, you and your brother, the Honorable Mr. Timothy Barrington, the Duchess of Lowell's new tutor. I do hope the travel was not too arduous for his…consumption, was it?"

"It was what my mother feared." With a little help from her children.

"And along the way, according to the duchess, your bosom friend, you have practiced healing arts on all and sundry."

This could not be about that, could it? She peeked up at him: he looked choleric and in need of a cooling tisane. "She is all that is supportive of my interests, Your Highness."

"You will have heard that Alwyn ap Lewin, the Duke of Llewellyn, has returned to the royal fold." The prince did not wait to assure himself of her knowledge or lack thereof. "He is suffering from his years of captivity, and I would assign him to your care."

"Captivity? In the wars?" Tabitha was sure she would have heard of an English duke held by the French. But what else could it be? "My brother and I met many veterans on our travels."

"He is not one of that illustrious company." The prince toyed with a button on his waistcoat. In her years of observation, this indicated nervousness to Tabitha, which was patently absurd. What had the prince regent of England to be nervous about? "We had thought him safely snug in his homeplace in Wales, but that was not the case." He looked down his nose at her, which he was well able to do: she was of middling height, and His Highness was very tall. And very broad. He continued, "I have heard nothing but praise regarding your capabilities. I am curious as to how you gained your knowledge of medicaments and suchlike."

Medicaments? Suchlike? She suspected he was condescending to her on purpose. Let her be very thorough. "I am honored, Your Highness. There is a tradition of engaging in the healing arts on my mother's side of the family. To be more precise, the predilection comes from her mother's father's mother, so it is a lovely combination of both the masculine and feminine principles of my family line. I learned what I could from my maternal grandmother before her passing, but seeing the desire I had to increase my knowledge, our house-keeper, who is, in fact, a distant cousin to my father in his paternal line, took me under her wing and taught me all she knew regarding herbs, the culti-vating of said herbs, the distillation of—"

"Yes, wonderful." Tabitha was cut off with a gesture of his lacy cuff. "I leave Llewellyn to your good offices. He has been installed in a cottage in the park at Lowell Hall and will put himself at your disposal."

"I would like to consult with him directly, Your Highness."

"That will not be necessary."

"I am afraid it is."

The prince drew himself up, seemed to grow in height and breadth, and he...drew all the air in the room around him? "I suggest you trust the will and opinion of your sovereign." Tabitha's ears popped, much like they had when ascending the Austrian Alps. Whatever it was weighted down her head and shoulders in an oppressive fashion.

Luckily, she had never been adversely affected by changes in altitude. "I trust you have the duke's best interests at heart, but I am not comfortable speaking about him behind his back or as though he were a child."

The air relaxed—what degree of fanciful was this?—and His Highness considered her. "He has not been free for many years. He has not had the company of those like him for all that time. His physicality is not what it once was. His demeanor is melancholy."

"I see. Melancholy very often prevents one from keeping one's form in fettle, which then exacerbates the dampened spirits. Is His Grace the active sort?"

"Oh, yes." The prince barked a laugh. "Active. Yes."

What was amusing about that, she had no clue. "I have a series of cures that have proven effective in the past, but ills of the mood are complex. Several of my tonics aid in a variety of ways, for example, a lack of sleep is deleterious to general health—"

Tabitha was cut off once again. "As to that." The

waistcoat button received renewed attention. "He is unlike your usual run of patient."

"Client," she dared to correct him. "I am not a doctor."

"You will not have met his kind before."

"A duke? Or a Welshman? I can assure you that I have spent the past ten years traveling far and wide and as such have a breadth of experience your common or garden apothecary cannot claim." Was she now arguing for this assignment?

The pressure hovered around the prince. "I would ask you to take me at my word."

"Your Highness." Oh, diplomacy, not her strong suit. "It is not your word I challenge but my ability to be of any use to this man unless I am apprised of the exact circumstances."

The prince stood still as a statue and yet another wave of that strange tension rolled off him. It had all the characteristics of waiting for the crash of thunder after the flash of lightning, a suspension that promised a shock, even as one expected it. She withstood it and he muttered something about *human females—human females*? That could not be correct.

He languidly extended an arm. "Regard, miss."

Tabitha regarded. And what she saw was unlike anything she had seen before.

One moment, she was observing the hand of the prince, as pale and pampered as one would expect from a person who had never done a day's labor, and the next—the next, she was looking at a paw. A massive paw, covered in brown fur, claws like knives fully extended.

His Highness flexed those claws as she continued to stare in silence. A comment was wanted, then? "Ah," she said.

"*Ah*?" He presented his palm, where she saw the pads common to...to animals, and in another instant, quicker than a blink, the paw changed back into his hand. "I will have you know, Miss Barrington, that only the most powerful of my kind can Shift a discrete body part." He huffed, part annoyance, part amusement. "I expect a sanguine demeanor is essential to one in your line of work but is that all you have to say?"

Speechlessness would be an acceptable reaction to what she had just seen. "I am, of course, amazed." It made her wonder about several acquaintances she'd made in her travels, the sense that there was something more to them than met the eye, the fact none of them encountered her and commenced cataloging their ailments. They had a glint in the eye, a robustness she could not categorize. And now this: a man turned, partially, into a beast. "You will know that confidentiality is key to any practice of healing," she said. "I would assure you that no one will learn of what I saw here. In this room and, and in this place, land, er, I doubt many of my, my kind, uh, human females, I see why you said that now, *human females*, eh, are aware of this, uh—" Perhaps she was a little shocked after all.

"You are now part of a small band of *homo plenem* who are aware of the existence of *versipelles*. To wit: a human who knows of the existence of Shapeshifters." She was grateful for the translation from what she guessed was Latin. "We are of every species you can call to mind and occupy every stratum of society. We are princes and dukes, housekeepers and butlers, solicitors and famous lady authors of Gothic novels. We contain two selves and are ever in communication with both sides." He hesitated. Imagine, a nervous prince who hesitated! "We have a law, and I find I must break it. Who but I may do so, without rebuke? We are never to speak of our dual nature, nor inquire as to the species of another *versipelles*…nor disclose our knowledge of another's identity once entrusted with it. But it must be done for you to do your work."

He looked at her expectantly. So it was up to her to help him break his own law. "The duke is a *versipellis*."

"He is a lion," the prince said, and an angry flush of color touched the apples of his cheeks. "He was held in a menagerie in his Changed Shape."

Had he kept the knowledge of his human self while in captivity? "That is horrific."

The pressure the prince exerted crested and

retreated. "We have an abhorrence for any animal held under such conditions and as such do not patronize that class of *entertainment*." He spat the last word as though it were a curse. "His identity was robbed, and I require you to aid him in retrieving it."

"I have questions, as you may imagine—"

"Her Grace of Lowell will see to the details."

Details the like of: What did he eat? Did he make a habit of chasing down prey for his supper? Would he condescend to be treated not only by a woman but also a mere human? "I would not know where to begin."

"Ply him with your tonics. Et cetera." The princely dismissiveness returned in full flow. "For he is, at least, half a man."

Would any of her cures work on the likes of his kind? She wouldn't know until she tried, but she doubted it. And yet she could not resist. "Speaking of tonics. Your complexion seems to be taxed with high color, Your Highness." She eyed his flushed face and rummaged in her reticule. "I have just the thing."

"Do you indeed?" The pressure was a building hurricane, and she flinched. He was truly cross.

"I have a soothing lotion ideal for those who suffer from a nature burdened with an excess of choler. I have seen it do a world of good—"

"All in my world is good, miss," His Highness all but growled at her, "and I shall leave it, and you, at that."

How utterly typical to insist someone else profit from her cures but refuse them himself.

The footman did a complicated backward step and turn on the threshold then came to attention as the regent swept out of the room. The royal attendant bowed with a fluidity that called to mind a salmon; before he could follow the prince, Tabitha slipped a vial of the lotion in the hand—or perhaps fin—of the footman, should His Highness change his mind. Felicity soon joined her with an Osborn retainer, whose wrinkly face and tiny hands made Tabitha think of turtles.

Later, the women gathered: she, Felicity, Beatrice, and Beatrice's sister-in-law, Lady Swinburn. There was brandy, a rare indulgence, and womanly discussion, a delight. Her advice was accepted without question, a rarity; she thought that being in one place, amongst friends, would not be so trying after all.

However, the palpable contentment radiating off the happily married women was enough to inspire her to seek a breath of fresh air. What a low emotion, to feel such gloom at the joy of others. There was an ottoman sitting beneath an open window, an idiosyncratic placement. The whole house had a feeling of lightness and play, which Tabitha would not have expected from an arranged, unwilling marriage. They were making a go of it, Beatrice and her duke, and it showed. Tabitha sat on the oddly placed hassock and leaned against the sill.

One moment she was regarding a rose arbor under refurbishment, and the next, a man. He stood motionless in the moonlight, his form swathed in what looked like outsize clothing from another century; his hair was hopelessly snarled, yet its abundance was breathtaking. She could not read his expression from the distance and instead parsed his stance, a method she had heard derided in more than one learned circle, but it had always proved informative: the man's shoulders looked like beams holding up a barn ceiling, his hands were loose, but she perceived tension in his elbows, surely the reason his shoulders were so taut. His feet were braced for fight or flight; either would suit, as he was more than prepared to move in an instant. His eyes did not settle for long in one place, and the overall impression was of a man uncomfortable in his surroundings, in his very self.

This could be no one but the Duke of Llewellyn.

Tabitha took in his stance, his stillness, his predatory aspect, and knew a moment of misgiving. Despite what she said to the prince, she knew little about dukes and even less about what aid she could lend to a *versipellis*. After rising from the ottoman, she stood in the window. He had not moved perceptibly, but she noticed his chest subtly expand with a breath, his chin tilt up, his left hand clench into a fist.

"Your Grace." She suspected a lion's hearing

was acute and did not raise her voice beyond her normal tones. "You would be welcome indoors."

He did not reply, but again, faster than her sight could reconcile, one moment he was in the distance, and the next, directly beneath the window.

Tabitha tried again. "We are to be made known to each other at some stage—"

"I know who you are." His voice was low and rough, more a growl than human speech. It resonated from deep in his chest, and it was as though it stroked her from cheek to neck, her skin erupting in gooseflesh.

"I look forward to furthering our acquaintance." An empty social remark such as she strove to do her best never to utter.

"Do you?"

"Well, not as such." Another sound emitted from the ducal person, akin to the grind of a rusty water pump. "His Highness has deemed it so, and I find myself constrained by his wishes."

He inched closer. "You have traveled the globe."

"Sadly not." Very sadly, not so at all. "There are great swathes I have not seen, nor shall I, I suppose."

"Will you not?"

Let them discuss travel, then. "I have no companion, as my brother is now content to remain on home soil. Even though companions may be hired, I cannot imagine traveling with a stranger." She could see this much human engagement was taxing his fortitude. "I, too, am to live at Lowell Hall," she said. "Shall we fix a time to, to meet?"

The duke crept closer still, his eyes uncannily bright even in the darkness. He tilted his chin again and appeared to assess the air. Whatever he scented had him backing up a step, then another, and then, as if he had never been there, he was gone.

A shiver of preternatural fear coursed through Tabitha's body. Even with the ill health he radiated, his power was palpable and his demeanor forbidding. She did not know where to start or, indeed, what use she could be at all. She suspected she had no idea what to do.

That had never stopped her before.

═══════

What had stopped her was the duke's unwillingness to be pinned down. His Grace was adept at avoiding the denizens of the Hall in general and herself in particular. He began as he intended to go on and eluded her during the great bonfire celebration at Arcadia. Once she and Timothy settled in the cottage, Tabitha sent His Grace several notes via eager footmen, of which Lowell had an inordinate amount. She hesitated to knock upon the ducal door, as humble as it was, but if the part of the park she now wandered brought her near to Llewellyn's sanctuary, then what of it? She had yet to investigate this particular grove—who knew what she would find?

Today, she found a duke.

A rustle in the shrubbery alerted Tabitha to his presence, and the rising sun cast just enough light through the trees to reveal Llewellyn's shadow. "Your Grace." Would she curtsy in the middle of a wood? No, she would not. "Good morning."

His husky voice rumbled from the perimeter. "You ought not to wander without thought to what lurks on this land."

That would be you, she thought. *Lurking.* "It is a paradox." She set down her trug and took stock of the place. "For even though the beings here are dangerous to humans, this may be the safest place on earth. Or one of them. I do not know if this is typical of *versipellian* culture, to bring together a variety of species to live as one..." She trailed off at the sight of—was that—oh! Digitalis! She slid her shears out of a pocket and reached to stroke the bell of the nearest plant.

"Do not!" the duke very nearly shouted, his vocal cords not equal to the strain.

Tabitha snipped off a stalk of the foxglove before laying it in the trug. "It is only somewhat poisonous."

"Under prolonged contact, it is more than somewhat."

"I am taking only one. Two." She hummed in consideration. "Three at the most."

"You ought to wear gloves." His eyesight was all it was vaunted to be if he could tell in this low light.

"They interfere with my perception."

"Of what?" Another rustle, this time from her right side. Goodness, he was fast.

"The health of the plant, the state of the soil..." She balked at admitting the fanciful notion that she could feel effectiveness or otherwise from what she touched and chose two more blooms.

A rumble of disagreement issued from between the leaves. "Gloves made of lambskin would suit."

"The porousness of kid would defeat the purpose." Tabitha set one last stalk into her trug.

"A trowel, then, for the love of Palu." His Grace moved fully into the glade, dressed this morning like a common laborer, in a formless coat and a muslin shirt hanging outside his trousers.

"A blunt instrument?"

"You may gauge the plant by eye and then touch the soil."

"Why should I uproot it, if it is not useful?"

"You may return it to its place! With the trowel!"

Tabitha could not stop herself: she smiled at him. How masculine he sounded in that moment, how like a man, exasperated at what he surely thought was feminine obstreperousness. He looked incredulous and irritated and...alive. She'd pat him on the cheek if she didn't think he'd snarl or run off. Or...or bite her. Instead, she asked, "Who is Palu?"

and turned away; he appeared to be discomfited by prolonged observance.

"A Welsh cat of legend, a goddess attached to my homeplace who protects those in her care from danger. What are you going to do with that plant?"

She would ask Timothy if he knew anything about Welsh mythological cats. "It is, of course, helpful for congested hearts. But an Italian apothecary showed me that the merest pinch in chamomile tea is a gentle purgative."

"I cannot believe even the smallest amount of poison is safe."

"Neither did I, until I witnessed how effective it was."

"Witnessed."

"Yes. Saw the results of its efficacy."

"Tried it yourself, I wager." This was delivered in a tone that had a lightness to it, perhaps of laughter?

"I cannot ask anyone to ingest something I would not." Tabitha was staunch in this viewpoint. "It was enough work earning the trust of others thanks to perceptions of the weakness of my gender."

"Others." His voice came from the opposite side of the grove. His nimbleness was truly astonishing. How swift would he be at full strength? "Men."

"Men, yes. And certain women. Some ladies preferred my counsel to that of a male physician, but many more would hear my advice and then allow a man to negate it. It was a waste of everyone's time, mine and theirs."

"The healing goddesses of the Celts are fierce. One does not call upon them for aid unless one is willing to be transformed utterly." The duke had moved again, swifter than thought, and stepped farther into the light. "Ceridwen is one such, and we felines also call upon the Egyptian pantheon, and thus, Sekhmet."

"How fascinating. So many gods and goddesses to invoke."

"Gods and goddesses, indifferent to my dilemma—" He cut himself off, visibly appalled at what he had almost admitted.

She would lose him if she pursued that line of thought. "The wolves follow the Romans, whom my brother Timothy says borrowed their pantheon and the terms for the pack hierarchy from the Greeks."

"Stole them, more like. Although, in truth, many on this island descend from ancient Rome. The wolves will do anything to hold sway."

"And by the Duke of Lowell doing so, many are safe under his aegis."

"As you and your brother are safe." The duke canted his head, assessing her. "You do not strike me as one who seeks safety."

"Who does not seek safety?"

"One who casually imbibes poison," he mumbled.

A gentle wind soughed through the branches of the birch trees, the air bitingly cold as it was wont to be in early spring in England. She tightened the scarf she had wound around her neck, over the shawl wrapped around her shoulders, over Timothy's heavy coat. She was sure she looked a veritable crone. Everything she owned was serviceable, made with longevity in mind. She suddenly wished for a brighter shawl, a frivolous scrap in a flattering color, that complemented her...hair? Did ladies wear things that enhanced their hair?

"You are forever out of doors." He hesitated and came closer.

"My work requires it. And it happens to suit me. The work and being outside. I dislike confinement." For one who was cautious in her language, she had erred grievously. "Oh. I apologize. That was thoughtless of me."

She left it at that and watched him watch her as though waiting for something. He said, "Her Grace of Lowell would be flustered to have made such a statement and deluge me with apologies."

"If anyone deserves to be swamped with those, it is you."

"While you are not. Flustered."

"I have misspoken and corrected myself." Years of needing to be as direct as possible to non-English speakers left her often sounding abrupt, but it had taught her to express herself precisely and simply.

"If you would like to discuss what I said, please do." Discussion did not occur. "And you may speak frankly to Her Grace. She is keen to become fully accustomed to *versipellian* ways."

"You have an instinct for them."

Tabitha didn't know if she did or she didn't. "Travel requires one to keep an open mind." She slid her shears back into her pocket and hoisted her trug.

"It is more than that." He reached out to take it from her like the gentleman he was, but stopped and backed away until he was once again hidden from her sight.

"Thank you, I am well able to carry it myself." This was more than she had hoped for from their first meeting in situ, as it were, so she made her way out of the grove.

"I remember it is the act of a gentleman." His voice sounded the roughest it had yet. "To make an offer of aid."

If it were not in poor taste, I would say you put your leg in that trap, Your Grace! "I am here to offer you aid, though I am no gentleman. You are aware it is my purpose at Lowell Hall, and yet this is the first time we have spoken."

"The second." That should not thrill her as it did, that he remembered the night at Arcadia.

"I must be honest with you, Your Grace." She shifted the trug up to her elbow; it ought not to feel any heavier than usual, but now that she had the image in her mind's eye of a duke carrying it for her, it very much did. "I don't know what I can do in aid of your difficulty. You are a source of worry to those near and dear to you, and my usual approach to healing matters is not useful in this instance.

"You may or may not speak of your experience as you see fit. I suspect, at this stage, speaking of it will reinforce the pain." She headed down the path that would lead her back to the cottage; he tracked her on the right. "However, I feel I must earn my place here, and unfortunately you are my means to do so."

"Shall we make a trade?" He prowled out of the underbrush and stood before her.

The sun had almost fully risen, and its light flooded the canopy overhead, limning him in gold. No matter his rough clothing, he looked like a fallen angel frescoed on the wall of an Italian church.

"Shall we? That is an unexpected proposition, Your Grace. What in the world have I to offer other than my tinctures and tonics, of which you seem reluctant to avail?"

A glint lit his eye. As for her, an old impulse stirred within, a carefree pleasure. "You have yet to attend the Sunday Meal," he said.

She could hear the capital letters implied. The duchess had been relentless in her pursuit of the Barringtons' company at this auspicious event. "My brother and I will attend this week."

"If it is true what you say, that I ought to be allowed to speak when I wish and not when I do not wish to, then I ask you to intervene."

"To draw attention from you?" Hmmm. "That does not sound onerous."

"Have we a bargain?"

"With my payment to be as I see fit?"

The duke nodded, and Tabitha extended her hand. He retreated, and she dropped her arm. Was a handshake too masculine a gesture? It wouldn't be the first time she'd made that mistake.

"Very well." She switched her trug to her unshaken hand. "This is much like a deal I would strike with my brother," she said.

Llewellyn's nostrils quivered. "I am not your brother."

"I am well aware—" And in a heartbeat, he was gone.

Three

Since she and Timothy had moved to Lowell Hall, great effort had been made to accommodate them and ensure their comfort. Timothy had overseen the refurbishment of the schoolroom in the Hall proper, as well as fulfilling the duchess's desire for one belowstairs. Tabitha's brother, egalitarian in his values when it came to education, leaped upon this opportunity like a spring hare.

As for Tabitha, Felicity assigned a fleet of Lowell Hall footmen the task of turning the former smokehouse, mere steps from the kitchen door of the cottage, into a stillroom. It was very impressive: the large hearth previously used for preparing meats now bristled with a series of swinging arms and pots for use over the open fire; tall oaken cases fronted by glass doors hosted a plethora of empty jars waiting for herbs and potions and extractions. It was very nearly wasted on her, as out of necessity she had condensed her medicinal needs to fit compactly into her portable carryall. Fashioned out of leather and canvas, with a variety of pockets inside and out, it served as a harvesting trug and an apothecary case. It was her most prized possession, one she'd designed with a cobbler, of all things, in Paris, of all places. She had everything necessary at hand, always, and no real need for anything else.

What would she do with all this room?

Tabitha set down her case on the high table in the center of the…the healing shed. Let it be known as the *healing shed.* "This abundance is not—oh." The stray cat that had adopted them in southern Italy was, of course, still abroad. Tabitha hadn't intended it to attach to her, but it had and became a feature around her ankles and on her appointments. Timothy had playfully called the creature her familiar and exhorted her to smuggle it back to England with them, but she would not do that to an innocent animal. Bad enough one of them was being transported against their will.

"Oh, dear me, Tabitha Barrington, that is a dramatic thought." If she had no Italian cat to talk to, she would talk to herself. There must be *cat* cats about the place; she might find a new audience soon enough.

Absent Italian felines notwithstanding, all these accouterments were poorly timed riches. It wasn't merely to do with her spartan way of working but also due to the fact she wasn't sure she wanted to continue down this road.

How invigorating it had been, building upon the skills she'd learned from Father's housekeeper. How satisfying as she and Timothy had made their way across the Continent, from France to the Netherlands to Spain to Italy to Greece, learning about local cures and emollients. No matter how few or how many days they spent in one place, there was always something new to learn and discover.

She had a repertoire of cures for common and not-so-common ills and the advantage, in the expatriate community they inevitably found in each place, of not being a foreigner even if she was a woman. Only grudgingly calling herself an apothecary and never calling herself a doctor, she had framed herself as a palliative vendor. During their time in Greece, Timothy had insisted she refer to herself as a Hygieist, in honor of their goddess of health. Try as he might, and to her relief, it did not take. In Italy, he had attempted to coin *Trotist*, based on the fame of an ancient female doctor who instructed men, but she had put her foot down, not wishing to find herself lashed to a stake in the *piazza*. Her skills often outpaced the common knowledge of the day, and the last thing she needed was to make even more of a spectacle of herself than she already was.

Tabitha sat on the stool that suited the height of the table. The enormous window faced north; in the summer she would be able to work well into the evening...if it was called for. As a rule, she had toiled every hour God sent but suspected that her days would be more her own than they had been her whole life. The time now afforded her would be welcome if she was to establish her practice in this new place.

She emptied her trug of the morning's forage, setting aside the foxglove with care, and headed for the cottage, yet another embarrassment of riches. It was two stories, and they each had their own bedroom, so no more sleeping on sofas for Timothy. The ground floor was one massive open space with a large, fully stocked kitchen that expanded into a lean-to; she could admire her brother's command of it from a table that optimistically seated eight. It was not on the level of the grandeur of the Hall, and they had both refused the cadre of servants Felicity was willing to assign them, but even so it was more than they'd had for years.

Tabitha entered through the kitchen door and watched as Timothy unpacked the last of his books, cooing like a mama dove at her bevy of chicks. As she had condensed the tools of her trade, his had expanded to the degree they needed a donkey and cart to transport them. Once they settled in Sorrento, the books had bred like bunnies.

Here, he had an entire wall of bookcases at his disposal, interrupted by the sitting room hearth and running from floor to ceiling. Two comfortable chairs flanked the fireplace, a tea table between them, with side tables prepared to accept cups of tea and piles of reading or a workbag. It was as cozy as an illustration out of *The Lady's Monthly Museum,* and it made Tabitha want to—

Want to sit down straightaway with a hot drop. Yes, indeed. That was the response of a lady and a contented woman: tea.

She thrust a poker at the fire in the stove and set the kettle on the hob.

Time to begin as she intended they go on.

A glance over her shoulder revealed Timothy sitting on the floor, absorbed. This happened every time he unpacked his library: his attention was caught by an old favorite, whatever progress he made came to a halt, and he was lost to the outside world.

So lost, the knock that fell upon the door went unheeded.

"Tim?"

"Eh—Tab?" He looked up, squinting like a bat at noon.

"Door."

"Door?" Another knock, stronger, sounded. "Ah!" Timothy rose smoothly to standing and opened the door to a little maid holding a tottering pile of linens. "Hello there! If these are for us, we are spoiled indeed." He beamed down at the girl as he relieved her of her burden, his big brown eyes sparkling.

"How d'ye do?" The girl bobbed a curtsy with the proper degree of deference required for an Honorable brother and sister. "Her Grace sends her compliments as well as the sheets and toweling cloths." She nibbled her bottom lip with two large front teeth.

"Good morning and thank you, miss…?" Tabitha asked.

"Oh, Mary Mossett. I'm from down the Hall, doing bits for Mrs. Birks."

"As well as being a talented seamstress, or so I hear." Tabitha had heard directly from the duchess.

"A seamstress?" Timothy set aside the linens and the book he still held; Tabitha watched the girl's eyes follow the latter like it was a sumptuous, laden platter being put out of reach. "I have several garments in need of repair. I am useless with a needle, and never mind my sister who, though she may stitch a wound as finely as a lady's hem, let her near a button and the less said, the better."

"Thank you for nothing, Timothy," Tabitha said. "What Mr. Barrington means to say is we are both in need of a talented needlewoman. What is your fee?"

"Fee?" The little creature—Tabitha guessed she was a mouse; the two front teeth and the large ears sticking out from her cap gave it away—looked as though she had been knocked for six. "Like, money?"

"The going rate in Southern Italy is equal to two English pounds."

"Two pounds?" Mary Mossett looked enraptured and enraged at the same time. "That's a fortune, that is. You got done, if you don't mind my saying." Any reservations the maid had in the presence of titled strangers flew out the window. Tabitha liked her all the better for it.

"A barter, perhaps?" It was a day for bargaining and haggling. "Since my dear brother has disparaged my skills—"

"Lack thereof, darling sister."

"—then I propose an exchange of your skills for his," Tabitha said. Timothy beamed; he, too, had seen Mary Mossett's fascination with his book. "Mr. Barrington will, of course, be conducting lessons in the servants' hall, but a few extra sessions here and there might be welcome?"

"Yes, miss! Yes, sir!" The mouse-maid treated them to a flurry of curtsies. "Although I reckon you could be charging more than two pounds for book learning."

"Value is in the eye of the beholder, Mary." Timothy took down a primer from the shelf. "I am paraphrasing Plato, who was a Greek philosopher. To many, the study of reading and writing is not worth the expense of time it takes to learn. Whereas to others, no price can be set on it, as it expands one's world far beyond its physical borders. Have you your letters, or…?"

As her brother patiently paged through the book with the little maid, Tabitha collected the largesse from the Hall and rushed up the stairs to exchange them for their mending. Timothy's room was the picture of chaos, as usual, and she tidied

as she gathered shirts, a waistcoat, and his heavy
jacket. They hadn't needed the latter for years. Oh,
Italy! As genial as France had been, as tolerant as
the Netherlands were, as lazy and hot as Greece
was, Italy had spoken to her even if she could not
return the favor—her grasp of the language never
advanced past remedial.

What a day for cataloging her lack of skills, and
yet she considered leaving behind the only thing
she'd ever mastered.

Tabitha's far more orderly chamber was a respite,
her pile of mending already assembled, with the
view to bribing Timothy into doing it. She piled his
clothes on her bed and stood at the window, seeing
all the way up the hill that was part of the Duke of
Llewellyn's domain. Should she draw the curtains?
For she was sure she had drawn his attention, finally,
and was certain he would learn as much about her
as he could. *Fair enough*, she thought. While his
plight called to her instincts, others had stirred in
that grove, playful, flirtatious instincts that had no
place in her life. She twitched the curtains closed
and left those thoughts to stew.

───────

After sending Mary Mossett on her way, Tabitha
deemed it time to roll out the big guns as far as the
duke was concerned. The kettle was boiled, the pot

was warmed, and the tray was arranged with plates and cakes and serviettes and the star attraction: the steaming pot of tea.

Always, perpetual, endless: tea.

The moment he heard the clatter of china, Timothy had taken his place in what would now and forever be his chair by the hearth. She poured out—she had no ingrained talent for this, but the only person she knew who could ruin tea beyond redemption was Felicity—and set her brother's cup and saucer on the table.

She had been approaching this challenge from one angle only. It was time for her brother to instruct her, as he was ever happy to do. "What do you know about lions?"

"Lions…" Her brother closed his book and set it carefully on the side table at his elbow. He folded his glasses with equal solicitousness. There was a time when they could not afford to replace anything broken, and certainly not expensive spectacles. Would they soon become inured to their relative prosperity? She hoped not, for what they had once lacked in coin, they had gained in resilience and ingenuity.

Timothy folded his hands in his lap, the sight of his ink-stained fingers suddenly filling her with grief and euphoria in succession: how she had feared for his well-being, how grateful she was he was safe. He smiled and rubbed the callus on his right middle finger, the one built up against his devoted penmanship. "Derived from the Latin *leo* and fittingly given our environs, the Ancient Greek λέων." He spoke a word in what she assumed was that language. "Order *carnivora*, family *felidae*, genus *panthera*, et cetera." He smiled, his cheeky wit gleaming through. "The males of the species, as you may have noticed, are blessed with an abundance of hair."

"His is in a wretched state. I wonder if it occurred in his animal Shape." Tabitha hated to think that was so. "And yet, inexplicably Welsh?"

"No, indeed. The Wild Lion of Wales figures in the traditional arms of the House of Aberffraw and on the personal arms of the current duke's ancient namesake. The reasons for this would be lost in the mists of history, as the family line is all but gone. Lions, for all their predatory and dangerous natures, are highly sought as hunting trophies and as the subject of ritual kills."

Tabitha tapped her fingers on the arm of what would now and forever be *her* chair by the hearth. "Do you recall that family in Munich? The ones who ran the guesthouse?"

"The ones you could not stop talking about?" Timothy topped up their cups. "Or talking to, quizzing them day and night? Thank goodness we were not meant to stay long, they were that close to turfing us out."

"There was something about them." Tabitha recalled their demeanor, fuller of life than anyone she had yet met. "I think they must be *versipelles*."

"Which you would not have been able to ask, according to their laws." The duke himself had explained the unique characteristics of their new neighbors to Timothy.

"Or had known to ask." Tabitha sipped at her tea. "I am surprised they find it necessary to do so. Once one knows what to look for, it is easy to tell straightaway."

"Not all of us have your powers of perception." Timothy considered the offerings and chose a slice of gingerbread.

"There is a healthfulness about them, unlike us. A vitality." Tabitha helped herself to a macaroon. "I expect that is why Llewellyn's condition is of such concern. The issue with his inability to Change cannot simply be physical. I am sure they must think themselves into their Shapes, don't you? Or feel into it—oh, they are an emotional lot, as we get to know them better. I do wish we had stayed longer in Germany."

"Not your opinion at the time," Timothy muttered.

"I heard tell of a physician, Dr. Reil, who thinks illnesses of the mind are not hereditary evils but a disturbance of the harmony between mind and body." The man had not provided any practical advice to follow, unfortunately. "The duke's instincts must be in his body as much as they are in his mind. Ought he to have something to, to hunt? Would that be part of his cure?"

"It is the female who hunts," Timothy corrected her. "The male is there for, er, courting purposes and as the last line of defense in the protection of territory. As I have said, they have always been hunted, and in the case of Your Grace—"

"He is not *my* Grace."

"—taken from their homes, never to return. Alive, if lucky. Or perhaps it is not so lucky."

"No. But he is lucky now to call this place home. And it must be the same for the rest, the mice and the colts and the badgers. Even if they live under the aegis of the wolf."

"The wolf and his wife, a human, who has taken to their ways with aplomb."

"Shall we do the same?" Tabitha asked. It wasn't so much a proposal as a consideration.

"I believe so. We are amongst very few who are in on the secret." Timothy, as ever, was delighted by knowledge of any kind. "And have so many things to add to what we know."

Tabitha ticked them off on her fingers. "Enhanced senses, longer-than-human life span, reproductive capabilities by choice, the power of the Alpha as expressed in the *dominatum*." That last was the oppressive power His Highness had exuded, and the first thing Tabitha had queried. "As well as bonding for life as fated mates. Or, to use the correct term, *vera amoris*." Why did that make her shiver so?

"The mating bite." Timothy waggled his eyebrows.

"It strikes me as rather unsanitary."

Her brother drank his tea. "I would accept one without reservation."

"Would you?"

"Oh, yes." He set his cup on its saucer and both on the tray. He took hers as well, since whoever did not cook or brew, cleaned. "To be visibly claimed by my mate before the whole world? Without censure or fear of reprisal? Yes, indeed."

"I did not think of it that way. Thank you." Tabitha grimaced. "Even so. A mark on one's person, so public."

Timothy took the tea things to the sink and added some hot water from the pot on the fire. "Not all of us are as independent as you are."

He made it sound like a bad thing.

Four

THE BARRINGTONS HAD ELUDED THE OBLIGA-
tion of the Sunday Meal one week too many and
could no longer defer. Timothy had been happy
enough to go, keen for society and comfortable in
it; Tabitha, not as much. He refused to attend without her, a stance that was not at all selfless: it was
his way of goading her into going, for she would
not deprive him of the chance to be in company.
To be fair, once she had made forays into the many
social circles they visited throughout their travels,
she'd enjoyed herself. This would not be any different, except for the fact they lived here now. They
would not be leaving here. Ever.

Tabitha tipped back her sherry, and the Lowell
butler, Mr. Coburn, was by her side in the blink of
an eye. She smiled with gratitude, sighed with resignation, sipped with pleasure. If this libation was
a weekly reward, it was another endorsement for
settling in Sussex.

She noticed that only she and her brother were
imbibing and remembered Felicity mentioning *versipelles* only lightly partook of wine with
meals. Tabitha suspected it had to do with those

heightened senses and shuddered to think of a Shapeshifter who had taken too much liquor.

The drawing room was a soothing chamber in tones of ivory and brown, and the Lowell Hall contingent was arranged decorously within it. The duke was dressed to a standard generally met in Carlton House, with Felicity not far behind in a gown that, while not *á la* current *mode*, spoke to setting future fashions. At first glance, Mr. Bates, the pack's Beta, or Second, appeared to be kitted out to the same high degree: the cut of his clothing was smart but did not hold up under scrutiny, as his cravat was wrinkled and his waistcoat a disaster of badly stitched seams. It was a poor showing for a lord of his status, given his brother Nathaniel was the heir apparent of their pack, and he, the spare.

Bates was outshone by O'Mara, Lowell's chamberlain and the pack's Omega, who was characteristically sporting her masculine attire. Timothy was quizzing her on the provenance of her tailcoat; as always, he, too, was turned out well, and for once Tabitha regretted her disinterested approach to fashion. The fabric of her garment was good stuff, at least according to the Florentine modiste who made it, but it lacked flair, which was not the fault of the dressmaker. Tabitha looked a very plain partridge indeed, but she was nigh invisible in comparison to Llewellyn, whose ensemble included a waistcoat the hue of a cluster of ripe cherries, not terrible on its own merits, but when added to the yellow coat... Tabitha laughed into her sherry. If Lowell's expression at the sight of his peer was anything to go by, he might require her *sal volatile*.

"I am delighted you have joined us, both of you." Felicity beamed at them, and Timothy left off interrogating O'Mara about her tailor.

"We had much to sort out after so many years abroad," Tabitha said.

"And I like to establish myself with my students before socializing with my employers," Timothy added. "Happily, there was opportunity to do so on the Continent, unlike the general practice in England to keep the help behind the green baize door. Or in the attics."

"We never did live with any of Timothy's charges," Tabitha added, "as the majority were adults keen to learn or improve their English."

"So no chance of being tucked away out of sight in some drafty Belgian *grenier*," Timothy quipped.

Tabitha squinted. "In a what now?"

"An *attic*, Tabitha," Timothy scolded. "Honestly, the context was right there."

"We are thrilled you are settled in to your satisfaction and have joined us at last." Felicity cut off the sibling spat without missing a beat; well done, for an only child. "His Grace has been our only new face at the table. I daresay you are relieved, Llewellyn."

Tabitha could not fault Felicity for attempting to draw out the Welsh duke but could see it agitated him beyond measure. He paced back and forth before a hearth whose mantel hosted a mélange of ceramic animal figures, plus one rosy-cheeked shepherdess. He paused by a window at one end of the room that overlooked the drive, paced past the hearth, and gazed out at the park from the window at the back of the Hall.

"I must say I am in sympathy with the duke. I am not at my best in company." Here, this was the perfect chance to fulfill her end of their bargain.

"Not at all, Tab—Miss Barrington," Felicity said. "Only think of the wonderful time we had at Arcadia."

"Partaking of the duke's brandy and likely speaking of feminine mysteries," Timothy guessed.

"I have a habit of defaulting to health topics no matter what the circumstances," Tabitha explained. "To the dismay of my brother."

"It is always illuminating, if not always comfortable." Timothy and Tabitha burst into laughter as one, and Tabitha cringed a bit at the politely inquiring faces that met their mirth.

"Timothy, we are rude. Apologies, all, my brother and I are somewhat rough around the edges for an English social setting. We adopted less stringent manners abroad. We are little better than feral." A cough issued from near the hearth. "Or not as feral as some." Good Lord, what was she saying? Even Llewellyn looked at her askance.

"I am thrilled to thank you in person, Your Grace, for our beautiful cottage." Timothy addressed the Duke of Lowell, covering her *faux pas* as usual. "And Your Grace, of course." He bowed his head to Felicity. "We received a wealth of linens just last week, and in turn, we sent Miss Mossett off with all our mending."

"Oh, she is a wonderful seamstress," Felicity said. "She tailored Miss O'Mara's waistcoat herself."

"Did she?" Timothy eyed the garment with interest.

"Miss Mossett was shocked to hear how much we paid for such services in Italy," Tabitha added. "Timothy is engaged on a barter with her, as she seems keen to learn."

"She is keen about everything." Felicity's smile was fond. "The preparations for the *cursio* at Ostara have her in alt."

Llewellyn froze at the front window, his fingers clutching the frame. Once again the company held their breath; they were so attuned to his distress, Tabitha did not know if it was helpful or harmful. "Ostara?" Tabitha asked, stumbling over the pronunciation.

Timothy set aside the sherry he had hardly touched. "Would that be a festival of some sort?"

"It is the lupine celebration in observance of spring," Lowell explained. "It aligns with the *homo plenus* celebration of Easter."

"There is to be a bonfire, and then all *versipelles* will Shift and run through the park." Felicity peeked at her husband through her lashes. "It is a common aspect of our practices, but it was not observed at Lupercalia."

"Due to the ducal wedding taking precedence." Lowell's husky tones brought a blush to his bride's cheeks.

"Are outsiders permitted to witness this event?" Timothy asked.

"The *cursio* is...rather daunting for those who are not Shifters," O'Mara said.

"I will only be present for the lighting of the fire," Felicity admitted, "and then must wait for my husband in one of the cottages in the park."

"Is it important to the health of the pack?" Tabitha asked. "To Change as one?"

"It is a practice we wolves have bequeathed upon all in our care," Lowell replied. "Our smaller species do not feel the need to Shift as often as, er, the rest of us." Another frisson of unease shuddered through the assembly.

"This sherry is lovely," Tabitha all but bellowed; she saw Llewellyn hesitate in his pacing and blink at her.

Felicity gestured to Tabitha's glass, and Mr. Coburn refilled it with alacrity. Oh dear, perhaps Tabitha ought to refuse, but the rooster—yes, he was a rooster, look at that comb of hair on his head—was so eager to serve, she hated to thwart him. "It reminds me of Córdoba," she continued. "We had arrived there after a journey made arduous by garrulous company and more than one broken axle, and our landlady greeted us with glasses of the most exquisite *amontillado*. Its making is far more complex than that of the sort found in Jerez and, well, it was delicious." She cut herself off—why would those who did not drink the stuff be interested in its making?

"And the brother of her husband's cousin-in-law provided us with casks for our entire stay," Timothy said, "due to the fact the distiller became enamored of—" Tabitha tilted her chin to her shoulder and shot him a look from beneath her lashes. "Oh, never mind. I shall refrain from sharing the anecdote. My sister has spoken—or grimaced."

The last thing Tabitha wanted recounted was the story of Senor Garcia's ardent pursuit of her. "Do forgive us, we have spent so much time in each other's company—" Tabitha began.

"We have an entire lexicon of facial expressions," Timothy finished.

"How I longed for a brother or sister," Felicity said. She turned to Llewellyn, and a threatening rumble emitted from the Welsh duke, whose pacing increased in speed. The air in the room compressed in the way it had in the prince's presence, and Timothy trembled as it peaked then faded.

Tabitha guessed Lowell was the origin of the disturbance, likely in protection of his wife. "I understand you have a sister?" she asked him.

"I do." Lowell nodded his gratitude at the diversion of the subject. "Lady Phoebe Blakesley. She has been away from us for some time."

"Abroad, in the United States of America." Felicity reached out and took her husband's hand. "I have yet to meet her."

The duke smiled at his duchess. "We are striving to bring her back."

"I am sure she is eager to be brought." Timothy sighed. "We ever yearned for home."

Speak for yourself, Tabitha thought. She was saved from uttering an anodyne sentiment by the strike of the gong, the sudden sound of which nearly sent Llewellyn out of his skin.

———

The typically excruciating Sunday Meal was made somewhat bearable by the presence of the lady apothecary and her brother; the addition of both created a distraction from his presence, and Miss Barrington was fulfilling her end of their bargain admirably. It was the least attention he'd suffered under this roof, and he hoped she wasn't as squiffy as she appeared, if only so she could continue to do her part. He couldn't say the flush on her cheeks and her general air of abandon weren't rather appealing. It was quite the contrast to her usual manner. In any case, it did the job; he wondered what she would charge him with in recompense.

He would find out, if the meal would ever, ever end. Every course seemed as if it should be the last but was inevitably followed by another. It was more food than he'd seen in all his years combined, certainly at Drake's and even at Georgie's. His memories of childhood meals were indistinct; his family had not had much call to entertain in the wilds of Wales, and if he recalled correctly, it was not his father who disliked society but his mum, unlike most females of their kind.

The lady apothecary seemed of that ilk. She hid behind her little glass of liquor during the farce that was the gathering in the drawing room. Shifters did not imbibe, although he couldn't recall why. Perhaps it made no difference to them, as they were unable to get foxed? In a manner of speaking. Or it was too dangerous for them to do so? Under the unflinching attention of the butler, the lady had become tipsy and nearly got into a squabble with her brother. Anything to keep them all from staring at him.

Although it was worse when they looked at him out of the corners of their eyes.

As they were doing now. It was impossible to ignore since they were sitting cheek by jowl at an intimate table rather than dining in state. Every move he made was observed, increasing his self-consciousness about his ability to feed himself in front of them.

The soup course had been manageable, and the cheese soufflé he addressed with a spoon, a spoon out of the correct order of utensils, which had sent a flutter of dismay through the footmen. Then another something or other, a casserole of vegetables which made the wolves groan good-naturedly and Her Grace ask for another serving of it to be doled out to those who complained. This was also to his advantage, and he dug in. A predator he may be, but greens were now a staple in his diet, and he'd become partial to them. It was nice to have them cooked and hot rather than foraged straight out of the ground.

The current dish contained delicately seasoned slices of lamb. The aroma hinted of rosemary and a touch of thyme, a heady scent that almost brought him to tears. In his mind's eye, he saw a flash of apron, a spit turning over a hearth; in the ear of memory, he heard a voice teasing him about robbing the spit-boy's job of tending to the meat. He breathed to calm himself, which only served to draw in the scent again and again. He grabbed for his glass, even though he had no use for wine. The tartness of the elderberry brought him back to his sour mood.

Alwyn wished to eat the meat.

He did not trust himself with the fork.

In Carlton House, mealtime was not unlike those he'd experienced in the beast wagon. A well-placed snarl ensured he was not required to dine with his betters. He suspected his sustenance would have been flung over the threshold of his rooms if not for the preservation of the royal porcelain.

It had allowed him the privacy to remaster utensils. The spoon was easy enough, but the fork still eluded him; even the knife presented less difficulty. He would not reveal how his hand trembled when he attempted the fork. He refused to struggle and fail before all.

For as polite and well-intentioned as they were, the coterie under this roof were highfliers. The Lowell chef produced a meal that would not shame the hosts should some lupine deity descend from the heavens to join them. Alfred was as fussy as Georgie when it came to his attire, and the entire company was kitted out in their finest. As was now customary, Alwyn took great pleasure in achieving new heights of sartorial idiosyncrasy. Alfred's thunderous brow was a sight to see, and the explosion was quashed only because his mate would not like it.

Alwyn had once wanted a mate and yet deferred seeking out the bond in his flirtatious youth. Had he met his *vera amoris*, would his absence have been discovered straightaway? Or would his beloved, seeking him, have fallen prey to the same foe, two souls rather than one caged? After all was said and done, perhaps it was for the best he hadn't found his true mate after all.

"Your Grace." The butler approached the table, and three came to attention. He saw the lady apothecary exchange a cheeky glance with her brother. They were alike enough to be twins, similar in coloring and build, with the brother more at ease in company than the sister. Mr. Barrington seemed better blessed in his looks, but the slightest spark of interest, of humor or mischief, and Miss Barrington was lit from within as if the sun rose not by degrees but in an instant.

Although Alwyn noticed her hesitancy to talk about her time abroad. She was vibrant and passionate when she began an anecdote and then snuffed it out as easily as she would a candle flame.

Everyone was looking at him. Why? Oh. He was the Grace queried. He grunted, and the butler said something about disliking the course and if he would prefer it replaced, the chef would be happy to do so. While the butler nattered away and everyone carried on staring, his fingers spasmed over the dratted fork, and the familiar frustration reared up within, as his essential creature once had, without thought, effortless. Now, no thought could reach his lion, no emotion, nothing. He was alone, alone with his body and his thoughts and—no, he could not think on this now, not in front of all these people looking at him. As he was one breath away from fleeing the room—

—that *lady* picked up a slice of lamb with her fingers and ate it.

===

Tabitha kicked Timothy in the shin, two short and one long, and picked up another slice of lamb. He glanced over at her and followed suit.

She smiled, closemouthed, at the variety of expressions that greeted her action. Lowell looked like a scalded cat; Felicity, bless her, attempted to betray no expression at all and failed; O'Mara was her usual sphinxlike self, and Mr. Bates, as was his wont, appeared to be parsing her action in his mind, teasing out her motive.

Timothy took his cue without faltering. He dabbed his lips with his serviette and reached for another piece of the delicious meat. "I suspect my sister is reminded of our time in Crete, where we often enjoyed a lamb dish seasoned very like this one. It was eaten quite casually with the fingers."

"Quite so, Timothy," she chimed in, "and without thinking, I fell into the traditional manner of consuming it."

"Is this the Greek way in all things? To use one's hands?" Felicity inquired.

Timothy, who was barely suppressing a guffaw, got an admonitory bash to his ankle. *Do not regale the party with your tales of Greek handiwork, Brother.* She glared and then had to stop herself from giggling. She quickly ate another piece of lamb.

"A dish such as *paidakia*, for example, would be too hot to do so, Your Grace, but much of Greek cuisine is eaten without ceremony. It is quite liberating, like a picnic at the dinner table. Although that may be a poor comparison, as it must be said that many an English picnic is conducted with as much ceremony as a royal banquet. After Crete, we spent several weeks on the island of Ios, where we…"

And bless him, as only one used to commanding attention could, Timothy drew all eyes and ears to his discourse on Grecian cooking as was found specifically in the islands north of the mainland.

Tabitha reached for the platter and was not equal to Mr. Coburn's eagle eye; he directed a footman to serve her. O'Mara went so far as to convey her reaction by the twitch of an eyelid and joined in. Mr. Bates looked to resist but was no match for Tabitha's stare. He considered her, noted where everyone's attention was *not*, and realization dawned. He, too, joined in.

The Welsh duke hesitated…hesitated…and proceeded to clear his plate. With a gesture from Felicity, Mr. Coburn himself retrieved the platter of lamb to replenish His Grace's serving.

Tabitha caught Llewellyn's eye, and his expression betrayed the usual reaction her innovations inspired in others: annoyance, reluctant interest, relief the issue was addressed, but irritation that the unique process was needed in the first place.

Timothy was concluding his thesis on Greek cuisine. "…and of course, as a result, there is a greater than usual need to wash one's hands, which results in two lucrative industries. Pottery, for the finger bowls, and rose otto oil."

"The latter restores the naturally occurring moisture lost in said handwashing," Tabitha said. She smiled at Lowell, who slid another slice of lamb into his mouth. "It is also effective as an emetic." Had she not been an old hand at embarrassing herself in public, she might have blushed, but the desired effect was achieved: the Duke of Llewellyn continued to eat in peace.

With any luck, this was the last course. Good Lord, how it dragged on. And yet it had served its purpose, and she had more than one question to put to the *versipelles* about their reluctant ducal guest.

Coburn, who was an absolute treasure, oversaw the addition of finger bowls to their place settings.

Conversation carried on, orchestrated by Timothy, who drew out Lowell and Mr. Bates on their own travels abroad. O'Mara remained stoic, and Felicity finally asked for the sweet course to be brought in; amongst the offerings was a trifle easily eaten with a spoon.

Five

AFTER-DINNER TEA DRINKING WAS A STEP TOO far for the Welsh duke: one moment he was walking down the corridor with the rest, and the next, not.

"That was ingenious." Felicity had taken Tabitha's arm as they processed down the hall. "I had not noticed His Grace was in difficulty."

"Fresh eyes." Tabitha patted her friend's arm. "And I am used to watching and listening from a detached perspective."

"But is it wise to reinforce uncivilized activity?" O'Mara stood aside and allowed the company to precede her into the drawing room.

"Would allowing His Grace's struggle to continue not have been worse?" As chummy as Timothy had become with the chamberlain before the meal, Tabitha and she had not properly spoken, despite having been introduced on the Barringtons' arrival. Was the Omega avoiding her?

In fairness, Tabitha had not made much effort to mix with those around her; it was time she came out of the high grass. She required answers, and there was no better time than the present.

The housekeeper, Mrs. Birks, wheeled in a tea

cart, and Felicity sighed with resignation. "May I?" Tabitha stepped forward. "It is the least service I can provide after such a wonderful meal."

"It would be a service to all," Felicity whispered in her ear as she ceded the place behind the tea things.

"You might sit at my side to watch and learn, you know," Tabitha countered; Her Grace laughed and joined her husband on a cozy sofa.

Tabitha duly poured tea and set cakes upon plates. Timothy and Mr. Bates distributed the treats; O'Mara gazed over Tabitha's shoulder and seemed to interact with the air. At one stage, the chamberlain's eyes narrowed even as her brows ascended her forehead; her jaw clenched, and she accepted her tea with a scowl.

"I suspect, Miss Barrington, that you have taken stock of our characters thanks to the way we take our tea." Mr. Bates smiled down at her, a dimple winking in his cheek. His green eyes were captivating, if one found that sort of thing attractive, all that dimpling and sparkling. She imagined his lupine coat was as light as his hair, which was exceptionally blond.

"What would I posit about one who takes theirs with several dollops of sugar?" She handed him his cup, made to that prescription. "I wouldn't dare to say." That they needed an infusion of sweetness in their life, perhaps?

"My sister reads the tea but sadly not the leaves," Timothy said.

Tabitha refrained from pelting him with a *petit four*. "My brother, for reasons known only to himself, wishes I were a witch."

"Tabitha's skills are often uncanny in their depth," Timothy said as he handed 'round the last of the treats.

"Do you find it uncomfortable being considered outside the pale?" O'Mara accepted a small plate of biscuits.

"You are far outside your own," Tabitha said. "I discern by your accent you are from Ireland."

"I am not from Dublin," the duke's chamberlain replied. "So, yes, very much beyond the Pale."

"Has O'Mara's role in our pack been explained to you, Miss Barrington?" The duke drained his cup and set it aside.

"I know her designation is *Omega* and nothing more than that."

"It is the final letter in the Greek alphabet," Timothy supplied, "and while one might think it the least, this is not so. Each letter, in lore, is imbued with a specific power, and the last is the bulwark against said powers losing their potency. It contains the strength of the entire alphabet."

"O'Mara acts as such for the Lowell Pack. It would be best if she were involved in your course of rehabilitation for Llewellyn." The duke looked at his chamberlain as though for permission; she nodded. "The Omega's role is to do almost exactly as Mr. Barrington said: to shore up the powers of the ones who go before. Without her, especially as we are such a diverse clan, we would fall into chaos. Preventing that is in her bailiwick."

"And how is this done?" Tabitha asked. The woman was as tall as Mr. Bates, nearly as tall as the duke, but rangy with it. Even though her physical strength was no doubt formidable, Tabitha suspected it was the least important factor in play.

"I am charged with ensuring that nothing escalates—no grievance, nor even an excess of joy." O'Mara took up the explanation. "*Versipelles* are powerful beings in all ways, and it lies with me to oversee the management of emotions."

"Or the control of them?"

The Omega shrugged. "If you wish."

"There is fear amongst the smallest of our kind that O'Mara must tend to," Lowell explained. "A strange predator in our midst is cause for unrest. Unlike us wolves at the top of the pack, who are known and trusted, he is not."

"Can they not do this themselves, by staying safely away? I believe they have been doing so. He is left very much alone."

"I am required to manage the general atmosphere." The Omega did not betray herself by word or tone, but Tabitha had the sensation O'Mara was gritting her teeth through this. "If I perceive a disturbance, I ensure it does not spread through the pack's *sentio*, thereby keeping the peace."

"And what of your own emotions?" Tabitha asked. Felicity hid her face behind her teacup, and Mr. Bates smirked.

"They do not enter into it," O'Mara said. Her usual calm tone was infused with a vein of impatience. "It is not me but a power working through me. In Irish it is called," and she said a word that sounded like *muh-HOO*.

Timothy perked up. "Would that be styled *m-o-t-h-ú*? And is your dialect from Connacht?"

"Yes to both." O'Mara did not elucidate further.

"So this…moohoo," Tabitha said, "is it like water flowing through a pipe? And you can manipulate it without being affected?" This analogy was not the best, but nevertheless: "Because even a pipe, inanimate though it may be, is affected by the flow of water over time."

A flash of anger showed on the Omega's face and was gone in an instant. "It is the way of my kind to be beyond such concerns—"

"Above them," Bates muttered.

"I have been entrusted with this gift. It is my birthright, and it is my responsibility to serve that gift and this pack." The ire seemed to be directed at Mr. Bates, but Tabitha felt firmly put in her place.

"I ask only because His Grace is doing nothing but

controlling his emotions, and I suspect that is part of the larger issue. But naturally, all help is welcome." Tabitha set down her cup and rolled the serving cart to the side. It would do her authority no good to be seen peering over the teapot. "The duke has avoided me up until this past week. In the time I spent with him, I found him to be discerning, protective, and canny. I feel he is grappling with, as would anyone, the loss of his years in that menagerie. What I am less versed in is how his being is informed by his lion self. I expect it takes quite a lot to prevent the emergence of one's animal state. Is that why His Grace reacted strongly to the mention of Ostara?"

"You are observant," Lowell's Second said.

"It was impossible to miss, Mr. Bates."

"The *cursio* is not only a celebration but a necessity," Lowell said. "When my mate first came to us, we had to keep our secret until such time as was perfect to disclose it." Felicity took his hand, and they exchanged a fond look. "It was simple enough for the small Shifters to find time and space to Change, for who would find it odd to come across a mouse or a stoat or a beaver in the park, doing what mice and stoats and beavers do?"

"One might come across a big doggie in the meadow and be taken by surprise," Felicity said, a comment that had even the stoic Omega smiling.

"I was so in need of Changing, Miss Barrington, that I was not thinking clearly," Lowell said. This earned an eye roll from his Second. "Her Grace came upon me in my Shape, and had she been anyone else, it would have gone very badly." He lifted their entwined hands and kissed the back of hers.

"The Change is also necessary for the well-being of the pack as a whole," he continued. "It is vital that the prey feel at home with the predators. When they see us regularly in our animal skins, when they mix with us without being harmed, it assures them we are there to protect them. When we run together, they understand they are not the object of pursuit, but are joining us in a show of unity. Hence, the *cursio*. We observe this on our ceremonial days and after milestone events like marriages and births."

"How spectacular." It sounded like nothing Tabitha had ever seen. "Is there no way we may witness this?"

"It is rather a lot for a *homo plenus* to experience," O'Mara said. "I would advise against it."

"Would this event appeal to all *versipelles?*" Tabitha asked. "Even if they were not part of the pack?" O'Mara nodded. "So, even if he wanted to, it will not be something the duke can take part in, as he is unable to Change. Or does not wish to."

"If he does not Change, he will die," Lowell growled.

They were finally at the crux of the matter. "Is that a certainty?"

"It is known amongst our kind," O'Mara said; her voice took on a light, soothing cadence that helped the duke relax and made Felicity scowl.

"Is it proven amongst your kind?"

O'Mara's tone turned abrupt. "You would not understand."

"Exactly!" The *versipelles* did not look as though they had expected that response. Tabitha continued, "This is why I am well-placed to address this. I do not understand, therefore I must strive to do so. I do this through inquiry. It is not my intention to anger you. I am not ignorant, I am uninformed. I will not suffer shame because there is no reason for it. Do you see how I framed this?"

Mr. Bates looked intrigued; the duke nodded; O'Mara cast a look over Tabitha's shoulder again and sighed, then nodded.

"I question perceptions," Tabitha said. "The inability to Change is perceived to be dangerous to *versipellian* health. It is clear the duke is suffering. Is it because he does not Shift?"

Lowell leaned forward. "If I do not Shift for a long period, I feel as though I shall die."

"Oh, I see. Feelings." Not *feelings* again. "You are fearful for your creature."

"Yes." The duke did not equivocate.

"Is your creature afraid?"

That made him stop to think. "Our connection

wavers and I cannot feel him as well as I usually would," he replied.

"I assumed—badly done of me, to assume—that you are in constant communication with your animal spirit."

"Not a spirit." This was relayed with conviction, and Bates and O'Mara both nodded at their Alpha's statement.

"No?" This was fascinating. "What, then?"

"An essence."

"What is the difference?"

"*Spirit* implies something ethereal," Lowell said.

"As in a novel by Mrs. Asquith," Felicity added.

"Whereas essence is shared between us," Lowell went on, "tangible in one form or the other, man-skin or Shape, and within reach always."

Tabitha beamed. "A wonderful distinction, thank you."

Lowell, against all odds, blushed at the compliment. "We hold them in our auras, and they chime in occasionally," he continued, "but we know when to cede to one another or when it is not appropriate to do so," he added.

"Appropriate?" Tabitha was nearly done with her questions.

The *versipelles* in the room looked at one another. "Safe," said the duke.

"Safe." As Llewellyn had not been. "How was it he was not discovered in his predicament?"

"Hidden in plain sight," said Mr. Bates. "We have deep, abiding pity for captive creatures, and thus we avoid such spectacles, not wishing to add to the attraction."

"There are those among us who devote themselves to the liberation of creatures unwilling in their work," O'Mara added.

"Oh, no." Felicity's voice broke. "I fear Himself was not willing in his work. It may be why we cannot find him." Her horse had been missing since her removal to Lowell Hall; neither hide nor hair of the Templeton stud had been seen for months. The duke nodded and set his arm around his duchess's shoulders, an astonishing gesture even among friends. "I had no way of knowing," she said. "A terrible excuse."

And finally, the thing Tabitha had wondered above all: "How was Llewellyn kept in his lionskin?"

The Alpha exchanged a glance with his Beta and Omega. "There is a way," Alfred said. "It is an old curse." Tabitha took a breath to dispute this nonsense. "It is ancient magic, Miss Barrington, and it is real."

"Beliefs are powerful things, Your Grace," she allowed.

"When proof is provided, it is no longer a belief but a fact," said Mr. Bates. "We wolves are responsible for some misdirection in that we have led the world to believe it is silver that may entrap or kill a *versipellis*, but in fact it is gold."

"As little as an ounce causes us to be held in our essential Shape," Lowell explained.

"It blocks our sense of our human selves," the duke's Second added, "and prevents other *versipelles* from perceiving the trapped being."

"The Shifter in question will, over time, lose all knowledge of their humanity," Lowell concluded.

"It is unbelievable that Llewellyn was able to come back to himself." Mr. Bates got up from his seat and paced the perimeter of the room.

"It is conceivable that his *feelings* of injustice were enough to bring him back," O'Mara said.

"Touché, O'Mara," Tabitha allowed. "Was he the only one of his kind in that place?"

"The only lion, yes," Lowell said.

"The only *versipellis*."

Mr. Bates, all out of character, gaped at her, then looked to Lowell, who nodded. Without another word, Mr. Bates bowed and left; if it were possible, O'Mara looked even more cross.

"How fortunate we are to have you here, Miss Barrington." Felicity stood and set about collecting cups and saucers.

"One last question, Your Grace." Tabitha knew this was the most important of all. "Why do you want him well?"

Lowell looked puzzled by this. "What?"

"Why?"

It was the Alpha's turn to rise and pace in

agitation. She saw O'Mara take a breath, and yes, well, the atmosphere in the room lightened, and Lowell calmed. He paused, and breathed, and said, "Because his life was robbed from him, his freedom, his essence as a human was stripped from him. Because he was very likely tricked into it through his status as an Alpha."

He turned to face her, exuding power in a way the prince had: in this case, not to threaten but to bolster. "I cannot think how it came about, who could have overpowered him, and by what means. He is not one I would like to come up against, even though we are both Alphas. His nature was used against him in some way, I am certain, and that is an abomination."

"A beautiful reason, Your Grace, one that speaks to your compassion and your protective nature. Thank you."

The duke blushed again. Tabitha took a breath and linked her fingers in her lap as she collected her thoughts. O'Mara was her mirror in stillness, though she once again seemed to be communing with something invisible over Tabitha's shoulder.

Far be it from her to question another's methods. She'd had enough of that herself. As opposed to the Omega, however, it had made her more flexible and open than not.

"I am not a doctor," she began. "My work and my methods have been passed down among women for generations. It is not solely based on what can be applied or taken into the body but how the mind influences what is being suffered. Modern medicine is backward in many ways, and in the case of the Duke of Llewellyn, too harsh for a soul who has known such cruelty. In Germany, I briefly came across the work of a man who believed the ills of the mind may be healed through the body. That is, by focusing on physical health, one may strengthen one's mentality. I have not had a chance to investigate this idea in depth but feel it is useful in this instance. It would be an interesting starting point."

Lowell crossed his arms over the great breadth of his chest. "I do not like the idea that Llewellyn is to be an experiment."

"I shall not force him to do anything," Tabitha vowed. "I will give him nothing but choice. He will return to his senses of his own free will. But I do not want him to change. Well, mostly."

———

Timothy and she declined the company of a footman to see them home. The path to the cottage was largely through a stretch of wood that separated a cluster of dwellings from the Hall: whether by accident or design, they were not isolated, but their nearest neighbor was some distance away. Tabitha resolutely kept her eyes forward and not on the night-blooming foliage that might reveal itself to be evening primrose.

As was their habit, they walked briskly, an excellent antidote to the lethargy the rich meal inspired and the seriousness of the teatime discussion.

Fraternal bickering did the rest to clear their heads.

"Oh, just a touch more of this delectable *amontillado*, Your Grace," Timothy warbled.

"Oh, Your Grace, far be it from us to reside in a grenade," Tabitha returned.

"*Grenier*! For the love of Venus!"

"*Venus*? Really?"

"Mr. Bates is forever invoking her. And when in Rome…"

They both snickered. Timothy offered her an elbow and she accepted it.

"What do you make of O'Mara?" she asked.

"An enviable fashion plate. She would not disclose the name of her tailor, which I find vexing. They are very cagey, these wolves."

"Oh, but—" Tabitha did not mention her insight into O'Mara's essential self; it was abundantly clear, to her at least, that the Omega was not a wolf. "Yes, I suppose all *versipelles* are circumspect by nature. I am not sure how she and I will work together. As if it weren't enough of a challenge."

"I have every faith in you. You, who managed to draw clientele in every country we visited despite an utter lack of ear for the languages." She started to defend herself, and he continued, "A feat I consider more prodigious than if you had mastered them all. Your manner and ability to communicate transcends mere vocabulary."

"Yes. Hmmm. Huh." Timothy rolled his eyes at her inability to accept a compliment. "Well. Thank you for pitching in. During the meal."

"I discerned your reason." He looked around and hesitated. Tabitha nodded: they were being followed.

"I thought Lowell would find it impossible to eat with his fingers," she said, "but it was Mr. Bates who resisted most strenuously."

"Mr. Bates is the wiliest of them all," her brother said. "I was much in his company during the refurbishment of the schoolrooms. He is gifted in winkling out all of one's opinions without expressing any of his own and manages to sidestep even a simple yes-or-no response."

Tabitha shrugged. "In the end, he followed suit."

"After much weighing of the reasons behind your action. He does not like to be caught on the back foot. Or paw." Timothy grimaced. "That is likely not well done of me."

"I have caught myself more than once. And not at all." She moaned, mortified. "*Feral*, Tim. Of all the words to choose. I would apologize for that," she called out to the underbrush.

"This is not comfortable," Timothy whispered. To no point, given the keenness of *versipellian* hearing.

"He is a lion, in fairness."

"You are not bothered." Her brother's eyes narrowed; it was the look he got when weighing a potential suitor for her.

Let her nip that in the bud. "He is only acting as his nature demands."

"I see why O'Mara would think us unable to witness their Changing *en masse*." Timothy shuddered. "Best to take them a species at a time."

"Remember how at odds we were at first, in France, as we tried to keep to our English ways in a foreign land? How much the better for us to immerse ourselves in *versipellian* culture, if we are to be here for some time, if not forever." Tabitha's heart stuttered at the thought of that. "For example, I long to see the *cursio*." She directed this statement to a grove of pine trees. "If only there were someone who might contrive a way for me to do so."

Timothy cast a worried gaze behind them. "Despite being told it is beyond the strength of a human."

"I do not expect to trot along with them as they race through the park. Just a view of the proceedings from the best vantage point, that's all." A stillness in the hedges signaled the receipt of her message, and the ensuing flurry of branches betrayed an exit at speed.

"Was that a yes?" Timothy wondered as they turned off the main path for their own.

"I suppose it remains to be seen." Her tone was diffident, the better to take the focus off her heart hammering in her chest and keep her brother's attention off of matchmaking.

Six

THREE DAYS AFTER THE SUNDAY MEAL, ALWYN was still wondering how to bring—well, not *bring*, it was not an outing in Hyde Park, it was not as though he were escorting her to a ball…

Alwyn was mulling over how to provide Miss Barrington with a view of the *cursio*.

If one were looking for a pattern card for providing, one need look no further than the Duke of Lowell. Alwyn stood outside the paddock that contained Her Grace's band of mares; if he knew horses, and he did, this was a string of very flighty, overbred creatures. Alwyn had lately heard that the horses had been at the heart of a dispute between the duchess and her uncle; the lady came out the better for it, with an entire premises at her disposal as a gift from her then-betrothed. Templeton Stud was established bang in the center of the Close and would soon be a going concern if Lowell had anything to say about it.

As dramatic a gesture as one would expect from a wolf, never mind a duke, it was especially extravagant. And all to prove his worth as a mate. Had Alfred no skills in the wooing department?

Constructing a building to convince a human female to wed him seemed rather desperate. How hard could it be to woo a *homo plenus*?

Lowell's efforts fell short, as there did not seem to be a male among this band, thus no stud for his duchess's mares. The horses managed Alwyn's presence with equanimity, even going so far as to blink their big brown eyes at the Alpha male in the vicinity. He did not intend to frighten them; in fact, he had a fondness for the silly creatures. *Horse* horses were greater in weight and heft than he, but so fearful. Lifetimes as prey would do that to a breed.

They may have batted their lashes at him, but they stayed well away, clustered for safety—all but one of them, that was: a rangy, dark bay equine paced the perimeter, ears swiveling, nostrils flared. When she spotted him, she whinnied; the rest scattered as she galloped to his side of the fenced paddock. Her mane flew, her tail floating behind like a banner, and the sight of it lifted his heart.

The only bright spot in his years at Drake's were the horses who performed in the equitation extravaganzas. There was a tableau he was required to participate in: he roared, under the encouragement of a harsh prod, and the horses involved would rear on their hind legs as if in fear. While *versipelles* struggled to communicate clearly with animals not of their own species when in their Shapes, and with *animalis pura* of like genus under very limited circumstances, Drake's horses seemed to understand his predicament. If he did not look sufficiently threatening, it went the worse for him, and he was convinced the herd did their best to appear terrified beyond measure.

Drake's horses appeared to find the nightly applause sufficient exchange for a lack of freedom. They were content, well-behaved, and placid.

Not this mare, who was close to frothing at the mouth. Ears pinned back and teeth gnashing, she prowled toward him, with as much fierceness as one of his own kind. He extended a hand for her to inspect, trusting her not to mistake his fingers for a delicious treat. "I mean no harm, fearsome one." He stepped back to—there was a movement one made, as a man before a lady, but it slipped through his mind like a trout through his hands. Was his leg involved somehow? It would not show to best effect in his baggy trousers. He had once dressed to reflect his high status, had he not? How shabby he looked.

"I apologize for the state of my valeting, for I have none. A valet, that is. I fear I am not fit for company, human or no." The mare had not taken her eyes off him. "Was I in the habit of conversing with *animalis pura*? Is it low of a duke to do so? I have forgotten much, you see. How I was in terms of style, or consequence, if I was cordial to your kind, or any kind, I do not know." He faltered. "I have lost everything, and I..."

She tilted her head, gaze suddenly soft; she huffed, and her ears twitched forward as she walked directly to the fence and hooked her chin over his shoulder. He stood, awkward, arms dangling like a marionette with cut strings. He had no recourse but to embrace her.

"What is it, *geneth*? I am so sad a case that prey pities me?" She didn't like that, no, she did not: she nipped him lightly on the shoulder and drew him closer. "Are you not the ferocious Delilah of whom your duchess speaks so fondly? And yet how soft you are. What is it, girl? I am a terrible human, I have no slice of apple for you.

"I am a terrible human in more than that, I fear. I have nothing to give any creature, neither man nor beast." Nor his essential self. Nothing to give to it nor take from that center of his being, for that center was void—

He pressed his forehead to her shoulder; in his head, his heart, all was in turmoil, a conflagration that threatened to burn him to a cinder. He could not let it roil, let it rage; he would not let an inno-cent fall afoul of his fury. He would not allow that spark to spiral out of control.

A spark of another sort had flared in the grove, when he watched Miss Barrington harvest fox-glove with no thought to her safety. It had been all he could do to stay calm, to resist flinging himself between her and the plant, a mental image that was patently ridiculous. She countered his every state-ment without fear and spoke to him as if—as if he were a man, a normal man. At the Sunday Meal she bickered with her brother before all, and it tore at his heart more than anything else, tore at it even as it lightened it. He had known at once: despite their wrangling, they were a brother and sister who were friends. He imagined the lady apothecary would do anything for her friends.

Blessed Palu, she was indefatigable. He won-dered if a lady would take offense at being described as such; it wasn't terribly feminine, was it? It was not like calling a woman *a diamond of the first water* or *an incomparable*. Not that he would have occa-sion to call attention to her feminine charms. Nor would he pass comment on her typical outdoor *ensemble:* she appeared to swathe herself in every coat and scarf and shawl she owned. Her face stuck out of the top of it all like a...like a flower in a bou-quet. A bouquet of cloth? Of wool?

He had much to recall in terms of flirtation.

He suspected likening the lady to a bouquet of wool was not it.

Not that was he interested in flirting with the lady.

The indefatigable and also unflinching lady. He had positively roared at her about the trowel. His voice had risen and risen, and the last thing he expected was to be greeted with a smile. And what a smile. It illuminated her understated beauty, beauty that must be sought out to apprehend, beauty that was like a secret only for him to discover.

And then—and then! Miss Barrington turned her back on him. Smiled at him and then turned her back and went about her business. She was rather splendid, for a human female. Not that he was interested in paying her compliments or squiring her about.

He sought only to hold up his end of their bargain. The thought of their bargain was enough to make him laugh aloud. *Feral*, she'd said. The looks on the others' faces!

The mare rubbed her jaw on his shoulder, and he stepped away. But not too far. The contact was soothing.

"You, my lady, are strong of heart and fearless. Very like another new acquaintance of mine." Each encounter with the lady apothecary was like a draught of cool fresh water after decades in the desert. Unlike the rest of that lot in Lowell Hall and, before that, Carlton House, he did not detect an ounce of fear from her, whether due to his species or his state of being. When she ate with her fingers! "Had I been the duke I was," he said, stroking Delilah's jaw, "I would waste no time in investigating the possibility of the *coniunctio*."

The mare's ears flicked with interest. "Amongst my kind—not the Welsh, the lions—we have an elevation of the *vera amoris* bond, which we have kept amongst ourselves. The *coniunctio* demands the bonded pair bring their example out into the world, to serve all *versipelles* together, no matter their species. It is a tremendous responsibility, one many are relieved to find they do not have. It is not for the faint of heart, oh no. It is the truest balance of masculine and feminine, discernment and empathy wedded with compassion and detachment. I had hoped, before I was taken, that I might..."

The horse pricked her ears and nudged his shoulder until he turned.

Speak of the lady and the lady appeared.

And she appeared to have attracted the attention of more than one *versipellis*.

One of Lowell's seemingly numberless footmen had brought a note from Felicity, asking for Tabitha's assistance with one of the stable lads. He'd run afoul of a patch of nettles and required a poultice.

While she did not wish the poor lad pain, she hoped this was an actual need for her intervention and not a sop to her supposed role. Busywork was not going to occupy her for long; she had started concocting creams and soaps with her healthful combinations of herbs for lack of anything better to do. She would not wish illness on anyone either, but she sincerely wanted to be useful.

Would she be any use at all to the Welsh duke? As gauche as her choice to eat with her fingers was, it had allowed him to feed himself. Eating well and properly would serve to increase his physical health; the health of his mind could only follow. She had neglected to pursue that line of thought over the teacups: Did he think himself into his animal skin—no, into his essential self?

She was so lost in her thoughts, she almost plowed into a man. "Oh! Do forgive me, I was walking and woolgathering."

"Sadly, I am not a sheep." Tabitha would never mistake the rangy fellow for one of that species. His smile seemed to be full of more than his fair share of teeth, and his scrap of beard waggled as he laughed. He was clearly a goat, from his bowed legs to his narrow eyes, which lit on her with pleasure. "Were I one, I would gladly donate whatever wool I could spare did you require it."

"You are, er, most kind." Oh dear, that was effusive. "Wool is an effective bandage, and one can never have enough of it."

"You don't want no truck with the sheep around here, dozy lads, the lot of them."

"I shall take your word for it." They stood. The man beamed and said nothing more. "I am Miss Barrington."

"I am Mr. Giles. Please accept this token as my way of welcoming you to Lowell Close." He thrust into her hands a log of cheese, done up with some flair in a brightly colored tea towel.

"How very kind of you. I will be sure to—oh."

The goat was jostled out of the way by a fellow whose roundness of shape and wideness of mouth indicated he was a frog. "Miss Barrington, you are very welcome to our little part of the world." He bowed and extended his hand. "I am Mr. Padmore, and here is a mere token of my army's—er, my clan's delight at your arrival among us." He handed her a muslin bag whose contents clattered; she felt it rude to examine it in his presence and put both the cheese and this offering in her trug.

"Oh, lovely, I will be sure to—"

"Miss Barrington," the frog began.

"Miss Barring—" the goat said; he was elbowed by the frog and gave as good as he got. "I was here first, Padmore, jog on like a good lad."

"Your hesitancy is not my fault, Giles, you sneaky little—"

"Miss Barrington, I would very much like to fetch you a cup of cheer on Ostara Eve," said the goat.

At the same time, the frog blurted, "Miss Barrington, if you would accompany me to the lighting of the fire and the *cursio*, I would be most honored."

"I am sorry, both of you, but O'Mara has cautioned against myself and my brother attending." The relief Tabitha experienced was mighty indeed.

"If I may trouble you, then, for a salve?" Mr. Giles gestured vaguely at his head. "I've the worst case of, of hives. On my scalp?"

"I am in need of a tonic something fierce, miss!" Mr. Padmore exclaimed. "My indigestion is troubling me. In the night? Destroying my sleep."

Neither sounded convinced of the legitimacy of their woes. "Leave that with me, gentlemen. I see the Duke of Llewellyn near that paddock and must consult with him."

The men bowed, disappointed but, by their expressions, undaunted. She picked up her pace and stopped short of a full-out run.

"Good day, Your Grace," she called as she came upon him at the fence. This was where Felicity kept her mares; the one in company with the duke was Delilah, against whom she and Timothy had been warned. The horse had an uncannily measuring look in her eye, and Tabitha was tempted to curtsy. If she didn't have the information of her senses, she would think twice before she named this one a *horse* horse.

As it was, she was compelled to greet the mare as well. "And good day to you, Delilah. We have not met, but your reputation precedes you." Tabitha held out a hand, and the mare made a show of judging her scent. She must have found it good, for she extended her muzzle and gave Tabitha a good sniff on the neck, enough to tickle her and send her crashing into—oh.

"So sorry." Tabitha's breath arrested as Llewellyn's hand steadied her. It was like a brand on her side, strong and warm, even through her multiple layers. For such a fleeting moment, it was enough to make her light-headed, like a green girl. She, who had never *been* a green girl.

But what an improvement: he had not even wished to shake her hand only a week ago.

"Not at all." The duke cleared his throat. "How lucky I was here to prevent you from tumbling to the ground and harming yourself."

"I doubt it would have come to that."

He brushed a hand down his coat, today's a full-length hacking coat likely from the seventeenth century, the placket secured with embroidered frogs. He looked up at her through his lashes, lashes that were, quite frankly, an injustice to be found on a man.

"As I have nothing to offer you as did those two fine fellows, I can at least prevent you from coming a cropper."

The mare snorted, and Tabitha agreed with that judgment. "It was most kind of them to offer welcome gifts."

"Kindness has nothing to do with it, miss. They are determining their chances of walking out with you." He gestured, and Tabitha headed for one of the many paths to the village.

"Walking out—as though they were—do not be ridiculous." Her face flushed. Was he making a mockery of her?

"Why is it ridiculous to think a man would see you and wish to court you?" Perhaps he was not: his voice was its usual rumble, but there was a velvety quality to it that seemed sincere.

A velvety quality? Honestly! "I am not of an age to be courted. I am well past it, in fact."

"There are more than a few males of every species who prefer a female who is not fresh out of the schoolroom."

She stopped dead and looked at him aghast. "If you do me no other favor in my life, Your Grace, you will say nothing of this to my brother."

"Will he tease the stuffing out of you?" A shadow of regret passed over his face.

Tabitha wanted to reach out to him at the sight of it—a glimpse of grief? He had reacted very poorly to the talk of brothers and sisters before the Sunday Meal. "He will, and it is insufferable."

"Will that be my part of the bargain seen to, then?"

"It will not." She resumed the walk to the Close. "I shall simply owe you another boon. I wish to watch the *cursio,* but only if it will not trouble you to do so."

"It will not trouble me. Running about the place in a gang is wolfish behavior, not at all leonine."

"I understand the males of your species laze about while the women do all the work."

"Not all the work…" The duke reached out, hesitated, and took her trug to carry.

That ought not to have flustered her as much as it did.

———

The lady apothecary was far too accustomed to doing everything for herself.

Alwyn was used to parting the Shifters of the Lowell Pack like a ship cutting through the sea: they saw him coming and discovered urgent business in another direction. As they neared the Close, the others saw him walking with Miss Barrington and calmed. He could perceive their heartbeats steadying as they passed, and one or two offered him obeisance, which was unexpected.

He flexed his fingers around the handle of the basket thing, an unusual piece of luggage that seemed rolled up into itself and yet covered in pockets. It was heavy enough, and as he was only gaining facility with his fingers, something of a challenge to hold.

Speaking of fingers. "You fulfilled your bargain with me above and beyond our terms." The lady muttered *something something feral*, and he—there was a bubbling behind his chest bone that loosened his shoulders and thrilled him as much as it frightened him. "I refer to the lamb course. Of course."

"Very clever, Your Grace." She blushed, two circles in the middle of her cheeks like two little nosegays...right beside her nose.

There was surely a more picturesque way of describing that.

"You were clever," he insisted, "and I must thank your brother for giving the action plausibility. It was, was it not?"

"Plausible? Oh, yes. You'd be hard-pressed to bother with utensils the farther south you go. The indolence of the heat has much to answer for."

"Ah, heat." Alwyn sighed, and the lady blushed again. How easily discomposed she became when she was not about her apothecary business. "You will not find much of it here. Weather-wise."

"You may have noticed I am not partial to the damp, given the number of garments I tend to wear." She held out her arms in demonstration.

Should he take this opportunity to compare her to a bouquet of wool and her face to a little flower? He imagined how his lion would react, the disdain it would inspire—no, he would not. His hand gripped and gripped the handle of the lady's basket thing as he fought down the remorse, the loss, the lack he carried within, his heart broken into a thousand pieces—

"...if I could run and warm myself, I would, but it is not done in England. Running, that is. Or more to the point, women running for exercise. I ran for my health in Greece, you see. Not only did we eat with our fingers, but we also raced like heathens along the beaches. It was quite wonderful. There was the marathon, in Ancient Greece—I wonder if the *cursio* has its roots in that. I must remember to ask my brother, who will pull every relevant book off the shelf to prove or disprove this thesis..." Her tone, despite the meandering of her words, brought air back into his lungs.

Alwyn switched the basket thing to his other hand. "It is unfortunate, then"—his voice was a barely intelligible rasp—"that you will not be able to take part in it."

The lady ably switched topics like a swallow in a susurration. "I don't wish to brag, but I am quite fleet."

"I suspect you succeed at all you undertake." An impulse flared to make a leg and kiss her hand; ah, yes, that was it: the courtly movement his muscles remembered and his mind only now recalled. He stopped and she stopped and—and nothing. She stood and waited. She did not pry. He opened his mouth to speak—

A droning kind of cough interrupted them.

Blessed Palu, not another one!

A fidgety gent appeared, as was the *versipellian* wont, from thin air. He stood with his hands behind his back; his eyes glanced everywhere but nevertheless seemed to remain on her. Tabitha found it slightly alarming.

"How do, miss." He bowed and beamed at her even as he kept one eye on the duke. "I am Beckett, of the coach house Becketts, and may I say we are all pleased to have you among us. And me, I mean I, most of all." With a flourish, he withdrew his hands from behind his back and held out a small clay pot covered with a checkered cloth.

"Mr. Beckett, how do you do? I am Miss Barrington, and this is the Duke of Llewellyn." Did one introduce a duke to a publican, or for that matter, a lion to a bee? "This is very thoughtful of you." She tucked the jar into one of the trug's pockets; in doing so, her arm brushed against His Grace's. Ah: he tensed but did not withdraw. Such progress.

The bee gave his obeisance and, in fairness to him, managed the presence of a predator far, far above him in the chain with impressive aplomb. "Miss, I would like to know if you require an escort on Ostara Eve, and if so, I would be honored to have you on my arm."

"I regret to say that O'Mara has deemed myself and my brother unready for such a celebration this early in our residence here."

The duke moved closer to her; the bee was not intimidated in the least.

"Then I shall patiently wait for a more appropriate occasion." He bowed to them both and hastened to leave, heading straight for the coach house, which was the site of much activity.

"I am wounded, Miss Barrington, that you did not tell Mr. Beckett you were already engaged."

He was teasing her, surely. "Will it not be our secret?"

"Oh, yes." If she wasn't imagining things, his gravelly voice took on a distinct purr. "Let it be that. A secret. Between us."

In her intent not to discomfit him, Tabitha had not truly looked the duke fully in the face. She had kept him in her sights, but she had not seen him full on, as it were. He was that bit taller than she, and while not as broad in the chest as, say, the Duke of Lowell, even in its poorly clothed state the impression his body made was that of many rangy muscles containing lithe force. They held a tension, but a fine one, an observant one, not one constructed entirely out of apprehension. She looked up into his eyes: hazel surrounded by that wealth of lashes, blond-tipped and unfairly lush. He hesitated to hold her gaze, but eventually, his rested on her face, his brows an expressive slash of dark brown, a contrast to his primarily blond...well, mane. And mane it was, as tangled and dry as it appeared. She suspected that if the snarls were worked through, it would rival even Lowell's for length and lushness.

Would he allow her to touch his hair? She raised one hand slowly, and one of his brows arched slowly, and boldness rushed through her veins and—

"Good day."

They sprang apart at O'Mara's greeting. Tabitha pulled her hand back, and Llewellyn's good humor drained away in an instant.

"O'Mara." Tabitha found she had to clear her throat. "Are you well?"

"A question I am sure you are used to asking."

"A question I suppose you need never ask, for you can sense it."

"I sense many things." The strawberry blond's complexion flushed, not a reaction one expected from the stoic chamberlain. She appeared to make up for it by doing that thing she did, gazing into the distance; this time, her object was the duke, and she appeared utterly puzzled and then somewhat bereft, no matter how she insisted her feelings were left out of her work. The Omega opened her mouth to speak, stopped, and looked uncharacteristically disoriented.

"In all seriousness," Tabitha was compelled to ask, "are you quite well?"

"Thank you, it is nothing a tonic can touch," O'Mara replied. The duke did not like this response and crowded against Tabitha's back. In defense of her skills? Perhaps she would be able to interest him in a palliative after all.

"I am at your service, should you change your mind." Good Lord, this was an uphill battle on every front. "I required a bracing tonic of milk thistle this morning. I found the Sunday Meal much richer than I am accustomed to."

"It is a privilege to partake of such a meal." O'Mara's big brown eyes flashed gold. "Not only with the duke and duchess, but with our kind."

"I do not mean to be ungrateful," Tabitha said. O'Mara did not treat anyone with kid gloves, but her conduct bordered on rude. "I enjoyed much of it, of course."

"The lamb course most of all," the chamberlain said.

"I hope you do not seek to criticize Miss Barrington for her behavior at the meal." The duke's *dominatum* drew around them; it was nothing like the prince's and only surged intermittently. In reaction to it, O'Mara took one of those portentous breaths of hers. This only incensed the duke further, and Lowell's Omega let out a low, whuffling sound of warning.

Tabitha stepped fully between them. "I do not fear criticism. If I did, I would not last long in the apothecary business." She looked over her shoulder, and the duke stilled at her glance. To O'Mara, she said, "My methods are often unexpected and require the flexibility of all involved. We have asked His Grace to keep company when it may or may not be his preference, and he has done so with, er, grace. I do apologize, sir—" Like a wraith, a wisp of smoke, he had disappeared.

"You have a champion, Miss Barrington." Tabitha could not tell whether the Omega approved, so flat was her tone.

"Whether or not that is so, O'Mara, I would like to discuss a mutual approach to the duke's recovery." She picked up her trug, which His Grace had taken care to lay gently at her feet before he disappeared. "I am headed for Templeton Stud, if you would walk with me?"

"I am going in the other direction." O'Mara's coolness was pure obstinance.

"It is not my intention to tread on your patch." Tabitha hooked the trug over an elbow. "Nor to thwart your Alpha's wishes. Let us meet, you and I and Lowell, if that suits, and determine a way forward."

"Our issues are beneath *my* Alpha's notice." The chamberlain's voice was a hoarse growl and her emphasis on *my* unnecessary. He was certainly not Tabitha's Alpha. "I would not call it an issue rather than—"

"Interference?" Tabitha asked. The Omega took one of her breaths. "Am I the only source of interference, or do you feel Llewellyn is a threat to your Alpha?"

"He is no match for Lowell's power."

"I agree, he is not. Nor do I think he seeks it."

"No, he does not," O'Mara admitted. The chamberlain looked around her, and in a heartbeat she appeared desolate—and young, so young, like a small girl. "There is…something disturbing. In the atmosphere."

"In the atmosphere." *For goodness' sake.* Tabitha forged ahead. "Is it to do with the duke?"

"No. It is a personal matter."

"And how do you perceive this unease? Is it from your way of consulting the ethers? I have noticed you seem to be connected to something that is not seen by a human eye or indeed a *versipellian* eye."

"It is part of my gift and not to be spoken of." Her composure returned as if her admission had never happened.

"With *homo plenum*, or—"

"It is not to be spoken of. Ever. Have I made myself clear?" O'Mara lowered her chin and all but bared her teeth; she looked as much like her essential self as Tabitha had yet seen.

"As clear as glass."

The chamberlain stormed off, drawing more than one eye. Tabitha hadn't realized how close they were to the village, nor how many had witnessed their contretemps. Angering the one who kept them all on an even keel would not endear her to the populace of the Close.

"I am failing on all fronts," she whispered to the memory of the Italian cat.

Perhaps she ought to take ship and travel on her own.

It was not nearly as daunting a thought as it had been in the past.

Seven

"WE CAN DO THIS THE HARD WAY OR THE EASY way, Ash." Mr. Marshall, the Lowell Hall stable master, clapped one of his lads on the shoulder. Tabitha held the bowl of poultice she had made, her demeanor calm. She could understand the young man's apprehension. Her recipe was tried and trusted, but to him, she was an unknown quantity.

She had some apprehension as well, having never had recourse to use this concoction on a Shapeshifter.

"It is more easily applied in your human form," Felicity soothed, "but it is understandable if you wish to Change."

"We do this all the time, missus," Marshall said. "This lot can't keep still when they're, eh, running loose, and that poultice won't stay bound if he's haring all over the place." He mitigated his salty tone by scrubbing the boy's hair.

Mr. Marshall was careful not to reveal the identity of his charge's essential creature but what could the lad be but a horse? Apart from his large eyes, Ash was leggy and loose in the way of a colt, and the hair on his head was long and coarse. And in fairness, they were on Felicity's premises with the stable master. The clues were in the context. *So there, Timothy.*

"I observe from the wrinkling of your nose that the smell is putting you off." Tabitha set the bowl down on the main counter and shook out a length of cheesecloth.

"Never scented the like, miss," Ash admitted.

"I do not expect anyone to follow my prescriptions unquestioningly." She heaved her trug closer to dig through it. "You have a good nose, young Ash, for you most likely have not come across this plant before. I have used a type of witch hazel distilled from a tree only found in southern Italy. Its odor is rather more pungent than those in our native land, and I expect in your Shape, it would be even more so."

"That it would, miss," Marshall agreed.

"It is also very dark in hue." She held out a small vial of the stuff for Ash to inspect. "It's better applied to your manskin, as I fear it might stain your coat."

"My coat, miss?"

"You are a gray, are you not?" She was greeted by a round of incredulous expressions. "Have I misspoken? I apologize for my carelessness if this is against your law."

"It's not that, miss, it's that a *homo plenus* oughtn't to be able to tell." Ash sounded impressed, so perhaps she hadn't made too flagrant a mistake.

"Nevertheless, I feel I have transgressed. I am

still learning your ways and am bound to err now and again."

"I've been here for donkey's years," Marshall said, "and my wife is a *versipellis*, and I still haven't quite got the knack of it."

"It's right impressive," Ash agreed. The young lad handed back the vial of witch hazel and extended his sore hand. "I reckon you know what you're about."

"That is high praise, indeed." Tabitha smiled, and with explanations for every move she made, she proceeded to tend to Ash's injury.

―――――――――

At the opposite end of the village, Alfred and his Third, Sebastian Gambon, headed for a disused building Matthias was intent upon refurbishing.

It was a recurring theme these days in Lowell Close. And in the park, come to that. Alfred had been bonded for less than a week when the request to lodge the Duke of Llewellyn had come from His Highness; he had overseen the work himself, though it meant his new bride was left alone in their bed in the early hours. What little he knew of lions, he hoped he put to good use: the dwelling backed on to the highest hill in Lowell's wild park, giving Alwyn vantage over all. He hoped the myriad windows were enough and at the same time not too much; were they too exposing? Alfred thought being unable to see out was worse and erred on the side of an excess of curtains. In the end, the cottage was compact and cozy and manageable for a bachelor living on his own.

Alfred and his wolf both cringed at the thought of living alone. By nature, lupines craved company, and if that need was not satisfied, well, then, to use Miss Barrington's poorly chosen term, they went feral. Alfred did not think isolation was the best choice for the lion Shifter, despite the natural feline drive for independence. However, Georgie had decreed this must be, and at least the Welsh duke had not run off or run rampant.

It was Alfred's duty to hold the health and safety of his pack as paramount. His *sentio* had grown more robust with his marriage to Felicity; as his bond with his *vera amoris* deepened every day, every hour, it strengthened the entire pack. A strange predator not woven into that web had an adverse impact on all and was the reason he sought Sebastian's counsel. Large in stature and gentle in spirit, the boar Shifter was responsible for addressing issues of the pack at ground level, and there was no one better to assess Llewellyn's effect on Alfred's people.

His people, whose presence in the *sentio* was muted.

It was not unknown that a Shifter could block

their connection to the Alpha of their flock or herd or clowder; in this instance, it was as though his pack was unwilling to allow him into their state of wellbeing—or otherwise.

"I do not understand why they are keeping their distance," Alfred said. "Are they afraid Llewellyn will challenge me, and thus seek to preserve my strength?"

"Your ability to protect us is not in question. It is confusion that is affecting the flow, not fear." Gambon hummed deep in his chest before choosing his words with care. "I can only speak for myself. I do not know what to think of His Grace, for if I think too long on what he suffered, I am filled with anger and despair." The boar looked around at the busy industry of the village, the shopkeepers and craftspeople and artisans all engaged as to their specific talents. "I believe this is the same for the pack. Yes, he is a great predator, and a duke as well. Keeping their distance from him, until he makes himself known to us, is correct. But first and foremost, Llewellyn is an object not of pity but compassion. That he is wandering among us, alone, after such an ordeal… Again, I cannot bear to think on it."

"Speaking of bears." Sebastian snorted, and Alfred continued, "His Highness is impatiently awaiting news of His Grace's rehabilitation."

"He no longer slinks about under cover of night," Sebastian said. "Today, he spent time with Delilah, who deigned not to bite him. He was seen with Miss Barrington earlier this morning. Several of our unmated lads have set their sights on the lady apothecary and came upon the two as they made their first attempts at courtship."

"I hope they conducted themselves with decorum?"

"Yes, as well as bearing gifts. Although what Padmore proffered is anyone's guess."

Alfred tried to picture the lady with the frog and could not. "I will let Her Grace know so she may offer up any advice. As a human female who was courted by one of us."

Gambon looked askance at that; Alfred knew his approach to wooing was held in low regard by all. The boar shook his head and said, "What could possibly go wrong."

A huge crash emitted from the disused shop that was their goal. The locus of the commotion proved to be Matthias; the source of the noise, a caved-in roof over a large lean-to at the back of the building.

"This place is in rag order, Gamma." Alfred's Beta brushed his soiled hands down his coat, a thought-less action that would normally send Alfred into a tailspin, but given Matthias's diffident approach to clothing, it made no difference.

Sebastian nudged a pile of rotten wood with his boot. "It can't help its reaction to a disturbance when it has gone unbothered for years."

"What was this place used for?" Alfred walked into the main part of the long, narrow building. It was divided into several chambers, and he could make no sense of what its purpose may have been.

"The manufacture of candles." Matthias looked up at the parts of the ceiling that remained in place. "I have an idea to resuscitate it and will get some footmen on the job. As it pleases Your Grace, of course."

"They being my footmen and all."

"If there are any left, as Her Grace dispatched the handiest in aid of the renovation of Arcadia," Matthias said as he led them to the front room. The door was flanked by two dusty bay windows, and he commenced muttering about displays and arrangements.

"There are plenty remaining who are eager to learn," Sebastian said. "And. Well, there is the sheepdog."

"The who, now?" Matthias asked. Alfred caught his Gamma in a blush and waggled his brows at his Beta. Matthias picked up his cue. "That young lad from up north? He's driving Coburn 'round the bend and charming himself out of all manner of tasks," the Beta said.

Sebastian straightened his waistcoat with an excess of dignity. "I would not know."

"Would you not?" Matthias was the worst for teasing, and he spotted an opening for relentless ribbing like an eagle spotted a hare. This trait likely came from being born second to his brother after an array of elder sisters.

The boar grumbled and retreated to tidy up the piles of detritus in the lean-to. Alfred and Matthias followed, hard on the scent.

"Tell me, this sheepdog, is he quite fit, Matthias?" Alfred asked.

"Oh yes, Alfred, Colin is fit and lithe and has the biggest brown eyes."

"You seem to have made a point of noticing his attributes," Sebastian mumbled.

"It is my job to notice things," Matthias was quick to retort. "If he is not to your preference, perhaps Mr. Barrington is."

"Oh?" Alfred hadn't paid much attention to Felicity's new hire apart from ensuring the stipulation in her marriage contract to secure a tutor was honored. At the meal, Barrington had prosed on about Greek culinary topics to cover for his sister, who was covering for Alwyn's apparent lack of skill with a fork. If Mr. Barrington was in line with his Gamma's desires, then that would be quite tidy. "Do we know for certain he would be amenable to such overtures as our beloved Sebastian may like to make?"

"Yes." The boar Shifter sounded glum. "One can tell when another is a…confirmed bachelor."

"The tutor is older than the sheepdog, if that is what's stopping you in the first case." Matthias picked carefully through a pile of glass.

"Mr. Barrington has lived all over the Continent and speaks seven languages." Sebastian started heaving the larger beams to the side. "I have journeyed fewer than one hundred leagues in my entire life and Chef Louveauteau despairs of my retaining the rudimentary French phrases he tries to teach me."

Alfred cleared his throat. "Sebastian, if I have learned one thing as a married man—"

"Oh, Holy Venus, not this again," Matthias grumbled.

"—it is that differences between mates are a heady aphrodisiac and keep things fresh. And there is only one language that the two are required to speak."

"The language of loooove," Matthias crooned and then hollered as Sebastian caught him in a headlock. Their scuffling finished what destruction his Second had begun, and Alfred howled with laughter.

Another tranche of ceiling gave way and clattered to the floor. "Lads, enough," Alfred ordered, and they broke it up reluctantly, neither conceding defeat. "Truly, Baz, you know we have no prejudices here. It would be rather ridiculous given the secrets we seek to keep from the human populace." It would be the height of hypocrisy, to Alfred's thinking. "Do you think he is your fated mate?"

"I do not know—hush, Bates, yes, yes, another thing in which Mr. Barrington may educate me." Matthias giggled as he had when he and Alfred were pups. Sebastian sighed again. "One simply knows, is that not true? And I have never heard of the *vera amoris* bond between men."

"It is common amongst my kind."

Alfred would vow to his dying day that he did not leap out of his skin in surprise; since his jolt put a glimmer of amusement in Alwyn's eye, he would not regret that he nearly had. Alwyn, who had joined them on silent feet, so quiet even *versipellian* hearing did not detect him. Alwyn, who was speaking of his own accord.

If they could lay this at Miss Barrington's door, then Goddess damn it, Georgie was right again. "Your kind? Who, the Welsh?"

Llewellyn did not move, but anyone familiar with felines sensed his ability to spring into action at a moment's notice. He made a show of looking around to avoid their gazes, and they gave him the courtesy of setting about the task of hauling more timber into the growing pile.

"Among lions and lesser felines," he answered. "We are not so hemmed in by convention. Like to like may love. It is of no consequence to us."

"I did not know that." Matthias did not sound the happier for it, either. He very much disliked being in the dark about anything. "And do you know this firsthand, as it were?"

"It is not delicate to ask," Sebastian scolded, delicately.

"Ah, I see. My apologies." Matthias was also quick to atone when he had erred. "Much like inquiring as to another's species, then?"

"It is one's choice to honor another with the knowledge, and it is made with care," Sebastian explained. "There is a lack of acceptance in the human world, which makes this necessary. Those who are not sympathetic can often turn dangerous. I suspect this is the reason behind the Barringtons' sojourn abroad."

Mr. Bates frowned. "I thought they had traveled for pleasure and for the brother to learn his many languages."

"Miss Barrington was difficult to convince to return to England unless we pledged to protect her brother from harm," Alfred said.

"And the lady?" Holy Venus, was Alwyn's voice no longer as guttural as it had been? "Did she not demand the same for herself?"

"You have spent more time with her than I," Alfred replied. "Does she have aught to fear?"

"She should be afraid of her lack of fear, paradoxically. She will go about at all hours and gather all manner of poisonous plants as it suits her. Not only to gather but also to test their efficacy. As though she were preserved from a debilitating reaction because she concocted it herself. She ranges wherever she wishes without any thought to the predators in the vicinity." Yes, his voice was much improved and smoother for the passion that infused it.

And yet: "Have I any predators about the place she should be protected from?" Georgie be damned, if she was not safe from Llewellyn…

"You do not." The lion Shifter trembled in his skin, not from fear but from the usual sort of aggression one Alpha accorded to another.

Alfred had not thought he would rejoice at such a display. "Just as well," he said. "I do not get the impression the lady appreciates being treated with kid gloves."

Alwyn snorted—with amusement? It was such a surprising sound, Sebastian and Matthias stooped in concert to lift aside a beam which either could have taken up with one hand, so they would not betray a reaction to it. Alfred also busied himself, though he wanted to erupt with joy and hope.

Alwyn had as good as laughed. At a joke only known to him. And perhaps to the lady.

"She does not appreciate that, no," Llewellyn said. "She has nothing to fear from me." As if his humor were not enough, Alwyn leaned down and lifted a length of timber, to help, to join in.

Alfred took the other end. "Has the lady anything to hope for, then?" he asked.

The lion Shifter muttered under his breath, "As if I have anything to offer a *lady*."

Tabitha saw off the colt and Mr. Marshall with stern advice and surplus dressing and poultice.

"That was a success." Felicity tidied the countertop, and Tabitha returned everything to its place in her trug. "I am not surprised to see how well you do at your work. You have authority and yet are kind with it. I am sure Ash will be back on his feet in no time."

"If only His Grace's ills could be treated as efficiently."

"Captivity for one such as he is a terrible thing."

"I would dearly love to know what class of villain would stoop so low." Tabitha cinched its straps and set the bag on the floor. "And how did it come about? I doubt he wandered around in his lion Shape, waiting to be taken. I am reluctant to inquire after the circumstances, as I fear my questioning will prompt further distress. It is up to him whether to speak of his experience or not."

They sat in the reception area. Felicity fiddled with one of the potted plants set out as decoration. "Amongst Shifters, great store is set by the heart."

"I insulted O'Mara prodigiously with my dismissal of *versipellian* feelings." Not to mention what had recently occurred.

"It is not feelings, or not only those." Felicity took a moment to gather her thoughts. "It is that the heart is the seat of their power. We look at them in their animal skins and see only brute force, but to keep everyone here safe, Alfred holds the well-being of all in his heart."

"That is very unlike Mrs. Anchoretta Asquith's stories." Felicity had insisted she borrow the lady novelist's latest volume, *The Ravishment of Miss Leticia Everington at the Hands of the Duca di Luperno,* a harrowing tale of an Englishwoman abroad in Rome. "It is astonishing to think she is a Shapeshifter."

"Oh, Alfred loathes her work. Once I started devouring them, he read one or two. He feels she comes far too close to betraying their secrets."

"She depicts *versipelles* in an unsympathetic light, that is for certain. They are nothing but horrible beasts intent on the destruction of innocent women." The atrocities implied in *The Ravishment of Miss Leticia Everington,* despite the obfuscating language, did not bear thinking about. "And yet you say their strength comes from their hearts."

Felicity nodded. "And the strength to hold a strong *sentio* is thanks to their essential selves, their animal aspect."

"And if Llewellyn's creature is absent…"

"Your Grace's heart is surely failing."

"I doubt that, in this instance, a dose of foxglove will suffice." A pity, as Tabitha knew what to do with that. "Nor is he *my* Grace. But do we know this is true? Is there previous evidence? Is the *sentio* common within all species and collectives? I cannot think how to help if all there is to go on are the rules for wolves or bears that may not apply to—"

A rousing cheer from the square cut her off, and both women hurried out of the premises.

Felicity clapped her hands at the sight that greeted them. A colony of beavers carted a large wooden sign across the green to the coach house. Its imagery, meant to be seen from a distance, was easily perceived, and its true ostentation became apparent the closer they came.

"That sign is…" Tabitha trailed off.

"Showy?" Felicity proposed, as they watched the head man, Mr. Beresford, set two of his colleagues to positioning ladders on the facade of the large, well-built edifice. The public house and coaching inn rose three stories, its windows pristine, its shutters a gleaming black against the clean white of the stone walls; boxes and planters awaited greenery and flowers. The impression of the whole was one of welcome, of home away from home, a place for all to gather and be merry.

"It's right impressive," Mary Mossett said, as she scurried over to stand with them. "You can't take your eyes off it. It makes you keep looking at it, it's so colorful and grand."

"Much like its namesake," Tabitha muttered.

"It is not as magnificent as my own," Felicity said, "but it is fit for purpose."

"I am amazed it has been allowed." Tabitha took

in the scrolling typography declaring the pub to be the Sleuth and Scepter; a brightly colored image of a large, glossy brown bear wearing a crown and holding the signatory of office grinned toothily down upon them. If one knew what to look for, the resemblance was uncanny.

"His Highness approved it from conception to execution," Felicity said. "Arthur thinks it hilarious, and Mr. Bates loathes it."

"Our Beta's fierce concerned about us keeping our secrets," Mary offered.

"He fought the construction of our offshoot of the London Road tooth and nail," Felicity added, and Tabitha wondered if that had been quite literal.

"That was made by me da and brothers, that road was," Mary said. "There's no one to work in a field like them. Day and night they cleared the way, and it is as perfect a road as you'd like to see, even better than the King's Highway."

"It opens up the pack to greater prosperity," added Felicity, "and the chance to share our gifts, in craftsmanship at least, with the whole world."

The bee man, Mr. Beckett, wandered out from behind the building. He waved at Tabitha, who felt her cheeks heat with a blush. Mary cooed and giggled, and Felicity wasn't far behind.

"Have you an acquaintance with Mr. Beckett, Tab—Miss Barrington?"

"You could do worse," Mary said. "Them bees is hard workers."

Tabitha gripped her trug in both hands as if to shield herself from the speculation. "I am far too old to be entertaining suitors."

"You're no age at all compared to them, miss," Mary insisted. "And *versipelles* like a bit o' years on a female."

"You sound like His Grace," Tabitha replied, which was a mistake if Felicity's rapturous smile was anything to go by.

"Which Grace?" A small, beautiful lady (*a dove*, Tabitha observed) joined them. Mary curtsied and beamed at the woman, who was not much taller than the little maid, while Felicity embraced her.

"What a wonderful surprise! But it always is with you. Wonderful and a surprise. Lady Jemima Coleman, if I may make known to you Miss Tabitha Barrington?"

Tabitha curtsied, without anywhere near the aplomb of Miss Mossett.

"How do you do, Miss Barrington?" The lady was dressed in a nondescript ensemble. "I have heard great things about your talents and your involvement with the Duke of Llewellyn."

"Only just now she has helped one of the stable lads with a poultice. I've never seen one of his kind stay so still," Felicity enthused. "It was all thanks to Miss Barrington's manner."

"And I have heard great things about your

talents, Lady Coleman." Tabitha was surprised at the soberness of the lady's ensemble.

"I made my way here under, er, my own power," Lady Coleman said, "and plundered the nearest vestment hut. Your Grace, I insist I be permitted to contribute to their stores."

Felicity explained to Tabitha: "Like many of our kind, we provide clothing for those who arrive to our lands in need."

Lady Coleman eyed Tabitha's serviceable walking dress. "That fabric is from Italy, the north of the country."

"It is Florentine." She ran her hands down the front of it, its tight weave smooth as glass, soothing against her palms. "My brother and I spent much time traveling abroad and found Italy most congenial."

"My own brother enjoys the freedom of the Continent," said the lady, and they shared a measuring glance. "He has for some time. As a confirmed bachelor."

Ah. "It is possible our brothers are acquainted, Lady Coleman."

"The world is small," she agreed.

"I have found it so, if one's interests intersect."

"Oh, indeed," Lady Coleman replied. "I myself have spent much time in France. Being abroad offered me the freedom to pursue my art, as I suspect it did yours."

"Yes, I did not fail to find those in need of succor

wherever we went," Tabitha said. "I learned much, and it kept the wolf from the door."

"A universal desire," Jemima agreed.

"I did not even consider that you two would find common ground," Felicity said. "I hope you will take the opportunity to further your acquaintance—"

Another stable master, or manager—how many people did it take to mind horses?—came running. "Miss!" he called, hailing Felicity and waving a letter.

"Are you now delivering post, Bailey? Do not let Mr. Marshall see you parted from your duties as his second-in-command." Felicity took the missive from the lanky fellow, whose exotic species took Tabitha by surprise. "And do not let His Grace hear you call me *miss*."

"Not at all, miss." He grinned cheekily and cast a sultry look at Mary before heading for the stable. The little mouse blushed and stuck her chin in the air the way Felicity was prone to do. Lowell Close was a veritable den of romance.

Felicity scanned the letter's contents. "Jem—Lady Coleman! This is from Mrs. Anchoretta Asquith. She is to pass through Sussex on her next research expedition." She turned to Tabitha. "It was Lady Coleman who introduced me to her work."

"Her Grace in turn has lent me her latest," Tabitha said to the dove Shifter.

"I do hope you will be here when she arrives."

Felicity slid the letter into one of her pockets. "I have never met an author. I will be delighted to welcome her."

"I am here now, which is all I can promise." Lady Coleman's response was serene but one sensed undercurrents. "I was not able to attend the ceremony at Lupercalia, so I am here to observe Ostara with you and your pack."

Felicity hugged her friend once more. "Again, wonderful and a surprise."

"It was spur-of-the-moment, as my aunt was called away to a house party. As a rule she requires my company, but happily not in this instance. And so I am here, without my trunks, alas," Lady Coleman said. "How convenient it will be to take a coach from Town."

"Perhaps you may seek to influence Mr. Bates's poor opinion on that score," Felicity said, a teasing look in her eye.

Any response the lady may have made was drowned out by yet another cheer as the pub's sign hung securely on its own.

———

It was Alwyn's turn to pretend he wasn't startled as another rousing cheer rang out in the village.

Lowell clapped Matthias on the back. "That sound is likely due to the Sleuth and Scepter's sign going up."

"That sound is the end of our safety," the wolf mumbled.

"Or the beginning of our prosperity," countered the boar.

"Increased prosperity, though I do not like to brag," said Lowell, who was shouted down by his Second and Third. And rightly so; all wolves did was brag and boast.

Lowell's pride was not baseless, for he was doing something good here, something strong and secure and welcoming. It was not hard to believe he could protect his pack from incursion, but the trust he was placing in his people to keep their secret and the humans not to see what he had and try to steal it away…it was a risk, but to what end? Surely not so the weavers could sell their cloth to the wider world. The wolf Alpha continued, "Increased prosperity and the chance to open up and make new, er, friends."

Ah-ha. "Mates." The three turned to Alwyn, only two faces showing surprise; Lowell looked caught with his hand in the biscuit jar.

"Alfred." Bates lost his decorum to the degree he spoke to his Alpha casually in front of a stranger.

"Matthias." Lowell looked at his Gamma. "Sebastian. You know this is the only way many in our pack have a hope of finding their *vera amoris*. The curse my parents brought upon us held sway for too long, and as quickly as I can see to my people's happiness, I will do so. Am doing so."

He turned his attention to Alwyn. "My parents lied about being fated mates, and due to this, the Goddess Diana called a curse upon the wolves and those in our care—"

"Yes, yes," Alwyn cut across him. "It is famous, the Lowell fertility curse."

"I will see every soul under my care mated, if that is their wish, and none will naysay me." Lowell sent a pointed look Bates's way.

"I am not a horse," mumbled the Beta.

"Let them not take you as an example of how to conduct an admirable courtship, Alpha," Gambon teased, leavening the atmosphere with far less portent than that Omega of theirs did.

"I have heard of this also," Alwyn said.

"If His Highness had anything to say about that—" Lowell snarled.

"It is a favorite topic of gossip among the tweenies in Carlton House." The howls of laughter from Bates and Gambon were gratifying, though Lowell's mawkishly optimistic expression at his joke, that he'd even made a joke, threatened to lower the tone.

"Your lady apothecary is being courted, although she does not think so," Alwyn said.

"Not *my* lady apothecary," Lowell teased as Bates led them back into the main body of the building; he produced brooms and handed them around.

Alwyn was not certain he could wield one and crossed his arms over his chest.

"Is it that *homo plenum* do not court as we do?" he asked.

"It is that they do not have our instincts for a fated bond, and thus we must work harder. I found encouraging Her Grace's talents worked greatly in my favor." Lowell's Second simultaneously mouthed the words behind his Alpha's back; this was a familiar refrain, then. "I genuinely do encourage them, and I believe it came as a surprise to her. One wonders what human men get up to."

"One wonders that you wish to bring them into our circle." Bates was like a dog with a bone. Alwyn sighed to himself: *Ha, ha. Dog.*

"It will increase my people's chances to have families, if that is their wish, and thus increase the pack. And if any new members are human, so be it." Lowell glanced over at Alwyn. "Do you recall the Osborn sleuth? Arthur Humphries's wife is human," he said.

"I was there. At the vows." Alwyn looked at Bates, who shrugged. Had he said nothing about it?

"If you wish to pursue the topic of courting a human woman," Lowell said, far too casually, "I suggest you write to Osborn and ask him."

Bates looked at Alwyn, dubious. "I can write," Alwyn said. In theory: Whether he was able to hold a pen in practice was another story. Much of human life, in practice, was returning to him: he would remember how to court, how to write, how to use a bloody fork. "I forgot nothing, trapped in my Shape. It was not forgetting that nearly sent me—"

"Sent you…" Bates urged, unexpectedly gentle.

Alwyn took a step back. "I have forgotten nothing. I am capable of being human. I am human. And human I shall remain."

Lowell's fists flexed on the handle of his broom, but his voice was calm. "I believe if you asked Osborn, he would agree with what I will tell you now: ignoring my essential self ensured my courtship went poorly."

"Arguably, if at all," Bates said.

"Yes, thank you, we wait with bated breath until it is your turn."

"What had your wolf to do with it?" Had Alwyn heard of this, known this?

"He knew, better than I, what was required to woo a female, even one who was human." Lowell brushed at the floor ineffectually; he had likely never held a broom in his life. "Only when I heeded his advice did I succeed."

"Did you allow yourself to be courted?" The men looked at him, dumbfounded; that was all the answer he required. They had no idea it was wanted or necessary. Alwyn had almost all the answers he had come for. "Will the *cursio* not reveal who is fated for whom?"

Lowell and Bates were not subtle in the look of hope they exchanged. "It can, of course," the Alpha wolf replied. "We would be pleased if you joined us—you are welcome in your manskin."

"Where is it to be run? Will I be kept up at all hours with you lot tramping about, hither and yon?"

"We race the circuit of the park, and once that has been done, sweep through the meadow to the eastern edge, away from the London Road. In this, I will not have my people exposed. We end in the meadow that lies in between the brook and the highest hill. You would be very welcome."

I will be there, only you will not know it...

Alwyn slipped out the way he came, through a hole in the wall Bates had yet to notice. As he made himself scarce, he heard Alfred say, "Here, take a broom, give it a try—bloody hell. Where has he gone?"

"Cursed felines," Bates swore in response. "Always coming and going."

Eight

KNOWING THE *CURSIO* WAS ABOUT TO TAKE place was enough to make Tabitha as edgy as a cat in a room full of rocking chairs. She could not settle and discerned a flaw in having the healing shed: she had become quite used to, and comfortable with, contriving within whatever space was available and having Timothy's company while she worked. She supposed she could fetch the cream she made, to decant into the little ceramic pots she'd gotten from Mrs. Grice, the ceramicist; it wouldn't be out of place to work at the kitchen table. In Poitiers, she'd had to work on the floor.

In Verona, she hadn't even had as much as that! She'd had to spread a waxed cloth on the bed!

She ought to fetch the pots and keep her hands occupied. Mrs. Grice had bartered for the cream, an excellent source of moisture for hands often dried out from working the clay. How these people survived on their skills, she did not know, if they did not accept money.

As to that, were she and Timothy even paying rent? Accommodation was her brother's responsibility—and he had gotten an earful regarding that flat in Verona—so she would have no way of knowing. They allotted a percentage of their wages for their lodgings, and it always worked out in the end.

Tabitha realized she didn't know exactly how it always worked out in the end.

"Timothy!" He blinked at her sharp tone, coming out of what had been a congenial silence. "Have you taken sufficient money from me for our rent?"

"The cottage comes as part of my wages." He had been perusing his books for what seemed an hour and finally selected a volume from the shelves.

"But what about Verona?"

"Verona?" To be fair, he had every right to look at her like she was spouting utter nonsense. "That was two years ago. And we lasted there less than a week. *How am I meant to work when there is not a table, much less room on the floor—*"

Tabitha got up to pace. "It has only occurred to me that I may have not paid my fair share."

"You have paid more than your fair share." His tone was light but with a tinge of bitterness.

"What is that supposed to mean?" she demanded, but they both stilled at the sound of a scratch at the front of the cottage.

The scratch was followed by a slightly more forceful tap. "Is that—" Timothy began; both jumped when a prodigious thumping followed.

"I'll answer, shall I?" Tabitha edged her brother

out of the way and threw open the door to reveal the Duke of Llewellyn on her doorstep.

"Your Grace." She dipped into a curtsy, and Timothy bowed. "Er. Hello. How unexpected."

She got a dig in her side as her brother went back to his chair.

"Hello," said the duke, and nothing further. They stood there, unmoving, as though they had looked upon Medusa. This went on for far too long; Timothy's sigh carried across the room and over the threshold.

The duke cleared his throat. "I found the plant. You were looking for." He raised his eyebrows and then waggled them.

"The plant?" What in the world—oh, subterfuge! "Oh! The plant. Yes." She repeated the gesture with the eyebrows.

Timothy muttered, "*Oh! The plant,*" in his usual, unfortunately faithful approximation of her voice.

"I shall fetch my cloak, one moment." She shut the door. Was she meant to ask him in? She opened it again. "Would you? Like to come in?"

The duke shook his head and wandered away from the dooryard, but not before jerking his head in an easterly direction.

She shut the door and piled on her usual complement of outer garments.

"Foraging? And on Ostara Eve, of all eves. Your work is never done, darling sister." Timothy blinked at her over his book. "I do hope you find what you are looking for."

"Thank you ever so much, dear brother. Enjoy reading *The Odyssey* for the one hundred and twentieth time." Her tone was only slightly less acidic than an Amalfi lemon. She wrapped one final shawl around her shoulders; after closing the door firmly on Timothy's snickering, she went to join the duke, who was half-concealed behind a hawthorn tree.

The entire enterprise was so ridiculous, she wanted to laugh. A giggle escaped and was greeted with a crash of eyebrows in her direction and a—well, it was a growl. A growl like a, a lion might make.

Llewellyn appeared as shocked as she; he turned abruptly and made his way up the slope that bordered the cottage on the eastern side.

It was only the beginning: they crept through underbrush, up and down a surprising number of hills, as well as a series of boulders. They forded a brook more than once as it wound its way around yet another hill, this one more like a small mountain. Her breath became labored and earned a look over the ducal shoulder. She grabbed up more skirt and overcoat and forged ahead. She would not be left behind; she was well able for physical exertion. However, this was nothing like climbing up and down Sorrento's streets the livelong day, steep as they were. She refused to be outfaced until they came upon a fresh crop of boulders running up the side of yet another hill.

Tabitha supposed that the duke and his cohort had placed these obstacles for the entertainment of the climbing *versipelles*. For example: felines. She watched Llewellyn glide up the sheer face of rock like it was little more challenging than a staircase. He paused at the top, and she swore he almost smiled when he looked down at her. Slinking back was the work of a moment, and he held out a hand. It hung there between them, and both froze. He snatched it back, and she set a foot upon the nearest stone, took a deep breath—and he extended his hand once more. She gave him hers, and a shiver ran down her spine.

"One step at a time," he whispered. She nodded and carefully began her ascent.

He led her up a way she could not see for herself, his palm warm and dry, the strength in his arm apparent. Her feet found purchase, one rock after the next, and in her exuberance at reaching the top, she was almost undone. Tabitha released his hand too soon, and it was as if the air at her back pulled at her, as though her body longed for the ground beneath, and she slipped on the final rock. In the instant she sensed her balance falter, an arm lashed around her waist, and she was lifted to safety, held hard against a lean, muscular side. Those muscles moved in an evocative manner as he placed her on the summit with the same ease as she would put a teacup in a saucer.

They leaned against each other until their eyes met, and once again the duke retreated...but not without a lingering brush of fingers to her side.

"Well," she said and was roundly hushed. "Well," she whispered, "here we are." The vista was astonishing. This was an entire tranche of the park she had not come upon in her wanderings. "Where are we?"

"The eastern edge." He pointed to a path leading off to the south. "That leads directly to your section of the park."

"Why did we not come that way?"

"For your protection. In case Lowell had mounted a lookout." That seemed unlikely, but Tabitha deferred to his greater experience as one who was more often the watcher than the watched.

The vantage was perfect, even with its wild outgrowth of tall grasses and undisciplined shrubbery; a ledge projected slightly from a prodigious tangle of growth that would provide cover...if they lay on their bellies like children playing on a rug before a hearth. The duke started to speak and then looked ashamed. Tabitha unwrapped one of her shawls and lay it on the ground.

"Is this what you had in mind?" she asked, and he nodded, those lashes hiding his eyes, a fan against his high cheekbones. "I can sacrifice one of my coats as well."

"I did not prepare for this as best as I could have," he admitted.

"Come, come. This is not a picnic."

"And not on the scale of a royal banquet. Perhaps it is more akin to what you experienced in Greece."

What now? Oh, Timothy's monologue from the Sunday Meal. "I assure you, this climate is in no way Grecian." She unbuttoned her overcoat, and the duke took it to lay over the shawl. He looked at her, his eyes glimmering in the light of the moon.

She ran her hands self-consciously down her sides. "I am thin, beneath all of that."

"You are a nymph, like to tempt Zeus himself." He extended a hand, and whether or not she needed his help to lower onto their impromptu blanket, she took it. To help acclimate him to touch as much as possible. Obviously.

He followed, and yes, they both needed to lie down to see into the meadow.

The sensation of that male body next to hers—no, neither of them had thought this through.

Tabitha rallied, as ever. "So. We are as far from the village as we can be."

"And at the farthest point from the London Road," he said. "Not that there was likely to be traffic on it at this hour. But there is no chance of intrusion."

"For the safety of the pack." The Alpha of Lowell

Hall had thought this through; at least someone had.

"For the protection of their secret."

And by extension the whole of *versipellian* society. And yet... "I understand Lowell Close is to be opened up to the wider world."

"It is a risk." Llewellyn rocked up on his elbows. "Lowell has his reasons."

"I doubt it is on Her Grace's account." If Felicity never strolled the perimeter of a *ton* ballroom again, Tabitha was certain she would be the happier for it; she also doubted anyone in the *beau monde* would be extended an invitation to her friend's pastoral idyll. "I believe His Grace wishes his people's talents to be shared with all."

"As long as that's all that is shared. He also plans for his people to—" He stopped himself and fell silent.

The stars shone in the night sky, and the surroundings were still; the blasted spring air stirred, and Tabitha felt the lack of her two top layers. She shivered; the duke hesitated and then incrementally edged over until his shoulder brushed hers. The heat coming off him was like a bonfire.

Speaking of bonfires... "Will we see the flames from here?"

"No. They have several ceremonial groves, and we are farthest from the one they are using now. It would not serve our camouflage if my eyes caught the light. They will have shifted well before they run past here, below us, through that meadow."

"How lucky the moon is full."

"Luck has nothing to do with it." He propped his head on his fist, and she could feel him looking at her. "The wolves are obsessed with the moon."

"Some would make that common knowledge. For example, I have been loaned one of Mrs. Anchoretta Asquith's novels, *The Ravishment of Miss Leticia Everington at the Hands of the Duca di Luperno*. If one knows how to read between the lines, it is quite dangerous for your sort." It also seemed to be based on Felicity and His Grace's societal scandal; if that truly was the case, the lady author had produced the volume nigh overnight.

"Not precisely my sort," Llewellyn corrected her. "She is as fixated on the wolves as the wolves are on the moon."

"Have your sort traditions you uphold in this fashion?"

"No. Again, the wolves are the only ones with numbers to make such things impressive. And Lowell gathering all these species under his protection makes him almost impossible to match."

"Is it a competition?" She lay her head on her crossed arms.

"It is, if you ask our prince regent. Thanks to the death of those like Castleton, who upheld the old ways, this new breed of wolves is going from strength to strength, from Dover to Aberystwyth to the Hebrides. And beyond. The farther their reach, the more influential their customs."

"Is there nothing the lions call their own?"

"Felines resist falling in with anyone too easily." He leaned back up on his elbows. Even in his shabby coat, the long line of his back was…long. "We have our ways of doing things, even unto the highest and most sought state of being among all *versipelles*."

"*Vera amoris*." When Felicity had explained it, the contradiction it awoke in Tabitha was unlike anything she'd known. How would one engage in such a thing and not lose one's self entirely? Was it only for producing young? It seemed almost too easy, this scenting and deciding and bonding. But she knew little of love; it could very well work that way for humans too, with fewer fangs.

The duke nodded and reached out to run a hand through the tall grass. "It is known amongst all our kind. But Shifter felines are not so obsessed with populating the world, unlike *cat* cats, and so we do not put restrictions on what is considered a proper couple."

"Or a conventional one."

"Better said. Amongst us lions, this bond can go deeper." He hesitated and sent her another one of those impressively lashed looks. "You may not know that the *vera amoris* bond requires the fated couple to build a pack or a sleuth or a pride around them. They must cleave unto each other and to a homeplace. But felines have another facet to this legend that we hold in the highest regard, a rare occurrence that only happens once a generation, if we are lucky. It amplifies the bond to the degree that the mated pair may move throughout the world as…as an Alpha pair for all. Those who are isolated or lost or the last of their kind may find the same comfort in them as they would in a pack or a herd or a clowder. It is known as the *con*—"

A rush of sound like thunder, a clamor of hooves and paws, of cries and growls and barks and ululation, drowned out the duke's speech. The *cursio* flowed into the meadow right beneath their ledge, and Tabitha wanted to shout with glee. She reached out and grabbed the duke's arm, unthinking, felt him tense then relax into her grasp.

It was as breathtaking as Tabitha had hoped: the *versipelles* moved in concert, sweeping around and around the meadow, the moonlight gleaming off fur and feathers, whiskers and tails. Even as high as they were, she could see the smallest clearly: for while murine *animalis pura* were tiny, a Shifter mouse was rather larger. She saw Mary Mossett with other mice, whom Tabitha could not name. She saw His Grace and Mr. Bates take it in turns to shore up those in the back of the crowd, those with smaller legs and slower pace. A brook ran around the edge of the field, and fish leaped in and out of the rushing water.

She saw Mr. Coburn strutting after a sheepdog who was intent on going against the flow of the run; she saw the feline footman who was Felicity's usual messenger...and several other cats whose human forms she did not know. Was it that she recognized the animal Shape if she knew the person?

"Interesting. I—" She turned to the duke, who instead of watching the *cursio* was watching her watch it.

"It is. Even for one such as I." His Grace narrowed his eyes. "But you?"

"I, what?" It likely wasn't very insightful, or he would find it boring, a pedestrian observation. When had she gotten so uncertain in her opinions?

A rumble issued from his person, not unlike the growl he let loose back at the cottage. "You have that look on your face that either presages an insight or a story you would like to tell but fear it will bore the listener."

"That is ridiculous—" No, it was not, it was exactly right. "Yes, well, I realized I can tell who is who, but only if I have met them in their human skins."

"Can you?" Llewellyn sounded astonished. "I have never heard of a *homo plenus* able to see in that way. Beyond the humanity to the very essence of a *versipellis*."

Maybe it was interesting after all. "Obviously there is only one rooster about the place, but there are several mice, and there goes Mary, oh, she is

wonderful, she's taking no nonsense from that cat."
As large as the mouse was, the feline was larger, and
the little maid was not having any of his cheek. She
used his greater breadth against him and slipped
underneath his belly, causing him to flip over on
his back as he twisted to pursue her, a pursuit that
was put to an end with the intervention from Mr.
Gambon, who was surprisingly intimidating in his
boarskin when he was so gentle as a man.

"And one can ascertain which is Lowell and
which is Mr. Bates by their coats alone. Oh, may I
speak so? It seems a very personal comment—"

The duke clapped his hand over her mouth the
very instant that Lowell looked up at their eyrie.
Llewellyn removed his hand to slip out of his over-
large, dull brown coat and swept it over their heads.
She cowered into his side, stunned by her reaction
which she acted on without thought: She must
hide and make herself as small as she could. She
must find protection however she may. The duke
lowered his arm around her and tucked her closer.

Through a very small opening between the
lapels, she could see the Alpha wolf cant his head,
ears pricked. His Beta joined him, sniffing the air
and showing his teeth; the light of the moon caught
every bristle of hair that stood up on his back. He
made to leap forward, but his Alpha swept his
paws from beneath him, and both started to tussle.
If it could be said the *versipelles* cheered this new

development, they did: the mice squealed and the birds crowed and the sheep bleated, each species to their own expression.

"Are you quite all right?" the duke whispered in her ear. Tabitha could smell his soap, earthy, rich, with a top note of bergamot, and his lips tickled her skin. She nodded and yet did not move her head from his shoulder.

When had her head fetched up against his shoulder? She trembled, and he tightened his hold, and then—and then he sighed, and his lips moved against her jaw. His nose tucked behind her ear, and he inhaled, gasped, inhaled again, said "Miss Barrington—"

A clatter of hooves on stone sent the duke leaping away like a grasshopper. One of the colts had left the crowd and come around the back way, presumably to sneak up on the rest to catch them off guard; when he loped into the light of the moon, Tabitha could not believe her eyes.

"Ash! How in the world did you make it up that rock?" she scolded, and the young horse ducked his head. "You will undo all the good that poultice did!" It had worked very quickly, and she reckoned it had more to do with his healing powers than hers. "I know I am not supposed to be here, but please do not tell on me? Let us make a bargain: I won't tell Mr. Marshall on you, fair enough? There's a good lad."

The colt slid with exuberance down the opposite side of the hill and galloped off to join his herd. "I only treated that young fellow's hoof the other day, and I—oh, for goodness' sake."

The eventful evening ended on a solitary note: the duke had evaporated like a morning mist. Tabitha donned the coat and scarf and picked her way down a less rocky side of the hill, studiously minding her feet and not her thoughts...and definitely not the pinch in her heart.

Nine

Tabitha's work had ever been her refuge: When circumstances threatened to sully her peace of mind, she turned to crafting and distilling and combining. Taking things that seemed contrary and putting them together harmoniously was utterly satisfying; perfecting the balance of a tonic, in its ingredients and its dosage, gave her an immense sense of accomplishment.

There was no relief in her concoctions today.

After being left to make her way back from the *cursio*, she had crept up to her room and risen before the dawn, to escape Timothy's inevitable curiosity. She walked and walked, well away from the duke's part of the park, returned to the cottage, smuggled some bread and cheese from the larder, and holed herself up in the healing shed. She made creams and soaps, distilled herbs into oils, even threw together some herbal sachets. She derived little pleasure and no distraction from the work: it was so ingrained in her, it allowed her mind to roam wild.

Much like the *versipelles* of Lowell Hall ran the *cursio*. How wonderful it had been to see such a thing; all the sights she'd seen on the Continent

paled in comparison. She had been impressed by the
Colosseum in Rome, by the Acropolis of Athens;
steeped in history though they were, those static
structures had nothing on seeing every species
inhabiting Lowell Hall in the skins of their essential
selves, in living, breathing, amazing freedom.

The duke surely missed being in his lionskin.
It had to be painful, on many levels, to be unable
to Change. On the other hand, he was becoming
more and more comfortable in his manskin. At
least he was last night. With his heat and his scent
and protectiveness.

But why would he run away? Had it to do with
her? Had she said something, done something that
made him go?

Enough was enough. This was unlike her. She
was as sensible as the day was long. Her bones were
knit together with prudence, their marrow a sober
core, her every thought and deed logical and judicious. She observed symptoms and gathered information as she gathered her herbs, organized her
thoughts as she did her trug, never jumping to conclusions, never foolishly hoping for the outcome
she preferred. She allowed nature to take its course,
the aid of her wisdom and experience a bulwark
upon which she leaned with confidence.

It would be most prudent and judicious to take
the advice she gave out so freely, her favorite being
that an overactive mind required activity of the

body. Therefore, she would take another walk, and perhaps she would sleep. As she had not the night before.

Valerian tea might be on the cards that night.

Tabitha banked the fire in the hearth and put everything in its place then draped herself in scarves and coats, including the one upon which she had lain with the duke. She held it to her nose, and there was that bergamot again, with—she sniffed again—a hint of mint? And a kind of…cake? How odd. She held the collar tight around her neck and wrapped another scarf around to keep it nestled against her cheek.

Thus swathed, she decided to head for the Hall.

Its forecourt was cultivated and manicured more in line with a typical big house, although the topiary carved as lunging wolves alluded to the pack's secrets, as did the fountain featuring a variety of statuary beasts, horses and bears and cats among them, cavorting in the flowing water. A massive hedge nearly two stories high shielded the wildness of the park behind from unwelcome eyes.

On the path ahead came her brother, radiant with a good day's work doing what he loved.

He opened his mouth to hail her, and she shook her head.

As he passed, he squeezed her arm.

She stopped and turned. He looked back over his shoulder and blew her a kiss.

How fortunate she was in her brother. Even though he would leave her alone only until he deemed it time for her to talk about what was bothering her.

Before she knew it, she stood on the terrace in front of Lowell Hall. Ought she to have gone to the kitchen door instead? She was there, so there was nothing for it but to knock.

"Good evening, Miss Barrington." For a rooster, Mr. Coburn exuded more than his fair share of dignity. If she had done wrong by not going around to the back, he would not say so, but his demeanor expressed his opinion.

"And to you, Mr. Coburn. I am here to collect my mending."

"I see." And he did not like it. Had she made yet another mistake? "As I am currently without an underbutler, you will find Lady Coleman and Miss Mossett in that pantry."

"I'll see her there, Coburn." As quiet as a cat, a comparison she suspected he would not like, the Duke of Lowell appeared at his butler's side.

"As you wish, Your Grace." The butler inclined his head and looked down his nose simultaneously.

"I have offended Mr. Coburn," Tabitha said as she and Lowell made their way deeper into the house.

"His standards are high," the duke admitted, "and I fear he is let down by all around him. We can only hope to improve."

Tabitha tutted. "Not too greatly, I hope, as his role requires he transform problems into solutions."

"I am of a mind with you, Miss Barrington." A series of turns led them to a green baize door. He opened it for her, and they descended the staircase. "When the pups start to arrive, he will have more than enough to keep him busy. As we all will."

"That will be a happy day for your pack."

"It will be. Long awaited and much desired." They passed the kitchens, and Lowell paused before a door. "We anticipate a happy day when Llewellyn will once again master his lion."

"You have rather less control over that, unfortunately." Tabitha wondered how much to say, if this was in the way of being a report. "The more time I spend in his company, the more admiration I have for him. By which I mean"—she was blushing, she could feel it—"he is becoming easier every day in company with others, in ways I did not foresee."

"It is your company specifically I believe he enjoys. We often met at Court as children, and he was always solitary but mischievous with it. Getting into things no one else did, for example, or finding hiding places no one would have thought of." The duke's eyes twinkled.

Tabitha rushed to Llewellyn's defense. "It was my idea entirely. He did it only for me."

"Did he?" Lowell rapped twice on the door and opened it for her. "How interesting." With that, the duke, who had greater knowledge of the depths of the Hall than one would think, slipped behind an unobtrusive door and away.

"Evening, miss." Mary Mossett curtsied even as she finished off a hem. The underbutler's pantry had been converted into a sewing room: it was not unlike her healing shed, with its high table and floor-to-ceiling shelves. These would have played host to silverware in need of polishing; now, fabrics in a rainbow of colors filled them.

Mr. Coburn's opinion notwithstanding, he had made it a useful and productive space. Lowell Hall was keen to adapt to the needs of its residents.

And its visitors. Lady Jemima Coleman unrolled a bolt of immaculate white fabric. "Miss Barrington. How nice to see you."

"And you. I was hoping my mending was ready, Mary?" She had two pounds for the little maid; perhaps Lady Coleman would act as her go-between.

"Oh yes, miss, I was going to give it to Mr. Barrington, but he was spending extra time with a few of the students, and then I had to do something for Mrs. Birks, and then he was already gone from the Hall." Mary collected a pile of folded clothing and set it on the large table. Just as she reached for a length of brown paper, one of the footmen, the one Mary had eluded during the *cursio,* stuck his head in the door.

"Here, Mary," he began then clocked the presence of the ladies. He bowed and blushed a bit, to

Mary's delight. "How do, my ladies, or lady and miss, or—look, Mary, Mrs. Birks says to come 'round to the laundry and sharpish."

"Thank you, Leo," said Lady Coleman. She took the paper from Mary. "Leave this with me, Mary."

"I meant to do that myself, I did," the mouse muttered, but went to do the bidding of the housekeeper.

"Miss Mossett has many demands on her time." In a trice, the lady had their clothes tidily parceled and wrapped with twine.

Tabitha leaned against the table and sorted out a pile of needles. "I have ruffled Mr. Coburn's feathers by coming to collect the mending."

This received a sharp look from the lady; Tabitha ought not to have mentioned feathers. "The less said about Mary's new enterprise, the better. She has the full support of Mrs. Birks, however, so it will not go too badly for her."

"I am relieved to hear it."

"Mr. Coburn is as high a stickler as Sally Jersey," Lady Coleman remarked casually, as if Tabitha had the acquaintance of that influential personage. "He is very concerned that our kind conduct ourselves impeccably."

"Yes, I am aware of his standards." If not able to meet them. "I suspect this is in a bid to keep all here safe?"

"Yes. In general, the less attention drawn to our essential selves, the better."

"They are key to your well-being, are they not?"

"They are."

"And the harmony between both is paramount." Would an outsider have a new perspective on this question? "What happens when you are at odds with your essential self?"

Lady Coleman lifted a length of cloth to drape over Tabitha's shoulder and considered its effect on her complexion. "I vow, this was dyed with you in mind." The color was a rich, deep orange, which she could not, in a month of Sundays, picture herself wearing. "I insist you allow me to make you something from it. A pelisse, perhaps."

It seemed the lady did not wish to pursue that topic. "If I do not allow it, will you proceed regardless?"

"I shall."

They laughed, and Tabitha recognized a kindred spirit.

"I, too, find my good advice overlooked at an alarming rate," she said, "but unlike you, I can't go forward regardless and enforce my will."

"Does the Duke of Llewellyn follow your advice?" Lady Coleman carefully set aside the fabric, and Tabitha had a pang of longing to be a woman who could wear orange, of any hue.

"He has asked for none. I have offered none. It is not... I do not feel as though he is a client such as I would consult with abroad. I give him my company, to accustom him to humans again, to his humanity again, and in this way, I hope to learn more about him and what his needs may be." Her needs did not enter into it.

"A young unmarried lady sniffing around an eligible duke?" The lady did a spot-on impression of a society tabby.

"I am not young, and I am sure fated mating is not on the man's mind." But speaking of sniffing: it had not been the lady doing it.

"Finding one's *vera amoris* is not the be-all and end-all of desire," Lady Coleman said, a daring statement to make in company with a mere acquaintance.

"I am well aware that sexual interaction is not necessarily about lifelong love," Tabitha assured her.

Lady Coleman picked up her shears and started slicing through the white fabric, a heavy, glazed, undyed chintz. "This is not a point of view one expects from a *homo plenus*."

"Is it different for *versipelles*?"

"There are certain formalities in place that prevent the indiscriminate production of young. Only the worst among us would overlook them." A particularly forceful snip of the scissors accompanied this statement. "All species honor the *vera amoris* tradition, which means once found, you will never know another. Thus, there is nothing to prevent us loving as we will, in our youth. Well, youth as compared to humans."

"I see." This was fascinating and in stark contrast to human opinions on the matter. "I have never held romantic notions, yet in order to communicate effectively with my female clients, I felt the need to investigate."

"Investigate?" Such a big laugh out of such a small lady. "Is that what you call it where you come from? What did you conclude?"

"It has its moments but is nothing to lose one's composure about."

"I agree. I wonder if we have both been failed by past partners."

"My investigation was exhaustive," Tabitha assured her. "Thanks to my travels, I was able to avail myself of lovers of many cultures, religions, social strata, et cetera, and thus create a matrix for comparison."

"A comparative matrix? That is *not* what we call it where I come from." They both laughed at that, and the sound breezed around them like a yearned-for zephyr on a summer's day. This was all that was needed to clear the malaise left by a man: shared laughter and confidences with a woman. With a friend?

Tabitha leaned on her elbows. "May we call each other by our given names?"

"Yes, please. I am Jemima."

"I am Tabitha."

"You will discover that my friendship is accompanied by garments." Jemima piled the cut pieces of the cloth to one side and took up another bolt of the white fabric.

"Mine comes with tonics. And lately, an abundance of soap." Jemima looked curious, but friend or not, Tabitha was not ready to speak of her day. "My brother will be envious, as he is the fashionable Barrington. His friendship comes with *bon mots*, and not only in French."

"Felicity's friendship comes with the wish we all settle here as family."

"I would not mind so much," Tabitha mused, "if my own experience of that condition had more to recommend it."

"I consider my brother my only family," Jemima said.

"We are alike in that."

"He left for France as many do, in search of a congenial, safer society."

"As did we. Timothy says I can say whatever I want about him, and yet I am careful."

"Protective."

"To a fault. Which may or may not be true. Or is both true and not true." Tabitha swept up the needles and poked them one by one into a pincushion. "It is the habit of a lifetime, and I find my respect for him and his ability to take care of himself at war with my desire that he never come to harm."

"I was given to understand, in no uncertain terms," Jemima said, "that if I loved my brother, I must leave him to his choices, the joys and the sorrows of them."

"Yes, I understand that here"—Tabitha pointed to her head—"but not here." She laid her hand on her heart.

"And has your heart been claimed, ever, during your investigations?" Jemima's smile was naughty. "For clinical purposes?"

"Not once. Not for my brother's lack of trying, nor my own, when I was young enough to think there was a future in it."

"Find a *versipellis* for a husband, Tabitha. I hear you are spoiled for choice as far as suitors are concerned. Would you not consider it?"

The door swung open, and Mary entered with intent. She'd clearly had ambitions of parceling up the Barrington mending, for she scowled at the package Tabitha swept into her arms.

"I must go," Tabitha said, and Jemima smirked at her transparent excuse to flee. "Mary, I am all that is grateful for your hard work." She'd have to figure out how to get those coins to her.

"I look forward to meeting again, Miss Barrington," Jemima said, "and furthering our discussion of your wealth of things to consider."

———

Would she consider it? How would she have answered Lady Cole—Jemima? As a personage or as a friend? Likely the former, awash with platitudes; she could not do otherwise when she did not know the answer herself.

Would she consider a *versipellian* match? Why should she? Surely at the age of five and thirty, there was no point. Her fertility was waning, and wasn't offspring the point of marriage?

Had she the company of the Italian cat, she would play devil's advocate and dispute that straightaway. For if the *vera amoris* bond was meant between two souls, procreation had little to do with it.

She was thrilled that Felicity's life was everything her friend desired. Having seen how happy and ebullient the stoic Beatrice had become upon her marriage to Osborn, Tabitha could not have wished anything else for her. She could look at their lives and be joyful for them, but she was sure it was not her path.

Why would the duke choose her, despite his compliment to her figure and his sniffing of her person? She ought to have asked Jemima about that—oh, but that would open Pandora's box!

Should she talk to Timothy? He had far greater experience than she at giving his heart.

When had her heart come into it? Her heart had nothing to do with it.

Nor the duke's heart, nor any heart. For the love of, of Palu, this was ridiculous. Swept off her feet by proximity and bergamot? Unlikely.

The frog and the goat, as pleasant and kind as

they were, did not suit her preferences. The bee was the closest she thought to encouraging if she was to give it any thought at all.

Mrs. Tabitha Beckett—oh dear.

Tabitha ap Lewin—

She almost stepped on something left on the doorstep as she charged through the door.

"All right?" Timothy looked up from his marking, still glowing from his day's work. She slammed the door behind her. "Not all right," he murmured and shuffled through the litter of foolscap on the dining table.

"This was on the porch." She held up a bunch of basil, roots exposed and tied imperfectly with string. It had not been dug up with a trowel. In her fanciful way of gauging the efficacy of plants and such, the stalks smelled hopeful and happy, the essential sunniness of the herb in no way dimmed by its English provenance.

Timothy hummed under his breath. "It was not meant for me."

"Basil is a common enough herb. What it is meant to signify, I do not know." Was she supposed to repot it? She set it aside with the parcel of mending and unraveled herself from her garb.

"I suspect it refers playfully to your plant searching the other evening." Timothy sighed. How Tabitha loathed that sigh of his, that long-suffering gust that despaired of her seeing past the nose on her face. Any intention to ask his advice went out the window. Especially when he continued, "Which on the night itself had appeared to have been unsuccessful. As regards herbaceous discovery, at the very least."

If she made faces behind his back, no one was to know but her. "Here is our mending, parceled by no less a personage than Lady Jemima Coleman."

"Had she made you feel your difference in rank?" Timothy removed his glasses and gave them a careful polish with a cloth.

"Not at all. We are to be friends. She resided in France for many years and is only lately returned to England."

Timothy donned his spectacles and blinked at her. "Is she as annoyed to be back as you are?"

"I am not annoyed." She ripped apart the string and tore at the brown paper of the parcel.

Oh, there, the sigh wedded with a roll of the eyes. "Are you not."

"No, I am not."

"You are becoming increasingly out of sorts," he observed. "Every day that passes, you stray further and further from the land of sorts."

"Do I?" She separated their clothing and bundled hers against her chest.

"After all this time, I think I can tell." He set his mended clothing aside gently, in contrast to her ill humor, his every movement measured. "One wonders what it would be like if you were to say what is on your mind."

"Or, as an example of the opposite, if one practiced discretion before saying whatever one thought." How had their conversation gone so dreadfully wrong?

"You might have stayed on the Continent, you know. I would not have been offended." If he had one besetting sin, it was his relentless need to teach her by example, to do the thing she was not doing to his approval. He would not stop *demonstrating* his feelings. "No need to shepherd me home."

"Might I have stayed? With no companion, no man to protect me?"

He snorted. "I'd like to meet the man who dared protect you. Or perhaps I have."

Was that what Timothy wanted, to marry her off to the first likely swain to darken her door, as their father had? Would he have preferred she hadn't joined him here in Sussex? Or even in the whole of England? It was like a stiletto to her heart. "Pardon me for interrupting your work. I'll take my clothing upstairs and wish you a good night."

Timothy's characteristic muttering would have been preferable to the silence in her wake.

The tension in her body threatened her with another restless night. And she had forgotten to fetch the valerian.

Too much of the herb was not healthy, but how was she to stop her mind from racing enough to sleep and thus improve her humor for the morrow?

She and Timothy often wrangled like cats in a sack, but this had been... Ought they to part and live their own lives? They did live their own lives, they truly did, each to their profession...but perhaps they were too old to be in each other's pockets. Did her brother feel she was preventing him from finding another partner? That must be what all the matchmaking was about, to get her out from under his feet. It was not as though she did not wish for a lover, but every man she met either quizzed her relentlessly about their conditions or refused to take her advice regarding their health.

Timothy had his eye on the duke for her, and who was less healthy than His Grace?

No, that was not correct. The duke was not unhealthy; he was unwell. That was not an improvement, or was it? Were health and wellness not the same thing? Oh, how she longed for someone to help her talk this through. Her whole philosophy had undergone great revision in the past year or so, and she did not think she would find an enlightened opinion here in England.

"Let me keep an open mind," she scolded herself

and then sighed. She missed the Italian cat, she truly did. It might be worth a trip to the stable to see if any in the clowder there would like to follow her home.

The Duke of Llewellyn was healthy in his frame, an opinion underscored thanks to their sojourn beneath his coat. He walked for hours and hours every day, much as she did, and seemed none the worse for it. His breathing was even, his color good, neither too pale nor too rosy; when he did not have to grapple with challenging utensils, he ate heartily. His voice sounded like a rusty gate, utterly lacking in the beautiful lilt to be found in a Welsh voice, and still it did strange things to her composure.

And yet...he was not well. Visits of long duration were anathema; the degree to which his hand had shaken attempting that fork tweaked at her heart. That he should struggle so with something he had mastered as a child, that he would do so before all, showed courage. Was it not well to be brave?

It was good of the others to care for his health, but Tabitha wasn't convinced they knew any more than she did. They had nothing to compare him to, apart from the fact he did not Change. Or could he not?

Was the issue with the lion and not the man? The *versipelles* emphasized how weak the human side was in comparison to the essential self, and yet Llewellyn was withholding the lion—and if he were truly weak, he would not have been able to Change back when freed from the curse, or the magic, or whatever it was...

Tabitha knew better than to tease this out further. Experience had shown that leaving a tangle to itself overnight would bring clarity in the morning. She would sleep on it, hopefully, and see what the new day brought.

After a quick wash and change into her night rail, she let down her hair. Not a curl to be found, a mere wave, nothing special except for its tidy length. How unfeminine she would be made to feel if anyone knew how short she kept it, only grazing the tops of her shoulders. Luckily the fashion to knot one's hair atop the head allowed for camouflage; it was impossible to tell its length when done up. It was so thick, no one could tell it didn't fall to her hips.

Would Llewellyn's hair fall to his hips? His slim hips... She had felt bone against her side when they lay on the ground. If that was indeed his hip and not his—she giggled.

All that talk of sexual activity with Jemima. It seemed to be the only thing ladies wished to speak of: men and their foibles and shortcomings and attributes, how all of it sat uneasily together to create an appealing objective. Her lady clients always asked how to enjoy the act without it becoming too enjoyable so the men did not think them loose in their morals or that they could have the bed things all the time. Tabitha suggested self-love as a means to those ends.

Again: perhaps she ought to take her own advice.

She climbed under the covers, slid her night-gown up to her hips, and unbuttoned the bodice. If only her favorite chemise weren't in the laundry; made of the finest muslin, it was so soft with age, it was like silk against her breasts.

Her breasts, which were not large by any means but very, very sensitive. She ran her fingertips around the sides, her skin appealingly soft if she did say so herself, thanks to the jasmine-scented lotion she made. Did the duke find the jasmine pleasing? Was that why he sniffed her? They had been lying together so close under his awful coat, creating a little den of warmth from their body heat and their breath.

His breath on her jaw, his lips on her ear… She slid a hand down her belly to her feminine place—she corrected herself immediately. She would not allow her clients to resort to euphemism, and she would not allow it in herself. Her fingers slid into her vulva and teased her clitoris. There. Adult terms for an adult woman.

But she mustn't be doing very well if she was thinking so clinically.

She rolled onto her side, facing the window,

open for a bit of night air. *Do not dwell on the health-ful benefits of night air, Tabitha!* she scolded herself. No: she'd think of how the night air had brushed over her face as the duke held her hand and led her up the rocks, how his palm in hers was so warm and firm, how long his back was and how muscular his side. How he had protected her from the gaze of the wolf, how his biceps pressed against her shoulder and flexed when he moved her closer to him, oh, and again, his lips on her ear, how they caressed her skin, and his voice, that gravelly, rumbling, manly voice, whispering her name… What if they hadn't been interrupted, and what if she had turned toward him, onto her side, and her breasts pressed against him, what if he had rolled her over onto her back, slid a thigh between her legs, leaned down, rubbed her cheek with his, oh God, those lashes fluttering over his changeable hazel eyes, brushing against her skin—

Her release crashed through her at the thought of touching his face, running a finger over those lashes, of his hips grinding against hers, and true to her prescription, she came and fell almost directly into a deep sleep.

Ten

"I THOUGHT IT AMUSING, TO LEAVE A PLANT? Because I attempted subterfuge on Ostara Eve and said I had located a plant she had been looking for. It is amusing, is it not?" As perceptive as Delilah was, there was only so far she could go to offer her opinion. At least as regarded speech; the mare's expression was dubious.

It was amusing, Alwyn was sure of it. Perhaps he would tell Miss Barrington how he snuck into the kitchen garden up at the Hall and sent that French cook into hysterics. What the man was doing out there in the middle of the night was anyone's guess. He had been pillaging the basil when the Frenchman appeared; Alwyn had risen to his full height and snarled (more embarrassed to be caught than anything else), and the chef had started in such shock, he fell over backward, arms windmilling wildly as he screamed at the volume of a chorine in an opera. The Frenchman had been unharmed; Alwyn had beat a hasty retreat.

"It is only my first foray, a gesture of my intent to court her. I assume the meaning of it was clear." He would have left a note, but as it transpired, he could write but was not in full command of a pen. "I left it on her doorstep. Where she would see it. Tied together with string."

Delilah snorted and nipped his shoulder. Miss Barrington had made herself scarce all day yesterday, which he knew because he was, in turn, making himself scarce. It was not well done of him to abandon her on the hill, but the moment a stranger clattered into their midst—"One of those rackety colts," he said aloud, and Delilah bared her teeth—he took flight. It was too much like the early days of his return to his manskin, of negotiating the London streets to Carlton House, every stranger a threat. Holy, Blessed Palu, was Georgie right in sending him here? Only think how nervy he would be, staying in the capital city. Even out here, with all this room to roam, he was too vigilant.

But he was improving. His senses were sharpening, his instincts returning. For it was a good instinct to fetch basil for the lady apothecary. It was Italian, and therefore she would find it pleasing. It was a useful plant, if nothing special... It was not as though he could offer white pimpernel, as he would find in great bunches along the waterways in Anglesey. That would have been a fitting tribute for his...

Blessed, Beloved Palu, was the lady apothecary his fated mate, and not only that but able for the *coniunctio*? As with all species, scent entered into finding one's *vera amoris*, but for lions, it was an awareness of the body as well. Even if he couldn't fully parse her scent without the aid of his essential self, he had perceived more than enough that fateful night. It had started from the simple touch of her hand in his, grown exponentially as they lay side by side, and nearly exploded as he hid them from Lowell's searching gaze beneath his awful coat. She was redolent of the astringency of rose water wedded with burning wood, a hint of cooling lavender, and the bracing air of a spring dawn. It wound through his senses like the path out of the darkest forest, and if that blasted colt hadn't shown up—

Alwyn would have kissed her. His entire being roused at the thought of those lips beneath his, kissing him in return. If the scent of her arousal had been any indication, she would welcome his attentions. He at least guessed she would... It had been a long, long time since he inspired desire in a female.

There: he was not entirely lacking notions of what was proper. He recalled his questioning of Lowell and his cadre; he must let her court him as well, and her version of that would most likely be tending to his ills. It was his ills that interfered with his capacity to know if she was his fated mate, and the intimation, the hope he had of her being more—

"I cannot be certain," he said, and Delilah made

a show of rolling her big brown eyes at him. "Not without being at full strength, and I require my lion for that state, and my lion—" No, he would say no more, not even to a creature who could not betray him. He must remain silent. The notion of being on the receiving end of the pity he would inspire in the others was enough to make him growl as if he were indeed in harmony with his essential self.

It made little impression, as Delilah didn't even flick an eyelash. "What do you think, my fierce one? Shall I let the lady tend to me? What harm can it do? I doubt it can do any good—"

The mare suddenly came to attention, ears forward and nostrils flaring. She whuffled deep in her chest, and the band, who always kept Delilah between them and potential threats, whinnied in distress and galloped for the opposite side of the paddock.

Now that he was no longer moaning about how to woo Miss Barrington, he heard what the horse did: a rustle in the underbrush, a scrape of hoof on rock, the slip and slide of leaves on muddy earth. He turned to see the shrubbery shiver, and that was all Delilah needed: she reared, backed up, and jumped the paddock fence in a smooth leap to charge straight into the wood. Alwyn followed, delighted that his endless wandering had rendered him more than fit enough to keep up with the mare.

When he came upon her, she was undertaking to herd a large chestnut stallion out of a ditch, and he in turn was unsuccessfully attempting to use a holly bush as camouflage. The state of the beast's mane spoke to a lack of grooming, and the muddy, torn rug straining to contain his great bulk bore the rubric for Templeton House.

"Templeton," he growled, and Delilah whinnied again, high and harsh. Alwyn's vision came over in a red haze, and slipping his fingers around one of the buckled straps at the horse's chest, he pulled the animal from the mud, across the field, and toward the village. Delilah capered in their wake, bucking and snorting until she jumped back into the paddock to soothe her band.

The horse had a powerful will. It dug its hooves in the dirt and threw its head around in a bid to shake off Alwyn's grip. A force surged through him, and in fits and starts as he reacquainted himself with it, it flowed free. His *dominatum* was not what it could be, but nevertheless it surged through him and around him, obeying his instinct to exert his will, and in this instance, to protect. Did this horse require protection? Her Grace was meant to be forward-thinking and compassionate in her animal husbandry. How dare she spout such empty platitudes when she knowingly...but did she know what this horse truly was?

Duchess or no, he would demand an explanation

as to how this captive creature came to bear her family's colors.

═══════════

"This is very impressive, Mr. Beckett, and we all look forward to greeting our first visitors."

The publican and his wife beamed as Felicity spoke, and she and Tabitha admired the common room of the coaching house. The tabletops were polished to a shine, and the brass gleamed; a massive hearth took pride of place. A long bar stretched to fill the side of the wall opposite the fireplace; this was currently receiving the devoted attention of a cloth wielded by another Mr. Beckett, he of the pot of honey.

"We will welcome each and every one," Mr. Beckett replied. "And we hear tell Mrs. Anchoretta Asquith may be first among them."

"Do you enjoy her novels, Miss Barrington?" asked the Mr. Beckett who was not the publican but the suitor, for lack of a better term.

"I have read only the most recent, Mr. Beckett." This would devolve into confusion in no time at all.

"I would be happy to lend you my sister's volumes," he offered.

"But would your sister be happy to have you lend them?" Tabitha asked.

"Archibald! If there's any lending going on, it'll

be your hands to the task you've left undone!" The shout issued from deep within the pub, and he waggled his fingers at her before he turned to go. Felicity snorted and turned it into a delicate sneeze into her handkerchief.

"Miss Barrington," said Mrs. Beckett-the-Publican, "Mrs. Grice cannot stop praising your hand lotion. I would like to offer some for our guests, but I am no apothecary! The simplest things are far beyond my abilities. Would you be willing to make some for us?"

"Of course, I would be delighted. I have also made soaps that complement the hand lotion, and both come in several scents." Making lotion and soap was better than wandering about behind Felicity day in, day out. "If you would give me a list of—oh, very good." Mrs. Beckett thrust a slip of paper into Tabitha's hand. "You are well prepared. That is admirable. Shall we not discuss this in greater detail? Do you wish to try some samples?"

Mrs. Beckett shook her head. "Any friend of Her Grace is to be trusted."

Goodbyes were exchanged, and once they crossed the threshold, a pinch at her elbow had her wincing. "Tabitha, you have truly caught Mr. Beckett's eye," Felicity said. "As Mary Mossett said, you could do worse than a bee."

If she were to go down the romantic road, she'd like to think she could do better, rather than do worse. "Mrs. Beckett's idea is clever and hospitable. I can't think it is good business to take what I give her without trying it for herself."

Felicity accepted the change of topic grudgingly, with another pinch at Tabitha's elbow. "You have a way about you that inspires trust."

"O'Mara does not trust me." They stood at the edge of the green, opposite Templeton Stud. Several lads were to-ing and fro-ing about with bits and pieces; she was no horsewoman, and it all looked strange to her, like lengths of leather longer than normal bridles and folded blanket things proudly bearing the Templeton Stud name. Another crowd of lads dragged troughs to the village pump and required the help of several of the men. As they pitched in, a handful of women gathered to offer advice and catcall. Mr. Gambon, as was his duty, soon interceded but managed to do so without ruining the fun.

Felicity gestured, and they went to join the milling crowd. "Her trust is not easily given."

It certainly was not. Tabitha said, "In turn, His Grace does not trust O'Mara."

"No. Her powers are so mysterious, even to other *versipelles*." Felicity shoved her hands in the pockets of her trousers. Apparently, part of her marriage contract, which she had written herself, deemed her free to wear them on Tuesdays. "I often feel she is too separate from the pack."

"Has she a suitor? Or…there are, of course, those who prefer their own gender."

"I am aware." Felicity looked proud of herself. "We spoke of this on my wedding day."

"Really?" What an odd topic to occur. "How in the world did that come up?"

"Lady Coleman and Miss O'Mara were helping me to prepare. The latter will not allow the former to sew for her. Not even a suit such as she is known for wearing. I pointed out that her preferences were all that mattered."

Tabitha halted them with a touch to Felicity's arm. "If that is your opinion, then I must say, I feel the need to correct you." This had been preying on her mind. "I believe O'Mara wishes to be addressed without an honorific. We had acquaintance with several people in France who preferred to have no specific designation as to their gender."

"Oh. I had no idea." Felicity looked stricken. "I thought it rude not to address her properly."

"*Conventionally* is a more fitting term than *properly*." Tabitha kept her tone light; this sort of thing provoked the oddest reactions in people. "It would be best, of course, to discuss it with her directly, but it is my instinct."

"I trust your instincts without reservation. Your experience of the world is so much greater than mine." Felicity slipped her hands out of her pockets and worried at the hem of her hacking jacket.

"O'Mara would not think it right to take me to task."

"As surprising as that is, given her general frankness, I think you're right."

"I shall do as you suggest. Oh! I am so unworldly. The *ton* is such a limiting place when you consider it. The same faces at the same events. I do not know what sort of duchess I shall make if my experience is so narrow."

"Your experience has expanded in ways unfathomable by most."

"True enough, and yet...I am a pattern card for conventionality." They walked on again; it now seemed the entire village had gathered around the pump. "And you?" Felicity asked.

"And I, what?"

"Have you a preference when it comes to gender?"

"I prefer men, but as a rule, they assume I do not when I don't fancy them as individuals under certain circumstances." Tabitha had to laugh. "Imagine having such arrogance."

"I had no love before Alfred." Felicity slipped her arm through Tabitha's. "Well, there was a vicar I fancied."

"There is always a vicar," Tabitha said.

"But no one else. So I had no experience to draw upon when I met him. In fairness, the abduction was out of bounds, but I held fast, and he was required to make amends."

"His courtship of you is still the pinnacle of *on-dits*."

Felicity grimaced at that, and who could blame her? "A part of me thought a simpler suitor might be preferable to one of such high status. I am curious if you feel the same."

Did she refer to the Duke of Llewellyn? And her? "I am not being courted."

"I wouldn't be too sure about that—"

A terrible noise interrupted Felicity's observation: a screech produced by the drag of a heavy object and a scrape of metal; whatever was causing it created such a cloud of dust, the source was obscured. People left their shops, and those gathered at the pump abandoned it; the Becketts soon followed, abuzz with anticipation.

As the cloud dissipated, a pageant wagon appeared, listing to the right and dragged forward by a bear, rather than a horse, in the traces. It was flanked by a troupe of players, comprised of one large muscular man, one tall slender man, and a woman who fell in between, all three looking the worse for their travels.

"How d' do," said the slender fellow, tugging his forelock.

"Welcome to Lowell Close." For a large man, Mr. Gambon moved with speed; he was at his duchess's side to make the introductions. "You are in the presence of Her Grace of Lowell."

An appropriately theatrical bout of bowing and curtsying was proffered by the actors. Mr. Gambon oversaw the introductions, and the players were revealed to be husband and wife, Moses and Molly Peasely; the strongman was the woman's brother, Mr. Quincy.

"You have encountered some trouble on your journey," Felicity observed.

"The axle broke on our way to Arcadia, as we heard the Humphries have returned," Mr. Peasley said. "Our troupe has long been welcome there."

"Or our fathers and grandfathers had been," said Mrs. Peasley.

"And you thought it kind to allow the bear to pull your broken cart," Felicity asked, her tone acerbic.

The slender fellow was quick to explain. "We had a horse—"

"Not for very long," said the lady actor. "He ran off the other day, and then the axle shattered—"

"And the bear stood in the traces and would not be moved," finished her husband.

"I am well able to pull the cart myself," said the strongman. He flexed his muscles and grinned beneath his luxurious mustache; this was greeted with a ripple of giggles from many in the throng.

"That bear is fierce stubborn," said Mr. Peasley.

"She is fierce intelligent and suffers no fools." Mr. Quincy stopped displaying his muscles, incensed at the aspersions cast upon the creature.

"My brother has the care of her," Mrs. Peasley explained, "and is very protective."

"Thank you for alerting us to the bear's gender," Felicity said, sharing a secret smile with Tabitha. "You are very welcome to Lowell Close. We would be pleased to host you until you can proceed on to Arcadia. Are the plays of Shakespeare in your repertoire?"

"Oh, yes, ma'am." Mr. Peasley slipped effortlessly into his pitch. "We are known the world over for our expertise in the works of the Bard of Avon and in our unique ability to distill them to their essence and to craft them for brevity."

"We do the Scottish play in half an hour," his wife said. "And of course *The Winter's Tale*." The bear raised her head. Tabitha was appalled to see the animal so fatigued after pulling the cart; exhaustion was only natural given the effort it took, but there was something unnatural about the beast. A prickle ran along the tips of her fingers, and a chill danced down her spine; she felt the urge to go closer to it, as large and intimidating as it was. She resisted the impulse, fearful of the large animal, and yet she also sensed no aggression. There was something very, very wrong, but she could not work out what it was.

"Let us see your wagon safely to our stables," said the publican, "and my good lady wife will see to your every comfort."

A rush of negotiation over room rates ensued as

the players followed along. The bear was released from her burden and led away by Mr. Quincy; several of the hardier village lads took up the dragging of the wagon under the direction of Mr. Gambon. No sooner had they turned the corner to the stable yard and the crowd made to disperse than the Duke of Llewellyn, face like thunder and body radiating fury, stormed across the green leading a gigantic chestnut horse.

Felicity gasped. "It's Himself, big as life."

Oh dear, Tabitha thought. If that was Himself, her friend was in for a surprise.

Eleven

THE HORSE ABANDONED ALL RESISTANCE IN THE face of Alwyn's sheer force of will, if not his attempts at drawing on his *dominatum*. The latter had little effect on the animal, which made him think the equine was an Alpha, which made him angrier. His fury churned through his body, lending him strength, thundering in his heartbeat, coloring his vision in a red haze. Had Alwyn been able to fight the people that had taken him captive, this was what he would have felt: righteous fury fueling his bid to break free.

If he could do this for another *versipellis*, it went some way to make amends to his lion.

As ever, all he passed on his way to the Close retreated; today, it was not out of fear but as a gesture of respect. The horse whinnied under his breath when he saw Her Grace and then sighed, long and gustily.

"I will protect you if that is what is required. The chain will be removed, and you will be freed, even if I have to force it done." The equine rolled his eyes and shook his head. He didn't seem bothered by the duchess's presence and whinnied louder the closer she approached.

"Your Grace! Wherever did you find him?" She reached out for the horse, and Alwyn stood between her and the animal.

"Madam. How dare you." The duchess took a step back, and he found he did not want to frighten her, only to *tell* her. "Knowing what you know about your husband and his people? Your people?"

"I do not understand—" She stepped forward again, and the duke turned his back to shield the horse with his body.

"To keep a man in his essential self against his will is deplorable. I thought better of you. His Highness thought better of you. Had he known you were keeping a creature like this, would he have sent me here?"

"A creature like—" Lowell's duchess was the picture of confusion, but Alwyn did not let her continue; he would say his piece.

"Every day that passes leaves less and less humanity behind. The struggle to remain balanced and in one's right mind becomes more and more arduous. The days I woke and wished I'd never risen at all, the days when I did not know how I would find the strength to keep my poor lion from wreaking havoc on all around him out of fear and rage and the loss of his agency. I will not see it visited upon another."

"Llewellyn." Miss Barrington stood between him and the duchess and lay a hand on his arm. "This being is not suffering the way you did."

He glared at her. "How can you say that, you of all people, who can see?"

"I say as one who sees and knows." Her voice swept over him like a cool hand, soothing a fever. "You would not be able to discern his essence if this horse were being held by way of gold. It blocks all sense of the essential self to other *versipelles*."

"That cannot be so." His hands were shaking, and his body would soon follow; he shut his eyes against this weakness, against being seen in all his feebleness. The horse braced his hooves, and shouldering into the duke's side, took Alwyn's weight.

"It is." Her hand gripped his forearm, lightly, enough to let him know she was there. "Mr. Bates said as much."

The rage flashed, once, and left him. "Oh, well, if Bates said so, it must be true." He took one breath, another; the horse lowered his head to rub his nose on Alwyn's knee. Miss Barrington did nothing more than hold his arm and stand in front of him, and yet her presence was like a balm for his senses.

"I don't believe it is well-known," she said.

"It cannot be, if none have come back from it to tell their tale." A communal intake of breath soughed around him. It was an unimaginable horror; he thought of his lost ones and trembled.

Miss Barrington ran a finger over Alwyn's knuckles, tense from clutching the strap on the horse's rug. Nothing wrong with his grip in this instance. He relaxed his fingers one by one and let go. The horse did not budge an inch until he moved, then the stallion nudged him on the side with his nose once he stood on his own. "My apologies, ma'am..." he began.

"Not at all, think nothing of it." Lowell's duchess came to stand beside the lady apothecary. "We honor you, Your Grace, and I regret most heartily if this brought forth the memories of your terrible trial." The duchess cast her eye around the gathered crowd, and they all cricked their necks, signaled their vulnerability to him, and gave him obeisance.

He kept his eyes on Miss Barrington, on her fine eyes, the only still point in his tilting, lurching world, until interrupted by the thunder of running feet.

———

His Grace of Lowell, followed by Mr. Bates and Mr. Gambon, pelted into the square. Tabitha had never seen the duke with a hair out of place; he looked as if he'd dragged himself through a hedge backward. His typically perfect cravat was all out of order, and he held a hand over his heart as though to prevent it bursting out of his chest.

She stood with Llewellyn at her back, as if she would shield him as he had tried to protect the horse. There was nothing to fear from the Alpha wolf, however; his eyes were wide with shock and a glimmer of...humor?

"What in the world?" he demanded. His pack offered him obeisance but no explanations.

Felicity raised her hands to stroke them down the horse's neck; he shied away, eyes rolling back in his head. "Is anything amiss? What's wrong, darling? Oh, please tell me you haven't had a terrible time of it, do."

The duke covered his face and made a noise like a snort, or a groan, or a snorting groan. It was undignified and not suited to his status as a peer of the realm.

"Alfr—Alpha?" Felicity looked over her shoulder at her husband. "What is wrong?"

"Nothing." His tone was as high and squeaky as Mary Mossett's.

"Well." Felicity braced her fists on her hips. "If not, then allow me to make known to you Himself, my stud."

His Grace scrubbed his hands over his face; Tabitha caught sight of a grin he immediately snuffed out. A snicker escaped, however, which served to relax everyone who had witnessed the spectacle of Llewellyn shouting at their duchess and borne witness to his brutal honesty. Tabitha guessed Lowell's humor ran along the *sentio*.

She could also, for the first time, discern the moment Llewellyn chose to slip away.

Felicity reached up to smooth her husband's hair back in place. "I am delighted for you to make his acquaintance, but Llewellyn alluded to something not quite right. I do hope he has not been injured in his time away—"

O'Mara erupted onto the scene and pointed an accusing finger at the chestnut. "Aiden MacCafferty! You misbegotten bastard of a gobshite!"

"Miss O'Mara—I mean, O'Mara! Language," Felicity scolded. "He is called *Himself*, although his papers say his bloodline name is Lord of Kinvara."

Felicity reached up again to pat his neck, and the atmosphere transformed in a way Tabitha had not yet encountered: there was a sudden compression of air around the horse, around her, around them all. It was unlike the sensation she experienced in the presence of the prince regent's *dominatum*, which had been loaded with incipient violence; this was a gathering, a promise of creation, of transmutation. A loud crack sounded, and all at once the duchess's stud was gone; in his place stood a man who caught his rug to his family jewels in the nick of time. He was of a size with Lowell, but half again as wide at the shoulders, and stood firm on long legs banded with muscle. His hair, copper bright, fell around his shoulders and down his back in great curls that yet had a masculine flair; the expression in his large brown eyes was a blend of joy and deep, deep misery.

"Ye bletherin' bastardin' shiteface of a bowsie!" The elegant, calm, impassive, imperturbable O'Mara was shrieking like a fishwife. "A stud! A stud! You arse-faced gormless wanker of a bollocks!" She huffed and puffed, her nostrils flaring; she bared her teeth and exploded into a gorgeous sixteen-hands-high strawberry roan then galloped away.

"I've not betrayed you!" he called. "Believe me! Fidelma!"

"Fidelma?" muttered every member of the pack.

"Oh, my goodness!" Felicity stood, enraptured, before him. "Are you a centaur?"

"That's a myth, missus," he replied as he secured the rug around his hips with one of its straps.

"Your Grace," said Lowell.

"Sure, I'm no duke neither," said Mr. MacCafferty. "My da's an earl, but only the Irish sort. I don't make much of it, myself."

"The lady is a duchess, and you will address her as such." The duke growled and flexed his hands.

"A duchess!" The horse Shifter threw his hands in the air and almost lost his rug again. "Well done, missus. Sure, you were far from a duchess when I met you at Tattersalls. Couldn't have happened to a lovelier girl, in fairness."

"How in the world did you get papers?" Felicity asked.

"Well, I'll tell ya, it was awkward in the extreme, missus. Your Grace."

"O'Mara is a horse?" she asked her husband. "I assumed she was a wolf, like you and Bates."

"I assume you are the reason she fled Ireland?" the Alpha wolf demanded.

"It wasn't like that, Alf. Can I call you Alf? No? Right." Mr. MacCafferty sighed. "It's a long story, and one I won't tell without Fidelma's permission. I'm that determined to make right by her."

"Well, let us acquire you some clothing," Felicity said to Himself—Mr. MacCafferty. Or with an earl for a father, was it His Lordship? "I shall send a footman ahead with the news of your arrival. Mr. Coburn will attend you, and Mrs. Birks will prepare a room." She nodded to one of the cats, who set off to carry her instructions to the Hall.

"I can't thank you enough, missus," he said, ignoring the duke's snarl. "If I could stay until I've sorted things out with Fidelma..."

"You honor us with your presence," Felicity said as she ground her heel on Lowell's foot. "If I may make you known to the Duke of Llewellyn? Your Grace—oh."

"He has gone," Tabitha said. "My lord"—the horse Shifter grimaced at the use of the title—"you look in need of a restorative. I shall put together a tonic for you straightaway."

―――――――

The Irishman did indeed look worse for his time away from the care of Felicity's stable yard. A concoction of angelica and the ever-versatile peppermint would at least refresh him after however long he had been keeping to his Shape. Tabitha combined the elements of the brew and put it on the hearthstone to keep warm while it settled; she was about to bank the fire when she heard and recognized the pad of a foot on the healing shed's step.

A cup of tea, as cliché as it was, would not go amiss. She put the kettle on the fire and opened the door.

Llewellyn held out a profusion of flowering nettle; he did not meet her eyes as he did so. She took it, cradling the bundle with care, and stepped back to let him enter at his own pace. "The duke and duchess expressed their appreciation for bringing Himself, er, Mr. MacCafferty to them. Her Grace would wish me to assure you she bears you no ill will, and if she had been harboring a *versipellis* unwillingly held in their Shape, she would have done all in her power to make it right."

"I did not know that one could not tell if a Shifter was trapped." He slid into a chair near the hearth, his back to the wall; he could see out the door, which he had not closed, and through the shed's large window. "Drake used to drag us around this godforsaken island in the summer months, and once in Penzance a colony of sea gulls passed through the sideshow. Foul creatures, sea gulls. I was not surprised they would take the opportunity to look down on *animalis pura*, but when they saw me, they did not *see* me."

"But you knew them for what they were."

"I did. Yes." He was taken aback by this. "Even without their squawking and scavenging, I knew."

Tabitha took down the everyday tea set from the shelf above the hearth: large, solid mugs suited for a day's work. "Was it—I was about to ask if it was your lion who knew this, but I am beginning to understand the sympathy between the two sides of you. It would have been both, even if the man was not at the forefront." The kettle started to steam, and she perused her jars of tea leaves. "And you knew that Mr. MacCafferty was not a *horse* horse and feared the worst."

"I thought he had been tricked as I had been." Tabitha moved as quietly as she could; the kettle bubbled, the fire snapped, and the duke spoke. "I was returning to Wales. I had been around and about, sowing my wild oats, and it was time for me to return to Anglesey. I sent a letter to Georgie saying he would not see me for some time as I was accepting my responsibilities at last, my wanders at an end. I passed through Cardiff and was anticipating the homely pleasures of the quiet life, even if I had no pride to go back to.

"I walked along the high street and heard, as only one such as I could hear, a baby's cry, a woman begging for her life, deep in a warren of alleyways in the seediest part of town. I ran and found her, covered in blood, bowed over her knees, protecting her child, her clothing torn, surrounded by ruffians. There were six of them, armed with cudgels and knives. I would have made short work of them all even in my manskin, but my lion—at the sight of the young, he insisted he show what happened to those who would hurt a child, even though we ought not to do so, never, before *homo plenum*. We Changed, and I thought the very sight of us would drive them away. I charged into the alley and leaped to stand over the woman to protect her, and she…

"She slipped the golden chain around my paw." Llewellyn rubbed his left wrist. "The men fell upon me and stowed me away into a beast wagon hidden around the back of the alley and drove me to my fate."

Tabitha took the boiling pot off the fire, poured the water into a teapot, and set out the cups, gently; she wondered if he could hear her heart beating like Wellington's drum corps. She reached to get the honey down and said, "A well-plotted ruse."

"My senses dulled almost immediately, but before I lost them entirely, I realized the blood was not human but that of a passel of hogs. What I took for an infant was a bundle of rags. The woman tossed it aside as she made a cry like a babe, mocking me, laughing like the villain she was. I never saw her face, but that sound, the cry, and the laughter, I have never forgotten it."

Tabitha took one shaking breath and willed her

voice to stay level. "There is no end to viciousness in men, or women."

"She was not only a woman," he said, "but a *versipellis* as well."

"What?" Tabitha was sincerely shocked. "But how can that be? Firstly, that she would handle the gold knowing its threat, and secondly, to do that to another like her… It is truly evil."

"I cannot know if there were others in Drake's like me."

"I asked that of the duke, and Mr. Bates is on the case, I believe."

"But he will have no more luck than I. I do not know who can tell or how they might."

"That is a problem for another day. May I?" Tabitha topped up his mug. Wonderful things, teapots, which one can wield to redirect a conversation. "I am honored that you confided in me." She spooned another dollop of honey into the duke's cup.

He sipped, and as he sipped, relaxed, and in his relaxation, he looked as though the weight of the world had rolled off his shoulders. He sniffed his brew. "Is this honey from that bee?" he asked.

"It is." Tabitha took more for herself. "Mr. Beckett and his family not only run the coach house and pub but also tend the hives. Of the *bee* bees."

"It is not bad," he said, begrudgingly.

It was the most delicious honey she had ever

tasted. "Mr. Giles's cheese is extraordinary but would not pair well with the chamomile."

Llewellyn huffed. "And the other suitor? What has he offered?"

"Stones from Edenbrook, which have no practical purpose but are very pretty."

"That which serves a practical purpose may also be pretty." He smiled into his mug. "One thing does not preclude the other. Things, and people, are complex."

Had they not been discussing cheese and stones? "What in the world are you talking about?"

The look he gave was one from his repertoire of male looks: a combination of teasing and humor and frustration. "That nettle I brought you—it is pretty and serves a purpose," he said. "The flowers are like drops of snow in a winter field, and the plant is good in soup and also helps when one's muscles are sore."

"I wish I'd had some when I was making up the tisane for Mr.—Lord MacCafferty? He did not explicitly say he doesn't use the title."

"He did not seem very happy with it. Nor, from what I could discern at a distance, O'Mara with him." They exchanged a wide-eyed look, and His Grace went as far as to waggle those brows of his.

"Her Grace was not apprised of her chamberlain's essential Shape," Tabitha said. "I knew, of course, O'Mara was a horse."

"A horse, of course." They snickered like children. Llewellyn added, "One did not anticipate the breadth of O'Mara's vocabulary."

"There were one or two epithets I have never heard, and I have heard many, and in foreign languages," Tabitha said; the duke responded with something that sounded very naughty. "I can identify that as French but can make no sense of it."

"It translates poorly into English." Must he peep at her through those lashes? She fussed with the teapot.

He cupped his mug with both hands. "Was that bee's honey any use to your tisane?"

"It was not." Llewellyn's crossness concerning Mr. Beckett's gift was paradoxically lightening his mood. "It is not a sweet cure. Many prefer sweetness when they need such things. I shall send it up to the Hall and whether his lordship takes it or not is up to him."

"I have a need."

Her great stores of control prevented her from startling at his request. "How may I help?"

"My hair." He ducked his head and gestured at it. "As you can see, it is not in its best looks. And for one of my kind, it is…it is a disgrace." He exuded shame, and every ounce of indignation she possessed rose up, then doubled, as he continued: "I was conscious of it when I dragged Mr. MacCafferty before the whole village, and I wished… It is of course meant to be my crowning glory. Is there a lotion you might apply?" Through the gravel of his voice came the first lyrical notes of the Welsh accent she had yet to hear, a lightness upon the words, like the notes of a song.

"I feared you meant to challenge me, Your Grace." She would invoke Hestia herself if need be. Luckily, however: "I have just the thing."

═══════════

Alwyn flexed his fingers over the handle of the mug. It was sturdier than a teacup—imagine trying to take tea with the Lowell Hall crowd, him with his big, ungainly paws. He'd crush the duchess's delicate porcelain into dust. A veritable bull in a china shop.

Miss Barrington rummaged around her stores with a vengeance, as though preparing to storm the Belgian front. He'd laid it on a bit thick about the hair but reaped the desired result. The lady's jaw had set, determined neither to deepen his shame nor take the situation lightly.

He had not stopped thinking about her slim body lying next to his on her coat. Of her face tucked into his shoulder. Of her scent, of how close he had come to kissing her. Would she welcome his kisses? He was not afraid to ask.

But first, a scene must be set. He balked at the

thought of hands in his hair, but up to now, her touch had been soothing. He would allow her to provide a solution to his dilemma and thus encourage her talents and begin his courtship in earnest.

Her healing shed was as good a place as any for such an endeavor. The sound of the water slowly bubbling in the pot over the fire, of the click of a glass jar on a wooden work top, the clean scent of tea leaves: it was a balm to the soul. The flames of the beeswax candles (had her eager apian suitor supplied her with those as well?) flickered gently as she moved about the place, and he relaxed his vigilance, going so far as to rise and shut the door.

As ever, the lady apothecary did not press, and as ever, silence descended—no, this was not silence, this was quiet. This was peace. A peace strong enough to contain his sorry tale, to allow him the relief of having told someone the truth, of not facing judgment for the mistake that had cost him his freedom.

He did not feel shame for what he had done. He would do it again, did he see a Shifter or human in danger or distress. Who would he be if he let fear rule him? Who indeed...

Alwyn joined Miss Barrington at her table, where she mixed Palu only knew what in a large bowl. "From which exotic stop on your travels does this originate?"

"You will be amazed to hear this is a good

old-fashioned English concoction that relies heavily on native marshmallow root." She set out a tea towel, a comb, a smaller bowl. "I have, however, tempered its scent with a pinch of foreign lavender from the south of France. When we were there, I—well. Do sit here, Your Grace." She indicated a high stool.

He sat upon it. "Do you seek to tantalize your listeners by never finishing an anecdote?"

"No one is interested. Not truly." She mixed cream into oil and swirled it about with her fingers. "When we were abroad, no one wished to speak of home. Now back at home, no one wishes to hear of abroad."

"I find myself tantalized." She dropped the comb to the floor and fussed over washing it off. "When you were in the south of France…"

"When we were in the south of France," she repeated, "we stayed for some time in Valensole. Timothy had students clamoring for his language skills—he could teach a stone to speak English— and while there, I was able to tend and harvest my very own lavender field."

"Was that your most memorable experience?"

"One of many."

"What is your first memory? Of your time abroad."

She smiled into the bowl and scooped some of the substance into a smaller one. "Dawn in Calais.

I am an early riser by nature, but waking there was like taking my first breath of life." She stood behind him, and he marveled at his acceptance of having someone at his back. "We were safe and free."

"Were you in danger?"

"My brother had a lover, of like gender, and it became prudent that we embark on our version of a Grand Tour." Her light tone did nothing to disguise the import of her confidence.

He was about to respond when she slicked some of the lotion onto the ends of his hair. It smelled like fresh grass in the height of August; it called to mind hazy days of idleness and adventure combined. She gently combed it through, holding a good portion of the length so it didn't pull on his scalp. Alwyn said, "This smells like summer."

"There is a dash of meadowsweet oil in it as well. I am sure that is common in Wales at that time of year."

"The two or three days we enjoyed of that precious season. Oh, the rain, the rain...though we did have meadowsweet to show for the damp, if not beautiful fields of lavender. Not much else to show for it at all." She drew the tonic through another lock of hair he'd thought was hopelessly tangled; her gentle touch convinced every strand to yield to her will. "Nor much to show for being a duke in Wales. Nor a lion."

"I had thought it an unlikely pairing, lions and

Wales," she said. "Timothy told me the lion is the symbol on the arms of your namesake, Llewellyn the Great. He said no one knew how it came about."

"The dukedom was conferred upon us by an ancestor of George's to make up for our kind forever being poached." He would not dwell on that, he could not. It was all he could do to surrender to the work of her hands. He breathed, and she breathed, and the scent of the summer and her essence, faint as it still was, soothed him. "Despite our superior strength, if we are set upon, alone by *homo plenum* in numbers, there is naught we can do but Change, and that is not permitted."

"Even to save yourself? Or a helpless child?"

"A hunter who has discovered a man may turn into a lion will not leave off the hunt for more."

Another application of the stuff, but with a caress to his skull. His courtship was making headway.

Oh, how his lion loved a pun. Alwyn was certain the whole world would be shocked to discover his dignified and lethal essential self adored a low play on words. He sighed and received another stroke to his scalp and imagined a purr deep within.

"Our line was elevated as an apology of sorts," he continued. "The old king, and the king before him, would not involve the Crown in disputes, especially with humans, so it is to be supposed he thought the title would protect my line." Which it had not. The unraveling of the tangles in his hair served to loosen his tongue. "I am not much fussed about it. There is a house, not a great one. There is land, but not enough to support a pride the way Lowell's does his pack. I have ceremonial clothing fit for my station but not much else. The title is empty. And—ahhhhhhh." The tips of her fingers exerted pressure on his scalp that sent a shudder through him all the way to his toes. "That feels rather, er, good."

"Doesn't it?" There was a smile in her voice as well as satisfaction. "I have discovered simply massaging the skull works to great effect when a client is suffering, for example, from a debilitating headache." She dug her fingers in at the base of his skull, and the guttural noise he produced was nigh on vulgar. She did it again, and he moaned almost as though he were in the throes of— "It is much nicer than bloodletting or purging, practices I do not agree with in any case." She moved to the top of his head and ran the pad of one thumb over the very top, over his crown, until he sighed and his shoulders dropped and his neck loosened and his head released into her hands.

———

Llewellyn's hair was as abundant as promised. Tabitha stroked her fingers down from his scalp, over and over, through the thick strands. The texture wasn't as coarse as it had looked when tangled, and the color was a stunning, unexpected mix of bright blond and rich mahogany. It was not quite down to his hips, but it was longer than Lowell's, longer than her own, well past his shoulders, down the center of his back.

That long, lean back was all but pressed against her as his muscles released and his head fell heavy against her shoulder. She stroked and stroked; if she hadn't known better, she would swear he was purring, deep within his chest, and almost asleep.

He tilted his head; his nose nudged her neck. He breathed in, then tensed, then roused.

His great hazel eyes blinked at her. Again, if she didn't know better, she would have sworn they'd flashed amber for a heartbeat. It was a trick of the fire, or something to do with those infuriating lashes which fluttered at her as he shook off his languor.

How loath she was to let him go, but she did.

Well, mostly. He rose and turned to stand in front of her, and she did not stop stroking his hair, brushing it away from his face. It would be badly done of her to leave so much as a knot, wouldn't it?

"Miss Barrington." Growly, low, smooth was his voice. "My gratitude knows no bounds."

"It was merely a homely solution anyone is able to mix together." She hid her fingers in his hair lest he see them tremble.

"It was a gift and privilege to be tended so

thoughtfully." He took a deep breath and held her gaze. "There is much I have forgotten about how to conduct myself with decorum. I find that in your company, I recover more and more of my past self and would pay honor to that. I must ask if I may kiss your hand."

He held out his, head bowed. Locks of lush, long hair brushed the sides of his face and fell over his shoulders; she left off rubbing the tonic through and wiped her palms on her skirt.

"I am not in the habit of accepting such tribute from a client." Not that any ever expressed such appreciation. "But you may." She held out her hand and found she needed to breathe deeply, the consequence of which was the inhalation of the familiar bergamot, the hair tonic, his maleness. "It is rough from the work I do, not the hand of a lady, or indeed the hand of a prince before it became a paw. Did I mention His Highness Changed his paw in front of me? To convince me to take on your case."

"I fear you have put me in the prince's debt." He stroked her fingers, nuzzled them. "Rough they may be, but as a result of helping others to become well in themselves. This is no small task. It is one to be respected."

Alwyn turned her hand over and set a kiss in the very center of her palm.

If she had a goddess of her own to invoke, she would do it now: the feeling of his lips on her skin set her to trembling. She had not gone unkissed, and the freedom she'd enjoyed on the Continent, gathering information for her comparative matrix, had involved kissing and more. But this simple touch turned her knees to water and her heart once more to a drum.

"You would allow a predator such as I was to be so close to you." Llewellyn held her palm to his face. "You defended me against O'Mara. You stood between me and the Duke of Lowell. How is it you are not afraid of those more powerful than you?"

"I faced the worst fear I could conceive of and survived." Those early days of Timothy's heartbreak and the attendant drama would never be forgotten. "Nothing else will ever be as terrifying."

"Your courage is quite stimulating."

Had she known he was so tall? Had she realized how changeable those hazel eyes were? Her heartbeat quickened, and he responded by gathering her against his chest. Her fingers slid up all along his scalp, down those long, soft and silky strands, and rested on his shoulders.

"Do you enjoy kissing?"

She adored kissing. "It is a passable diversion."

"Oh, *cariad*, you must have been kissed poorly." He stroked one finger down her cheek. "May I?"

Oh, yes, please! "You may."

And he kissed her.

Alwyn kissed her like he was posing a question,

gently and yet with authority. He ran his mouth
over hers, lightly, slowly, as one might gauge the
temperature of a cup of tea. He brushed her lips
with the tip of his tongue, once, twice, a teaspoon
of sugar added into the heated mix. He gathered her
closer, and she could feel his heart beating in his
chest; the strength of his embrace wedded with the
gentleness of his inquiry made her head spin. She
tightened her hold on his shoulders, and one of his
hands slid into the hair at the nape of her neck; he
turned her head and slanted his mouth over hers.

Tabitha must indeed have been kissed very
poorly, for it had never inflamed her like this. She
wrapped her arms around his neck and nearly
climbed him like they'd climbed that hill of rock the
night of the *cursio*. She nipped at his mouth in turn,
laved it, until he slipped his tongue fully between
her lips, and oh, holy Palu, it was glorious, sending
her up into the boughs even as she plumbed depths
of arousal she'd never thought possible.

Llewellyn's mouth was hot on hers, his strong
hand cupping the back of her head, his fingers
teasing her scalp, much as hers had done his. She
pressed against him and ran her hands through his
hair again, both palms cradling his skull; the shudder that ran through his body inspired one in her.
His hands ran down her back, gripped her hips, and
she rolled against him, restless, wanting, wanton.

Tabitha nipped his lower lip again, sucked on

it until he moaned. *She* had done that, it was her kisses, her touch, that inspired that glorious, seductive, decadent sound, and she wanted more, more, and more—

A cursory knock fell on the door, and they hurriedly released each other as it opened. Timothy took one look at them and smiled like a shark.

"Your Grace." Her brother was capable of an exceptionally elegant leg. "I am pleased to find you here."

"Are you?" the duke replied; how lucky he always sounded as if his voice were the presage of an earthquake, low and rumbling and gravelly.

Tabitha grabbed several bags of cheesecloth stuffed with red clover and thrust them into Llewellyn's hands. "His Grace was only saying the other day how he was keen for some sachets."

"Yes. Sachets." The duke lifted them to his nose and blinked at her.

"Yes." She turned and banked the fire and gathered heaven only knew what to keep her hands full, to stop her reaching out to the duke, or shoving Timothy out the door, or doing that in reverse order.

"Oh, *sachets*," Timothy said. Out the door they would all go: she herded both men over the threshold and into the back garden. "I see. Is that how His Grace's hair came to be so smooth and shiny?"

His blasted Grace waggled his godforsaken

eyebrows, and Timothy, if it was at all possible, grinned with greater mischief. "Basil has recently been added to my kitchen," he said. "Dare I presume it was a gift from you?" Llewellyn nodded. "I hope my sister has thanked you accordingly. There is a dish I learned in Italy that requires it. How I have longed to make it since returning home."

"I have often enjoyed dishes made with basil," His Grace mused.

Timothy laid a hand on his heart. "What a coincidence. I intended on making it for tomorrow's evening meal."

"How *I* long to try food from Italy," Alwyn replied. "My travels did not take me there."

"We would be most honored if you would join us, Your Grace."

"I am pleased to accept your kind invitation if it is also the wish of your—oh."

Tabitha, having slipped away during the disingenuous byplay between the two men, hid behind the cottage's kitchen door.

Let her be the one to flee the scene for once.

Let him have a taste of his own medicine.

Twelve

ALWYN LOOKED IN THE MIRROR, WHICH HE HAD kept covered with a cloth until that moment. His hair was no longer looking as well as it had, even one day after Miss Barrington had tended to it; he pawed at the tangles, snarling it further. Would it be that arduous to engage the services of a valet? His entire being rebelled. No, he would not allow anyone touching him, ordering him about, touching his hair.

Well. Not just anyone.

Looking at himself was worse than being looked at by others...or it had been. Even when less than perfect, his hair now did him justice. His ensemble for the evening made a change as well: the jacket was a castoff Weston winkled out of Georgie's astonishing surplus of clothing, and while it did not cling like a second skin, it fit better than usual and was a sober hunter green. He remembered the color to be flattering to his eyes.

He looked his reflection in the eye then turned away.

The trousers were workmanlike and secured roughly. He ought to practice with buttons, but it galled him to have to relearn as basic a skill as that. And yet if he wanted to look well for the lady—if he wanted to look like a duke, like a man—he would need to hark back to his childhood.

His childhood, when he had a pride, a father, a mother, brothers, and a sister—no, no, no, he would not, he could not think on that, not now, not when Miss Barrington might look at him and see.

Miss Barrington, who claimed to be ambivalent about kissing. Untrue, he thought, pleasure rushing through his body at the mere remembrance of her mouth on his, her fingers in his hair, those places she touched on his scalp that made him want to melt at her feet and give her anything. Give her everything.

What had he to give? Nothing, no pride, an empty title, the barest grasp of his humanity, nothing. And yet he rebelled against that, for he had his heart to give. If she was his *vera amoris,* and on top of that his *coniunctio*, he had himself as a place of rest to offer, a lifelong companion, lover, and friend. Never mind that he still had to walk for hours to find any rest in the night, that he was alert to the slightest change in atmosphere—

He heard footfalls approaching. No one came here. Who would come here?

Who else would come here? Alwyn had ceased wondering why the lady apothecary ended up where she did, so finding her on his doorstep wasn't that much of a surprise. Nor did her curiosity regarding his abode; what took him aback was the flash of hurt on her face when he essentially barred her from entering by stepping out and closing the door firmly behind him.

"It is a bachelor's accommodation," he said. "I wish to make a better impression on you." Her expression couldn't decide whether to be peeved or to preen. "What brings you to this neck of the woods?"

"Mr. Giles left his flask in the shed, and I brought it back to him." She pointed to a craggy heap of stones in the distance. "He and his tribe reside on that hill."

"*Left* it did he? How forgetful. It does not say much about his intelligence."

"I believe you know exactly how intelligent it was. He has received his flask full of a healthful cinnamon tonic, which he assured me he will imbibe at the earliest moment."

"I suspect he would imbibe something far less pleasant than cinnamon to impress you." Alwyn gestured her before him; that was gentlemanly, or was it? What if she came upon a stone and fell?

Miss Barrington set off without hesitation. Their way through the outer edge of the park led them to a culvert, and he rushed in front of her and extended his hand without thinking. She laid her hand in his, and the thing he sensed between them fluttered in his heart at their contact. None of it had been his imagination, then. Not his tolerance of her touch, not the cuddling under the awful coat, not the hair combing, not the kiss. No wonder Delilah had been so scornful: there was nothing wrong with the mare's instincts. He made a sound; to his ears it was as if his lion were agreeing with him, an even deeper rumble than usual. Miss Barrington looked at him askance.

"Her Grace's mares are a flighty bunch," he said, "but if I did not know better, I would think Delilah a *versipellis*."

She accepted the non sequitur with aplomb. "I agree. She responds to one's speech and actions with true comprehension."

"Horses, in general, are rather more perceptive than most *animali purem*, or at least they give that impression," Alwyn said. "The horses at Drake's were my allies, which is astonishing given their status as prey."

"Perhaps they sensed the humanity in you." She paused beside a flowering bush, hesitated, then forged ahead. "And do tell me if this is insulting, as they are the least of felines, but the cats around the Lowell stables are great friends with both the lads and the *horse* horses."

"It is not insulting. We larger predators feel protective of *cat* cats."

Her laugh, no longer so rare, rang through the

glade. "You would have only to meet the cat from Sorrento and you would not say as much. He was as fierce as any of your sort, I can tell you."

"Your cat?" Predisposed to felines, was she?

"Oh no, I had no illusions on that score. He had us—me, primarily. Timothy tried, but the creature preferred my company."

She sounded pleased about that. "What was its name?"

"The Italian cat."

"Yes, as you have said. What was it called?"

"The Italian cat."

He stopped walking and pinched the bridge of his nose. "Miss Barrington."

She burst into laughter again. "That was what I called him. The Italian cat. Timothy is terrible at naming things, and I refused to address the animal as Diocletian or Pope Leo the Thirteenth, even though the latter fit rather well." Bold, she ran a finger down his forearm. "That is my favorite joke."

"I am honored you consider me a fit audience." Alwyn's face felt odd, stretched, his jaw loose, his eyes slightly pinched but in a comfortable way.

She reached out, hesitated, put her hand in her pocket. "Making even an audience of one smile is all the reward required," she said.

Oh. Smiling. He touched his cheeks. That's what that was. *Oh.*

It affected a change in more than his face: his

chest opened, his shoulders released tension he hadn't known was nigh constant, his entire body lightened. A simple smile, accomplishing all that?

He gestured her forward, and they carried on.

———

The Italian cat prevailed again. How many skittish clients had that cat soothed, how many bilious types made to laugh at his antics? Even in memory, he succeeded in amusing the duke, had made him smile! How she missed that cat.

How she had missed Timothy's Italian cooking. As they entered the cottage, the kitchen was redolent of the sunbaked hills of the south, thanks to the duke's basil. Water boiled, promising pasta, and the scent of garlic promised pesto. While less ambitious than the Sunday Meal, Timothy manned several pots and pans simultaneously.

The duke looked around with less vigilance than he usually had when indoors, and she was proud he felt safe.

Proud, as his progress was clearly...progressing.

"We do not have a room for dining and will sit here if that is acceptable." She divested herself of her layers and started to set the kitchen table.

"I am not so high in the instep," he replied, the gravel of his tone taking on a playful cadence.

"We were offered footmen but prefer to do for ourselves," Timothy said.

The duke picked up a fork Tabitha had just laid down. "I see we shall not enjoy Grecian fare this evening."

"You may use it or not, as you please." Tabitha fetched down some wineglasses as a bottle was cooling in a bucket of icy cold water from the nearby stream. "I have no idea what to expect of the meal, as that is my brother's domain."

"You would not be faulted for assuming, Your Grace, that if one should spend much of her time over bubbling pots, it would translate to sustenance," Timothy said. "Alas."

"You make me sound like one of those Macbeth witches." Tabitha snapped out a serviette and refolded it, it had to be said, with little flair.

"They were not explicitly called such in the play," said Llewellyn.

"Do you enjoy the theater?" Timothy strained the pasta and billows of steam gusted around him.

"I have been exposed to it." The duke cleared his throat, voice gone guttural as it had in weeks past. "And reluctantly played a part, in the menagerie."

Timothy put aside the pot and faced the duke. "I did not think before I spoke. I regret mentioning something you must find painful."

"The ills begin to fade the longer I am in my manskin." The duke held the fork with ease and went so far as to flip it around his knuckles. "I may have practiced that." He placed the fork on the table. "I must speak of my time in Drake's, or else it will fester in my mind. So: the very fact of my existence required I be shown to all. I figured largely and inexplicably in *Much Ado About Nothing*."

"Oh, Sicily!" Tabitha cried. "I—well, yes, a lovely place. Your Grace, please sit." She received a look of ducal approbation wedded with a pair of muscular arms crossed on a chest that looked larger than it had last week. "Sicily was warm and bright. We found the place to be most congenial."

"Congenial but bereft of lions," Timothy said. Several chops spit in a pan; while they seared, her brother popped a sliced loaf into the oven to warm. Tabitha was handed the caster, which contained the seasonings her brother deemed necessary at every meal: salt and white pepper, powdered mustard seed, and garlic. Vinegar and oil in cruets joined the everyday butter crock, so no standing on ceremony, despite their exalted guest.

The wine, chilling in a bucket, smelled like citrusy stones. Tabitha knew as much about wine as she did about languages and left its choice to Timothy's superior grasp of these matters.

The duke took a small sip. "Despite the lack of my kind, what might one find to enjoy in Sicily?"

"A lifestyle so relaxed, it was rather decadent." Timothy set to work with mortar and pestle. "We found Englishmen and women there, as we did everywhere we went. We also became acquainted with Sicilians who soon came to trust my sister, and she learned from them. I was quite busy in work and made many friends." He glanced at the duke over his shoulder. "Home of macaroni, after all."

"*Bonaroo!*" Llewellyn exclaimed. "*Toda bona, mona omie?*"

Timothy lit up like a chandelier at a ball. "*Mais oui, ducky, dinna nish* the chat!"

The duke leaned forward, elbows on the table. "It's been *donks* since I've had a *cackle, savvy?*"

Her brother took a breath to respond and bless him, looked at her with tragedy writ all over his face, for what reason she did not know. Due to being left out by yet another foreign language, perhaps? "Was that Italian? Mine never came up to scratch."

"It is not quite that language, or not solely Italian," Timothy said. "It is called *Parlyaree*, a lingo often used amongst...myself and my dear friends."

"It is common parlance for many classes," the duke said, "including the roustabouts at Drake's. It is indeed well-known amongst the mollies"— Timothy hooted with laughter—"but I am not attracted to my own gender."

"Plain speaking. How refreshing." Timothy set the toasted bread on the table. "I, for one, am attracted to my own gender."

"As I explained to Lowell, lions in particular, and felines in general, do not put limitations upon with whom one may or may not bond."

Timothy mixed the pesto into the pasta. "Did Lowell require the explanation?"

"His Gamma required the reassurance."

"Oh, Mr. Gambon." Her brother spooned the pasta into a large shallow dish. "He is a lovely man," he said lightly. "So helpful about the place."

Tabitha and Llewellyn winced in concert. "Just as well he holds out no hopes for you," the duke said.

"Oh, but Timothy, he is truly lovely," Tabitha said.

"We all have our preferences, and those preferences, in turn, involve criteria. What might yours be, Your Grace?"

"I expect His Grace prefers to be fed as promised." Tabitha whipped her serviette open and placed it on her lap.

Timothy handed out serving dishes, and Tabitha arranged them on the tabletop. "My sister's preferences include travel," he said, "and happily this coincided with a need to broaden my horizons."

"Tim."

"It is my story to tell, Tab. And my instincts to trust." He set the last platter on the table, pork chops done to a turn in rosemary and sage. "We dine *á la française*, Your Grace. One may take what they like without being obliged to eat what they dislike."

His Grace laid his serviette in his lap. "I am honored. By the meal and the trust."

"I am glad to hear it. Now. Need I explain how my desires are illegal in the eyes of the powers that be and those who do not mind their own affairs?" The duke shook his head even as he dished up a healthy serving of the pasta. "Very well. My lover was to marry, as many do, and there was to be a send-off amongst our friends of a certain kind. Jasper has an elder brother who did not mind his own affairs and, in a fit of pique, alerted the local constabulary as to a gathering of *omepalonis* in the area. Amongst whom, thankfully, was a friend of a certain kind. To add insult to an injured heart, I escaped the pillory by the skin of my teeth."

Tabitha stabbed her pork chop. "That man would not desist in his pursuit of Timothy—"

"In a decidedly unromantic fashion, with many protestations as to his true motives, although I have my suspicions—"

"He then turned his attentions to me—"

"And tried to compromise Tabitha to force her into marriage. It did not go well for him." Timothy's grin was pure mischievous satisfaction, and he bit into his buttered bread with relish.

"Once he recovered, he intended for it to go badly for me." Still, she shared Timothy's smile.

"So, with both of us in need of broader horizons, we engaged upon a stratagem in which Tim became consumptive."

"Overnight. Such a shock," Timothy said. They both snorted. "Fortunately, our parents had long ceased to remark upon our existence—"

"Timothy!" Tabitha protested and then reconsidered. "You are not wrong."

"Due to the fact I was not a manly man on the verge of repopulating our little corner of England and Tabitha was a woman intent upon working with her unnatural skills—"

"Never mind that father's heart congestion was managed entirely by me, and I abandoned my Season to go to his aid."

"—we departed for the Continent to little fanfare and much relief."

Relief did not begin to describe it. Tabitha was well used to Timothy's gloss of the situation, but the reality had not been nearly so tidy. That loathsome lord had made a show of her before the whole world and threatened her safety, on top of his wandering hands and unwelcome (and poor) kissing. If she had anything to thank him for, it was that she took command of her sexual education; he provided her with a very low bar to step over in the intervening years.

Llewellyn's kisses were not so much a step up as a vault into new heights. How easy it was to talk to him after such intimacies: no embarrassment, no awkwardness, no unsavory allusions to what might come next—unless he had not liked kissing with her or because he thought of it as a minor exchange of affection?

He and Timothy were back at it with that language, which sounded much the same as any to her. Should they not speak it? It might be a painful reminder of the duke's time in captivity... He seemed not to mind. In truth, he had been much easier in himself for having spoken the truth about his time in Drake's. Much as the lancing of a wound released painful pressure. But ought she to suggest they stop?

No, she ought not to: the duke was an independent soul capable of saying what he wanted or did not want. Tabitha cut her pork chop into tiny pieces as she composed herself, for she was experiencing fear for him, and it was not her place to do so. How had she gotten so afraid, so concerned with what was affecting him, in such an unprofessional manner?

After another flurry of incomprehensible chatter, the duke said, "I understand you speak many languages, Mr. Barrington."

"I do. Had you known Parlyaree before..."

"Before Drake's? No, I learned it in my Shape."

"Did you? Is that possible?" Tabitha took a slice of bread to conceal her shredded chop.

"It became so. Apparently." He said something

to Tabitha, who looked blank and then handed him the salt.

Llewellyn smiled, again. How easily one could become used to that expression on his face. "Thank you. However, I said, *It may be my lion who was adept.*"

Timothy offered around the pasta. "My sister has not got a head for languages."

"Perhaps Miss Barrington requires *un dictionnaire d'oreillers.*" Her brother and the duke laughed and laughed.

"Tiresome polyglots," Tabitha groused. "And yet I still do not know what it means."

"It means, roughly, a pillow tutor," the duke said.

"One who will rest their head next to yours and whisper in your ear," her brother explained. "The shared intimacy and the lowered defenses before sleep are likely to aid one in grasping basic grammar, as well as grasping other things within reach—"

"Fine, Tim, thank you." How wonderful to be teased, to see the light in her brother's eyes, his ease in himself. "I do not think a thousand pillow tutors would have helped me conquer Greek."

"I will allow you that," Timothy said as he rose to clear the table, "but after all that time in Spain, Italian ought to have followed."

"How could it, when I never mastered Spanish?"

"You are a fine example of English womanhood." Llewellyn's voice rumbled.

"No, no, that makes me like the numberless English abroad who refused to even learn so much as *grazie mille.*" Her accent was as inharmonious as ever. "My brain simply does not work that way."

The duke leaned forward and held her gaze. "Your brain works in wonderful ways."

Timothy batted his eyelashes at her over Alwyn's shoulder. She jumped up with enough force to knock the chair over.

"Yes, well. Hmmm. Most kind of you to say so. Tea?" Tabitha fired up the kettle and made a start on the dishes. She elbowed her brother out of the way; he set her chair to rights and sat with Llewellyn to review the languages they had in common, exchanging phrases and, if their laughter was anything to go by, salty idioms. The sounds made no sense to her, but the tone of both their voices was pure harmony: Timothy's a clear, lyrical tenor and the duke's a gruff, throaty bass, a joyous chorale of shared knowledge.

Timothy sat back, satisfied. "That counts as nine languages between us."

"Mr. Gambon reckoned only seven," the duke teased her brother. "But come, let us not exclude your sister."

"I exclude my sister at my peril." Timothy reached for the tea things Tabitha laid before him and poured out as she searched for the last of Mr. Beckett's honey.

"I had a sister." Tabitha stopped clattering around the cupboard and exchanged a look with Timothy, who stilled. "I had three brothers and a sister. And a mother and father."

Silence reigned until Tabitha judged it acceptable to ask, "Were they taken as you were taken?"

"I do not know. I would not know, would I? Not if the gold blocks one's perception of a captive *versipelles*." Llewellyn flipped his fork over his knuckles then clenched it in his fist. "We were on the move, as an alliance was to be struck between my sister and a pride from the Continent, through marriage. We were eager to meet others of our kind and set off with no thought to any danger. How could we be in danger? We were in the British Isles, in modern times. We were as safe as could be.

"At Milton Keynes we broke our journey, though it was nothing for the likes of us, going from Anglesey to London. I was the eldest and keen to continue, so I did and made for the city. And the next day, I waited and waited. I asked amongst the *versipelles* I knew of, ran back and forth on the London Road, looked everywhere, and I never found them. His Majesty had no time for me, no matter the ills done to my kind by his." His hair cloaked his expression, and Tabitha thought she might weep and never stop.

"What a terrible loss." She had never felt so useless in her life.

A regal nod acknowledged the sentiment. "And so, I roamed. I know Lowell searched far and wide for his *vera amoris*, but I did not have his means to travel the whole world. Nor did I want to do so alone...but alone I did, searching high and low." He took a breath. "For my family, yes, and also for the one I would call mine, daring to hope I'd find not only my mate but what amongst the lions is considered an immense blessing. An aspect that, if its locus is found in the fated mate bond, transcends even the *vera amoris* in legend." He looked up at her through those lashes, eyes flashing in the candle-light. "It is known as the *coniunctio*."

Timothy rose the moment the duke finished pronouncing the word, even as he drank down the last of his tea; without a wasted movement, almost like a dance, the cup was returned to its saucer, coat collected and donned, hat and scarf in one hand, walking stick in the other.

"I trust, Your Grace, you will continue to behave with the highest discretion where my dear sister is concerned." He jauntily tossed his scarf over his shoulder. "I am off to embark upon my evening constitutional."

"I am sorry my sad tale has driven you away," the duke said.

"Not at all. My sympathies for you are sincere, and I am honored you, in turn, trusted me with your story." Timothy set his hat on his head. "And I hope my sister will trust you with the whole of our history, despite her habitual reticence."

"Tim." Tabitha would not burden the duke with their past, which was nowhere near as painful.

"Tab." He turned the knob and stood on the threshold. "It is your story as much as it is mine. *Nos da, Dy Ras*," he said with a smile for Llewellyn and left.

Thirteen

THE DOOR CLOSED; SILENCE REIGNED. THE DUKE said, "Your brother speaks Welsh flawlessly. It is not often the case with outsiders."

"What doesn't he speak flawlessly," Tabitha grumbled as she bashed the tea things onto their tray and ferried them into the sink. "What did he say?"

"*Good night, Your Grace.*" That enchanting lyricism entered his tone again. "It is a treat to hear the sound of my first language in my ear."

"Then I am glad his tiresome ability to master any dialect came in useful." She plugged the sink and sparingly added lye. Even with her bespoke hand lotion as an antidote, the harsh soap was an unpleasant sensation on the skin. She put the dishes into the water one by one, and the occasional splash of water was soothing and homely.

Once again, the duke seemed better for having spoken of his past. His chair scraped the floor, her only warning, and he was at her shoulder. "Instantaneous consumption?" he asked.

"Quite easily managed." Tabitha handed him a tea towel; he held it as he would a dead fish. "I made some spirits of Saturn—"

"Blessed Palu, woman!" He took the dripping saucer she handed him and dabbed the towel against it.

"Yes, yes, it is poisonous, but only when used with regularity. Nevertheless, we applied it with great care to his face. He clutched a handkerchief already prepared with carmine—that was his idea, not mine, but it proved to be an excellent flourish. He quietly coughed his way through breakfast, and when that failed to attract the required attention, he fainted, holding the hankie to his mouth so it looked like he was leaking blood all over the place." She snickered at the memory, and the duke made that rumbly, scratchy sound that seemed to originate deep in his chest, reluctant to be released.

"Very dramatic." The duke conquered the saucer, so she handed him a cup. "I wonder that your mother was not disturbed?"

"It was as Timothy said. We did not come up to snuff." Tabitha watched Llewellyn address drying the cup with greater confidence. "Neither my mother nor my father exerted themselves when it came to us. My father was forever pronouncing upon my attributes or lack thereof and insisting on ways I must improve myself. And despite many attempts and many losses, my mother did not produce any more children."

"Many losses. Is that why you pursued your craft?"

"Very perceptive, Your Grace. As her daughter, I was to tend her through her recoveries and found I had a talent for it." She handed him a large bowl, and he held it carefully as he dried it. "And thank you, it is a craft, although Tim has more than once joked in poor taste that it is a capital-C Craft, like witchery."

"An enchantress, then," Llewellyn said. "Akin to Ceridwen, who combined many ingredients in her fabled caldron and produced magic. You may be more powerful than she, using fewer ingredients to greater effect."

"An enchantress, honestly." Why he said these things to her, she could not fathom. "When it came down to it, we were not useful to their ends. Timothy thought we would not be missed, and so it was. Letters were not answered, and I gave up after a while."

"All are not best disposed to have young. The lions know this, no matter that *cat* cats reproduce indiscriminately." He set the bowl to the side and accepted one of the platters. "Having said that, we were larger than most prides, and my mother was still keen to bring forth young."

"I am truly sorry." Tabitha left the utensils to soak and dried her hands. "I hope it has done you some good to speak of them."

"More good than I can say. It is like when the chain slid off my paw and I was freed. The moment it was removed, the impediment gone, my Change flowed through me." His amused huff would be the death of her. "To the alarm of the thief who had seen the gold and wanted it for himself."

"It was as simple as that?"

"I suppose? There is much that seems to be unknown." Llewellyn shrugged, a boyish gesture not remotely ducal. "My usual handler had taken ill, though now I think on it, the thief may have ensured the man sickened. He must have thought to feather his nest, but little did he know."

"You Changed instantly?"

"From one breath to the next. The thief…lost his composure, shall we say? Even in my weakened state, I managed to divest him of his clothing and made for Carlton House. It was a swift departure. And yours?"

"Mine? Oh, swift, but with fewer thieves and ensorcelled golden chains." She busied herself putting things away, while the duke seemed to take great pains to ensure the last platter was dry as a bone. "The lord I shall not name had been feral, if you will once again forgive me the term, in his pursuit of Timothy. Utterly relentless, a law unto himself, which is not unusual, I suppose, in the upper classes. On top of this was watching my brother struggle with his grief. Oh, he vowed he understood the reality of the situation, but the loss of his beloved cut him off at the knees. He didn't have the vitality to be looking over his shoulder. So I did it for him."

"With no thought to your own safety, I imagine."

Tabitha ignored the comment. "The unfortunate result being it brought me to this lord's attention, and he attempted to court me, with my father's permission, in order to compromise me. To what end, who knew, as he would have been quite stuck with me. We reckon he meant to leave me at the altar as if it would shame me or break my heart. It was decided that drastic steps were to be taken."

"I do not think you would dose him with foxglove."

"Oh, no, it is far too easy to miscalculate the dosage." He closed his eyes in disbelief, and she had to laugh. "Rose otto, you may remember, is an efficient emetic, and one can use as much as one likes, to no ill effect. Barring the hours spent curled over the chamber pot."

"You are a formidable foe." He did not seem put off by that. "And then you left."

"And then we left. Before the emetic was administered, we made sure we had enough for the fare and some ready money. Timothy had a small legacy, and we both had skills we could put to use in the wide world. Life was cheaper abroad, everyone said so, and everyone was correct if, like us, they were used to making do. We did, and did nicely."

"And your brother was safe and happy."

"On all counts. Mind you, it was not as though the Continent was a paradise where confirmed bachelors were completely free to live their lives without censure. There is no such place, but there were plenty of towns and cities where we both found peace of mind. I had not reckoned on how much the release from fear would do for him. It was like watching a bird fly from a cage. He was already warm and friendly and sociable, but with freedom, he became expansive and charismatic and urbane."

"And you? What did you become?"

"Less cautious, less concerned." These adjectives paled in comparison to Timothy's. No matter. "I became adept at many new approaches to healthful living and have seen things I never thought I'd see."

"Has your brother given his heart again?" The platter was dry to His Grace's satisfaction, and he laid it down.

"He has been enjoying his freedom. Not unlike you or I would do under the same circumstances, never minding that our desires are more in line with what society deems conventional."

"Are your preferences conventional?" He leaned back against the sink. Nothing about this action ought to make her tremble, and yet. This evening's coat was a dark green, far less eye watering than recent choices; while it fit better than those previous, it still hung off him like washing on a line; his trousers appeared to be fastened with a sliver of wood wound through a loop; his boots were made of scraps of suede sloppily stitched together and tied closed at his knee. All of that, and yet the posture cast his body into a sinuous line of potent masculinity. His hair still held the shine her tonic had given it, and it was all she could do to refrain from working out the growing tangles. He leaned closer. "If I am to succeed as your suitor, I must know what you prefer."

"My what, now?" She turned away to wipe down the table and stack the plates and cups they had yet to clear. "You are not—there is no suiting going on here."

"Tell that to the bee. And the goat, and the toad."

"He is a frog, that is rather different. All toads are frogs, but not all frogs are toads," Tabitha corrected.

"Do you prefer toads to frogs?"

"I have given no thought to the matter." What in the world was he on about? "One is much the same as the other."

"Not to a lady toad or a lady frog." Was he smiling again? She attacked a stubborn spot on the tabletop. "So preference regarding amphibians is ambivalent, then," he said. "Have you any decisive preferences that come to mind?"

"I cannot think what you mean."

He swiveled to hitch his hip on the table's edge. The posture did shocking things to the placket of his trousers.

"What do you enjoy or not, as the case may be."

Did he mean bed things? "I abhor black currant in all its forms."

The skin around his eyes crinkled, a new devastation to her nerves. "No jam for you, then, nor cordial."

"As though you had the patience to make any of that."

He rose and followed her around the table. "I have acres of the stuff."

"Acres of blackberry bushes?" She knew she was being obtuse...but also teasing him. "I find it hard to believe it would not be beneath a duke's dignity to cultivate such, nor have you had time to do so." Somehow he had passed her and was now blocking her progress around the table.

The scritchy-scratchy amusement sound evolved into a pleasing thunder that emitted from deep in his belly, a rich, rolling thing. He leaned in, lips close to her ear. "My very literal lady. I cultivate what I please, as I am a duke."

"I thought you said you were not much of a duke."

"I have decided to apply myself and improve upon my deficits in that arena and expand upon my skills. Take Lowell, for example. He excels in clothing himself as though his ensemble must be recreated for the broadsheets, and yet it is known he made a shambles of his courtship of Her Grace. I do not suffer such a lack."

"Is that a corollary? The less well-set, the better with the ladies?"

He extended one long leg, a leg that, when the loose trousers pulled tight, appeared strong and muscular and intriguing. His thighs, imperfectly revealed in the dull stuff of the fabric, hinted at being very impressive. She ran her tongue over her lips, and he followed the action with those hazel eyes. Lord, she felt like a milkmaid as she casually inserted herself in the space between his knees. He looked at her appraisingly through those maddening lashes.

"I don't care what *ladies* think," the duke said, hands braced on the table behind, making no move to, to grab her. "I care what one lady thinks, a lady apothecary who has not given any thought to what she prefers."

"It truly has not come up. Not in any abiding sense."

"Good." How pleased he sounded.

Lest he think otherwise: "I am not without experience as regards sexual congress."

"Good." He sounded no less pleased about that.

"I have not agreed to anything."

"I am aware." The timbre of his tone made the hairs on the back of her neck stand on end. "I believe you ought to be courting me as much as I would you. Should you agree to do so, of course."

"Like our bargaining." Tabitha reached out and

laid a finger on the middle button of his coat. "We both took part, both had equal returns on our, uh, desired outcomes. It was not merely the case of one party, generally the woman, holding back the ultimate prize for a series of smaller gains along the way."

He smiled, fully, freely; if he asked, she would give him everything. "You inspire me to give you as many great gains as you wish."

"I wish to kiss you again." Desire had simmered beneath everything she'd done that day.

"That is my wish as well."

"Then we are both the victor."

He laid his hands on her hips, leaned back, and pulled them onto the kitchen table. Whatever had been left on top smashed to the floor, plates and cups, and oh, she was done for if the caster was damaged; Timothy adored the blasted thing and had hauled it around with them since France.

She leaned up on her hands, his hair a wreath of blondish brown luxuriousness around his head. "Before you kissed me…"

"Before I kissed you…" It was a miracle his voice alone did not divest her of her petticoat.

"I was not honest with you. I adore kissing. But I have not kissed many who liked it as much as I did." Tabitha ducked her head and rubbed her forehead on his sternum. "I feel you enjoy it as much as I do."

"Before I kissed you," he murmured, "I had not

kissed anyone for many, many years, and it was as though I had never kissed anyone before. As though you were the first and now have ruined me for anyone else."

Kissing Alwyn ap Lewin while standing was exhilarating but a vastly different proposition to kissing Alwyn ap Lewin while lying down; when one lay on top of him, it took on a whole new light. She spread her knees to rest on either side of his hips.

He set one hand on her ribs and the other cupped the back of her neck. He drew her down slowly, his eyes on her mouth, and they both sighed when their lips met.

Oh, a different proposition entirely. He was careful of his hands, of where he moved them, unlike more than one potential lover who, once she was in their grasp, turned into octopuses. She smiled against his mouth. He urged her back and nipped her chin. "Funny?"

"You are not an octopus." She laughed at his confusion and shook her head. "I wonder if I have ever, in the past, kissed one of those."

He blinked, perplexed. "They tend to live close to the ocean, as one would assume."

Did she want to laugh or kiss? Kiss now, laugh later… She leaned down again, and he decided to take this kissing seriously. An arm wrapped around her waist, the other behind her shoulders, and her knees slid farther apart until she fully lay upon him. She could feel every movement of his muscles and that…that was not his hip, or not just his hip she felt against her belly. She wiggled once, and his moan reverberated through his body, made her shiver, which caused him to rock them both with a shift of his pelvis, and they were heading down a very slippery slope indeed.

"Wait, I—" she said, and he pulled back immediately, held her away from him; if his head hit the table with force, it was gratifying to know he was as overtaken as she. "It is not that I am not enjoying this—"

"If you wish to stop, then we shall stop." He stroked a finger over her cheek, where she knew she blushed.

"This is not—I am meant to be treating you, not cavorting about on the table with you."

"I am no longer your client. I would be your suitor." He lifted her off his body and set their feet on the floor. "I am aware you have other considerations. You may find, with time, there is much to like in the toad."

"The frog!" She took a step back but kept hold of his coat. When had she taken hold of his coat? "I doubt I am able to juggle suitors like a diamond of the first water."

"I will not make the mistakes my ducal peers did." He laid his hand over hers, his fingers tracing over her knuckles. "How we proceed is entirely up to you."

She lifted her chin as she had seen Felicity do when she wished to appear resolute. "I require time to consider and the solitude to do so."

He stood, and honestly, every time she looked, he seemed to grow another inch. He made her an elegant leg that rivaled those of the *ton*'s Corinthians and employed those lashes in aid of his brand of courtly dark arts. "Then you must take as much as you need." He blinked at her and said, "I am entirely at your service."

Fourteen

At her service, was he?

Planned to court her, did he?

Tabitha woke very, very cross.

As stimulating as their kissing and whatnot had been the night before, she woke contrary and annoyed and very, very tired of men declaring things at her.

Father; that loathsome lord; the Prince of Wales; and now His Grace of Llewellyn.

She couldn't settle; she didn't want to see him, but she wanted to know where he was so she could avoid that place. At least that's what she told herself as she stalked around the fringes of the park and the village.

How she wished she could run as she had in Greece. She could not convey in words how it made her feel, how it settled her, how the fatigue of her muscles relaxed her mind. She'd had more than one breakthrough after a race down the beach with those Greek women, women of all shapes and social classes, united in their love of the invigorating sea air and of racing down the sand.

Even in this place that defied society on so many levels, Tabitha did not feel free to do so.

So she wandered from dawn until sometime between the noon hour and teatime. Wandered alone, as she wished, all the while annoyed Llewellyn was respecting her wishes and had not sought her out.

Timothy was right: she was out of sorts.

The duke was only doing as she asked.

As she came over the crest of yet another of the park's hillocks, her heart leaped when she saw him chatting with Delilah.

How gratifying that his shoulders tensed, and he did her the courtesy of not looking over his shoulder, though he sensed she was there.

Tabitha turned on her heel and headed for one of her new favorite places to brood.

Had she always been a brooder? She must have, as she could call to mind several well-hidden places in every town and city they'd traveled in, where she went to think; most times she was thinking, but just as often—

She brooded. And this was prime ground for such an undertaking.

It was a vantage point like one she and the duke had lain upon to watch the *cursio,* like the one His Grace's cottage perched on; if she turned around completely, she would see his summit. She did not do so. *Her* summit sat to the west of the Close, the distance between them no farther than the length of beach she used to run in less than four minutes. An ancient chestnut tree held court, the spread of its branches so wide, it was likely as old as England; beneath it, a conveniently placed boulder provided the opportunity to sit and rest. She saw yet another high hill making up the last compass point, surely intentional; the park yielded yet another of its secrets. Nothing here was left to chance.

Chance would be a fine thing, she huffed to herself. To be courted by a duke. One who did not seem to think much of the disparity between their lots in life. Which ought to be a mark in his favor, for what would she do with a proper duke?

What was she to do with a suitor who insisted she give all her options consideration? Whoever heard of such a thing.

The bee and the goat and the frog had not declared at her; a mark in their favor.

The very notion of breaking crockery with any of those? She could not picture it.

Oh, but Tabitha could easily recall the picture His Grace made, spread out on her kitchen table like a gruff banquet, those eyes lambent in the candlelight, the feel of his strong body beneath hers. His mouth, his tongue—Blessed Palu, his tongue. The sensation that flooded her being when their hips had rocked together, the sheer sensuality of everything about him: the heat of his body, of his hands running up her back, the sounds he made, a cat purring its satisfaction at getting its way, all that hair, and his eyes and those godforsaken lashes.

Or goddess-forsaken. What did she know about him that she hadn't discerned as a practitioner? "Tabitha Barrington, what do you know about him as a woman? Quite a lot, I'd reckon, for the—for the love of Palu. Oh, dear." She moaned. Sulking and talking to herself aloud. What was wrong with her?

"I don't know what to do." She *always* knew what to do. She had years of experience making decisions and choosing the appropriate courses of action. She, who did not hesitate to pursue knowledge, was embarrassed she had no frame of reference for this at all. It must be a failure of her femininity… although if the bee, the goat, the frog, and a duke of the realm were to be trusted, nothing was lacking there.

She would ask Felicity if they might speak in confidence. And Jemima as well. There, that was a plan.

Tabitha's stomach rumbled, alerting her to her forgotten breakfast. She had not brought sustenance, as she had not expected to be sulking and lurking the livelong day. It was out of character, but if she were being truthful, it came as a relief. How relaxing, to sulk and to lurk, to throw off the need to be productive and available. She slid off the boulder to the ground, leaned against the tree, and closed her eyes; even this early in spring, even under the cover of the chestnut, the sun that drifted through was hard on eyes that had hardly shut for yet another night...

A noise in the distance woke her. She squinted at the sky; how long had she slept? Long enough to see several coaches had pulled into Lowell Close—oh, it was Beatrice and her new family. Everyone gathered around them, bar Llewellyn, who kept to the edges as usual.

Tabitha stood and stretched and started to make her way down, despite the presence of the Welsh duke, to greet the newcomers. Now she had three friends to ask what to do.

With that rather more optimistic thought, she brushed herself down, indulged in an unladylike yawn, and set off for the Close.

———

Alwyn had sensed when she saw him and avoided him. Delilah had an adverse opinion about that, but he was thrilled.

The faint of heart might find this troubling, but not he. The vitality surging through his veins was unlike any he had felt before.

It was time he let her do what a lady lion would do—hunt.

He was in her sights, and it was up to her to pounce.

Thus, he found himself at the disposal of the Duke of Lowell, as well as his Second and Third as they guided a cart laden with sheets of glass to the disused building they'd been cleaning the other day. That Irish horse moped around after them.

The lengths of glass were unlike anything he'd ever seen. "Is this to be a conservatory?" he asked.

Bates looked at him over his shoulder; he had insisted on taking the lead. "No."

"Do not bother trying to get more out of him than that, Llewellyn," huffed Lowell. "He is keeping his secrets regarding this venture."

"It is not our lot to be the brains of this undertaking, merely the brawn," added Gambon.

An outbreak of banter followed, peppered with myriad insults to Bates's brainpower or lack thereof; it even managed to raise a smile out of MacCafferty.

"Take care with this and bring it around the back." Bates stood with hands on hips and considered the reconfigured roof of the lean-to. It looked like it had been built with speed yet precision, even to Alwyn's untutored eye. A fleet of footmen set ladders in place, and still others unloaded the carts to hand up the glass.

Every *versipellian* ear perked at the sound of a carriage in the distance.

"Expected?" Bates looked ready to Change at a moment's notice.

Lowell scented the air then smiled. "No, but not unwelcome."

Leaving the footmen to their work and MacCafferty to his brooding, and lacking anything better to do, Alwyn followed the trio down to the coach house. If only he could scent the air himself and know not only who had arrived but also where Miss Barrington—dare he think *Tabitha*—was.

An array of coaches lined the square, all emblazoned with the escutcheon of the Osborn duchy. The bearer of those arms—*Ha, ha, bearer,* Alwyn said to himself—erupted from the first vehicle and swept his duchess down in a showy swirl. She beamed up at him, and look at that: they must be in harmony, unwilling marriage notwithstanding.

Alwyn held back as Lowell rushed forward and embraced Arthur.

"Lowell!" Osborn thumped his peer heartily on the back; as an Alpha bear Shifter, it was not a love tap. "I hear you have given our players shelter in their difficulties."

"Your players?" Lowell made a show of neatening his ruffled cravat. "We knew you had a love of the theatrical but no idea you had a troupe at your disposal."

"*We*? Have you been elevated equally to the highest among us?" Osborn rolled his eyes. "Yes, our dear mother loved a play above all else and had long supported the Peaselys."

"Where is your duchess, Your Grace?" Beatrice asked. She was half the size of her husband, yet her demeanor gave the impression of a much larger figure, helped in some way by the extraordinary height of the ostentatious bonnet she wore. It was covered in bows and feathers and ribbons, and to his manly eye, distracted from her lovely face. Or was that the point?

The men bowed to the lady, Alwyn one beat behind. "Hard at work in her premises, Your Grace," Lowell answered her.

"All this Gracing, we cannot go on with it," the little duchess pronounced. "At the very least, not in private."

Osborn smiled down at her and toyed with one of her ribbons. "My Second's word is law."

Ah, yes, she was his Beta: Alwyn hardly recalled her *initiatio*, though he had been present. It had been early days, and his unwilling attendance at the ceremony following Osborn's confrontation with Hallbjorn had been a blur. All he remembered was eluding the lady apothecary—dare he say, *his* lady apothecary—before he fled the scene.

The Duchess of Osborn seemed more than equal for the challenge of her role; Alwyn could not think of a better outcome for the little firework. He felt immensely proud of her, for no good reason at all.

"Is that you, Llewellyn? Lurking as only your kind can?" At Arthur's words, Alwyn revealed himself, and Osborn started. "Oh. How well you look. Bloody Georgie, right again, was he?" Osborn and Lowell shared a long-suffering grimace.

"Children, come greet His Grace as you have been taught," said the little duchess. Three small-ish creatures lined up in front of Alwyn. "Your Grace, here are Bernadette, Tarben, and Ursella Humphries." The cubs' parents were otherwise occupied: Lord Swinburn, Osborn's brother Ben, and Gambon were off discussing Gamma matters, while Charlotte, Lady Swinburn, was gossiping with the publican's wife. After the children's introduction, their aunt had been approached, as though she were a wild beast, by Bates, who had never seen a human female Second in all his days.

The children gave an obeisance so elaborate, their tutor could only have been Lady Frost. The girls' curtsies wobbled but held, noses nearly touching the ground, while the boy bowed and twirled a handkerchief near the size of a bedsheet, profuse with lace.

Alwyn laughed. "Rise, children." They beamed up at him and he down at them, and he laughed again, rich, deep, full, from his belly—from his heart.

He looked around the suddenly silent square, the cynosure of every astonished eye; before he could inquire as to the cause, the littlest one came up to him and leaned on his leg.

"Hello there," he said. Ursella looked up at him and canted her head, considering, bunching the excess fabric of his coat in her little fist. "I perceive the influence of Lady Frost in your tribute."

"I do not know who that is." Tarben scowled. How like his mother; Alwyn remembered her as a child from days spent in Court with Georgie. She forever wanted to know everything.

"Our Aunt Beezy taught us," said Bernadette, her composure rivaling that of a seasoned dowager.

He crouched to their level. "Your Aunt Beezy is known as *Lady Frost* and is famous throughout the *ton* for her curtsies."

Tarben bounced back and forth in front of him. "She is not frosty to us," he declared.

Ursella transferred her grasp from the hem of his coat to his sleeve. "She was frosty because she was sad," she whispered.

"Was she?" Alwyn did not expect such insight from a little child.

"Like you are sad," she replied, and no, not that degree of perspicacity at all. He studied her as she did him; was she an Omega? It would be a blessing for the Osborn sleuth if she was.

"Your Grace?" Bernadette asked. "It is said you were in the circus."

"Which sounds magnificent!" Tarben leaped once into the air. "But our papa said it was not. He said it was a crime like no other and the villain ought to be taken to the highest authority! Who is the highest authority? Is that the king or my mum?"

"Your mum, I would think, without question," Alwyn replied. Ursella rubbed her face against his arm. He supposed he was spoken of amongst his kind as a cautionary tale. Maybe their parents had brought it up so they would not ask, but children were children and curious above all things.

"I am sorry such badness befell you, Your Grace." Bernadette cuddled up on the side opposite her sister; she played with the ends of his hair and proceeded to work out the tangles.

"Thank you kindly, Bernadette. It was badness, the sort one would think was only found in a story." His lion would take it amiss if he did not warn them himself, in a way they would appreciate. "Once upon a time, long ago, an evil sorcerer worked his terrible magic and made it so even the tiniest bit of gold could keep a *versipellis* caught in their Shape forevermore. Those who know the spell can employ it against Shifters of all species. The sorcerers were a cunning lot and used devilish ploys to capture *versipelles* unawares. They tricked them into taking their Shape so the gold might be caught around their necks or their paws to trap them in it." There was yet another aspect to it, a way to lull them into immobility, one he could not easily recall; his mind rebelled and refused to pursue it further.

"How do the Shifters escape?" Tarben asked.

"They must be freed by a human. I was released by a greedy creature as may be found in any species. He saw the golden chain on my paw and wanted it for himself."

"How lucky he was greedy," Bernadette declared.

"Who was greedy?" Charlotte asked as the children's parents joined them.

"His Grace told us about the sorcerer and how they bewitched the gold and how you are the highest authority, Mum!" Tarben threw himself around his mother's knees.

"Did he? I like that in a duke," Charlotte said. Alwyn rose, and the lady smiled at him while hugging her cub. She and her husband showed their necks to him. "I cannot manage a curtsy, Your Grace, and certainly not as well as my daughters."

Ben tugged lightly on his son's ear. "I do hope you have been introduced properly to the Duke of Llewellyn and did not take it upon yourselves."

"Aunt Beezy did the pretty," Bernadette said.

"No one does it better," Charlotte agreed.

"And they, in turn, did very prettily," Alwyn said. "They are lovely children."

Ben set his hands on his hips. "What, these children?" Their mother and father exchanged exaggerated, incredulous looks while their two eldest protested their prettiness with great volume. His parents had teased him and his siblings so, had looked at them with all the love in their hearts, as these two did their cubs. Grief coursed through him, and his perception of the world around him grew hazy, as it had not for weeks. His time with the cubs had drawn attention. As crowded as Lowell Close could be at any given time, there were greater numbers than usual, thanks to the addition of the Humphries. The pressure of all the people staring was oppressive; he felt the equanimity he'd achieved start to drain. His breath arrested, and his head swam until a little hand gripped his arm. Ursella tugged until he looked down at her; she put her hand in his, and he squeezed it in gratitude. They both held still as he inhaled deeply, once, twice, and nodded, calm once more.

Until yet another coach rolled into the forecourt of the public house.

Its postilions bounded into action as soon as the vehicle drew to a halt.

One of its attendants let down the steps and handed down a lady.

She was unknown to all, causing a murmur of speculation to break out.

Well...not quite unknown to all.

"Oh, my goodness!" Charlotte gasped. "It is the lady author, Mrs. Anchoretta Asquith."

Fifteen

ALWYN GENTLY REMOVED THE CHILD'S HAND from his.

As Lady Swinburn rushed forward to greet Mrs. Asquith, he edged away.

Lowell and Osborn, as well as Bates, Gambon, and Lord Swinburn, moved to stand in front of the citizens of the Close. Taking their cues from their Alpha and his cadre, the villagers clustered together, shielding one another against whatever had raised the protectiveness of their duke.

Alwyn slipped behind them.

He did not like the look of that lady author.

"Mrs. Asquith." Lowell drew his power to him, a *dominatum* waiting to be unleashed.

"Your Grace." Her polished obeisance was all it should be; Alwyn preferred the children's effort. "I wrote to your duchess but found I could not wait to see the developments in Lowell Close for myself. I notice you have been joined by the Duke of Osborn."

Arthur's bear rumbled, and the lady duly offered him tribute. Her smile, as fine an example of a restrained expression fit for society, was not reflected in her eyes, which avidly took in her surroundings.

Alwyn wanted to charge over and knock her down—or incapacitate her to ensure she came no nearer to anyone in the gathering; he wanted to run in the other direction, flee her presence, put the whole world between them. His confusion built and built, the tension between the two choices too much to contain. His instincts screamed that she was a threat. How could this elegant lady be so? He was imagining it; it could not be true.

He would stay and gauge her behavior—no, he could not, he could not stay one more moment in a place she inhabited. It went against his nature to abandon the weak to danger, but how dangerous could this lady be, here amongst the greatest predators on this island?

A battle raged within; its fury held him captive, unable to act.

———

Distracted by a glorious overabundance of lovage, Tabitha's meander to town came to a halt while she harvested as much as she could carry. She thought she spied a patch of hyssop nearby when yet another coach rolled in. Mr. Bates's fears regarding the village's future may not be so far-fetched, given the increase in traffic to Lowell Close. She saw

Llewellyn, who had been entertaining children (of all things!), start to sidle away after a lady stepped down from the carriage.

Tabitha did not know who she was, but she could see the newcomer was uncommonly beautiful. Of dainty height, her figure was sheer perfection, bosomy yet slender. Shiny hair the color of rich mahogany hugged sleekly to her skull in a low chignon, and as her gaze cast about the Close, Tabitha saw her eyes were a pale green, like the sun shining through one of her tincture vials. The lady's clothing was in the first stare of fashion, from the top of her head to the tips of her toes, with exceptionally fine gloves in between.

The lady was an Incomparable, and Tabitha took against her on sight.

She was too far to hear, but she could see: as the new visitor spoke, it was obvious Lowell and Osborn were protecting their people, the pack gathering as one behind the bastion of their strength. Tabitha's unrest grew. As Llewellyn slunk farther to the back of the crowd, she wondered what he sensed...

For she sensed all was not right with this woman.

———————

Why did Lowell not expel her from his lands? It was clear he was not pleased to see her, that she was unwelcome. Alwyn was not an avid reader of novels, but he recalled Miss Barrington saying her books came very close to giving away *versipellian* secrets. Georgie devoured them even as he castigated her, but the prince did nothing to stop her or rein her in.

The lady author was baiting those who were more powerful than she, but to what end?

On top of all that, she was rude to the publican and his wife: when they made to greet her, she dismissively gestured to her excess of trunks and cases, to be given into their care via the postilions.

"You do not travel light, Mrs. Asquith," Lowell observed.

"I assume I am welcome to stay at least one night, Your Grace?" Her mien was all that was submissive, her tone pure conciliation—yet as she ran a hand up one of her full-length gloves, it was an oddly aggressive gesture.

"It is to be expected that you travel so, as you are known for your style throughout society," Lady Swinburn remarked. "I have never seen the like of your gloves."

"You would not have. They are the only ones of their kind." Mrs. Asquith raised a slim arm, and the wide bell of her pelisse's sleeve fell back; sunlight caught the scales that comprised them, a shimmering rainbow from the tips of her fingers to the crook of her arm. "I have earned a rather good wage from my novel writing," she said, glancing at Charlotte's less-than-fashionable walking dress, "and I do like to indulge myself. These are rare, the rarest of all—dragonskin."

"Dragonskin!" Tarben exclaimed, and only his father's *versipellian* reflexes prevented him from rushing to the lady for a closer look.

"There are no such things as dragons," his father said.

"I have heard—" Charlotte began; Mrs. Asquith turned her back on her and addressed Beatrice.

"Your Grace," she said, "how I adore your bonnet. We appear to have the same extravagant tastes."

Osborn's duchess did not deign to reply; Alwyn swore he could see the mantle of Lady Frost enfold her in its chilling embrace. She treated Mrs. Asquith's figure to a slow sweep, head to toe and back again, that paid twice what Mrs. Asquith had accorded her sister-in-law and gave the lady author her shoulder.

"My dear Lady Swinburn, let us fetch Her Grace." Osborn's wife and Second linked their arms and drew her away. "The duchess must be very absorbed in her work."

The women swept past her, noses in the air. Unfazed, Mrs. Asquith's smile did not waver as she scanned the crowd. "I was made to understand there is yet another duke in Sussex—"

Shouts issued from behind the inn: the performer's bear charged out of the stable yard and into the heart of the crowd. Rested after her trials, she appeared larger than when she arrived and the villagers fell back farther, leaving it to their leaders to sort out.

The bear made straight for the lady author and was headed off nimbly by the Duke of Osborn. Mrs. Asquith was unperturbed, and if she looked cross and surprised, it was perhaps due to the spotlight veering from her to the rampaging beast. The strongest of the *versipelles* herded the bear gently toward the strongman, who spoke to her softly until she calmed.

In the melee, the lady author wandered through the crowd, looking about her intently, and rather than catch her attention, Alwyn fled.

———

It would take the spectacle of a loose *animali puri* to draw attention from the newcomer. Tabitha's unease doubled as the bear charged into the green. Lowell and Osborn corralled the creature, and Mr. Bates and Gambon did their best to help. The bear ignored them all until Mr. Quincy came on the scene, distraught yet calm, gentling the animal until she allowed him to put on her harness.

How had the creature gotten loose?

Lowell and Mr. Bates conferred, heads together, leaving Mr. Gambon to urge the pack members back to their shops or homes, while Ben and Osborn took the lead in helping Mr. Quincy soothe the bear. She had seen Charlotte and Beatrice disappear into Felicity's premises, and they had yet to return.

With the adults thus occupied, no one was watching the children.

In all the milling about, the newcomer had maneuvered her way over to them.

Tabitha started walking faster.

The lady extended an arm and allowed the boy to inspect her exotic-looking glove. The older girl looked unwillingly fascinated, but the littlest one glowered.

In a feat of legerdemain, one moment the lady's hand was empty, the next it held a long chain. She let it dangle from her fingers and a stone pendant hanging from it began to swing, back and forth, back and forth; as it did, it seemed to glow, as if lit from within by an eerie fire.

Tabitha ran.

She ran as she had never run in her life, scattering lovage in her wake. Despite her skirts, she leaped over a low stone wall, and uncaring of the eyes she drew, she pushed through the crowd to stand between the children and the lady.

As quickly as it appeared, the chain vanished.

"How fast you are!" The boy, like a little magpie, diverted his attention to the newest interesting thing he noticed.

"I have never seen a lady run like that," the older girl said, her tone unsure whether she should admire this or not.

"I did so every day when I lived in Greece, on the shores of the Aegean Sea," Tabitha said, only slightly winded.

"You must be the lady apothecary I have heard so much about," said the visitor. "You will have heard of me, I suspect." She fluttered her lashes, as if out of modesty.

"Will I? And yet I do not know who you are." *I know* what *you are*, Tabitha thought and put the children at her back. The smallest would not stay there and stood next to her, exuding stubbornness.

"She is the lady author, miss," said the boy.

"*The* lady author, oh my, I am hardly the only one of my sex scribbling away at my little stories." How foul Mrs. Asquith was when she simpered.

"I remain unenlightened," Tabitha said. The small girl looked up at her, assessing then admiring.

"You are very much in the dark, Miss Barrington." The lady author's eyes flashed red, and her smile evaporated. "Unenlightened in oh so many ways. In ways that speak to grave danger in your future, whether or not you become the wiser."

Tabitha and the little girl exchanged dubious glances. "That sounds like the plot of a Gothic novel."

"Art often imitates life," the lady hissed.

"She is Mrs. Anchoretta Asquith," whispered the girl at her back.

"Ah, that lady author. I have read a book of yours." Mrs. Asquith touched her heart as though humbled, yet if looks could kill… "It is true," Tabitha went on, "life often does imitate art. I have heard it is common in novels that an unaware heroine must conquer more than one travail to learn and grow. Is that so for your books, or…?"

"Do you not like stories, Miss Barrington? You do not speak as if you do."

"Not as much as my brother does." The child took a handful of Tabitha's skirts, an oddly soothing gesture.

"I have a legion of fans amongst his…sort. How I adore them. They seem to identify with those helpless heroines." Despite her gratified air at the thought of her ardent admirers, her tone mocked them.

"Children, let us join your family." Tabitha herded the two eldest in the general direction of their mother then waited for the smallest, who was occupied with glaring at the lady author. "Come, love, I am sorry I do not know your name—"

"It is Ursella, is it not?" Mrs. Asquith said. "The Omega of the Humphries sleuth, if I am not mistaken."

"You are not," Ursella replied. "But you are misbegotten in your ways and will soon be thwarted."

With that, she spun on her heel and ambled over to her family.

Mrs. Asquith began, "I vow, the rearing of that child leaves much to be desired—"

And in the rudest action Tabitha had ever taken in her life that did not involve emetic herbs, she turned and walked away.

"Yes, go, Miss Barrington, flee while you can," the lady author called, "but thanks to you, that which has slipped through my fingers will eat from the palm of my hand."

━━━━━

"You have missed all the drama," Tabitha said as she approached Felicity and Beatrice outside Templeton Stud. She turned to keep Asquith in her sights just as the lady made a show of inspecting every trunk and case before she let them be carried into the coach house. Charlotte was gathering her children and calling for Ursella, who had drifted over to the stable yard to look at the bear.

"If I left my office every time a shout let out in the square, I would get nothing done," Felicity replied.

"Well, let us hope Mrs. Asquith does not see fit to abandon her career as a writer," Tabitha said. "She is not fit for the stage."

"Did said drama originate with her?" Beatrice

slipped her arm through Tabitha's as they strolled across the green.

"She favors portentous half thoughts dropped into conversation to tantalize the listener."

Felicity took her other arm and pouted. "Oh, do not say she is an awful person. I so enjoy her books."

The Peaselys rushed to greet the Duke of Osborn, who proceeded to make much of them. As the ladies passed, he asked, "What play shall you give us?"

A flash of inspiration had Tabitha suggest: "Let us have *Hamlet*, Your Grace."

"The Melancholy Dane?" The bear Shifter hummed regretfully. "It is a play of deep thoughts, Miss Barrington, and not as much of an entertainment as others in our beloved Bard's oeuvre."

"Oh, we can do it in less than three-quarters of an hour," said Mr. Peasley.

"All the while sustaining the tension and pathos," added his wife.

"Now that I have to see!" The duke proceeded to quiz the Peaselys on their approach to the play.

"This will be the first performance I have ever hosted," Felicity said as she herded them off to the side of the crowd. She continued to chatter about theater and Shakespeare and Edmund Kean until they could be private.

Tabitha kept her eyes on the whole of the square. "My friends, I need your help."

"Anything," Felicity said.

"We are at your service, of course, Tabitha." Beatrice's perfect little face wrinkled with a scowl. "Has it to do with the lady author?"

"I saw, from a distance, that Asquith was holding something out to the children. The way it caught the light sent a tremor down my spine. You know I do not speak so fancifully, ever, but it was as though a dreadful event was about to transpire." She recounted her run to the Close and finished with her turning away from the lady author. "She knew Ursella's name and that she is an Omega, and then threatened me with who knows what."

Beatrice laid a trembling hand on Tabitha's arm. "Was the chain she lured the children with—was it gold?"

"I believe it was." She laid her hand over her friend's. "I am aware gold is anathema to Shifters."

Felicity set her jaw. "I find I do not trust Mrs. Asquith."

"Only one with dire motives would visit Lowell Close with gold at their disposal." Beatrice shook her head. "As she is *versipellis*, I would be amazed she exposes herself to it."

"I fear she has use for it." Tabitha's mind reeled with the possibilities, wedded with the timing of Asquith's visit, and came up with nothing good.

"That is a very serious accusation." Felicity lifted her chin, and Tabitha took heart: nothing stood in the way of the Duchess of Lowell when she did so. "We must be able to support it without question. If only O'Mara were here."

"Ursella is young and very knowledgeable," Beatrice said, "but I do not know if dealing with this person is beyond her abilities. I shall speak to her parents, but it is their decision as to whether the child can help."

"I believe Asquith will not hesitate to boast of her successes," Tabitha said. "I shall write a speech for the players to speak, trippingly off their tongues, and trick her into exposing herself."

"The play's the thing," Beatrice supplied.

"To catch the conscience of a…whatever she is," Felicity finished.

"A snake," Tabitha said, without hesitation. "I am sorry to break the *versipellian* law, but it must be said."

"Are you certain?" Beatrice asked. "Even after all this time amongst them, I can spot a *versipellis* but cannot discern their species."

"Tabitha has a gift for it," Felicity said. "Lowell says it is quite uncommon."

"Speaking of uncommon gifts, my brother's is equal to that of Mr. Bates. When he seeks knowledge, it does not elude him for long." Once asking for help began, it was the easiest thing in the world to do. "If I may borrow some footmen, Felicity? Timothy will set them on the scent of Asquith's antecedents and see what that reveals."

They watched as Mr. Beckett-the-Publican ushered the lady author into the building. Mr. Beckett-the-Suitor gave Tabitha a little wave.

"I do not like her staying there," Felicity said. "Or anywhere near us."

"I shall warn Mr. Beckett and ask him to spread word amongst those in the village to be on their guard," Tabitha said. "Let us tell our—well, you tell your dukes and I, I shall—"

"You shall tell yours." Felicity grinned.

"Oh dear, I am quite behind the times." Beatrice attempted to look innocent and failed utterly. "Have you a Grace to call your own, Tabitha?"

"He is not *my* Grace."

"Such protestations are familiar to me," Felicity mused. "And I daresay Mr. Shakespeare had words to say about a lady doing too much of that." With that, she and Beatrice flounced away.

"Perhaps you ought to retire from duchessing and take to the stage yourself!" Tabitha called.

One final glance around the village green revealed Asquith was not wandering at will; Tabitha strolled through the inn's forecourt and peeked around the corner into the stable yard. The bear's lead was tied to a post while Mr. Quincy mucked out her stall.

Tabitha looked at the bear, and the bear... looked back.

She took a step forward—and Mr. Quincy did not hesitate to put himself between her and his charge. "Sorry, my lady, but she's had enough excitement for one day."

"It is *miss*, not *my lady*." But why should he know that? "I am Miss Barrington and would like to discuss a matter with you and your company tomorrow. Shall we say midday? It would be my pleasure to give you lunch."

As she suspected, no actor worth his salt passed up a free meal. "Thank you, miss, we would be delighted." He winked and flexed his biceps, as unthinkingly as anyone else would blink.

"Until then," she said. He bowed; she nodded and turned to leave. As she did, the bear peeked around his back and *looked* at her. At a loss, Tabitha waved, and she swore the creature rolled its eyes and sighed.

Sixteen

LOST IN THOUGHT OVER THE BEAR, AND SUS-pecting the worst, Tabitha wandered back to the cottage—back home. She ought to be thinking of it as home by now. *Home,* she thought as she stood in the dooryard…it did not resonate.

Inside, a note from Timothy informed her he had gone in search of the gossip around what had transpired in the village, with a pointed reference to another gift on their doorstep which he had laid on her pillow.

It was a hair ribbon, a hue of mustard that did not look pretty, but once she held it up to her hair, it glowed like gold. So ladies did wear things that matched their hair…or rather brought out the best in both the hair and the ribbon. Another feminine thing she did not know.

What was feminine? She could not accept it had only to do with ribbons and frocks. Some of the fiercest women she had ever met had been about the work of childbed, as dauntless in their mission to bring forth life as any man on a battlefield was to end it. Added to that, the other women in the room doing everything required in support of the imminent mother—nations of the world wished they could inspire that kind of unity.

The turmoil in her head was not helped by the stuffiness in the room; throwing open the curtains revealed Llewellyn below. She raised the sash and leaned on the sill.

"*What light*, et cetera." He did not continue and shrugged.

"Not the aficionado of the theater that Osborn is?" He didn't quite smile, but his face threatened one, revealing crinkles at his eyes that were a dastardly accompaniment to those lashes. While she was not the devotee of dimples her brother was, Llewellyn had creases alongside his mouth that were far more appealing. No callow youth, he. "We are to be given *Hamlet*, not *Romeo and Juliet*."

"I dislike that play."

"As do I!" Tabitha leaned forward precipitously, and he was at the side of the house in a heartbeat.

"I find that surprising given your penchant for poisons." Laughter helped settle her mind and was like the breath of fresh air she was taking. "The ribbon looks well in your hair," he said.

It was all she could do not to fuss with it. "I do not often wear ribbons."

"They are pretty and serve a purpose." He leaned a hip against the low wall behind the kitchen lean-to.

"Pretty is nothing in comparison to elegant and

fashionable and…" She trailed off and received the familiar scowl in response to her unfinished thought. "Nothing. Thank you. Though I cannot imagine what you were thinking."

Had she thought the lashes an outrage? Those eye crinkles would be her downfall. "I was thinking you might brush out your hair and tie it back and then touch yourself again."

"Your Grace!" Tabitha almost fell out the window. "Hush! How dare you lurk and watch me in a vulnerable moment."

"I did not see." Unfair deployment of lowered lashes ensued. "I heard. I…scented."

"Hush, hush!" She covered her face, more appalled at her missish dithering than anything else.

"Must we discuss it in this fashion?"

She dropped her hands to glare down at him. "Would you like an invitation indoors?"

"Why, thank you kindly," he said. Llewellyn leaped onto the wall, scaled the side of the kitchen, vaulted off its roof, and landed right on her window-sill. Tabitha fell back to sit on the bed. He shook his hair out of his face. "I tire of haunting the periphery."

"Like *The Savage Specter of Crowell Mall*, by our illustrious visitor." Thinking of it, that novel also seemed to take the Lowell Pack as its pattern. *Crowell Mall* was a terrible name if one considered it too closely.

"One of the equestrian masters used to read

aloud to the others, tales of the dead come back to life. I have no way of knowing if any of them were hers. She is quite—" He started to say more but stopped and shook his head.

"She is talented and beautiful." And possibly perfidious, but did Tabitha think so out of envy? Perhaps she had been wrong in her assumptions about the lady author.

Arms crossed over a chest that seemed to be expanding by the minute. "I hope you are not comparing yourself to her."

Tabitha curled her toes into the rug beside her bed. "Of course not, she is rather perfect."

"You sound cross." Llewellyn settled on his heels, perfectly balanced on the sill.

"I am out of sorts, according to my brother."

"You were out of sorts with me. After we kissed at the meal."

They did rather more than kiss. "Yes."

"Why?" He wrapped his arms around his knees.

She kicked out her legs and shook her head. "I do not know how to do this."

"Do you not?"

"I know how to do bed things, but not…courtship or, or any of that." She wiggled in place. What in the world was wrong with her? "I find this awkward. I—I don't know about proceeding in the usual way. The man and woman way. I had no desire for more than brief liaisons. I mean to say—though it was merely research for my comparative matrix—I chose carefully, I was not profligate, but I did not…"

"Did not?"

"Care."

He grinned slowly, slid off the sill, and prowled the few steps to stand before her, and said something that was likely saucy in—

"Welsh?" she guessed.

"It is. My language is coming back to me. My senses are restoring themselves. I was so far gone, I did not think I would return. I wanted Georgie to put me down as he did that rogue of Osborn's, as his father failed to do with Castleton." He reached out and toyed with the ends of her ribbon. "Now, I wake in the morning and feel the beauty of the world around me as I have not since before Drake's. I lay that in your lap."

"It was merely the work of my instincts." She clutched her hands in that lap lest she reach out and wrap them around his slim hips. "And time. Time heals all wounds."

"It was more than that, but I will say nothing else on that score, at this stage." He knelt before her. "As I have said, I am no longer your client."

"You would be my suitor." Where had he gotten that coat? It fit him well, and the dark blue made his mane look like wheat ripe for the harvest. Tabitha ran her hand down one of the lapels.

"I would be your lover if you would choose me."

The duke held out his hand, and she placed hers in it. "I do not like to hear you compare yourself to that lady author. I would not like to hear you compare yourself to anyone." He laid a kiss on her palm. "Your instincts are worth following. They are excellent and exhilarating"—he kissed her hand again—"compelling, alluring"—and again and again.

Kiss by kiss, her envy dissolved, her sulk faded. "I have never been accused of being alluring, of causing exhilaration."

"*Homo plenum* see through the eyes of tiresome convention, which deems what they are meant to find appealing." His Grace—Alwyn—released her hand and laid his arms on either side of her thighs to rest on the bed. His upturned face looked healthy, and *oh*, he was so handsome. "Their greatest fear is to run against the opinions of the pack. Or herd. They are more like cows, clustering together in fear of the unknown. You are as sleek as a gazelle, my lady, yet exhibit the ferocity"—he punctuated this with a nip on her knee—"of the females of my kind. Lionesses...and the Welsh."

Tabitha framed his face in her hands, ran her thumbs down the creases by his mouth, evidence of a history of smiles. Her fingers sought out the tangles in his hair, and his eyes warmed, the changeable hazel edging toward amber rather than the usual green. She tilted her head down just as he rose on his knees, and their mouths met.

Kissing him was as natural as breathing, as the sun rising, as fields greening in the spring. No one's kiss had ever inflamed her so, made her want more, to take more, to give more.

His hand cupped the outside of her thighs, his thumbs rubbing against her *vastus lateralis* and evoking feeling in a way quite different to when she tried to release cramping after a run. She smiled and imagined those hands helping her after her usual ten miles. He murmured inquisitively.

"When I was often impatient to run..." she began.

"You? Impatient?" He nibbled on her lower lip. "Never."

Tabitha pinched his ear, and he shivered. That invited further investigation: she ran her thumbs around the outer edge, and his hands convulsively grasped her thighs. She smiled again. "When I was impatient, and I did not take care to warm my muscles before exertion, the pain afterward was almost beyond the help of arnica. A massage at your hands would be an excellent tonic."

Llewellyn leaned in and kissed her, sucked on her lower lip, wandered over to nip her jaw. "Hmmm," he murmured. He sat back on his heels and ran his hands down to her ankles, then back up to her calves, and squeezed. He tickled her knees and lay his hands back on her thighs, now under her skirts. He squeezed there; her arousal rushed in, and he grinned again, a roguish thing she found she adored.

Back up on his knees, he nuzzled at her jaw. "You say you have experienced lovemaking?" His tongue rasped underneath her ear, an invigorating sensation. Ears: so sensitive, yet she had not known. She wanted to moan like a wanton—so she did.

"I have," she managed. "It made no sense to remain uninformed if I was to advise others regarding their, uh. Senses. No sense. Nonsense. Ahhhh…" His tongue continued on its tour of devastation, down the side of her neck to the inch of collarbone that peeked above the neckline of her dress.

"So you were merely on the hunt for knowledge." His hands gripped her hips and slid her across the bed; he nuzzled her belly as he rucked up her skirt and petticoat. She wiggled to help the process along.

He diverted his attention to her garters and untied one, then the other, with his teeth. "Oh!" Tabitha's head fell back. "I learned—huh, uh"—he rolled her stockings down with his nose—"that the fuss seemed unsubstantiated."

"What poor tutors you employed," he said and ran his tongue up the inside of her thigh.

"Alwyn." Oh, the look on his face when she called him by his name. "It is the middle of the day."

"I admit, it is not the common hour for

lovemaking." He nosed his way around her knee and stopped. "If you are more comfortable waiting for a more conventional time…"

Tabitha jabbed her toes in his ribs. "A statement guaranteed to ensure my participation."

"*Cariad.*" He nuzzled her *vastus medialis.* "Have you experienced this aspect of love in the past? When the man uses his mouth?"

"Not to any great effect." Blessed Palu: lashes, smile creases, and eye crinkles conspired to bring her to release before he'd even touched her.

"Let me make my best effort." He lapped at her inner thigh. "You have only to say if you wish me to desist." He lapped at the other, rubbed his cheek against the sensitive skin, and shouldered her knees farther apart.

It wasn't the heat he gave off, the strength of his hands, the texture of his hair—it was everything, all at once: these elements taken discretely were intoxicating enough but together held her senses in suspension, in tension, in the anticipation of his mouth on her—*oh*.

His shoulders slid up her legs and spread them farther as she arched her back. No tentative touch from His Grace of Llewellyn, no hesitation: his tongue stroked and delved, found her clitoris without wavering, and laved it over and over like it was the sweetest thing he had ever sampled.

The duke's hands cupped her bum and tilted her

hips closer; every muscle in her body felt as though turned to water, the blood in her veins rushing to support the thunder of her heart. She reached down and sifted her fingers through his hair. When he used his lips to suck, she closed her fingers suddenly enough to evoke a growl—not a warning but encouragement. Tabitha's hips began to rock in a fluid rhythm to match his, and if not for the ribbon in her hair, it would be as snarled as his was a few days ago.

His Grace—Alwyn—ran his hands over her ribs and expertly loosened her front-tied soft corset just enough to slip his hand beneath and cup her breasts. For the first time, Tabitha was not embarrassed by their size; they fit perfectly in his palms. Her nipples stiffened to the point of exquisite pain, and when his thumbs brushed over both, her hips came off the bed. He turned his head and smiled into her thigh.

Keeping one of her breasts in the care of a palm, he slid his other hand down to join his lips and tongue, licking and stroking until she lost all sense, all sense of time, of place, of anything but his mouth, his hands, and his complete devotion to her pleasure. She whispered his name, once, twice, as it built, *le petit mort,* every inch of her skin afire, every limb quivering, unlike any release she'd ever experienced. The muscles of her legs tightened around his shoulders, her heels dug into his back, both hands gripped in his hair until the final tension, and then over the precipice she went, shuddering and shivering with it. He was relentless and chased for more, one more quiver, one more gasp, until she begged, "Stop, stop," and he did.

He wrapped his arms around her waist and pulled her into a soothing embrace that was the perfect complement to his efforts, his hands stroking up and down her back as she came down to earth.

She sighed and wriggled, his arms tightening around her before releasing. He laid his head on her belly, and she stroked his hair and wished for this moment to carry on forever, that they may never have to leave this bed, this embrace.

"You appear to be all that is satisfied," he murmured at her hip.

"If there is a way to be more than satisfied, I am that." She used both hands on his scalp and he made noises the mirror of her own in the throes. "Your skull is very sensitive. I have never come across such a responsive cranium." She pressed again at the area above his ears, and he moaned. "I would say you had a hair trigger, but that is a terrible pun."

"My—" He tensed and paused before continuing. "There are many who like a good pun."

"That's not what we call it where I come from." She encouraged him to lie beside her and whispered in his ear, "May I return the favor?"

Downstairs, the front door flew open as only

Timothy could make it fly; she heard it slam against the wall behind it even as he called, "Tab? Are you in?"

"I—uh." She stood and shook her skirt and petticoat into place, her hair at sixes and sevens despite the ribbon, all her lovely looseness lost. She heard Timothy take the first stair, the second, and cracked open the door to shout, "I'll be right down, uh, yes, just—caught napping," she called.

"Alwyn—" Gone. No surprise there. He had not stirred the air with his departure, and no sound issued from his leap to the ground.

———

Mr. Quincy had the responsibility of the bear, and it was work he took pleasure in. It had been a strange thing, coming across this tame beast as they made their way south from Scotland. They had not been long on their journey out of Inverness when they encountered the poor thing, her skin hanging off her, dying of thirst. It was not as though they could drive on; what sort of folk would do so? It was Quincy's opinion the bear had been abandoned by a circus, for no one else would have the keeping of such a creature. It was a disgrace was what it was, and while his brother-in-law and sister agreed they could not leave her, they were less keen to tend her.

But Quincy had a gift for it, and the bear seemed to prefer him.

"You do prefer me, don't you? You listened to me over all them dukes and lords and whatnot. What set you off, my friend? Were you frightened? I think you were." He added more straw to the horse stall in which the bear was being kept and laid out an extra share of feed; anything drenched in honey was welcome. If the price came out of his pocket, what of it? He lacked for nothing, was living his dream of performing across the British Isles, so a few quid here or there to give the bear something she liked was nothing to him.

"You seem full of life. I have not seen you so alert since you joined our little troupe." He set the cleaned and filled water bucket next to the oats before he stepped out. "Now, then. That ought to set you right until the morrow. Sweet dreams, if dreaming is something you sort can do."

He slid the bolt home even as the bear rose to her hind legs and snarled. "Here, here, what is it? You need your rest if we're to do a play for the dukes and duchesses on the morrow. Imagine that, us playing before the highest in society—oh."

Was the bear angry a stranger entered her territory? For someone had come upon them: moonlight limned a figure standing in the doorway of the stable. Quincy walked toward the intruder to prevent them from coming closer to the bear. "Hello there. May I help you?"

"Oh yes," came a sibilant hiss, "you may."

Seventeen

THE DAY OF THE PLAY WAS AT HAND. THE LADY author had been circumspect in her movements within the Close; Tabitha had lunched with Mr. and Mrs. Peasely, the strongman oddly absent, and quizzed the coach house Becketts about Asquith's behavior, which was apparently above reproach.

Tabitha was not taking any chances, given *versipellian* senses, and decided her brooding place beneath the chestnut tree was the best spot to meet her putative suitors. The footmen Timothy set to their tasks had no sooner returned to the cottage bearing the fruits of their labors than Tabitha asked them to deliver three notes.

The recipients approached from different directions with glowing faces, but the closer they came, the less pleased they looked. Mr. Padmore's face naturally lent itself to dolorousness, and Mr. Giles looked more cross than upset. Mr. Beckett sighed with resignation.

"I hope I did not give the wrong impression by corresponding with you." As direct as her wording had been—*I have concerns regarding the lady author and would discuss them*—who knew if that could be construed as romantic to a male of any species.

"If we had hopes, they are dashed," said Mr. Beckett.

"The duke has made his claim." Mr. Giles stamped a foot.

"Without going into too much detail, miss"—Mr. Padmore blinked his great big eyes at her—"you are redolent of lion."

"Didn't think he could manage a scenting without his essential self in good nick," the goat whined.

"For if he were in harmony with his lion, there would be no question as to his ability to Change," Mr. Beckett explained.

Here was an opportunity for another point of view she had not thought to consult. "I had been told if His Grace didn't Change, he would die."

Mr. Giles shook his head, his little beard quivering. "Us prey don't be Changing all over the shop, willy-nilly," he said. "It's not the end of the world if we don't Shift even for a month at a time."

"And if we Shift due to a big fright, like if we've been taken unawares by a predator," Mr. Padmore explained, "we like to keep to our human Shapes for a good while."

"Often, after a shock, our essential self goes off on its own to recover until they can come back to us," Mr. Beckett concluded.

"Goes off?" Tabitha asked. "As on a journey? To a physical place?"

The three gents looked at one another; the frog shook his head, and the goat shrugged. Mr. Beckett grimaced. "Well, just goes to a place where it takes time," he said. "To feel...not afraid anymore."

Tabitha cast an eye at the canopy of the chestnut tree. "Yes, I understand that impulse."

"If you don't mind my saying, it is not impulsive but instinctual," Mr. Beckett said. "The higher-ups would have a different view of it."

"Like it was cowardly." Mr. Giles scoffed. "But it is a necessity if one is to return to full strength and trust. In one's instincts and the world."

"And is it known amongst all *versipelles*?" This was knowledge she could have used. How was it that O'Mara was not aware of this? Or had she withheld it on purpose?

Mr. Padmore laughed. "We don't be knowing what the Quality knows."

"Even though you are connected to your Alpha, and through him, the pack?"

"That's in the heart, not the head, miss," Mr. Beckett corrected. "There's no words in the *sentio*, only feelings."

Feelings. "Gentlemen, I have learned much today. I am very grateful," Tabitha said. "And now I must ask more of you."

"We are at your service, miss," Mr. Giles said.

"You are aware gold is used to entrap *versipelles*," she began. She explained the threat presented by the lady author; it was all supposition and frankly sounded like a fairy story. She had no real evidence to support any of it, but the three fellows listened carefully and did not seem to find it outrageous. She impressed upon them the unease she felt at the sight of the pendant Asquith had made to appear and disappear, like a conjuror. "Please do take care. I believe she uses that chain for nefarious purposes."

"The likes of us aren't what she's after," Mr. Padmore said.

"I'd like to see her try for me." Mr. Beckett puffed out his narrow chest.

"I can be right stubborn when the situation calls for it," Mr. Giles boasted.

"I am sure your Alpha has alerted you to his discomfort through the *sentio*," Tabitha said.

"Discomfort is right," Mr. Padmore groaned. "If only O'Mara were here to temper it. We do miss her something fierce."

"I am sorry I didn't get to know her better." Tabitha truly did regret it. "We did not agree on how to help His Grace, and I tread on her patch. I am going to go even further and tread on that of your Alpha and ask you to spread the word of my concerns throughout the village and anywhere else on Lowell lands you think is best. And please, keep a weather eye on the Humphries cubs." The three easygoing gentlemen suddenly looked as fierce as any wolf or bear or lion.

"I expect we will meet everyone from the pack at the performance," Mr. Beckett said. "Once there, we shall split up and do as you ask."

With one last woeful glance from Mr. Padmore, the three *versipelles* made for the Close, and she turned toward the cottage.

Tabitha would have to revise her thoughts about feelings, if that was not a contradiction. Had discomfort with her own emotions prevented her from being as helpful as she could have been in the past? She admitted to impatience with the ladies who only ever wanted to talk about gentlemen and now saw she had not been as compassionate as she might have been.

How did it feel to be connected to a *sentio*, as the Lowell Pack was? It must be a relief to know that another's heart was not one's sole responsibility, and conversely, to know one's own was held in reverence, in community.

Ought she to have told the Lowell Alpha of her plan to alert the pack? She was so unused to consulting with anyone apart from Timothy. She at least should send a note to Mr. Gambon. This was in the Third's remit, going between the greater body of the pack and their Alpha. Tabitha would let him know what she'd done. It was better to have the process started sooner rather than later. It was better to have done something rather than nothing.

At least O'Mara's absence could not be laid at her door. That Irish mister-lord must have erred prodigiously to inspire such fury in the cool and calm Omega. Now that Tabitha felt like less of an outsider, it would have been good to try working with O'Mara again, each to the best use of their talents. That thing the Omega did, the *moohoo* or however it was called—drove Tabitha wild with curiosity; but otherwise, O'Mara was as close to a colleague as she was going to come across in these environs. Particularly given Tabitha's departure into the world of fantasy and speculation, populated with vile lady authors and their chilling pendulums.

She was living in a world of fantasy, for the love of Palu—to the degree that she had begun to invoke foreign goddesses! She had always followed her instincts, only to be ignored; here, amongst the *versipelles*, she was sought out even if her usual cures were not needed. Little she had ever relied upon had come in useful with Llewellyn, bar the hair tonic; and yet, how far he had come in almost no time at all.

Tabitha sniffed her wrist: How was she *redolent of lion*? She had washed quite thoroughly last night, given the events of the afternoon, and scented nothing but the almond of the soap she made. Her senses were most likely not elevated enough to, to smell him on her. Her comparative matrix had no data when it came to the scent of another, as she'd never paid it mind before, beyond being part and parcel of the act. She had rolled herself in her sheets after Alwyn had left so precipitously and reveled in them but had not lingered and now regretted it. She'd bustled the sheets into their little laundry and set them to the boil. Luckily it was her dedicated chore, even though Timothy gave her a look, as it was not even close to washing day.

Maybe if one took a Shapeshifter as a lover, some of the essence was shared? If so, it was a wonder he could share it if, as they explained, his lion was… away. How far away? And for how much longer? Did the larger *versipelles* know what the smaller knew? One would think so, as any good predator must know the mind of its prey.

Lost in thought, she was steps from her door when Mr. Quincy charged into her path.

"My lady!"

"That is not the proper address—"

"Your Grace!"

Neither was that, by a long chalk; nevertheless, it gave her the tingles. "Mr. Quincy, I have already introduced myself as Miss Barring—"

"You are needed in the wood! This wood, this deep, dark expanse of, of trees! For the Wild Lion of Wales has returned and is running amok!"

Her first thought: *He has Changed and will not die!* Her second: *Has he? Really?* For Mr. Quincy's gaze was unfocused, as though he were not fully present in the moment. His movements, for a seasoned performer, were unconvincing and awkward, his speech overblown and halting.

It was entirely possible he was a poor actor; either way, Tabitha was not convinced.

"And who sends this message?"

Mr. Quincy goggled at her; she had apparently gone off script. "You must follow me, for you alone can tame the Wild Lion of Wales!" He threw his arms wide, imploring; then he flung them to the left, into the wood she and Alwyn had hiked to view the *cursio*. When she did not move, he flung them again in the direction he wished her to go.

She should take the time to leave a note for Timothy but reckoned that would ruin the narrative flow of the showman's production. This was not the work of a friend and was likely driven by malice, but the need to know what this little drama was about was too much for her.

"Lead the way," she said, and he did.

Once out of sight of the cottage, Mr. Quincy veered off west and into a part of the wood that did not invite trespassers, at least not of the two-legged variety. The deep underbrush and the closely grown trees would suit the smaller Shapeshifters, the mice and the squirrels and the ferrets. Her foot slid on the mulch of leaves, on earth that never saw the sun. Brambles—again, lovely for the mice—tore at her skirts, at her coat. Having such a large figure to follow did not help, as Mr. Quincy, despite the size of his frame, wafted through the narrow spaces between trees and bushes like a vapor. Low-hanging branches slashed at her face, she slipped and slid again, into the oppressive dark, and up ahead, in the first example of a clearing they'd yet to come across, the actor stumbled and started to fall to his knees. Tabitha darted forward; as she reached for him, he eeled out of her grasp, and she lost her balance and tumbled into a pit.

A pit. That had been camouflaged with cut branches. A pit dug in the middle of the wood where no one her size would wander. She picked up one of the branches, from a tree she'd never come across. She sniffed it, and it smelled like nothing, chewed on a leaf (she could hear Llewellyn's outraged growl in her ear) but tasted nothing. She stood and felt her ankle give; she had turned it just enough to be painful. "Wonderful," she muttered. "Mr. Quincy? If you would lend a hand? I find myself in difficulty—"

A figure appeared at the edge of the pit to perch like a gargoyle. "Oh, yes, you are indeed in difficulty."

"Asquith." Tabitha would not bother with the title she suspected was wholly fictional. "How unexpected."

"Barrington. How easily you fell into my trap, figuratively and literally."

"I won't say this comes as a complete surprise."

Tabitha took another step and did her best to suppress a wince.

It was not missed by the sharp eyes of the snake Shifter. "Oh, no, have you come to harm? Whatever will happen when the Duke of Llewellyn finds out? It is well-known he does not Change. Will he do so, to save his sweet virgin bride?"

"I am none of that," Tabitha muttered. She waved a branch of the strange plant. "What is this?"

"It is called *neem*," Asquith said. "It is known to hide the scent of those who wish it hidden. For example, a *versipellis* who does not wish to be known as one. It will prevent your scent to be discovered."

Except for the fact her scent could be followed this far and thus lure Llewellyn straight into Asquith's clutches. "And it grows wild in this place? I wouldn't think it was allowed. That sort of deception could prove dangerous."

"I cultivate it myself and brought it with me."

"In one of your trunks? That was well plotted." Tabitha tossed aside her branch of neem after slipping some leaves in her coat pocket. "I suppose that comes from churning out those novels at the rate you do."

"You think yourself so worldly with all the traveling you have done, but when it comes to commerce, you know nothing."

Tabitha heard Mr. Quincy mutter, "Where

am I?" and saw Asquith strike, whipping out her chain and pendant and letting it sway until the man settled. Tabitha looked away, for even as far down in the ground as she was, it had a dreadful effect on her.

"As I was saying," Asquith began, and the chain once again vanished from sight, "I require far more to sustain my lifestyle than I can earn as a writer, despite my devastating popularity. You would be amazed at what a lord or an earl would pay to avoid being exposed in one of my stories."

Tabitha tried her ankle again; she had wrenched it comprehensively. "No one would believe it."

"No human." Asquith left simpering behind; her voice was as hard as the rock at the bottom of the pit. "But a *versipellis* would read the truth between the lines, and it would not go well for the lord or the earl."

"I understand His Highness does not involve himself in these matters. Whose authority would you expect to render justice?"

"It would be a very rough form of justice, Barrington, and nothing to do with the crown." Asquith brushed her hands, encased in those scaly gloves, down the front of her expensive pelisse. "I have risked my ensemble to come here to you. You will be guarded by that easily influenced *homo plenus*—it was child's play, really—until I release him from my power. I will put it about that you have been abducted. Perhaps your suitor will become paralyzed by grief, and therefore easily snared by the sort of poachers his kind often attract."

"He will look for me." She knew he would, and it was an equally terrible outcome.

Even in the dim light of the deep wood, Tabitha could see the lady author's nasty smirk. "That, too, is an acceptable twist of plot."

Eighteen

THE PAGEANT WAGON, AXLE REPAIRED, STOOD IN all its glory on the edge of the village green, transforming the heart of Lowell Close into a theater. While many larger vehicles of its kind had a second story to double the playing space, this one was modest yet by no means the lesser for it. One of the long sides of the wagon folded down in front to form a platform; curtains hung from the base to the ground on all sides to conceal the wheels and provide a changing room and a place for props to be easily retrieved during the run of the show. A painted garden hung as a backdrop, and a bench was set in the center, with banners concealing offstage left and right. It looked as any traveling playing space would but for the bear crouched in the corner.

The bear, who was becoming increasingly distraught. Alwyn wanted to ask Miss Barrington—*Tabitha*—what she saw when she looked at the creature, for she would see that something was not right.

Every stratum of the Lowell Pack was represented, from the servants and footmen in the

Hall to the shopkeepers and crafts folk of the Close, to their Alpha and Gamma, who moved throughout the crowd greeting one and all. The Humphries were present, and it was all Ben could do to keep his cubs from running onto the stage to get a closer look at the ursine participant. The Duchess of Osborn had a composed look on her face that Alwyn perceived as boding ill, or at least unusually watchful for a pleasant day of entertainment. Lowell's duchess had the same stillness about her, like an eagle in an eyrie, waiting patiently for its prey.

Alwyn discerned a counterpoint to Lowell and Gambon's movement: that bee, and that goat, and that frog, in a pincer movement, whispered into the ears of all they met. Nods and determined expressions fell in their wake, and casually, but with purpose, the multitude drew in a protective phalanx around the Humphries cubs.

There were far too many gathered for his comfort, but Alwyn could not resist a production of *Hamlet*, and one that ran less than one hour at that. He scanned the crowd once more: Where was his lady apothecary? Had he put her off? There was no doubt he'd gotten her off. He rasped a laugh to himself and heard—

Felt, inside—

An answering snort.

He retreated from the green until his back hit the

base of a mighty oak; without a second thought, he scrambled up into its branches. His foot slipped, and his essential self corrected for them before he could even consider the likelihood of falling.

My friend. Alwyn wrapped an arm around the trunk and placed his free hand over his heart.

I am here.

His lion expanded to fill his aura. *I thought... they thought it was willful of me, to resist the Change, but I feared...*

There would be nothing to Change into.

My friend, my friend, forgive me. I abandoned you. He rested his head against the trunk of the tree, and the sounds from below faded as their connection strengthened. *I did not want to pursue you merely to allay the fears of others.*

His lion huffed in that familiar way that said he heard his human's reasoning and found it wanting. *We did what our prey does when it eludes us and still contains the terror. I retreated until I came back to myself. Thus I have and now come back to you.*

The sense of rightness was like to make his heart burst. *Was there anything I could have done?*

What a joy to feel the exasperation of his essential self. *All was done according to the will of Palu. And*—a purr rolled through Alwyn's aura—*our reward is to defer to the will of our* vera amoris.

I hoped that was so. Alwyn tipped his head back and breathed, long and deep, and for the first time in a long time, both breathed in concert, in freedom. *She has a gift: she can see the essential self of a Shifter without being told. What do we know of this?*

Silence met his query, not the silence of absence but of thought. Blessed Palu, there was nothing to stop him now.

This is not known in our lineage, his lion said. *Is it due to her humanity, perhaps?*

We shall discover the meaning of it, Alwyn vowed. They settled onto the tree branch, in harmony once more. Alwyn's heart opened, and a tension quivered, released, then snapped like a fishing line pulled taut. Was that Tabitha? She was very cross indeed. The connection was not fine enough to tell more than that.

Be wary of vexing our lady, his lion teased. *She will repay you in kind.*

I am wary of that lady author. The snarl that statement evoked alarmed him. *What is it, friend?*

She is not what she seems. I can say no more than that.

Alwyn would not trouble his lion as he had been troubled. *In your own good time, then.*

Someone has learned patience. His creature sounded amused and pleased.

He gave it thought. *It was a lesson learned in a contemptible way. I had nothing to do but wait and hope you would not forget me. I was worthy of being forgotten, falling for that low trick.*

No, his lion said, resolute. *I would do nothing differently, even unto captivity once more. For what sort of man, what sort of creature are we to abandon one in need?*

If it was possible, Alwyn's heart expanded even further; his connection to Tabitha—for who else could it be?—blossomed further. *You are far stronger than I am.*

Impossible, for your strength has given me this time to rest. We will need all our power, for our lady apothecary is quite the match for us.

Exhilaration ran through them both at the thought of her. Alwyn said, *My friend, I am convinced it is the* coniunctio—

A gong sounded.

The assembled crowd, rather than stand about as was customary, had set themselves down on blankets, with picnics; all applauded the appearance of the Peaselys.

The lady actor set the gong aside as her husband stepped to the lip of the stage. "Welcome, one and all, to today's performance of *The Tragedy of Hamlet, Prince of Denmark.* The Peasley Troupe of Traveling Players is renowned for our precise presentations of the classics of world theater, and this is no different—"

"It is, I'm afraid," Mrs. Peasley cut off her husband. "One of our number is unable to perform."

Arthur popped up like a vole from a hole. "If

it would be any use at all, I confess I have the text down by heart." Osborn's little duchess beamed up at him, and his nephew and nieces cheered as the lady player waved him to the stage.

"It is unlike any Hamlet you may have seen," she cautioned him, as he joined the diminished company.

"I am particularly well acquainted with the solil-oquies." Osborn drew a deep breath. "*Oh, what a rogue and peasant slave am I—*"

"You're to play the secondary parts." Mrs. Peasley cut across him. "That is, Your Grace. Sir. A walking gentleman, like, with a word or two here and there."

"Ah, yes, well, each role is part of the whole, as they say," Osborn mumbled.

"Then let us begin. We have been asked to start with 'The Mousetrap,'" Mr. Peasley announced. He closed the curtains that flanked the proscenium.

"The what now?" asked Mary Mossett. "I don't like the sound of that, sure I don't."

Footsteps and muttering were heard as the company took their places. A trill of a harp sounded as the curtain parted to reveal a king taking his ease on the garden bench, sleeping the sleep of the just. Osborn stood upstage, holding a wooden box; the lady actor, garbed as a sinister masked figure, removed something from it and turned to address the crowd.

"*Thoughts black, hands apt,* ehhh, oh yes, *golden*

chain, and time agreeing—" Mrs. Peasley lifted her hands to reveal the necklace, to shocked gasps from the entire assembly. Neither she nor her husband had expected such a reaction from a seemingly simple adjustment to the text; consummate professionals that they were, they milked it for all it was worth. She drew out the rest of the speech, all the while lifting the necklace, lowering it to drape over Mr. Peasley's neck, who shook violently in his "sleep" each time it came near. As she delivered the line, "*Thy natural magic and dire property/On wholesome life usurp immediately,*" she lowered it for the last time to shouts from the audience that she desist—

When the lady author ran in front of the stage and threw out her arms. "I bring disastrous news!"

"Shush!" Mr. Peasley cracked open one eye. "This is the important bit."

To cover the disturbance, Arthur stepped forward. "*Why, let the stricken deer go weep/The hart ungallèd play—*"

"No, no, that's been changed as well," Mrs. Peasley said. "I mean, Your Grace, if it's all the same to you, you're to say the *stricken lion—*"

"Woe is me!" Asquith's moan carried across the green to where Alwyn lurked. "There has been a disaster!"

She lies, his lion rumbled.

Mr. Peasley flapped a hand at her. "Hush, lady, you are out of order."

"A lion?" Arthur looked confused. "Have you a text I might consult?"

Mrs. Peasley shook her head. "It was the lady apothecary who gave us the notes."

The lady author gasped. "It is she of whom I speak!"

"What news, Mrs. Asquith?" Lowell's duchess cried as she rose and approached the stage. "I fear the worst!"

"I suspect Miss Barrington has been abducted! And for nefarious reasons, not those under which you were taken by the duke." Mrs. Asquith gestured to Lowell, who had joined his wife.

Alwyn could not believe what he was seeing. *Does no one else suspect she lies?*

His lion sniffed the air. *They do, but they are cozening her to discover her plan.*

Alwyn and his lion slid down the tree without shaking a single leaf, prowled around the back of the pageant wagon, and crouched behind one of the wheels.

"Another abduction?" The Duchess of Osborn added her voice to the tumult, a cool dash of water in the face of the unfolding drama. "We have only recovered from the one last visited upon us when Hallbjorn captured Ursella."

"What an astonishing coincidence," said Osborn, who stepped forward to the edge of the stage.

"Such as one taken from the pages of your

books," Lowell said. Mr. Barrington stood some distance from them all, wringing his handkerchief.

"My novels do not rely upon such low devices as that," Mrs. Asquith was quick to retort. "It is true that I may be mistaken. I went to consult with her as I had slept poorly the night before and sought one of her concoctions. Her little shack was at sixes and sevens, herbs tossed hither and yon."

"Was there perhaps a letter lying about the place?" asked Lowell's duchess.

Mrs. Asquith squinted suspiciously and produced a scrap of parchment from behind her skirts. "There was, Your Grace. I did not like to read it myself."

"I shall do so." Osborn's Second snatched the paper out of the lady's hand. She commenced reading it aloud, in a tone one reserved for reading a shopping list for the mercer. "My dearest brother Timothy, I find I cannot accept the attentions of His Grace the Duke of Llewellyn and must flee. I shall take ship to the Antipodes, for his passions overwhelm me so—I cannot fly far enough away. Do not think to follow me, as I will be beyond your reach by the time you read this. Sincerely, your sister, Tabitha Barrington."

"How strange that she would write such a formal note," Mr. Barrington observed.

The lady author shouted, "We must act, this is nonsense!" Alwyn made to spring from his concealment, and his lion held him back, surging into his aura with sufficient strength that Osborn and Lowell looked around for the threat.

Patience, friend, his lion cautioned. *We shall receive our cue.*

"If Miss Barrington were to take ship for Australia," Mr. Peasley offered, "she would have left yesterday, and we were only consulting with her this afternoon."

"Miss Barrington shared our midday meal and offered us some delicious cheese as an accompaniment," Mrs. Peasley added.

"The latest she could have left would have been at least by teatime," said Mr. Bates, who had kept his presence at the entertainment well concealed. "I am very familiar with the timetables, thanks to seeing off several of the Duchess of Lowell's relations."

"I am appalled that my word should be questioned so." Mrs. Asquith voice quivered.

"I agree." Lowell's duchess tapped her chin in an unconvincing manner. "I remember this exact sequence of events unfolded in one of your early novels, *The Mysteries of Woldolpho,* with dire consequences for the heroine. Have any of you read it?" The multitude shook their heads. "Ah, well. It is not amongst your most popular titles."

"How faithful a reader you are, Your Grace." The lady author did not sound pleased to say so.

"As far-fetched as this appears," said Lowell, "we would be remiss did we not search for the lady."

"Do allow me to help as best I can." Mrs. Asquith clenched her hands at her bosom to convey her sincerity. "I would be happy to attend to the younger Humphries."

The crowd stirred, and as one, formed a barrier between the lady author and the children.

The upper echelon put themselves between the crowd and the cubs. Alwyn could see, even with Lowell's renowned control, his claws had sprung from his fingers; Osborn had no control to speak of: as he leaped to the ground, his back to the players, he allowed his fangs to drop. Alwyn's instincts were all in a whirl, and through the tentative, not-at-all-reliable, minor *sentio* of his, he knew Tabitha was nearly upon them.

Alwyn sprang from behind the wagon. "Wait," he said. He held up a hand, and all obeyed, even the other Alphas, and he did not fail to see the nasty—triumphant?—look on the lady author's face.

———

The pit was just deep enough that Tabitha could not pull herself up over the edge. Had poor Mr. Quincy been made to dig it? If so, he had done it in such a way as left the roots of trees to act as handholds and footrests. It was not easy on her ankle, but she contrived and freed herself.

The actor, who had been staring off into the

distance, saw her emerge and threw out his arms as if to block her progress.

"Do forgive me, Mr. Quincy." Tabitha slapped him hard about the face.

He blinked once, twice, thrice, and looked around him in confusion. "What are we doing out here, miss? I did not lure you into the woods, did I? I am sorry to say you're not my preference." He winked and flexed his muscles, out of ingrained habit, for he immediately looked confused again.

"I believe you have been mesmerized by Mrs. Asquith." Tabitha touched the back of her fingers to his forehead; his skin was cool. "What is the last thing you remember?"

The strongman's brow furrowed as he thought. "I was putting the bear to bed as I do every night. She got quite fussed, and I turned around to see who was there, and that is all I know."

"I do not trust that woman. We must hurry back to the village." She took one step, and her ankle let her know it was not going to support a run through the wood.

"The play!" Mr. Quincy tore at his hair and howled to the sky. "I have missed my cue!"

"Come, come"—she waved him over—"lend me your arm and let us make haste. I fear the worst for the Humphries cu—children."

Why would Asquith say *child's play* if she did not mean to capture the cubs? Tabitha would not put it past the lady author to create a disturbance in order to mesmerize the little ones. Even as canny as Ursella was, she was still small and no match for an adult *versipellis*.

Mr. Quincy was an able prop, and while not as graceful as when he was under the power of the pendant, what he lacked in sure-footedness he made up for in sheer strength. They rushed past the Barrington cottage, and he all but carried her down the road to the village. As they approached, they could see the show had been halted and Asquith stood at the foot of the pageant wagon's playing area; the pack subtly gathered around the cubs. Her erstwhile suitors had done the job. She heard Lowell say, "As far-fetched as this appears, we would be remiss did we not search for the lady."

"Do allow me to help as best I can." Mrs. Asquith made a mockery of genuine emotion by clutching her hands at her heart. "I would be happy to attend to the younger Humphries."

"Wait." Tabitha's heart thundered in her breast at the sight of Alwyn so near that woman, at his voice carrying so commandingly.

"That will not be necessary." Mr. Beckett put himself at the front of the crowd that had closed around to protect the children. "The entire village will mind them."

"Again, in *The Mysteries of Woldolpho*—and I am, of course, aware this is true life, not fiction—it transpired that the letter had not been written by the heroine," Felicity said. "I must demand proof my friend wrote the letter."

"I will be able to judge if it is in her hand," Timothy said.

"That will not be necessary." Asquith snatched the letter from Beatrice. "How dare you accuse me of foul play."

"We have not done, as such," Lowell conceded, "but now I feel the need to do so."

"What a weak accusation leveled without proof," Asquith scoffed.

"I present myself as proof," Tabitha said as she limped forward. "As well as the formerly mesmerized Mr. Quincy."

His relations made much of the strongman, and the bear looked happier by the turn of events. Timothy came nearer her side but was cut off by Alwyn, who wrapped an arm around her waist. "You are hurt," he said. His eyes flashed amber, and his brows lowered as he assessed her well-being. She gestured to the stage, and he helped her up onto it.

"I fell into a pit in the middle of the wood, one that had been dug with the express purpose that I fall into it so the Duke of Llewellyn would find me. Mrs. Asquith covered the pit with branches of neem"—this produced a reaction from the audience—"with the intent of forcing His Grace to Change—"

As one, they all looked at the players, who squirmed under the scrutiny. Mrs. Peasley took off the mask she was wearing and had a silent exchange of meaningful looks with her husband. Mr. Peasley cleared his throat.

"Change?" he asked. "Do you mean like the animal-people?"

"We know all about that," Mrs. Peasley said. "Her Grace the Duchess of Osborn, may she rest in peace, took my husband's dad into her confidence. She let us leave our store of costumes up at Arcadia and all."

"It was my granddad," Mr. Peasley corrected.

"Or your great-grandad." His wife shrugged. "At any rate, it is a secret that has been entrusted to us for generations."

The bear let out a sorrowful whine.

"Excellent. Then I may speak freely." Tabitha looked to Lowell for permission, which he granted with a sweep of a hand. "She intended to force His Grace to Change so she may trap him in his Shape."

"This is a serious accusation." Lowell nodded to Mr. Bates, who gathered a fleet of footmen around him. "I will send for His Highness, the Prince of Wales, to lend his gravitas to these circumstances."

"What nonsense." In the blink of an eye, Asquith also mounted the stage. Mr. Quincy put himself between her and the bear; Charlotte and Ben took their children in their arms and gladly accepted the protection of the pack. "I marvel that the word of a *homo plenus* is held in higher regard than one of us."

"You are one of us, and yet you have more than enough gold on your person to hold many here in their Shapes," Alwyn said. "Why would that be, unless your intentions were dire? This is very like the way I was tricked into my captivity. A female in distress called to my essential self, and thus Changed, I was caught."

"What a moving testimony, it makes me want to cry." Asquith made a sound, as Alwyn had described the cry made by the woman in the alley; he fell to his knees as the lady author produced that dratted pendulum and held it aloft.

It did not affect the *homo plenum* as it did the *versipelles*, who, as one, dropped to their knees as Alwyn had. The players' bear howled, and Mr. Quincy struggled to calm her. Mr. and Mrs. Peasley looked to Tabitha for direction, and she found she was as frozen in place as the rest of the assembly. Even with the strength of the Alphas in their midst, none could move a muscle at the sight of it.

Had it to do with that blasted stone? As Asquith swept it 'round, the stone shone brighter and brighter and was somehow more threatening than the gold chain from which it hung. Tabitha could not look at it, for though it was designed to subdue the Shifters, it affected her as well. What was her course of action to be? Panic would not do, she must focus, but her breath arrested, her heart fluttered, her pulse raced—her heart fluttered again, as though it were being nudged for attention. She placed a hand on her sternum, and it pulsed again. She took a breath, deep, breathed again, and felt the thrall of the pendulum lessen, just as the lady author made her way downstage to where Alwyn knelt on the ground.

Tabitha limped forward, one step, another, until she set herself between Asquith and the duke.

The lady author raised her arm high. "You are no match for this, Barrington."

"Am I not?" Tabitha had a choice: stay where she was and protect Alwyn from the mesmerism, or take a risk to save them all.

She knew which choice he would make.

Despite a head-spinning giddiness, Tabitha reached out and grabbed the chain. Both women froze when her hand made contact: the pendulum stopped dead and hung as though drained of its power. The crowd roused to a degree that the lady author sensed the threat. Asquith tugged on the chain, but it would not cede, even to her greater strength. There was another nudge at Tabitha's heart, and with both hands she wrenched it out of the villain's grasp. Tabitha tucked it away even as the Alphas, released from the sorcery, rushed Mrs. Asquith.

No sooner had the chain been taken than the snake Shifter slithered away, stage right.

Tabitha's ankle had taken all the abuse it could, and she sat down, hard. The players' bear roared without ceasing in the background, and the children shrieked a thousand questions at the top of their lungs. More than one of the smaller Shifters had Changed in a panic and fled in a rush of feathers and fur.

Mrs. Peasley threw her mask to the ground. "If you think we're following that, you've got another think coming."

Nineteen

THE MOMENT THEY WERE RELEASED FROM THE thrall, the Lowell Pack rushed to Tabitha's aid. Hands reached to lift her, to pat her shoulder, to straighten her skirts, to inspect her ankle, which was where she called a halt. "It is a mere sprain, nothing an application of a poultice and propping up on a pillow won't cure," she insisted.

Lowell and Osborn returned after failing to hunt down the lady author—lady villain, more like. Mr. Gambon was busily moving amongst those gathered, promising a meeting at the convocation stone, whatever that was, in due course.

Alwyn was nowhere to be seen.

That was not a problem of the first order. The pendant was: the effect that tiny stone and chain had on the populace was not to be denied. "Mr. Gambon," Tabitha called, "I must ask you what just happened."

The boar Shifter urged the crowd about their business and lent her an arm to lean on. "I suspect the stone is a locus of power for the serpentine class," he said. "As you saw, none of us can get near enough to examine it."

"I shall do so in private," Tabitha said. "I would go to my healing shed and see to my ankle."

"Let us help you, miss," Mr. Padmore begged, blinking his large eyes.

"It is the least we can do," Mr. Giles insisted.

"Gentlemen, you rallied the village and protected the cubs. You have already done as much as anyone could do." They beamed at her praise. "I assure you it is not necessary."

"Not necessary but well deserved," said Mr. Beckett, in the way he had of reframing things. She hoped they would be friends; his insights always presented a unique perspective.

Tabitha's erstwhile suitors made a basket of their arms, and Mr. Gambon set her gently into the center. Applause rang out, and the men carried her back to the cottage, her brother leading the way as though he were the lord mayor at the head of a parade.

She was set on a chair in the shed as gently as a baby was put into its cradle; there was jostling in the yard as more villagers sought entry. She made a face at Timothy, who herded everyone out with thanks and promises to keep them apprised of her recovery. Her escorts bowed and left, and she allowed herself to slump against the cushions, the pain in her ankle reaching its peak. She fumbled in her pocket for the pendulum when her brother returned.

"This stone, Tim, I am sure I have never seen—"
Yet it was not Timothy in the door but Alwyn.

She hurriedly put it out of his sight. "Your Grace.
I hope you were not affected by the sight of that
odious gem."

He said nothing. He stood there, simply looking
at her. The clothing he sported was out of the usual
run of his idiosyncratic regalia and more what any
man would wear, even if still slightly too loose.
He had eschewed a cravat as well as buttoning the
shirt; his exposed throat was oddly evocative to
gaze upon.

"Must you loom?" She rose, and he took a step
forward.

"Must you throw yourself into danger without
thought?" There was an increase of power around
him she didn't recognize. His eyes flashed gold, and
his voice reverberated throughout the shed, deep
and resonant, clear as a bell.

"I was the only one who could stop her."

"You were not—"

"The entire company stood like statues, Alwyn,
utterly enthralled. Even the Alphas could not move
a muscle." She limped to the high table and pretended to lean casually against it when, as a matter
of fact, her ankle was throbbing. "Whatever sorcery
she has at her disposal was enough to render you all
powerless. And she escaped." What if Tabitha was
the only one who could pursue her? Even on two

good ankles, she doubted she had a patch on the nimbleness of a snake.

"She can do no more ill, now that her crimes are known to all." Alwyn's characteristic growl had a depth to it, an added layer of gruffness.

"I will not take that chance. I will never take the chance with anyone I—" No, she would not say that, not like this. Whether or not she knew for certain. "You must go away from here, to escape her fate for you. She is relentless in her pursuit, and she is still at large."

He shook back his hair, lusher than it had been even the day before. "You would be on the precipice of a declaration and then shun me?"

"I think only of your freedom, your safety."

"I shall not take advice about safety from you, woman." He looked to the side and seemed to be lost in thought. He canted his head and nodded, as though reaching a decision, and pinned her with that flashing amber gaze. "No, but I must admit, you did what I would have done in your place."

"Then I shall leave." This proposition did not please her as it once would have. "For whatever that is worth."

"Your worthiness is beyond question. You are the only one worth anything to me," he said. She moved away and winced. "Tabitha. You are in pain, and I would help you."

"I can take care of this myself."

"But must you?"

She turned her back on him and thought she heard him laugh, of all things. "Leave me be."

Fingertips traced the back of her neck and trailed away, leaving gooseflesh in their wake. "As you wish, my dear." He paused on his way to the door. "There is no fleeing from what is between us. We shall discuss it at length soon. A heart-to-heart, as it were."

Timothy was through the door on the heels of Alwyn's exit. "Where is His Grace going?"

"I sent him away." She gathered cornmeal, cayenne pepper, mustard seed, nutmeg, Epsom salts, and a length of bandage; as she reached up to a high shelf, she turned her ankle again.

"Here, let me." Timothy took down the bowl and set it aside.

"I can do that."

"I don't doubt it." He led her over to the chair everyone seemed to want her to sit in and sat her in it.

Her brother made short work of combining the ingredients into a poultice with water kept warm on the fire. He pulled over a short stool and sat in front of her; after laying a towel on his thigh, he propped her ankle gently on it. "Allow me to do something for you, for once in your life. No matter where we go or what we do, you will not let me help you at all. Not overtly."

Tabitha banged a fist on the arm of the chair. "You *were* paying more than I in rent, I knew it—"

"It is not about money." Timothy applied the mixture, and his soothing touch in addition to the herbs resulted in blessed comfort. "When that loathsome lord turned on me, you would not step back. You left England so I would not be alone in my grief—"

"Your heart was shattered. Do you think even I, who had never loved anyone like you loved Jasper, did not realize? You were bereft, and his horrendous brother would not leave you alone."

"And in turn, you took him on and almost got yourself married to that creature."

"He never would have gone through with it." The poultice soothed her ankle immediately. "I knew this mixture would work without spending a fortune on saffron," she said. "The mustard is an excellent substitution if I do say so—"

"I often wondered if you wound him up only to contrive a reason for us to run." Timothy talked over her as he wrapped the bandage around her ankle. "No more running for you, Tab. In more ways than one, perhaps."

"That appears to be the consensus."

He held her ankle, applying and releasing pressure as she would do if she were not the patient. "You must know you are the fated mate of the Duke of Llewellyn."

What? "I am not."

"You are. Everyone can tell."

"How do you know they can tell?"

Timothy applied greater pressure. "I had more than one Shifter draw me aside after today's drama, certain his lion will return because His Grace has chosen you."

"That is neither here nor there." It wasn't, it mustn't be, it was not the time. "He is in grave danger. He must go away until that woman is caught. But will he? No, he will not. He will put himself at the forefront, I am sure, and draw her out—"

"If I hadn't known for sure you two were fated, then I would now," Timothy interrupted. "Both of you endless fonts of sacrifice to the disregard of your own needs. As you sacrificed yourself for me." He rose and set aside the mixture, muttering, "Endless sacrifice, endless gratitude..."

"I do not want your gratitude," Tabitha said.

"That is somehow worse." In his methodical way, he prepared another round of poultice she would need later.

"As if everything I have done for you has hampered you—" Tabitha began.

"It has hampered *you*." He fisted a hand on the tabletop. "Forgive me if I am not grateful to have been used as an excuse to flee your fate. How noble to have sacrificed your childbearing years for the sake of your nancy brother."

"Do not speak of yourself like that."

"Do not tell me how to speak, how to call myself. My friends and I derive immense satisfaction from usurping the slurs used against us. And do not turn the subject. Do not continue to make me your excuse." Timothy cut another length of bandage. "I am well able to take care of myself. At least admit you had desires of your own."

"I desired to see you safe." This conversation felt more dangerous than Asquith's pendulum.

"You desired to see the world. We never stopped because you wanted to keep moving. France was workable, Belgium and Germany interesting. The Netherlands! I could have lived in Rotterdam and counted myself content, but you wanted to move and so move we did."

"We had to take advantage of our opportunities." Tabitha was incredulous. "What was the point of having such freedom, and the skills to support ourselves, if not to take in as much as we could?"

"I wanted community," Timothy said. "I wanted a home."

"We found it in Italy."

Her brother covered the bowl with the towel and laid the length of bandage beside it. "You found it in Italy." He turned to her, arms crossed, where Alwyn had stood and loomed.

"You adored Italy. You were happy there. Having said that, you would be happy in a ditch," Tabitha groused. "You would befriend every rock and root around you."

"You make that sound like a bad thing."

Tabitha's pulse stuttered with unease. "You had only to say, Timothy—"

"To say what? When you had already displaced yourself for my sake? It was all for my sake."

"And I would do it again." The first stirrings of real anger set in and drove out the fear.

"So you have." Timothy smirked. "Here we are in England, and you are furious about it."

"I am not furious!" she shouted; any other time this would have sent them into hysterics, but not now, not tonight.

"For the love of Venus," Timothy hissed, "admit to a true feeling for once in your life."

"I have feelings. I have feelings all the time." How she wished she could get up and pace or, better, leave. "I simply choose not to flail them all over the place. They are private and—"

"Private even from the man you love? Don't even think to deny it, for it is written all over your face," Timothy said. "Does he know you love him? You took on that vile woman whose strength exceeds yours exponentially and did it for he who loves you. You do know that he loves you?"

"You have no way of knowing." But was it true?

Timothy ran a hand over his face, impatient. "He named you his *coniunctio*."

Her heart contracted in her chest. From fear? Or longing? "He did not, he merely mentioned the concept in, in passing."

Her brother ignored her feeble equivocation. "It is Latin, as most *versipellian* terms are. At face value, it means *conjunction*, as it applies to verbs. Its deeper meaning," Timothy's voice shook as he continued, "comes from medieval alchemy and speaks to the ultimate union of souls. Of the perfection of balance as well as the perpetual adjustments required to sustain it. It is the paradox of two unlike elements combining to make something greater than themselves."

No, no, now was not the time for this. "There is the lady villain to be dealt with, and then..."

"And then? What will your excuse be after that? Will it be that your poor little brother is back in England where it is not safe for him to love as he wishes? I will not allow you to use my nature to keep yourself shackled to me, to both our detriment."

"Tim." She was appalled, and frightened, and numberless other things her brother would not believe she was feeling. "I would never use your nature against you."

"Then I suggest you accord the same privilege to the duke."

He left her there, in that blasted chair, with the fire and her thoughts, her chaotic, stunned thoughts, for company.

Twenty

THE VERY NEXT DAY, THE VILLAGE GREEN teemed with pack members delirious in anticipation of the arrival of the prince regent. Tabitha's seat on the boulder beneath the chestnut tree provided her with a view of the entire landscape: Mary Mossett was practicing her curtsying to a hydrangea, and a cheeky clowder of footmen was winding up the stable lads, who in turn gave as good as they got. The artisans of Lowell Close had set up displays of their accomplishments in front of their shops, and several of the workers on the home farm walked through the crowd, offering their wares: Mr. Giles offered samples from a tray of cheese, and Mr. Beckett handed out tiny pieces of honeycomb.

Mr. Coburn and Mrs. Birks directed the more dutiful footmen in setting out a massive tea service, should anyone be in dire need of a cuppa, with Felicity overseeing the laying of the table. The Duke of Lowell moved throughout the crowd easily, openly, speaking with one and all and, Tabitha suspected, dispensing his strength for the good of his pack. Never far behind, especially as O'Mara was still among the missing, Mr. Bates stood at his Alpha's shoulder and seemed to be scanning the gathering...for danger? Or for a certain *versipellian* modiste who had arrived that morning?

This was why she did not truck with exclusive lovers, or suitors, or any of it. She would hazard a guess that many of her lady clients had come to her not with a malaise of the body but of the heart. Her tonics were effective in giving the women ease in terms of their sleepless nights, her facial lotions went some way to soothe cheeks raw from endless tears, but they had not come to her for practical advice, rather for a willing ear... Or for someone to tell them what they wanted to hear. How close she was to such a precipice.

Had she not fallen into one? An evening of arguing had led to another sleepless night, and the cool cover of her brooding place did little to soothe her. Harsh words had been exchanged, but there was truth to them; no one knew better than she what relief there was to be had once an injury was cleaned and bound.

She'd had plenty of time to think on what was said. Tabitha behaved like a good patient: she did as she knew she must and left her ankle alone, replacing the poultice when it was necessary. She wrapped up in a blanket and stayed in the chair, the lesser of two evils when compared to attempting the stairs to her bedroom.

There was always the sofa, but she wanted Timothy to have the cottage to himself.

How long had her brother carried those wounds? At least since Rotterdam, or else he had done her the courtesy of not listing every country they'd visited, every single city and town they'd traveled through.

What was done was done. But now what would she do?

She would apologize to her brother.

And then she would pin him to the wall about the fated mate nonsense.

Nonsense? Tabitha Barrington, with all the evidence to the contrary? In addition to the delirious kissing all over her person, there was the way Alwyn ceded to her as though her preferences mattered. It was the way her heart had responded to direction when disarming Asquith—had it been his heart? How could that be; did an Alpha not need a pack to have a *sentio*?

Was she enough of a pack—a pride—for him?

How could it happen so quickly? But here, she had evidence at her disposal: Felicity had been wed in less than a fortnight; Beatrice had been married off to a total stranger and seemingly in no time they were in total accord. At least Tabitha had had the good fortune to get to know her duke—not her duke—

She covered her eyes. He was her duke, wasn't he?

The part of her that resisted that possibility was in direct conflict with the part of her that wanted it, so much.

A breeze blew that notion into a swirl in her head. She tucked her tender ankle across her lap and massaged the residual soreness. It was much improved, and should she take on this Welshman, Timothy could cover her duties until Their Graces found someone else. If they needed to.

If she chose Alwyn, would they go to Wales? He did not seem attached to it but said there was a house there. Would it be in disrepair as Arcadia had been before Osborn gave its care to his wife? Did she see herself as the chatelaine of a great ducal manse? She did not.

Nor did she wish to be known as a lady apothecary any longer, so he could not give her a premises, as Lowell did Felicity.

Would he give her the world?

The badgers had hung the last length of bunting and scurried away with their ladders just as the first horsemen of the royal cavalcade trotted into Lowell Close. A spontaneous cheer erupted, and she saw Lowell and Mr. Bates exchange a rueful glance. Felicity smoothly took her husband's arm and led them to the forecourt of the coach house, where they awaited their regent's arrival.

At the same moment, Timothy appeared to perch beside her. He looked around him, up at the tree, and down at the boulder they sat on. "This is one of your more magnificent *boudoirs*."

"I do not sleep here."

"It is from the French, *bouder* which means *to pout*. It's very like the ledge in Valensole above your lavender field."

"I am predictable," Tabitha grumbled. "How lowering. Sulky and predictable and cross and out of sorts."

Timothy clearly hesitated to refute that, and she was saved from further ignominy by the prince's entrance into the village. The royal carriage was as ornate as one would expect, gilded within an inch of its life and well in tune with the style of the coach house's flamboyant trademark. As a footman opened the door and lowered the step, His Highness popped his head out the window and beamed up at it. "That," George declaimed, "is a magnificent sign."

As he descended, all present bowed and curtsied, and where appropriate to their species, bared their necks to the greatest among them. Tabitha noted His Highness was in no rush to release the Lowell populace from its obeisance. The footmen stood immobile as statues, and the very air stilled in his presence.

As he negligently waved a hand and all rose, His Highness's valet ran up with a brush and flicked the dust of the road off the princely ensemble.

"Speaking of magnificent," Timothy said, "that coat deserves such praise."

"That coat is the work of Lady Jemima Coleman, I suspect." Tabitha worried at her skirts. She had never been so unnerved around her brother, ever. "You came upon me as silently as a wolf. I wonder whose example you have taken as your pattern card."

"Speaking of pattern cards." If she didn't know him so well, she'd think he hadn't a care in the world, but the way he kept plowing his fingers through his hair belied his unease. "I suspect Lady Jemima Coleman has the eye of the one whose I would catch."

They took a moment to observe Lowell's Beta as he smoothly orchestrated a receiving line of sorts; one imagined the prince had little patience for such things. "Fit, blond, clever, and dimpled," Tabitha said. "I should have guessed. No wonder you disliked Italy."

"That wasn't the only reason." He sighed. "Mr. Bates and I are not to be, and thus I pine."

"Do you? Really?"

"No. You know I do not exert my affections where it will do me no good."

"Nor do you ever use anyone's nature against them."

"Ahhh, I said that. I cannot believe I said that." He rubbed his hands roughly over his face. "This is the first quarrel we've had since the doll and the penknife."

"I shall never forgive you for that. The wanton destruction of Lady Bastable-Clark's hair at your hands will live in infamy." She reached out and tugged on the hem of his coat. "But as for last night…I hope you can find it in your heart to forgive me."

"Tab." Timothy knocked his shoulder against hers. "I cannot believe the words I spoke. I, who know so well the great damage they can do. I am appalled, and I am heartily sorry."

"As am I." She took his hand. "But there is truth in it."

"We have been each other's only bulwark against the vagaries of the world since we left England." Timothy squeezed her fingers. "I am amazed we didn't fight before last night."

"It would not have felt safe, I suppose. As we were each other's only bulwark, et cetera." Tabitha forced herself to continue, "And there were many times I was sure I was surplus to your requirements. You were a shining star in any social firmament we found ourselves in, and I held you back, I know I did. What I didn't know was that you were so homesick. It never would have occurred, you were so happy and free."

"I only wanted you to be out amongst people who wanted more than your healthful advice. I wanted you to star in your own social sphere."

He linked their fingers together. "I thought being home again might make it easier for you to branch out. No language barrier and all that."

She must tell him the truth, the truth of her *feelings*. "I am afraid you wish to be rid of me."

"In a manner of speaking." He yanked on her hand until she met his gaze. "I wish you the life you threw away without even trying for it, the life apart from your baby brother whom you do not trust out on his own."

"It's the world I don't trust."

"That's beyond your power. Well, mostly. You can be quite doctrinaire when the mood takes you." They leaned into each other and watched the Lowell Pack drift toward the playing area. The prince was escorted to an elevated pavilion, constructed overnight, that he may enjoy the performance at a comfortable distance from the crowd. "Holy Venus, I do hope someone has warned the Peasleys that His Highness is in attendance—"

"I didn't *throw* my life away."

"You did, you scarcely had one Season!" Timothy slapped the boulder for emphasis. "It was your first chance to find your place away from the benign neglect of our parents, your first opportunity to enjoy sophisticated company. But no, you ran home at the slightest indication that Father was unwell. And then you insisted upon coming to my rescue. You didn't have a chance to find your way—"

"Or every step I took off the conventional path led me here, where I am meant to be," Tabitha said. "Stuff that into your philosophical pillow and sleep on it."

"Into my what now?"

"I know you abhor a pipe."

"*Au contraire.*"

They both roared with laughter, loud enough to draw more than one look from the green beyond.

"Timothy Barrington." She laid her head on her brother's shoulder. "I love you exactly as you are."

"As I have always known. And I you, Tabitha Barrington." He rose and extended a hand. "Come. I am sure this is one performance we shall not want to miss."

Beatrice waved them over to join her family on their blanket just as the harp signaled the parting of the curtain. Alwyn was nowhere to be seen. Mr. Peasley, as if the events of yesterday had not occurred, repeated his introduction to the play.

"I understand a traveling company seeking to make use of everything at their disposal," Osborn grumbled, "but I cannot justify a bear in *Hamlet.*"

"I doubt Mr. Quincy will let her out of his sight for a good while," Tabitha said. The strongman held the bear's harness, and the look on his face dared anyone to venture near them.

Tabitha found she must dare, for again it seemed the bear was looking straight at her. Even across the distance that separated them, she knew it was she who was being stared at. She knelt up, to the annoyance of the folk on the blanket behind. "Pardon me," she whispered.

She crawled a little to the left and knelt up again. More hissing ensued from the next blanket. "So sorry," Tabitha said and was hushed roundly. Timothy shot her a look that said, *Now what?* Which she ignored.

The players soldiered on, quite efficiently conflating the scene featuring the ghost of Hamlet's father with the stabbing of Polonius through the arras in Gertrude's chamber. Tabitha rose and quickly moved out of the crowd. The bear turned her head to follow her progress.

Mr. Quincy glowered at her as she approached. His sister and brother-in-law spoke louder to draw attention back to the performance.

As if mesmerized, Tabitha drifted to the front of the crowd. The bear broke Mr. Quincy's grasp and crept toward her. Mr. Peasley, in the midst of being stabbed as Polonius, threw his hands in the air in disgust. "Miss! What must a humble player do in these parts to properly perform his role?"

"I am sorry, I am so sorry, forgive me, but I must see to the bear—"

Despite her still-tender ankle, Tabitha climbed onto the stage and sat next to the creature. The bear laid her head in Tabitha's lap, and she stroked her fur, ran her fingers between the ears and down around her neck—

"There is a chain," Tabitha said. She looked up, around, and Alwyn, as was his wont, appeared out of the ether. "There is a chain, Alwyn, what do I do?"

A whispered chorus of *Alwyn?* soughed through the audience, to whom the duke turned. "Has anyone a small blade or a sharp object?"

Beatrice removed an enormous hatpin from that day's elaborate bonnet. Ursella took it and ran up to Llewellyn, holding it carefully out in front of her. She, too, scrambled onto the playing area and cuddled up against the bear's shoulder after passing the pin to Tabitha.

"Undo it, my dear." Alwyn laid a hand on Tabitha's back, and she did so.

The Change was slow, nothing like Mr. MacCafferty's transformation from Himself: it was silent, soft, as watercolors bled when touched with a dampened brush. Mrs. Peasley took one of the silks off Gertrude's couch and laid it over the bear—or what was once the bear, as the Change revealed the woman whose Shape it had concealed.

Her hair was tangled and unkempt but a deep, rich brown; her eyes were an emerald green that wavered with the yellow of her essential self. She blinked at the child at her shoulder, at Tabitha, at Alwyn, and turned her head to look out at those assembled.

"Arthur? Garben?" Her voice was little more than a rasp in her throat, as Alwyn's had been when he had newly resumed his manskin.

The Humphries brothers froze. Charlotte gasped and surged to her feet. "Armelle," she said as she charged through the crowd. "Blessed Freya and all her Valkyries—Armelle? Oh, gracious Thor, Armelle…"

Arthur and Ben followed in her wake; Tarben shouted, "Granny? Is that my granny?" as he and Bernadette joined their sleuth and huddled around the newly Changed figure.

The Humphries sons helped their mother backstage; Tabitha stood only to wobble on her feet, and Alwyn jumped to the ground to hand her down. Just as their hands touched, Asquith appeared from the opposite wing and in short order grabbed Tabitha by the hair and held a knife to her throat.

"The last mistake you will have made was to let me go." Despite her delicate frame, the snake Shifter was, as expected, very strong. Tabitha did not bother to struggle. Alwyn made to spring to her aid, and the snake wrapped her other arm around Tabitha's waist and slid the knife over her jugular, where it would do the most damage, most quickly.

"The first mistake," Asquith continued, projecting to be heard in the back, "was to think we would allow one prize to escape us, much less two. Oh, yes, we have had the Duchess of Osborn—now the

Dowager Duchess, one supposes—in our possession for ages, as well as the Wild Lion of Wales. Do not, Your Grace." Lowell had come forward with his Second and Third, who halted at the lady author's word. "Regard my blade." She jerked Tabitha's head back farther so the gold caught the light. "Nothing less than this for one such as you, Barrington, a *homo plenus* who, once let into our secrets, can see the truth beneath the skin."

"Is that known?" Tabitha asked. Alwyn had not dropped his eyes from hers, and she directed this to him. Someone ought to write all this down and send it around the *versipellian* community.

A pity its most renowned writer was a heartless villain.

"It is known among those who seek to avoid your kind like the plague." Asquith laughed. "Do you succumb so easily, Barrington? Not even the slightest struggle?"

"I am not your equal in strength. I see no point in needless drama."

"If you insist on disrespecting the narrative, then you will have to pay dearly for it." Asquith drove Tabitha to her knees with little effort and pulled her head back so she could no longer see Alwyn. "His Grace was meant to search for you high and low, and thus fall into my hands, hands holding another golden chain at the ready, as once more he played the hero."

"Played?" Tabitha would not give Asquith the satisfaction of betraying the fear coursing through her. "There is no playing when it comes to the duke's heroism."

"Women in love," the lady author spat. "So predictable."

"And yet you did not predict my ability to save myself?"

"How will you save yourself from this, eh? I will have you know I am adept with weapons—"

"Due to growing up in the itinerant troupe that evolved into Phineas Drake's Equestrian Spectacular and Exotic Traveling Menagerie. Your brother, I believe, Mrs. Asquith?" Timothy stepped forward, cool as could be, as if his sister had a knife held to her throat every day. "Your many duties, apart from minor female parts as sadly you had no skill in that arena, were in the weapons line, shooting things off other things, throwing knives, and sundry magic tricks. The troupe began to lose business hand over fist until the family diverted its talents in nefarious directions, to renewed profit."

"Years on the road and nothing to show for it," Asquith snarled. "It was not playing to the masses like cavorting monkeys that made our fortune."

"Ah, here now," muttered Mr. Peasley.

"With the breadth of our serpentine knowledge and our skills at subterfuge, we were able to capture the likes of the bear and the lion, as none on this island could boast. It set us apart from the rest of the riffraff, and we were ready to depart for a grand tour of the Antipodes, until both of them escaped."

"How can one such as you pursue this dire occupation?" Timothy asked.

Asquith tightened her arm around Tabitha's waist. "My dragonskin gloves are my protection from the thrall of gold. The stone in my pendulum is from the diadem of Medusa. The crystal itself gave her the power to petrify those who gazed upon her until one of my lineage stole it from between her very eyes."

"There is no such thing as dragons," scoffed someone in the crowd.

"Diadem of Medusa?" muttered another. "What is she on about?"

"Things far beyond your ken, you who have not ventured five leagues from this village." Asquith's voice took on a decidedly East End timbre. "I shudder to think I was once as unworldly as you lot."

"All the worldliness that came from, oh, being a traveling player?" Mrs. Peasley mused.

"Enough." Alwyn's voice rang out over all. "You cannot threaten the life of my *vera amoris,* my *coniunctio,* and go unchallenged. Here I am. Take me."

"Alwyn, do not!" Tabitha struggled against the snake Shifter's hold and found it as pointless as she suspected.

"Men in love," Asquith crooned. "So predictable."

Without hesitation, Alwyn Changed in front of everyone into his magnificent lion: he shook his spectacular mane and roared, his fangs like razors, his paws enormous and bristling with his claws, his shoulders and chest wide, his coat gleaming a tawny brown. He stood head and shoulders above all present, his height and breadth bigger than that of a *lion* lion—muscular, lethal, enraged.

Asquith laughed. "I shall simply kill two birds with one stone." She pricked Tabitha's neck with the blade and coaxed a line of blood to flow down her neck.

Alwyn leaped in front of her, paws on the edge of the stage, roared again; the other large predators in the crowd Changed, wolves and stags and one enormous chestnut horse, in an explosion of aggression, as each snarled and howled and reared up on their hind legs. The show of force concealed the actions of three small creatures gone unremarked during the spectacular transformation: all at once, a frog hopped onto the hem of Asquith's skirts, a bee swarmed around Asquith's head, and a goat nipped her on the knee. In that second of inattention, Tabitha slipped out of the snake's grasp. The bee stung Asquith in the eye; she screamed and dropped the knife; the frog promptly sat on its handle.

"That will do." His Highness, entirely forgotten,

stood and gestured to his nearest attending foot-men, who took the lady author, shouting and thrash-ing, into custody.

The wolves and the stags and the horse bowed to the bee, the goat, and the frog; the audience followed their lead to honor their ingenuity. His Highness nodded his head in tribute, infinitesi-mally, it had to be said, but it was noted by all.

The lion stood at her feet as Tabitha rose; she touched the graze on her neck, the blood flow already slowing. She waved off her brother, her friends, and stood at the edge of the stage. The lion shook his mane and growled.

"Silence!" Tabitha exclaimed. The lion froze. "Were I able to growl, Your Grace, it would be I who ought to do so. How dare you? How dare you put yourself in such a position when you knew her intent? You are reckless and thoughtless and rash." The lion looked to his comrades, who backed away slowly, then looked to his liege, whose slowly blooming smile promised no help from that quar-ter. Tabitha limped one step forward, winced, and the lion growled again.

"Hush! You accuse me of such rashness, of not considering you and your feelings, and did you even for one instant think of me, what it would do to me if you were taken? You claim I am your *vera amoris* and your *conio—conincto*—that Latin word, and make the choice you made? You claim

me before all without allowing me the same courtesy? All of that, and yet you would throw it away in
a fit of, what? Pride? Arrogance? If this is how you
behave—"

To the astonishment of the audience, who had
watched Tabitha as avidly as though she were Miss
Elizabeth Yates enacting the role of Rosalind, the
beast rolled onto his back, exposing his belly. He
tilted his head, showed her his neck, and purred at
her. All of a sudden, she was in complete and utter
sympathy with O'Mara: she raised her voice as she
had never in her life.

"Do not! Do not do whatever that is you are
doing, in front of all here, not after the risk you
took!" Oh, dear: that was far too strenuous on
human vocal cords. "We shall speak, sir, believe me
we shall, and it will be at my discretion and at my
convenience."

Tabitha's exit was impressively executed, and a
burst of applause saw her off.

As she limped away, she heard Mr. Peasley cry,
"Is there any need for traveling players in this local-
ity at all?"

Twenty-One

TABITHA STOOD AT THE PADDOCK FENCE. Felicity's alpha mare was making a show of ignoring her, letting her know whose turf she was on. Tabitha respected that. She had come with an appropriate offering; she knew who owed obeisance here.

Tabitha unwrapped the chunks of carrot in her handkerchief. She had dressed with some care, as after she visited with the mare, she was expected at the Hall for tea with the Osborns, by request of the dowager duchess.

No complaints from her: anything that put off the inevitable confrontation with Alwyn was welcome.

"Here, lady," Tabitha called. "I bring you tribute as one who is an admirer of the Duke of Llewellyn yet also lacks patience with masculine hijinks."

It was the carrot, not the sentiment, that drew the mare over...wasn't it? "Honestly, if I did not know you were a *horse* horse, Delilah..." The mare nipped the proffered treat and chewed slowly, assessing its quality and, Tabitha imagined, her own character.

The next chunk was duly accepted, and Tabitha was bold enough to reach out and pat the horse's neck. This resulted in a nuzzle of her shoulder. She gave Delilah a good scratch on her withers, and the horse laid her cheek against Tabitha's own.

Tabitha leaned against the fence and the horse, who had moved as close as she could. Slowly but surely, she let the mare take her weight along the breadth of her neck. What a relief, to lean on a creature so much bigger than she, so much stronger, who invited it, welcomed it. Tabitha inhaled the scent of horse, of grass, of earth, breathed again, and the events of the previous day and weeks slotted themselves into perspective.

It was as she had said to Timothy: every step along the way had led her here. Every time her mother had been in danger of dying in childbed, Tabitha learned how to tend her more effectively. Every time she was treated as less than by her parents, or by those who sought her aid, she determined to learn a better cure, a more palatable tonic. She expected to be loved by her mother and father in return for her facility, but that had not been the case. So she thought the world might at least reward her for her knowledge, and it had and brought her here, where nothing she had learned was useful in its practical sense but more in the essence of it: in her approach to talking to people, through her calm, and—*yes, Timothy*—her composure.

It was in her nature to be all these things because circumstance had deemed it so. She would no sooner let a villain hold sway than she would allow someone to remain in pain if she could alleviate it...if they asked her to do so. Both were choices, the first hers, the second theirs.

So she had no right to dictate anyone else's choices.

"Oh, Delilah," she sighed. "More apologies are in order today."

The horse nibbled at her shoulder as if in agreement and stepped away. Tabitha produced the last portion of carrot and stroked a hand down the mare's face. "I think you are a greater healer than I could ever be." Delilah snorted and, with one last brush of her muzzle, pranced off to boss around the rest of the band.

———

Was this place good enough for his mate? Alwyn had asked favors throughout the Close and been met in excess of what he asked: the bee had provided candles and honey for her tea; the goat brought his excellent cheese as well as offerings from other farmers and cultivators in the pack, so there was food enough for a day and a night and a morning; the frog, to Alwyn's everlasting surprise, had arranged beautiful sprays of long grasses and wildflowers set in ceramic vases thrown by Mrs. Grice the potter, with whom Tabitha had bartered.

The sheets were pristine and delivered by a bold little mouse, and he'd replaced the utilitarian curtains with the delicately embroidered set she'd brought. How they had been sewn up so quickly, he did not know. He wished he had a coin or two to give, but she was able to practice her curtsying on him, so he reckoned they were even.

He must wash. Should he bathe in the brook? His essential self rolled in his aura; how he wished they could run there in their lionskin, but he'd only just landed in the good books of all here and would rather not frighten even the smallest fly.

Ought he to light a fire? It wasn't terribly cold, and yet he knew Tabitha suffered from the lack of heat. His lion snickered even as Alwyn shushed him.

He stood in the center of this haven, hand on his heart, and reveled in the trust shown him, by Lowell and his duchess, by the hierarchy and the pack, to live amongst them, untroubled, until he was able to accept their welcome. To be welcomed when he had been so misused, to be accepted when he had thought he was so lost. To heal, at their hands and through the good graces of Miss Tabitha Barrington.

Soon to be Your Grace, his lion quipped.

"My Grace," he agreed. "Mine."

———

The Lowell Hall contingent gathered in the drawing room whose mantel was covered with figurines. Mr. Coburn announced Tabitha in his typically stentorian tones, but today his visage was so warm and welcoming, he seemed on the verge of winking at her.

The room was full to bursting with personages: the hierarchy of both the Lowell Pack and the Osborn Sleuth were present, as well as His Highness and several of his attendants. Palu forbid he should mix with even his most exalted subjects without sufficient evidence of his consequence.

"I apologize for my lateness. I was talking to Delilah," she said after the flurry of greetings and bows and curtsies and embraces died down. "She sends her regards."

Lowell huffed, sounding very like his wolf; Felicity had told her, on pain of death if Tabitha let it be known, that she called him *Alfie*. "I would not be surprised to learn you can speak with *animalis pura*," he said.

"Miss Barrington has a great gift." The Dowager Duchess of Osborn sat in state in the corner. As Alwyn did, she ensured she had full view of the door and was next to a window. Tabitha suspected the vigilance would be with both of them for some time to come.

Despite her years trapped in the Shape of her bear, the dowager had lost none of her presence as a woman of the upper echelon; yet for all of that, the warmth of her character shone through. Her sons sat on either side of her on the sofa, with their wives standing behind them, and her grandchildren leaned against her legs. While she was exhausted by her travails, she was the picture of contentment with her family around her.

"Your Grace." Tabitha approached and wished she had Beatrice's facility with deep curtsying, for no one deserved that tribute more. "I am honored to have done you service."

With a wave of a duchessy hand, a royal footman produced a chair. Tabitha sat and could not help herself: she reached out and took the woman's pulse; the rate would have been dangerously lethargic in a human. "Interesting," Tabitha remarked. "I find *versipellian* pulses run rather slow."

"Except when they don't," Charlotte mumbled.

"And depending upon whose pulse," her husband added.

"Hush, you two, you haven't changed a bit. Always a saucy comment," the dowager scolded, and both blushed and smiled and fought happy tears. "My gratitude knows no bounds, Miss Barrington."

"I was merely following your lead, ma'am," she replied. "I am curious to know how you knew I was able to free you?"

"It is pure chance I was able to escape at all." The dowager, as frail as her voice sounded, sat strong and tall. "The roustabouts were up in arms, as their wages had been shorted once again, and they chose to spend what they had on drink. The night handlers were lax in their duties and failed to close my, my cage"—here her voice stuttered and her entire family leaned in to her in support—"so it was the work of a moment to free myself. I had only the sense of my beloved bear to carry me forward, for weeks on end, until I came upon the Peaselys." Her countenance lightened. "As we had left Drake's farther and farther behind, my human senses slowly returned, and while I did not know who they were precisely, I knew them for allies."

"They will be rewarded." Osborn's voice was husky with emotion, and Beatrice rubbed her hands over his massive shoulders. "They will be known herewith as the Peasley Troupe of Traveling Players, by Appointment of Her Grace, the Dowager Duchess of Osborn."

"That is rather a mouthful, Arthur," Beatrice said. Charlotte and Ben burst into hysterics, curbed in a trice thanks to another censuring glance from the dowager.

"I am sure they will be gratified beyond words," Tabitha said.

"I hardly think Mr. Peasley ever finds himself beyond words." The dowager smiled. "They were so kind, especially Mr. Quincy, who took such wonderful care of me. The farther we journeyed south, the more impatient my bear and I became, and then when we arrived here, and we saw you..." She took Tabitha's hands in hers and held fast. "It was the first time my bear and I had spoken to each other since we were caught. We saw you and knew you were not one of us but able to see us."

"Are humans able to do this?"

"Only humans who are capable of the *vera amoris* bond, which is not as common as you might imagine, despite the recent bondings in this part of the world. It is a particular gift that is only brought to bear—" *Ha, ha*, said her entire sleuth. Her smile lit up the room. "Is only brought to bear once in a generation, if at all. It is extremely rare, and the knowledge of it has fallen out of circulation. What times we live in that we should see this."

"Thank Freya you knew of it," Ben said.

"Thank her and all her Valkyries," the dowager agreed. "When we saw you, we started to come back to ourselves, despite the gold. So we looked and looked until you saw."

"Thank you, Your Grace." Her insight was helpful, if not entirely instructive. "I wish I knew how to use this gift, to be more aware—"

"You have simply to be, my dear." The dowager squeezed her hand. "That is more than enough."

Charlotte's glare over Tabitha's shoulder alerted her to the royal presence.

"I must steal Miss Barrington from you, Your Grace." The prince's tone brooked no refusal.

"You have ruined a beautiful moment, Georgie," Osborn muttered.

"We shall speak again, Miss Barrington." The

dowager opened her arms for an embrace and rocked her back and forth; once again Tabitha was grateful for her stores of composure, for it was a hug like none she'd ever known, pure maternal love and acceptance and pride.

Before she could follow His Highness, Ursella tugged on her skirt. Tabitha crouched to her level.

"He was sad, and you are afraid. If he changed"— and the girl smirked at her pun—"so can you."

"Miss Ursella, may I give you a squish?" Tabitha asked, and the Osborn Omega threw her arms around her neck. The child exuded calm; it hovered in the air, waiting to be plucked out of it, and Tabitha took what was so kindly offered.

The prince stood near the window overlooking Lowell's wild park; Llewellyn's cottage, on its high hill, was framed in the panes. "You have our gratitude." The regent did not sound very grateful, but she suspected it was his way. "It is tiresome for us to continually be called upon to intervene in such affairs that could be nipped in the bud, as it were. We require you and your mate do the nipping." He held up a hand. "Do not think to protest, miss. Or, as I have done with your peers before you, I shall be presumptive and address you as *Your Grace*." He looked down at her from his great height. "A lion Shifter only shows his belly to his mate. To do so before all is to name you before all..." Prince George's smile was as devilish as any Timothy might raise. "You are as good as married. In an unconventional sense, if not the proper sense."

"Not until I have consented," Tabitha retorted. "Your Highness."

"I would expect nothing less." On a signal invisible to anyone but his footmen, they fell in line in such a way as created an aisle to the door. Mr. Coburn opened it, and as he took his leave, George continued, "Not from the mate of one such as he."

───────

Tabitha's way to Alwyn's cottage was impeded, pleasantly so, by greetings and thanks from the Lowell Pack. Each of her suitors, she was happy to see, found new loci for their attentions: the goat, the bee, and the frog were respectively walking out with a hare, a sparrow, and a trout. She made much of the three gents and the part they played in bringing down Asquith; how fortunate for Mr. Beckett and his little bird that an apian Shifter was able to survive the deployment of his stinger.

As she climbed the hill to his cottage, Alwyn was sitting on the doorstep, in trousers and a light linen shirt, his feet bare. He rose when she neared, and she stopped in the dooryard. She lifted her chin. "Georgie said we are as good as married."

"Georgie?"

Tabitha smiled. "Beatrice said it is a rite of passage."

He leaned in the doorway and crossed his arms. Gone was the tentative presence, the excessive vigilance, the rusty tone, the inability to meet her gaze. As casually dressed as he was, he exuded health and heartiness—and power. "I apologize for my valeting." He indicated his rough trousers, which were still an improvement on the sartorial choices of his recent past. "I was preparing my home for you, if you choose to enter. But I must tell you, should you do so, then yes, we are as good as married."

"I cross the threshold, and it is done?"

He shrugged. "Lions do not truck with all that lupine lighted-torch nonsense."

"The bears did so as well." Tabitha recalled Beatrice's investiture as Second in the Osborn sleuth with awe and also with the thought she would hate being the center of such carryings-on.

"Nor ursine nonsense. Our bond requires you make my home your home, the acceptance of my bite, and that we tell each other every day we choose each other." He smiled, that slow, roguish thing that threatened to destroy her presence of mind. "It's along the lines of a daily bargain. But if you prefer a public proposal—"

"I do not." Blessed Palu, no. "But a proper one would be welcome."

Alwyn approached her then dropped to one knee with the grace of his kind: feline, definitely;

Welsh, possibly. He reached out a hand, and she took it, her fingers trembling until they lay safe in his grasp. "I was an arrogant youth. I had all one could hope for and more, with the addition of the consequence of my station. While I did not lord myself over others, I took it for granted. It was all taken from me, in such a stunning storm of loss that if not for the strength of my lion, I would have been undone. And once I was captured, I had lost not only my past and my present but my future. I had lost the chance of finding my fated mate. I had lost the chance of ever knowing if I was worthy of the *coniunctio*. And then I saw you in a window at Arcadia, I saw you wandering the woods, I caught you gathering poisonous plants, I huddled beneath a coat to protect you from a threat..."

The headiness of the bergamot, the thrill of the proximity. "I had never felt safer in my life," she admitted.

"I had never felt stronger, even at that stage, in my persisting weakness. All of that, and I suspected but did not know for certain until I knew you could see. Then I knew we were able for the *coniunctio*, a match beyond the strength and the power of the *vera amoris* that takes the best the fated pair has to offer and elevates it for the good of all."

"As an Alpha pair for all."

"Only a pair who can be Alpha for all is able for

this union." His voice was as gravelly as when they first spoke those weeks ago through the window of Arcadia's drawing room.

How much had changed, and so swiftly. "So the lost may find comfort, the isolated be embraced, the captured be freed."

"And as one, build a family, its members as they are found along the way."

It was overwhelming, an enormous responsibility, and well out of her sphere of knowledge.

She had never let that stop her before.

"Yes. I will be your mate, your *coniunctio*." He raised those brows of his at her faultless pronunciation. "I may have practiced that. And you will be mine. My *coniunctio*, my mate, my duke." She knelt and held their hands to her heart. "And I will be your duchess and wield the power of that position for the most imaginable good."

He kissed her lightly, rubbed his face all along hers, and wrapped her up in his arms. She in turn buried her nose in his neck, and his warmth spread as if into her veins. Pressed against him, she could feel his heartbeat adjust, and then hers until they matched in pace. She leaned back and laid a hand over his chest, even as he did hers.

"It is the *sentio*. It opened of its own accord, in response to your tumble into the pit," Alwyn said. "Osborn told me it was easier to allow it to open than fight to keep it closed."

"Everything about this is so simple." Surely such life-changing events should be more complicated.

As if he read her mind, he said, "We can make it more difficult, if you prefer."

"I do not." She laid her head on his heart. "My preferences include selfless lion-men whose eyes crinkle when they smile, who laugh at the worst puns ever made, whose endless reserves of patience will be handy in the years to come."

Alwyn undid the ribbon, his ribbon, she'd tied around her hair and loosened it from its bun. "Mine include selfless, if not reckless, human women who would stop at nothing for the one they…"

"The one they love." That was easy to say, once risked. She cuddled into his chest. "That was manipulative in the extreme, Your Grace."

"Do not fear the feeling is not returned, my love. My mate. Mine."

In a seamless move, he hooked an arm under her bum and raised them both to stand. Tabitha could not be blamed for squealing, a sound that produced such hilarity in the duke—her duke—she did not regret making that highly regrettable sound.

Which she reproduced when he brought her into his home and dropped her on his bed, and then himself beside her. He ran his hands down her side over the buttons there. "I received a trunk full of clothes," she said, as with dexterity he slipped each out of its button-hole. "From Lady Jemima Coleman, I can only assume."

"As did I." Alwyn slid his hand through the gap in the garment and tickled her ribs. "She has a gift, for it all fits and I can dress myself. No valet for me ever, I fear."

"I am happy to take on such duties." She shimmied out of her walking dress and treated the placket of his trousers to the same treatment he had given her buttons. "Oh, my." Her comparative matrix was to be found lacking in yet another area. She slid her hand around his cock and bit her lower lip. "I know what I would prefer to do with this."

He stretched, exposing that belly, and had she ever seen such a well-defined example of *rectus abdominis* in her life? She had not. "Have you had experience of this? A woman using her mouth on you?" Tabitha demonstrated her meaning, and the sinuous roll of his hips, in turn, demonstrated his appreciation.

"Do not. Not now. I won't last, I can't—" One last application of her tongue, a promise of future efforts, and she knelt up to fling her chemise to the side, even as Alwyn followed suit with his shirt. They tumbled into each other and down onto the covers. She wrapped her legs around his hips and used her heels to tug at his trousers, which made him laugh. She took it one step further and hooked her toes in the waistband and slid them down his legs, which had the excellent byproduct of bringing their hips together. She thought she scented mint, the heat of sun on stones, something like a bun stuffed with currants—oh, his essence. She tucked her nose into his neck and breathed deep. They were the most delicious things she'd ever smelled.

Tabitha tilted her head back as she arched up and ran the tips of her breasts over his chest, making him shudder. He slid an arm beneath her hips, the other hand tracing down to her cunny. "How I want you," he managed as his fingers settled into the source of her heat.

Her hands flew to his hair as he laved her nipples, stroked her flesh, sucked, and kneaded. His eyes were hot with passion, and gripping him harder by the hips, she guided him into her even as she trembled. She wrapped herself around him, body and soul, and rose to meet him, as he plunged into her, again and again, heedlessly, wildly, and she urged him on, luxuriating in the feel of him against her, inside her, this man, only this man, here and now, forever. Feeling him reach his peak filled her with a sensual, magnificent power, and she stroked him, caressed him, ran her hands everywhere she could reach. In the aftermath they breathed as one, hearts beating as one, whispering words of love as one.

Alwyn spread a blanket on the floor before the hearth, the firewood within lit for her benefit. She sat wrapped in the duvet and leaned against the foot of the bed. Was this to be her future? Decadent lovemaking in the daytime hours and the unwavering attention of her mate? He made her a plate of assorted tidbits from a larger platter full of fruit and cold meats, bread rolls, and cakes. "I can help myself," she protested, sleepily, it had to be said.

"It is an Alpha's honor to tend to his mate." He set her plate and a cup of wine beside her and joined her on the floor. "I have planned ahead, and our picnic is complete."

"This is Mr. Giles's cheese." She took another bite. "I see you have made your peace with him."

"And the others. Easily done, as I have won your favor." How smug he sounded.

"I was impressed by the quick thinking of Mr. Giles, Beckett, and Padmore."

"That was my work."

"Was it?"

He nodded and grinned. "They had already done your bidding and were prepared to do mine, to your benefit."

"You could not know that would happen."

"You could," he countered, "if you had been tutored by one Mr. Timothy Barrington in the lady author's oeuvre. Knives figured largely."

"I would not be surprised if he read them all in one evening. I have never seen anyone devour a book the way he does."

"Will he stay here?"

"Yes, as we have agreed it is time we parted company and pursued our own ways through the world." Her voice caught, and she bit her lip to keep her composure. She told him of their argument and then said, "I owe you an apology. You were only following your nature, and I took you to task before all."

"And you will continue to do so." He took her chin in his hand. "We shall be an Alpha pair to all we meet. We may discover our Beta and Gamma as we go on, but we shall always be each other's staunchest supporters and critics as well. It would have been rash to Change as I did, without having laid the groundwork for overwhelming Asquith with numbers. Which you did not know, and for that I owe you an apology."

She nuzzled his palm. "May we consider both accepted?"

"Yes, and thus, we move on." He served her more cheese and slices of apple. "Mind you, a feline can hold a grudge like none other."

"And a Welshman?"

"Is powerless before his beloved." He nestled closer. "You will miss your brother."

"Yes. But I will have the comfort of knowing where he is. Alwyn." She slipped an arm around his waist. "We must look for your family." He rubbed his face in her hair and nodded. "And keep a lookout for O'Mara." He leaned back, and they waggled their brows at each other.

"What does O'Mara do when she looks off into the distance?" Tabitha asked. "She looks like she's conferring with the air."

Her duke took a breath, bracing himself. "We do not think death is the end. *Versipelles,* not dukes. Or not only dukes."

"Alwyn, no." This was the outside of enough. "Do not tell me she is speaking to ghosts."

"Very well." He reached across to hand her a small, flat cake, dusted with sugar and studded with currants. "I will not tell you. Try this. Lowell's French chef deigned to follow a Welsh recipe—"

"Alwyn!"

He tore a piece off another and devoured it with relish. Dusting his hands of the sugar, he said, "We believe the essence of our animal selves and our ancestors prevail over time and space—"

"Holy, Blessed Palu." Tabitha took a bite of her cake to prevent her from saying any more. Happily, it was delicious.

"—and the powers Omegas have are a mystery to us all," he continued. He peeped at her through those lashes, as if he knew how it disarmed her. "I suspect she can talk to them."

"To your ancestors."

Alwyn tapped her on the nose. "To anyone's. It may be her specific power."

"Her gift." Tabitha polished off the cake. "The *moohoo*."

"The what now?"

Tabitha explained what he'd missed at tea, that Sunday Meal. "Oh, Alwyn." She drew back and took his face in her hands. "If that is the case, she sought to help you in that way and could not. It must mean your family is alive."

"I wonder if none of my ancestors could sense them even from beyond, thanks to that infernal sorcery." He laid his forehead against hers, and they breathed in tandem.

"And how does the Irish mister-lord fit into this picture?" Tabitha wondered.

"They may be fated mates. One cannot imagine that melancholy horse exerting himself to thwart her to the degree she fled her homeland, but"— Alwyn shrugged—"still waters run deep. We will put word out in London. I doubt she is there, but she may have passed through."

"We must go to Drake's and free any who may be captive. Mr. Bates went to look despite having no way of knowing. He said there is a leopard he suspects is not an *animali puri*."

Alwyn shivered. "I had a terrible thought that Jack Bunce might have an ability such as yours, but he did not *see* me. Or else he would not have lost his mind when I Changed."

"The Dowager Duchess of Osborn said it was a

matter of *vera amorum* meeting, and that is why my, my gift realized itself. I suspect my natural inclination to observe lent itself to it."

"Lucky for all involved."

"Luck!" Tabitha objected. "One cannot base a future on luck. Or a gift. A gift I had no notion even existed."

"Then let us not call it a gift, for I suspect you are as awful at receiving them as you are with compliments. Am I wrong?" Alwyn asked. She growled and saw his lion flash in his eyes. "Let us see. How is your new skill different from the usual application of your knowledge?"

She tipped her head back and thought. "In apothecary matters, I have numerous hypotheses based on what I have previously observed, I have the experience built from having seen what is useful and what isn't, and I extrapolate from there into other avenues of ingredient combinations, dosages, and substitutions."

"While you have had only one experience, you trusted your instincts, experimented, were given proof of your conclusions, and now have that to build upon."

Tabitha could not find fault in his logic. "You are as good a confidante as the Italian cat. Although his silence was often his strongest recommendation—ah!" Her duke wrestled the blanket down to rub his face on her belly, which, with his abundance of hair, tickled mightily. "Your Grace. Your Grace! I accept your gloss of the situation. I had not considered it that way." She smoothed down his hair, and her fingers teased the crinkles around his eyes. "Thank you for your insight. I will rely upon it."

He rolled over and settled her on his chest, heart to heart, and she asked the one question she dreaded. "Will we go to Wales, after London? To settle there?"

———

Alwyn rested his cheek on the top of her head. "If you wish." His mate did not sound as though she wished it. "I rather thought we would travel the world."

Her heartbeat kicked up, and his matched it. "The whole world? That will cost a fortune."

"There is no need for concern. The Llewellyn title may be empty, but the coffers are full."

"We shall fill the title with new pride. In more ways than one." Tabitha's whole body relaxed. "I do not understand money, which as a grown woman is ridiculous, but it was always Timothy's forte. How do you have money if you didn't earn it?"

"Dukes do not earn money, *cariad*." He explained the circumstances around his family's royal stipend and their investments until, having clearly lost interest, Tabitha sat up to run a finger over his belly muscles;

she seemed enamored of them. "Do not distract me," he rumbled. "Here, now, speaking of money. Did you charge a single client for your services?"

"Do not distract *me*." Tabitha peeped up at him, her big brown eyes sultry. "Is there to be a bite?"

"Any old bite?"

"Your old bite. What age are you, I'd like to know."

Alwyn lifted her onto the bed, while mumbling into her neck, "You wouldn't, not really," and snuggled between her thighs, leaning on an elbow and trailing the fingers of his other hand up and down her side. "You know of the increase in lifespan you will gain, once bitten?" She nodded and tucked her nose in the dip of his collarbone. "You will also gain the ability to have as many cubs as you wish, if you wish."

"I do not wish." She hesitated then lay back, holding his gaze.

His fearless mate. Alwyn ran a finger over the little round patch of blush on her cheek. "That is understandable, given your mother's woes. I would have you know that you will be gifted with strength uncommon in *homo plenum*, should that make a difference."

"It does not. Not at this moment. I cannot say whether my mind will change." She trembled against him, and he held her close. "Does this disappoint you?"

"Only insofar as I foresaw more than one gray hair in my future, at the thought of a daughter of yours as a lion cub." He smiled into her shoulder.

"You may prefer a mate who wishes to give you that."

"It is your decision, and I honor it." Alwyn ran his fingers through her hair, thick and lush and straight as a pin. "I have the mate I prefer, and when our desires do not align, then it is well we are able for the *coniunctio*, for we shall ever be finding our balance, for the rest of our lives."

"Until death do us part."

He recognized the words from the human bonding service. "That is a long way away, for we have much work to do." He cupped her breast and idly swirled his thumb around her nipple. "But let me apply myself to the task at hand. My love, my mate."

Tabitha wrapped her arms around his neck and her calves around his hips. "Where will you bite? Felicity's is hidden, while Beatrice's is not."

"It will be as you prefer."

His mate lay a string of kisses around his throat. "It must be seen. If we are to earn the trust of those we find, it must be seen by all."

Alwyn ran his lips, then his tongue, low on her neck, where it met her shoulder. "It may be seen when you wish to show it. It is yours to make known or not. If you wrap yourself up in shawls and coats as you are wont to do, then here"—he nipped lightly, and her entire body shook—"can be covered as you see fit and displayed when you think it required."

"Then I choose that place." Tabitha leaned up for a kiss. "As I choose you."

He had no idea what it would feel like when he gave his bite to his *vera amoris*. His father had not thought to tell him; Alwyn's time to consider it had been so far in the future. It was too personal to ask his peers. Since Tabitha was his *coniunctio* as well, he did not know how that would affect the process.

Time to trust his instincts. His lion rolled once, twice in his aura before withdrawing, to wait until it was a *fait accompli*.

They moved together with the ease of seasoned lovers and the thrill of new love. Her scents rose to tantalize him, her arousal wedded with her signature scents of the rose water, the fire, the bracing cool of the spring dawn. She hitched her hips, and he slid home, her sighs of pleasure sending him higher until suddenly, he knew: he knew to cradle her protectively in his arms, to wait, wait, wait, until she was about to reach the crest; to whisper words of love and encouragement in her ear as she did; to allow his fangs to drop and to trace them on her neck that she may be accustomed to them, and then, only then, when her release was upon her, and his was upon him, did he bite.

His fangs slipped into her neck as though the grooves were already there. She flinched, for it could not be without pain; he felt hers through their *sentio*, and surely his exultation roared down the connection to her to alleviate it. He bit, and their release was the most exhilarating yet as their bond took and set, forever and ever.

Twenty-Two

To rise at dawn, with a lover, with her *mate*, was a joy unlike anything Tabitha had ever known.

To watch him Change and then run and run throughout the park was beyond her capacity for expression, even more breathtaking than the *cursio* had been. His speed took her breath away, his agility stunned, and his playfulness, once he returned to her, was more than she could have hoped for. He was a fearsome predator, but he was her fearsome predator, and it was thrilling to know his essential self recognized her and enjoyed her company. He sat at her feet and allowed her to thread her fingers through his mane, welcomed her hands running over his powerful shoulders, and rubbed his nose against hers. She would never confuse him with a *cat* cat, and the purr he raised as she scratched him on the skull was not too far away from Alwyn's reaction when she did the same.

With Alwyn back in his manskin, both of them wrapped in a quilt and perched on the step, they watched the sun ascend over Lowell Pack lands. As usual, Tabitha was bundled up to her nose, but the heat Alwyn exuded was prodigious, so she had no complaints to level against the frosty spring air. With Ostara in the past, the days would warm, and she found she would miss the finer English weather. She laughed to herself and shrugged when he poked her with his nose inquisitively, not unlike his lion had when he wanted more scratching of his mane.

"I was thinking I would miss England in the summer when all I had wanted was to be elsewhere."

"We shall come and go," Alwyn said. "Or we can wait if you like. We may do as we please."

"What a thing, to do as we please."

"It would please me to do this." And he kissed her.

Sometime later, Tabitha asked, "Shall we go soon?"

"When your brother sent the footmen on the scent of that snake, I gave one of them a task as well. If you do not wish to delay, then we have passage on a ship making for France at the end of the week."

"We should leave this afternoon, then, to address our business in London and make Dover in good time."

"Your heart is beating like a rabbit's," he murmured.

"I am excited and a little terrified. You may prove to be as efficient as I. It is a maiden's dream."

"Is it really?"

"Well, it does depend upon the maiden." They

excelled at kissing while smiling. "And whether or not she is a maiden. That ship has sailed. As ours will. At week's end."

"We are decided, then."

"Yes. But we cannot depart without letting everyone know."

"Nor can we miss finally seeing the play." He rose effortlessly to his feet, the blanket falling away to reveal that belly of his, and if they whiled away another hour or two until it was time to meander toward the village, there was none to say them nay.

———

"*Now to 'scape the serpent's tongue,*" declaimed Mr. Peasley as Puck, tapping the side of his nose and looking comprehensively 'round the spectators in the front rows, "*we will make amends ere long…*"

Puck's epilogue was more apt than usual. In place of *Hamlet*, the Peasley Troupe of Traveling Players mounted a rousing and precise production of *A Midsummer Night's Dream*. Bottom's transformation was played with an insider's touch of proprietary knowledge, and His Highness was heard to guffaw more than once.

"*Give me your hands if we be friends!*" Mr. Peasley sang; he, Mrs. Peasley, Quincy, and the company's day player jumped from the stage and urged the audience to its feet, convincing them to all take hands. As one, players and watchers chorused the last line: "*And Robin shall restore amends!*"

The ovation was rapturous, and the troupe returned to the stage to bask in it fully; the response had to do as much with the quality of the performance as it did with the players seeing the thing through to its end with no interruption.

As ever, watching the audience was as diverting as the play; Tabitha would not be so ill-mannered as to take her attention away from the stage, especially given what the troupe had gone through, but once concluded, the attendees created their own spectacle.

The contingent from Arcadia was especially rapturous: Osborn, serving as the day player, had acquitted himself with great vigor in his myriad roles of few words but great presence; his wife was heard to compliment him on his spear carrying, which sent her in-laws into gales of laughter.

Timothy had no sooner begun to mingle than he was surrounded by his pupils, who followed him to the tea table like a brood of ducklings; he encouraged them to share their opinions of the production. The Duchess of Lowell asked him if he thought Shakespeare, given the themes of this play, had been a man of more than one nature, and a lively debate followed.

Mr. Quincy was beckoned to join the Humphries; the Dowager Duchess took both his hands in hers, and they spoke quietly while her grandchildren swarmed around their feet. Tabitha hoped the Peaselys took their good fortune well and that their elevation in the theatrical ranks did not inspire them to change their style one whit.

Beyond the dowager duchess, Mr. MacCafferty sulked around the edges of the crowd; Tabitha considered bequeathing him her brooding boulder beneath the chestnut tree. The colts capered around him, seeking to shake him out of his dolor, and the merest quirk of a smile sent them into greater efforts to be even more amusing than the actors.

And if one knew what to look for, one would notice Mr. Bates and Jemima making an effort of their own to avoid one another's company and yet never letting the other out of their sight.

As turnabout was fair play, Tabitha's ease on the duke's arm did not go unremarked.

"As I said to Beatrice only weeks ago, we must not *Your Grace* each other to death. Your Grace." Felicity smiled like all the lupine festivals had happened at once.

"I was admiring your coat so thoroughly, I almost missed my husband's efforts." Beatrice toyed with the cuff of Tabitha's new pelisse.

"It is a Lady Coleman original." Tabitha ran her free hand down the front and slipped it into the pocket. "It is also very orange."

"Not *orange* orange—it is like the deep auburn stripes of a tiger," Felicity said. "If that is not an insult to your duke." She smiled at Alwyn, who smiled in return.

"Jemima made Alwyn suits of clothes that he can dress himself in. And she made me several very practical...pieces of clothing? That I am to change about, from one ensemble to the other? I have never seen such a thing."

"We are fortunate in our friends, whose skills enrich all our lives," Beatrice said.

Felicity clapped her hands. "As my skill lies in organization, I must organize a larger abode for you both."

Tabitha bit her lip just as Alwyn slid his arm around her waist. She did not think couples went about expressing affection like this, but she suspected her duke was a power unto himself.

In any event, Lowell took one of his duchess's hands in his and twined their fingers, and Osborn absently played with the furbelows on his wife's bonnet.

"We will not be stopping here, my friend," Tabitha said.

"There are souls in the world who need my duchess's skills." Alwyn went so far as to give her a squeeze.

"We cannot express our gratitude enough," Lowell began.

Osborn huffed. "*We*, again, Alfred?"

"I speak for my duchess, Artie," Lowell said, "and for all in my pack, if not beyond."

"Indeed." Georgie descended upon them. "The Duke and Duchess of Llewellyn have the gratitude of the Crown."

Oh, that was rather a lot to hear for the first time, and Tabitha leaned into her mate's side. He was well able to take the weight.

"In return, you two may express your gratitude," the prince went on, "by liberating any of our kind who are trapped under sorcery such as that lady author practiced."

"I would know that she is not going to slither out of your grasp," Alwyn said.

"The snake Shifter is securely held, and I have a business of ferrets engaged in winkling out her connections and associates," the prince assured him. "And thanks to your mate, that vile pendant is secured."

"And we will be taking it upon ourselves to locate and liberate any *versipelles* who have fallen afoul of Drake's menagerie before we go." Tabitha could not wait to get there.

"Will you remain in London?" Felicity's hope warmed her heart.

"We leave for France in three days and are for Sorrento, ultimately," Tabitha said.

"I have heard only good about the place," Alwyn said. "And there is a certain Italian cat whose acquaintance I wish to make."

Lowell extended a hand to Alwyn, who took it and, beyond all expectation, pulled his peer into an embrace. Osborn joined in and patted both on the backs to the subdued delight of their duchesses. When they stepped back, Lowell said, "You may send any you find to us, if they do not choose to roam with you or need a place to rest until their pack or clowder or herd are found."

"And a place will be held as a home for you here," Felicity added, "whenever you wander back to us and for however long."

Promises were made, of correspondence and visits, even as hugs were exchanged. A familiar hand touched her elbow, and Tabitha was drawn into her brother's arms. Before she turned her head to Timothy's shoulder, she saw Alwyn herd the others away.

"If I had to send you off with anyone, it would be His Grace," Timothy said. "Your Grace."

"That will take some getting used to." Tabitha closed her eyes and clutched the back of her brother's coat.

"I don't know about that," he joked, "you've always been high in the instep."

Timothy made to release their embrace, but she shook her head. "I cannot look at you and keep my composure."

"You and your blasted composure." Despite his caustic tone, he tucked his face into her shoulder.

"We have already had this argument," she scolded.

"Then let us have a new one when we meet again." They both sobbed once, and the tears rushed in.

"I have packed your trug, and it is ready with your trunk." Timothy sniffled. "One trunk, honestly, how will you cope?"

"How shall I cope, without my truest friend?" When she decided to have feelings, she discovered, she did not go about it halfway. She had them all at once.

Her brother stood back; he did not let go but took the opportunity to give her a shake. "Very well, I suspect, for you have your fated mate."

"Who would have ever thought?" Tabitha accepted his handkerchief and dabbed at her eyes.

"I would have if I had known to think it. For you deserve all the good the world has to give."

"As do you." Tabitha took his face in her hands. "I wish you students and books and community and friends and, most of all, the love of your life."

"If you say so, then it will be." Their eyes filled with tears again, and Tabitha was certain she was going to blub like a baby but for the approach of a certain duke.

Alwyn cleared his throat. "Mr. Barrington, I neglected to do you the honor of asking for your sister's hand."

The threat of tears was banished in an instant. "My what now?"

"Your Grace, I appreciate your respect for the proprieties, but you must know my sister's hand is hers to give herself." Timothy offered one of his sharklike grins. "*Gardy loo, mon bone omee.* You'll make her happy and keep her that way, or I'll know the reason why."

Alwyn replied in kind, the lingo sounding like so many languages all mixed up into one, she had no hope of making head or tails of it.

"We must go before I lose my nerve." This pronouncement received incredulous looks from Alwyn and Timothy; Tabitha tugged her *vera amoris* away before his disbelief resulted in more incomprehensible discourse, and after one last embrace of her brother.

She and Alwyn reached the edge of the village green and Tabitha cast a longing look over her shoulder. If any place had ever felt like home, it was this one. She had no idea what lay ahead and wondered at her willingness to leave Lowell Hall behind—until she leaned into the man next to her.

Tabitha took her mate's hand. "Alwyn," she said, "I choose you."

He squeezed her hand, then kissed the back of it. "Tabitha," he rumbled, his voice resounding with that of his lion, "I choose you."

Hand in hand, the Duke and Duchess of Llewellyn took their leave for now, though not forever.

As they made their way to collect their things and avail of the Lowell state coach, His Highness was heard to say it was time to turn his sights on the next couples in line to mate...

Start from the beginning of the Shapeshifters
of the Beau Monde series—a delicious mix of
Regency romance and shapeshifting adventure
from Susanna Allen

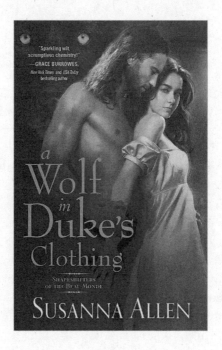

One

IT WAS A VERITABLE CRUSH.

In the year 1817, with the Napoleonic Wars well and truly won and the American Colonies well and truly lost, nothing less than an utter squeeze would do, not when the hostess was the Countess of Livingston and well able to put the wealth of her husband's earldom on display. The ballroom was spacious, framed by its gilded and frescoed ceiling; impressive with its shining wall of mirrors; fragrant from the banks of hothouse flowers set about the vast space; and yet... Nothing about it was unlike any other ballroom in London, where hopes and dreams were realized or dashed upon the rocks of ignominy. Packed to the walls with the great and good of the English *haute ton*, the society ball was as lively and bright as any before it and any that would follow.

Despite having traversed a well-trod path of lineage and reputation all their lives, the guests gave themselves to the event with an abandon that appeared newly coined. They came to the dance, and to the gossip, and to the planning of alliances and assignations with the energy of girls fresh out of the schoolroom and young lords newly decanted from Eton and Harrow. Those undertaking the lively reel threw themselves into it as though it were the first opportunity they had to perform it; the watchers congregated at the sides of the dance floor observed it as though they'd never seen such a display in all their lives. Though the room was lit by more than two thousand candles in crystal chandeliers, shadows lurked in the farthest corners; the gloom was not equal, however, to the beauty of the silks and satins of the ladies' gowns or to the richness of their adornments. As the multitude of jewels and those eddying skirts caught the light, the setting looked like a dream.

Unless it had all the hallmarks of a personal nightmare. Alfred Blakesley, Seventh Duke of Lowell, Earl of Ulrich, Viscount Randolf, Baron Conrí, and a handful of lesser titles not worth their salt, found the Livingstons' ball to be an unrelenting assault of bodies, sounds, and most of all, scents. This last was a civilized term covering a broad range of aromas that encompassed the pleasant—perfumes, unguents, and those hot-house arrangements—to the less so, among them the unlaundered linen of the less fussy young bucks and the outdated sachets used to freshen the gowns of the chaperones. If he wouldn't look an utter macaroni, he'd carry a scented handkerchief or, in a nod to the Elizabethans, an orange studded with cloves. Whilst either would save his sensitive snout from the onslaught of odors, it would defeat the purpose of his presence this evening.

As usual, said presence, after an absence of five years, was causing a flurry of gossip and conjecture. With jaded amusement, the only amusement he was able to muster these days, and without appearing to do so, he eavesdropped on the far-ranging theories regarding his person that were swirling around the ballroom, much as the dancers spun around the floor itself. If the gossips only knew how acute his hearing was, they might hesitate to tittle-tattle...

"My Lord, he is divine," last year's premiere diamond of the first water sighed.

"That chiseled face, that muscular form." Her friend, at best a ruby, fanned herself vigorously.

"If only my dear Herbert would grow his hair until it touched his collar," Diamond said.

"If only my Charles would pad his jacket. And his thighs. And his bum!" Ruby laughed wickedly.

"I doubt very much that there is any padding on the duke's person," Diamond said.

Ruby peeked at him over her fan. "If only he would stand up with one of us so we could get a hand on those shoulders."

Two bucks of vintages separated by at least twenty years waited out the current set. "He may be among us, but he will not stay as much as an hour. My valet would thrash me did I not pass at least three hours allowing the entire *ton* to remark upon his prowess," the aging young buck opined.

"And yet, he is dressed to a turn, his linen pristine, his coat of the latest cut," the actual young buck replied.

"His linen may be," scoffed his elder, "but there is something queer in the lineage."

"Lineage!" One old gent bleated to another as they made their way to the card room. "Hodgepodge more like. A ragbag of dependents of no known origin, a mishmash of retainers, a mélange of—"

"Yes, yes." His companion flourished his cane. "My own family claims quite a healthy acreage near to Lowell's shire, and ne'er the twain shall meet, I can tell you."

"I do not take your meaning," Gent the First said.

Gent the Second put his hand on his friend's arm and leaned in. "My nephew's housekeeper's brother's wife's granddaughter is from the neighboring village and says there is never a house party, never a ball, and never a need for outside help. And we all know what that means."

"Penury."

"Not a groat to his name."

Along the mirrored wall, an older matron rustled

her organza. "He is rich as Croesus, although the origins of the fortune are suspect."

Her bosom friend gasped. "Surely it does not come from trade?"

"He keeps no sheep, he tends no crops—well, he has no people to do such things. Even he is not so far gone to propriety to engage in animal husbandry firsthand."

"Some say the entirety of his holding is a gold mine, a literal gold mine." Bosom Friend looked ecstatic at the notion.

"Hardly," Matron replied. "There's not a nugget of gold on this island; the Scots mined it eons ago."

A merry widow and her ardent admirer lingered near the drinks table. "No one I know has had him, and I know everyone who has had anyone of import," Merry grumbled.

Ardent moved closer. "Is he…?" He gestured to a group of *very good* male friends clustered in the corner.

"*Quelle tragedie*, if so," said Merry. "It is true that he is seen nowhere without his steward, Bates, by his side."

"He, too, is a favorite amongst the ladies."

"No one's had him, either."

And so the ton *sups from the same old scandal broth*, thought Alfred. He'd heard every word without having moved so much as an inch from his place near the entrance to the ballroom. No creature with hearing such as his would need to do so. The rumors and speculation built in strength the longer he did not take a wife, but it was not merely a wife for whom he searched.

Searched he had, far and wide, all across Europe, as far as the Far East, a duke of the realm wandering the earth like a common journeyman—but it had to be done, for no one could find his lady for him, identify her for him, take the place of her. He found himself back in England after five years of endless travel, thwarted yet somehow not disheartened despite being here again. Here, almost to the man and woman, were the same faces he'd seen upon entering society after coming up from Oxford, faces that were beginning to resemble one another; he feared they'd all been intermarrying rather too closely for comfort.

His own family line was a different breed, and to explain his clan's uniqueness to most in this room would result in panic, fear, and an atavistic desire to obliterate any trace of him and those like him, for all time. To expose their distinction would put all under his care in the most perilous danger—a paradox, as that difference made him more powerful than any human being.

Yet, here he was among them, bracing himself for the possibility that the one sought by him and his inner creature, his essential self was of their number. His wolf stirred within him, impatient, vexed by the delay in finding their mate, held in check when all it wanted to do was hunt and hunt until they found the one whose heart and soul called to them, belonged to them, whose presence would set things right at Lowell Hall.

"Your Grace." His steward, Matthias Bates, appeared at his shoulder.

"Animal husbandry..." Alfred murmured, and Matthias gave a low laugh. Alfred regarded his closest friend and right-hand man—the perfect second-in-command, aligned with him in thought, yet with enough independence of spirit to challenge Alfred as needed. Bates stood as tall as he, at several inches over six feet, although the steward was blond where he was dark, lean where he was excessively muscular. None of the gossips had gotten around to that criticism this evening: What well-bred male of his status sought to gain such brawny proportions?

"I believe the *haute ton* needs to stop marrying itself." Alfred began to wander, Bates at his side.

"Indeed," Bates replied. "And it is, of course, a discussion relevant to your own situation."

A sigh soughed through Alfred's entire being. "It is enough to make one wish to take a ship and sail far, far away—had I not already done so and visited every corner of the globe."

"There are always the Colonies."

"The United States of America," Alfred corrected. "I am not well acquainted with any of our sort from out that way, despite their being one branch from whence we all came. My sister has not written to me of discovering such, in any case."

"One imagines such outliers to be as poor a choice as one of these women."

The air around the two men became oppressive, as though all the heat of the room had coalesced to envelop Bates. He struggled for his next breath, and his body trembled as he fought an outside force for control of it. It did not affect Alfred, as this elemental energy generated from him; known as the *dominatum*, it was the ultimate expression of his power as Alpha of the Shifters of Lowell Hall. This power was his and his alone, the essence of his authority, the manner in which he held sway over the beasts within his people, the way in which he protected them from outside aggressors, and if need be, from one another. To him, it was akin to the dynamism of the Change: held entirely within and called upon with a thought. Its use was judicious, never mindless, but in this instance, it was excessive; he blamed his wolf, who was surging under his skin, seeking release. Even the slightest insult to his future mate was enough to incense them both, and at this precise moment in time, when the search looked to be a failure, he did not need the reminder that his true mate was no longer likely to be one of his kind.

Bates was not the only one to experience the potency of the emanation. Though invisible to the naked eye, it had an intensity akin to a lightning strike; the ladies who had ventured closer, hoping to catch the eye of the duke, came over rather faint and repaired to the retiring room. Nor were the men unaffected: the more delicate youths swayed as though they had visited the punch bowl several times too many. Alfred's face showed no effect or exertion but for the tightening of his jaw and an increased ferocity in his gaze.

"Your Grace." Bates managed a stiff bow and turned his head, baring the side of his neck. "I misspoke. We will welcome any female you bring to us as your bride, regardless of her provenance." He held his posture until the pressure receded but still did not meet Alfred's gaze.

"What must be done, must be done," Alfred said, and they continued their perambulations. "The issues that arise when lines too closely related produce offspring is, in the case of the *ton*, a weakness that expresses itself in illnesses of the body and of the mind. This is happening far too often amongst our own branches of society, and it must be addressed. The bloodlines of our...family must be strengthened, and our only hope may be found by my marrying one of 'these.'"

"Which will endow permission to do so for those among us who also wish to marry and to be, er, fruitful," Bates replied.

"Permission must be endowed sooner rather

than later. Enough time has been wasted in my jaunts across the Continent. The continents, in fact. My wish to marry one of our own is not to be. I despair I have wasted time and endangered our people in trying to do so. I wanted my ma—my wife to be of our lineage."

"Alpha—" Bates dropped into another bow. "Alfred, that is to say, Duke, Your Gr—"

"Matthias." Alfred reached out and touched his steward on the arm, bringing him back up to full height. "If a secure future for our people is achieved through marriage to a society lady, then any sacrifice will be worth the cost." He swept his glance around the room and met a domino-effect of lowering glances. *How difficult this undertaking will be,* he thought, *if she won't look me in the eye... But surely the one meant for me is as strong as I, no matter her genus?* "My entire existence walks this fine line between our ways and the ways of society. The paradox is that in choosing my bride from the *ton*, I will have to hide my true self from her, regardless of our customs."

"Impossible," said Bates. "You will no more be able to hide your true self from your wife than the moon could fail to draw the tide."

"That sounds almost romantic, my friend," Alfred teased.

"Certainly not." Bates's offended expression inspired Alfred to indulge in a short bark of laughter.

"It does not fall to me, thank all the Gods, to subscribe to this fated-mate nonsense." He coughed and lowered his voice. "But the notion you could spend a lifetime pretending to be something you are not? The expense of energy this would require?"

"I have neither the time nor the energy for romance."

Which he would feign, like it or not. His interactions with the ladies of the *ton* had always been marked by a social duplicity that was anathema to him: the little white lies, the sham emotions, the manners that in fact betrayed a lack of gentility and integrity. But there were far too many in his care, and they had gone too long without a strong sense of cohesion and community for him to indulge in stubbornness. He must lead the way, though it seemed unlikely he was to find happiness on his path.

Happiness! Had he ever thought happiness was in his future or was his birthright? In every clan he met, of every breed, he saw what a world of difference it made when they honored the ways of their kind. When a pack or a clowder or a flock were led by an Alpha pair who were *vera amorum*, they thrived, and it pierced his heart with regret, even as it strengthened his resolve. His mother and father had lied about their status, claiming one another as true mates, and the reverberations of that falsehood were still serving to hurt his people and endanger their future.

"I will do what is needed, whatever that may be." He took the glass of champagne that Bates offered, and both pretended to drink. "I will find a lady before the Feast of Lupercalia, and we shall go forward from there."

"Your Grace, I must remind you of what O'Mara made plain upon our return to England. Nothing less than a love match will satisfy your people." He sounded dubious; since puphood, Matthias had scorned the tendency of their breed to mate for life. "As well, you will have to proceed as a male of the *ton* and observe the customary formalities."

Alfred half listened to Bates prose on as regarded the necessity of *billets-doux* and floral tributes and wooing and instead assessed the women who came close, but not too close, to him. They treated him as though he were unapproachable when all he wanted was to be approached; unlike the majority of the young aristocratic males in the room, he yearned to marry. A failed pairing could destroy the morale and robustness of a pack—he had only to look at his parents: the disaster that was their reign had all to do with disrespecting Fate and allowing their ambitions precedence. And yet, he dreaded the notion that he might not find her by the Feast day and would thus be consigned to searching one ballroom, one garden party, one Venetian breakfast after another, for another year, all in the hopes of discovering—

He thrust his glass into Bates's hand and froze, nostrils flaring. There. Where? He let his instinctual self scan the ballroom, his vision heightening to an almost painful degree even in the soft candlelight, his focus sharp as a blade. He fought to turn without the preternatural speed with which he was endowed and struggled to align the rest of his senses. His ears pricked, such as they could in this form: he heard laughter, a note of feminine gaiety that made his skin come out all over in gooseflesh, a sound that landed into the center of his heart as would Cupid's dart. His inner self rolled through his consciousness, eager to explode into life, and he held it at bay.

The set concluded; the next was to be a waltz, and the usual flutter of partnering unfolded around him. That laugh rang out again, and he turned once more in a circle, uncaring if anyone noted the oddness of his behavior. It was as if every one of his nerve endings had been plucked at once, as if a bolt of lightning were gathering its power to explode down his spine. He scented the air again, and between the candle wax and the overbearing scent of lilacs, he divined a hint of vanilla, an unexpected hint of rosemary, a waft of sweet william...

"We are very near the wallflower conservatory," joked Bates as he set their untouched glasses aside. "Shall you pluck a bloom from there?"

Alfred held up a hand and focused on the wall of palms screening the corner in which the undesirables mingled and hid, homing in on a bouquet of fragrance he'd despaired of scenting, a combination of familiar elements he may have experienced singly but never before as one, not with such rapturous force. He turned to face the greenery; Bates moved to protect his back. He inhaled, and yes, there it was, a collection of mundane notes that combined to create a glorious symphony of attraction, desire, lust, yearning, and possibility; a concoction of lush skin, that hint of sweet william, fresh air, horses—and an excessive amount of lemon? His heart beat like thunder, and as the violins tuned for the upcoming dance and the crowd's murmur built into a roar, he swept, heedless, through them to reach the source.

Author's Note

It was so much fun to bring everyone back together for Tabitha and Alwyn's *vera amoris* journey, and I am so lucky to have a team that brings it all together for me: my agent Julie Gwinn, my editor Deb Werksman, and the design, copy, production, and marketing departments of Sourcebooks. Thank you all!

Quite a lot went into this novel and led me down rabbit holes—ha, ha—I hadn't reckoned on.

Apothecaries had been organized as a professional body since the seventeenth century in England (aka the Worshipful Society of Apothecaries) and were as likely to act as general practitioners as much as dispensers of powders, tonics, and sundry drugs for a client's ills. Very few women would have found themselves in this role; the ones who did were widows of professionals whose businesses they were entitled to after their spouses' deaths. It wasn't until 1865 that a woman entered the profession on her own merits, when Elizabeth Garrett Anderson earned her license to practice in Britain. The techniques Tabitha employed were passed through the feminine ranks of families and households, and much of contemporary natural approaches to healing, including aromatherapy, have their roots in home remedies. Herbs played, and still play, a significant role in soothing aches and pains, but ingredients such as urine and earwax have fallen out of favor.

You wouldn't find many women able to run long distances, or at speed, either. Tabitha's love of running is antithetical to common thought at the time, which deemed exercise dangerous for women, whose feeble bodies could not handle the exertion. It was believed femininity was destroyed on a cellular level by exercise. This was disputed by the medical profession, but the power of societal thought held sway. Walking, dancing, horseback riding, and calisthenics were permissible but only up to a point, lest one perspire one's womanhood out of existence.

Spirits of Saturn is also known as Venetian ceruse and was used by the likes of Elizabeth I to whiten the skin. It is extremely poisonous and only appears in Tabitha's apothecary kit in service to the plot.

Despite not having found Germany a place to stop for long, Tabitha added to her metaphysical apothecary case while there, and she would have been exposed to ideas that led to what would become the discipline of psychology. Tabitha references Johann Christian Reil, who thought the treatment of mental illness ought to be less reactionary and more preventative and is considered a leader of German romantic psychiatry.

Macaroni was a thing in Regency era cookery and served much as we would do so today; an early nineteenth-century recipe for mac and cheese floats free on the internet. Pesto has been present in the Italian diet since Roman times; its first recorded use comes well after Timothy cooked it here, but that's not to say the use of basil in pesto hadn't been employed in folks' kitchens just because Giovanni Battista Ratto didn't write it down in a cookbook (*La Cuciniera Genovese*) until 1863.

Coming across Parlyaree, or Polari as it has been known since the 1950s, was the happiest accident I have ever had as a writer. The insider lingo was lingua franca not only in gay culture but also amongst theater folk and roustabouts, the perfect meeting point between Timothy and Alwyn. It's a vibrant language, the vocabulary of which remains robust in common parlance, at least in Ireland, where *slap* (makeup), *naff* (dodgy), and *scarper* (flee) are used with frequency. Having said that, it was a challenge to come up with dialogue that wasn't exclusively saucy, so any mistakes are mine and mine alone, *savvy*?

No one in this book except for Timothy seems to be earning a wage in actual money, and it takes Tabitha some time to work out she's been bartering her skills as well. Dukes, as a rule, lived off the labor of others; since Alwyn had no lands to speak of, as luck would have it, the Regency era version of the stock market was a plausible source for his wealth.

Speaking of: I am obsessed with how much old money is worth in contemporary times. An English pound in 1817 is comparable to roughly £88/$120 in today's money (via the online UK inflation calculator). Mary Mossett's astonishment at what the Barringtons paid for mending is not surprising: as maid of all work, she would be lucky to earn a maximum of £3 in an entire year.

Spear carrier is the time-honored title given to a minor player in a theatrical production and a perfect opportunity for Charlotte and Ben to exercise their bawdy wit. Finally, I had as much fun naming my humble players as I have had naming my *versipelles*, and they are based on the fairies and the rude mechanicals of *A Midsummer Night's Dream*, who also played to a duke and duchess and had their own challenges along the way.

About the Author

Susanna Allen is a graduate of Pratt Institute with a BFA in communication design and counts *The Village Voice*, *New York Magazine*, and *Entertainment Weekly* as past design experiences. Born in New Jersey, she moved to Ireland for twelve months—in 1998. She is the author of *Drama Queen* and *The Fidelity Project*, both published by Headline UK, and *That Magic Mischief*, recently rereleased via Ally Press. Susan is living her life by the three Rs—reading, writing, and horseback riding—and can generally be found on her sofa with her e-reader, gazing out a window and thinking about made-up people or cantering around in circles. She loves every minute of it. Follow Susanna on Facebook, Instagram, and/or Twitter: @SusannaAWriter

THE DUKE WHO LOVED ME

The Duke's Estates series brings you sparkling Regency romance from bestselling author Jane Ashford

When James Cantrell, the new Duke of Tereford, proposes a marriage of convenience, Cecelia Vainsmede doesn't understand how he can be so obtuse. He clearly doesn't realize that he's the duke she's always wished for, so his offer is an insult. But when a German prince arrives in London and immediately sets out to woo Cecelia, James will have to come to terms with his true feelings. Is running away worth the cost of losing her, or will the duke dare to win her once and for all?

"Impossible to put down... The story crackles with clever dialogue and humorous scenes."
—*Historical Novel Review*

UP ALL NIGHT WITH
A GOOD DUKE

A new sparkling and sexy Regency romance series
from award-winning author Amy Rose Bennett

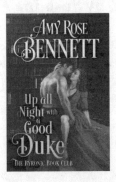

Artemis Jones—"respectable" finishing-school teacher by day and
Gothic romance writer by night—has never lost sight of her real
dream: to open her own academic ladies' college. When Artemis is
unexpectedly called upon by a dear friend to navigate her first London
Season, she comes at once. Perhaps she can court the interest of
a wealthy patron for her school. As long as she can avoid her aunt's
schemes to marry her off. Little does she realize she's about to come
face-to-face with a Byron-esque widowed duke determined to find a
bride…

"Infused with heat, energy, and glamour."
—Amanda Quick, *New York Times* bestselling author,
for *How to Catch a Wicked Viscount*

For more info about Sourcebooks's books and authors, visit:
sourcebooks.com

Also by Susanna Allen

SHAPESHIFTERS OF THE BEAU MONDE
A Wolf in Duke's Clothing
A Most Unusual Duke